Kezza, an aerialist in the Martian circus, can never return to Earth – but she can assassinate the man she blames for her grim life on the red planet. Her murderous plans take an unexpected turn, however, when she comes into contact with a strange infection that might have alien origins... an infection that could spell her death or her salvation.

A thousand years into the future, Azad lives a safe but controlled life on the beautiful desert planet of Nabatea. When he discovers that his runaway sister may still be alive... and in danger, he joins her former crew, a band of space-traveling historians seeking to learn the true reason that their ancestors left Mars.

Although separated by time and space, Kezza's and Azad's stories will collide in the vast Martian desert.

NADIA AFIFI

A REBEL'S HISTORY OF MARS

FLAME TREE PRESS
London & New York

This is a **FLAME TREE PRESS** book

Text copyright © 2025 Nadia Afifi

FLAME TREE PRESS
6 Melbray Mews, London, SW6 3NS, UK
flametreepress.com

US sales, distribution and warehouse:
Simon & Schuster
simonandschuster.biz

UK distribution and warehouse:
Hachette UK Distribution
hukdcustomerservice@hachette.co.uk

Publisher's Note: This is a work of fiction. Names, characters, places, and
incidents are a product of the author's imagination. Locales and public names
are sometimes used for atmospheric purposes. Any resemblance to actual
people, living or dead, or to businesses, companies, events, institutions, or
locales is completely coincidental.

Thanks to the Flame Tree Press team.

The cover is created by Flame Tree Studio with elements courtesy of Shutterstock.com
and: ART-ur; klyaksun; Un.imajinasi; Vyshedko.
The font families used are Avenir and Bembo.

Flame Tree Press is an imprint of Flame Tree Publishing Ltd
flametreepublishing.com

A copy of the CIP data for this book is available from the British Library
and the Library of Congress.

PB ISBN: 978-1-78758-944-5
HB ISBN: 978-1-78758-945-2
ebook ISBN: 978-1-78758-946-9

1 3 5 7 9 8 6 4 2

Printed and bound in the UK by CPI Group (UK) Ltd, Croydon CR0 4YY

NADIA AFIFI

A REBEL'S HISTORY OF MARS

FLAME TREE PRESS
London & New York

Part One

The Civilizationist

When the good people of Mars let me name our planet, my choice was immediate: the Planet of Nabatea, for the people who dwelled within the ancient city of Petra. My mother took me to Petra after the war. Though she intended to reconnect with her own roots, I was the one who left changed forever. In a city carved into the rose-colored cliffs, with homes burrowed from rock, the Nabateans lived in harmony with their environment. They traded, they farmed, they warred with their neighbors, all the hallmarks of civilization I had not yet learned to leverage for my life's work, but there was something different about them. They thrived, and then vanished. Nothing remained of them but their hallowed homes, broken pottery and scattered tombs. An old Bedouin man spoke to me in front of the Treasury, noting that only these barren traces of them remained. He was not as impressed as I. "What remains of these cliff-dwellers?" he sneered. "Where are they now?"

As we arrive on the other side of our galaxy, I finally have an answer for him. They are here. They are us.

From **The Journals of Barrett Juul, Founder of Nabatea**

Awake! For morning in the bowl of night
Has flung the stone that puts the stars to flight
And Lo! The hunter of the East has caught
The Sultan's turret in a noose of light
'Rubaiyat', Omar Khayyam

Chapter One

Azad

NABATEA CITY, PLANET OF NABATEA
YEAR OF SETTLEMENT 1208

The Vitruvian woman burst through the Central Nabatean Hospital doors, saucer-eyed and staggering, before collapsing backward into a pot of synthetic hydrangeas. The clay shattered. Blood ran in a thin trail from her forehead.

Azad's jaw dropped. He stood, dumbfounded, for a solid ten seconds – a lifetime in an ER. It wasn't every day that a Vitruvian showed up in the hospital, especially in that state. They were notoriously difficult to weaken and injure – it's what made them Vitruvian. The signature snake tattoo coiled around the woman's neck, its scaled body dancing across her heaving chest. Artificial dirt from the potted plants flecked her white tank top, which contrasted with her choppy black hair and bronzed skin.

Azad snapped into action, reaching her before the emergency medmechs had finished calculating the situation. No obvious signs of injury, apart from her violent spasming and the bleeding cut on her forehead. No fractures or broken bones. He checked her pulse – racing. Her temperature – burning. He pulled her eyelids up, revealing dilated pupils that darted like insects across her milky sclera.

A knot twisted in his stomach. He didn't know what would happen to him if a Vitruvian died under his watch, but it wouldn't be good.

The medmechs loaded her onto a gurney, which directed itself to the nearest available treatment ward for triage. Azad ran behind, running his hands through his dark hair in a daze, his eyes rounder than the Nabatean high moon.

What could have happened to that Vitruvian? They could survive space exposure. Not forever, of course, but rumor went that they could last a solid hour until rescue arrived or luck ran out. In addition, Vitruvians were intelligent, their risks calculated, making them a rarity among the Central Hospital's usual visitors – regular Nabateans like himself with regular human impulses, wheeled in after vomiting up inedible plants, breaking bones from wandering into transport lanes, or screaming from blister burns after daredevil runs into the Sulpherlands, the yet-to-be terraformed half of the planet. Natural selection was Azad's daily foe, who, despite humanity's twenty thousand years of existence across the stars, retained the upper hand.

In the ward, a small army of medmechs went to work on their new patient. Monitors covered the walls, projecting a dizzying array of vitals, neural scans and 3D body images. There wasn't much these days to being a doctor. Medmechs did the heavy lifting, with their precise, unwavering fingers and nanosecond-based decision-making algorithms. Azad existed to hold hands and offer reassuring words, to put a human face on the whole operation. A side character in his own play.

A gurgling sound escaped from the woman's throat. Instinctively, Azad reached for her hand. She stirred at the human contact, lacing her cold fingers around his own. Her head continued to jerk in every direction, but her eyes found focus, searching her surroundings.

"Diagnosis?" Azad asked the nearest medmech.

"Determining," it replied. "Uncertain cause. Prognosis poor based on declining vitals."

His insides turned to icy liquid. No one had ever died on his limited watch. She couldn't be the first. What would they even do to him? Prison? Exile? Something even worse?

The woman shuddered under the onslaught of needles and neural scans. Her dark eyes shone with unmistakable fear. Blood leaked from tear ducts as she shook on the gurney. Red streaks ran down her cheeks, joining the blood coming from her injured forehead. With shaking fingers,

Azad enlarged the wall monitor displaying her vitals, searching for some clue a computer might miss. Forcing himself to stay in the moment, to push fear aside. Through his churning thoughts and thundering heartbeat, he breathed. He had to focus, to be present in this critical moment. The Vitruvian's life, and his, depended on it.

He blinked. A live, three-dimensional map of the woman's body hovered directly above her. Vitals plummeted. Organs liquified before his eyes. The scanner detected a black, viscous substance coursing through her system, seeping through her digestive tract and pooling in her spasming stomach. Bile rose in his own throat. The machines revealed several months of illness, a prolonged assault on the body that even a Vitruvian could not survive.

The woman was dying. But that wasn't the most shocking part.

No foreign infection. No virus, no bacteria, no external contaminants. A body free of a diagnosable problem, despite the gruesome visual evidence to the contrary.

Baffling, even by Vitruvian standards.

"Run the scans again," Azad said to the nearest medmech. "Is everything configured to a Vitruvian body, not an orthodox Nabatean?"

If the machine could blink, Azad suspected it would have in that moment. "Patient is Vitruvian. No infections or cause of affliction detected."

"But she's dying!" Azad exploded, gesturing wildly from the spasming woman to the array of data hovering above her. "It's not possible. Keep running the scans, figure it out."

He pressed his hands against his temples, as though an answer might seep out of him. How could the medmechs not detect a cause? A normal Vitruvian, a normal *anyone*, did not have organs disintegrate within minutes, tar bubbling through their lips.

"You must have the reading wrong," Azad said, verging on tears as he rounded on the nearest machine. "Your algorithms aren't designed for Vitruvians."

Right on cue, two unsmiling visitors pushed through the ward's door. Vitruvians, a male and female. These Vitruvians were the picture of health, with the stern scowls that accompanied a not-so-random inspection. Azad's heart sank. With clenched fists, he dipped his head into a curt bow.

"We should have been flagged immediately," the man said, fixing cold eyes on the only functioning human in the room. Though not a Vitruvian, Azad possessed something the medmechs never would – accountability, which was a nice way of saying he could be punished.

Azad tore himself from the monitors and his thrashing, dying patient. Arranging his face into a neutral mask, he addressed the female Vitruvian official, whose uniform indicated a higher rank.

"We're in the middle of an emergency," Azad said. "Attending to the patient is always first priority."

"Not this patient," the man said. He passed Azad without eye contact. Azad bristled but stood aside. The nearest wall turned red with declining vitals, static beeps filling the windowless room. With a wave of the male Vitruvian's hand, the emergency medmechs paused their work.

On the table, the woman's back arched in a violent spasm. A low rattle escaped between her clenched teeth. Azad pushed past the two intruders and grabbed her wrist. A dangerous move, but he couldn't help it – his patient needed him. Her pulse fluttered, alarmingly weak.

"We don't know what's wrong," Azad said, his voice quavering. "It's nothing we've seen before."

"We need to Archive her," the female Vitruvian official said in a calm, clipped voice. "She can't be saved, but we can at least salvage her neural imprint."

"But she still has a chance," Azad said, but he wasn't even convincing himself. The Vitruvians responded with stony scowls.

Azad stood upright, hovering defiantly near his patient. He would obey, but no more than he had to. The medmechs lined the walls, passively awaiting instruction. The Vitruvian officials proceeded with characteristic efficiency, attaching an Archive Band to the patient's forehead. The thin, metallic crown's lights flashed in a circular pattern. Only the patient seemed willing to fight for her own existence, struggling for each breath.

"Believe me when I say there is no chance," the female Vitruvian official said. Her voice remained dull and edgeless, but something softened in her eyes, a gentleness she wasn't required to display to an insubordinate doctor.

Azad gasped at the cold grip on his wrist. The woman on the table turned to face him, looking directly in his eyes for the first time. Her mouth, bile seeping from the corners, stretched in a wide, dreamy smile. Thin streams of blood leaked from her forehead, running down her cheeks. Azad swallowed but leaned closer, clutching her hand.

"You look just like her," the woman said, barely above a whisper.

The room tilted. Azad's heart plummeted like a lead ball. His knuckles whitened as he squeezed the dying woman's hands, but her smile only widened.

"Wha-what do you mean?" he said, stammering. "Who do I look like?" He wanted to hear the name. Needed to hear it.

A loud beeping sound filled the room.

"Quick, start the download!"

"Stand back, doctor."

"Same face," the dying woman said. "Same eyes."

"No!" Azad yelled.

The Archive Band glowed, spinning around the woman's forehead. Her eyes, cloudy with blood, withdrew across the wide, black chasm between life and death before they turned dull and unseeing. Gone. Azad pressed his palm to the base of his throat, thinking but not uttering the Dusharan final rites.

At last, the surrounding equipment silenced, the screens turning black except for a single string of text, spanning the wall.

VitruviaAxel3247, Nenah. Time of death 16:08 p.m., Nabatean YOS 1208, 125 Sols.

Azad finally let go of Nenah's hand. Even seconds after death, it felt heavier.

The Vitruvian man closed Nenah's eyelids with gloved hands. While his partner instructed the medmechs, he turned to Azad with flinty eyes.

"You're not to blame for this," he said in a low voice. "This is a Vitruvian matter and we'll investigate it fully. I suggest you forget what happened here. Don't talk about it to anyone, even the authorities. Wash your hands immediately. In fact, do a full body cleanse. We don't expect you to be compromised from this limited contact, but if your operating system detects any symptoms, you'll be hearing from us."

Azad swallowed but nodded. Relief warmed his chest – he wouldn't be imprisoned or exiled. At least, not today.

The crisis over, formality returned to the ward. The medmechs wheeled the body of Nenah VitruviaAxel3247 through the door, clearing the area for the next patient.

You look just like her. The words rang in Azad's ears. A dying Vitruvian's words, as her brain fired off its last, desperate signals. Who had she seen that looked just like him? Was it possible? A name he hadn't spoken aloud in years, too painful to utter even in private, became a mantra in his mind.

Ledo.

Only one person in the known universe could have looked just like him, but she was dead. She had to be. A girl who abandoned her twin, her planet and everything she knew for a life of space wandering. A criminal's life, an existence free of the rules and structure that allowed Nabatean society to thrive.

Azad closed his eyes. It wasn't possible the woman had seen Ledo. If the dangers of space travel hadn't killed her, she would likely have been Blanked.

Azad's skin crawled at the thought. Blanking, a fate worse than death, meted out to those who made the mistake of trying to live like a Vitruvian. A few strategic electric pulses to specific parts of the brain and Ledo would become a soul trapped in the present, devoid of memory or abstract thinking. Blanked Nabateans wandered through the bushes during Azad's shifts at the Central Gardens. They performed the same task over and over until directed elsewhere, unable to recall their own names or where they had been an hour ago. Humans stripped down to biomechanics. At least the medmechs had machine learning, the ability to become smarter and anticipate the future. The Blanked were prisoners of time.

No, Ledo was dead. Azad had buried her in his mind years ago. Recited the Dusharan funeral rites by himself, since no one else would bother praying for a girl who died somewhere far away, with no chance of Archival, to share wisdom with future generations. He imagined her death summary.

of Khazneh, Ledo. Time of death unknown. Place of death unknown.

After his full body cleanse, Azad stepped out of the hospital, the curved domes of Nabatea City bright and shimmering under the afternoon heat. A dusty, red world offset by piercing blue skies. His footsteps echoed along the stone roads as he fought to push the past away.

The Vitruvian woman's hideous, bile-caked smile seared itself into his brain, but even harder to shake was the glowing recognition in her eyes. She must have seen Ledo at some point on her travels. Knew her. Why else would she have said those final words?

Could Ledo actually be alive? Alive and unBlanked?

Alive. An idea, now planted, that he could not kill. The word buzzed in his ears, drowning out the sound of traffic, the chatter of pedestrians along Nabatea City's spiraling walkways. He barely registered the glaring sun, harshest in the high summer, illuminating the rust-colored hills that stretched across the main city. They reached the height of the tallest buildings, forming an interconnected wall on the city's western side. Parks rich with flowered trees spread across the highest points along the Jebel Road, houses and complexes carved into their sides, a hidden ecosystem that provided relief during the sun's peak hours.

He joined the teeming throngs along the central walkway in the direction of home, the Khazneh Zone. The ochre houses formed winding tributaries across the low hills, their round windows dark like olive pits. He inhaled, tasting sugar and sumac in the air from a nearby bakery. His stomach growled. He had grown softer and rounder around his middle in the last few years, a lifelong love of sweets finally catching up to him. Ledo used to run with him to the Souk after Township, where they would eat syrup-coated pastries and lick their fingers under the shade of rowed palm trees. On nights when he didn't have to work, Azad baked alone at home.

Now outside of working hours, he reactivated Osbourne, who came to life with a warm pulse down his neck. Words echoed in his ear, accompanied by text that stretched across his thoughts when he closed his eyes.

Welcome, Azad of Khazneh. How was your medical shift? Choose one: Perfect! One of those days where everything goes right.

A typically great day helping the people of Nabatea.

Not great, in all honesty, but tomorrow's another day!

One of Nabatean society's seminal achievements was the abolishment of open-ended questions. A Juulian concept, as most societal breakthroughs were. Humans functioned best when given a defined set of options. Easier to paint over an outline than try to create art from a blank canvas, Azad's first counselor in Township once proclaimed. Through Barrett Juul's trial and error back on the mother planet, three had been proven to be the optimal number of choices for any routine decision.

Ledo never understood the choice of threes. She looked to the sky and saw an infinite canvas to fill, a blank space to mark with her own equations. She was odd from the very beginning. *Imbalanced,* Township counselors pronounced. How could someone like that function in Nabatea City?

Osbourne waited in silence, accustomed to Azad's meandering thoughts. With a blink of his eyes, Azad chose the third option, the least false of the three. A person had died on his table but resurrected Ledo in the process. No line on an algorithm could summarize that day.

Osbourne chimed in his ear.

I'm sorry to hear that, Azad. But you're right – tomorrow is indeed another day. And this one isn't over. This evening, would you like to:

Join Light Night at Khazneh Arena? Tonight's show is titled 'Soundless Migration: The Founding of Nabatea'.

Go to the library and study the theories of gardening?

Spend the night at home and bake sumac cakes? You ran out last night.

Although every orthodox Nabatean who came of age lived alone, every night had an event of some kind where people could mingle. Another by-product of Juulian theory. No one on Nabatea was ever lonely unless they chose to be, went the saying. But after Ledo ran away, Azad learned that even when surrounded by others, one could still be lonely.

Azad sighed. A breeze whistled through his dark, curled hair, carrying the smell of baked bread and canal water from Palmyra Street. Water was everywhere in Nabatea, the city's critical ally against the heat. It ran in dark rivulets along streets and sidewalks, formed narrow moats around each house and coated the rocky surfaces of the hills. The sun had finally set, dissolving over the Sulpherlands, but the humidity always lingered. Ahead of Azad, other Nabateans loosened their clothes like an irritating second skin, beads of sweat forming chains around the back of their necks, from which their own Osbournes spoke to them, planning their evenings in fates of three.

Though it carried a dark appeal, Azad knew he couldn't spend his evening alone. He had already used a third option today, usually the unspoken, socially unacceptable answer. A voluntary detachment from society, coupled with a bad day, would unmask him as having a Problem, which could trigger a visit from the authorities. And in truth, he didn't want to be alone. He chose option one – a night at the arena.

Crowds filled the stone seating around Khazneh Arena. Always popular with the city's orthodox inhabitants, Light Night performances celebrated Nabatea City's history. Heads turned at the sight of a rare group of Vitruvians attending tonight's show. They gathered in a small circle, drinks in hand, separate from the larger swarm of orthodox Nabateans migrating to their seats. Their necks were free of Osbournes, unconstrained by choices of three. They didn't work shifts like regular Nabateans and their options were limitless. They traveled and traded across planets, like Ledo dreamed of doing.

The group drew curious stares, even looks of outright hostility, from the surrounding crowd. *This is our world*, their expressions said. *Go rule and explore the stars and leave the caring of Nabatea City to us.* It was the hard work of orthodox Nabateans, after all, that allowed Vitruvians to power their vessels and supply their journeys. An ecosystem, with everyone in their rightful place.

The rows of rock-carved seats glowed with phosphorous light. Azad and Ledo used to play in the arena after Township classes each afternoon, jumping from row to empty row under the high heat. Every time they raced, Ledo beat him to the stage. She ran with abandon, all skinny arms and flying black hair. Azad would follow, always holding back. Always afraid to fall.

Osbourne directed Azad to the upper level of the arena after he ordered a glass of chilled apricot wine. His grip tightened at the sight of Averro, a slick-haired man in his thirties, waving at him. Azad nearly turned back, but he already had a seat picked and it would draw attention to retreat.

He sat between Averro and Maece, a woman in her forties with impossibly large, glassy eyes.

"I heard you had a rough afternoon, Azad," Averro began. Of course he had. Averro made it his business to learn everyone else's business. At least, in the Khazneh district. "Just remember, tomorrow is another day."

Maece snorted and Azad warmed with affection toward her.

"How did you know, Averro?" Azad asked, doing his best not to sound defensive.

"I'm on Problem Patrol," Averro said, his chest puffing slightly as his cheeks turned the same color as the apricot wine. "Applied and got in! I get to miss my farming shifts all month while I work. I see all the neighborhood's data. Medical stats, Choice of Three selections, activity logs. You came up on the report because your pulse and blood pressure spiked today. Heavens to Mars! I was worried about you."

Azad's stomach knotted and the blood drained from his cheeks. So he'd been flagged on a report. It had begun.

Averro unleashed a low giggle. "Azad, your face! You're not in trouble, if that's what you're thinking. Not everything that shows up on the report gets acted on – there are only so many cells in Saydar Prison. That's where people like me come in, to give the authorities some context. Now, if you had a Problem every day, that would be a different matter."

Azad's heart rate slowed back to a normal human pace, but a coldness traveled down his spine at the mention of Nabatea City's infamous prison. A place spoken of in whispers. Azad knew little about it and wanted to keep things that way. He exhaled.

"Something at work today reminded me of Ledo," he said in a low voice. He chose his words carefully, mindful of the Vitruvian official's warning. "It made me think about her, wonder if she's still alive."

Averro gasped, nearly spilling his glass.

"Who's Ledo?" Maece asked to no one in particular.

"Azad's deviant twin sister," Averro said. "I remember her from Township. There was something wrong with her. Full of strange ideas about seeing Mars. Got suspended who knows how many times. Used to run off to the edge of the Sulpherlands and come back with blistered feet. Broke every rule put in place for her own good. And then, she ran away."

"To another district?" Maece asked, frowning.

"No, off the planet!" Averro said, morbid glee creeping into his voice. "Disappeared. She might be on one of the moons with other weirdos, but most likely, she joined a crew of space wanderers. Which is fine if you're Vitruvian, that's what they do, but imagine a normal person being completely adrift like that. Anchored to nothing, every day unpredictable, not knowing where you're going or who you even are. Or she could have done something illegal and gotten Blanked," he added callously.

Maece shuddered, muttering a Dusharan prayer. Azad glowered. Any respect he'd felt toward Maece melted away, but his hands itched to toss that sticky, sickly cheap wine into Averro's face. Averro was only saying what everyone in the district whispered behind his back. The difference was they had the sense to whisper it.

"Maybe she wouldn't have been happy here," Azad said. "Maybe it's not just Vitruvians who can't live this way. Maybe some orthodox people get the same urges to leave the planet and explore. Not that I'd want it," he added quickly.

Dangerous words, but heat, wine and grief had made Azad feel dangerous. He'd already been put on a report. Why not go all the way? Call the Vitruvians' bluff and make them arrest him. As expected, Averro leaned forward, wineglass tipping precariously.

"Azad, there's a reason our structure exists," he said. "When people lived in other ways on the mother system, they destroyed themselves. Mars is a graveyard. Everyone and everything on Mars is dead. Even Earth became a wasteland. Juul saw where the human race went wrong and corrected it. And it's not that the Vitruvians are better than us – they're just different. Anointed by starlight, as the saying goes. It's the confused and troubled people like your sister who won't accept that fact. She was just self-hating, unable to accept what she was."

Azad opened his mouth to protest but held back, considering Averro's words. Only Vitruvians thrived outside the city, wired as they were to explore and discover. They learned that in Township. Different but equal. That was what made Ledo's departure so inconceivable, so contrary to all they had been taught. But Azad recalled the dreaminess of the dying Vitruvian's last smile. Perhaps Ledo's life wasn't so solitary and horrific.

The lights along the aisles dimmed and the hum of the crowd died down. A few Nabateans remained in deep conversation, but were quickly silenced by loud hisses.

The Light Show always began with sound, music emitting from an auditory system woven into the rocky arena itself. Azad's seat vibrated beneath him as a sad, lilting melody pulsed from the cool stone. He shivered. Through the pitch black, a voice, smooth like sand, boomed over the music.

"Our story, the story of Nabatea, begins with a man made of fire," the voice narrated, and the crowd gasped as heatless flames rose from the center of the arena. Twisting and dancing in red and blue, the flames formed the shape of a man, raising his fist in triumph.

People rose from their seats. Nearby, the Vitruvians grumbled, gesturing the group in front of them to sit. The Nabatean orthodox complied with low bows. Azad grimaced at the exchange. Separate, but definitely not equal.

Fingers pointed to the other side of Fallow Lake, where a giant, glowing shape emerged from the water. Shimmering limbs glided into place, forming a female figure that advanced toward the flaming man and the arena.

"The man left the decay and destruction of the mother system," the smooth voice continued, "and migrated across the stars with the fortunate, worthy few, until they found a home under a fiercer sun. On the journey, a new people came into being."

A smattering of Vitruvians clapped appreciatively. Though Nabatea never dwelled on the past, under the advice of Juul's teachings, everyone learned this elemental story in Township. A ragtag group of survivors, led by the civilizationist Barrett Juul; his mother, Saadia Hamza; and their allies, abandoned a dying colony on the planet Mars, escaping disaster. Through one of the colony's founding mothers, the more evolved Vitruvians came into being on the interstellar journey. The ones who didn't evolve, the majority, shared the same traits as their human ancestors on the mother system. Both groups settled together on the planet of Nabatea. Orthodox and Vitruvian. All Nabateans, despite their diverging evolutionary paths.

Even by Light Night's standards, the show was spectacular. Averro and Maece clapped feverishly as towering beams of light danced above them, figures wandering through a barren wasteland and making it new. Sandwiched between them, Azad's shoulders stiffened.

The cacophony of sound and light overwhelmed his senses. His eyes drifted beyond the luminescent shapes to the stars scattered across the sky, their light millions of years out of date. Ancient signals of the past, blinking down at him in conspiratorial silence. The crescent of Cerata, the Shadow Moon, hung low above them, like a scythe had cut into the black fabric of the universe to reveal light beneath its skin. Its moonlight coated the waning crowds in a celestial frosting. Infinite matter and beauty was all around him, but all Azad could think of was Ledo, the deviant and wanderer. His sister. A longing tugged at his heart, an invisible hook cast from the night sky.

He had to find her. The solar system was big, the galaxy too big to fathom, but if she was out there somewhere, he needed to see her again.

Azad lingered after the show with the intent of walking home alone. The night left him dizzy, drunk with possibility. Clouds of smoke hovered around the center of the arena, ghostly remnants of the pyrotechnic display with nowhere to dissipate in the muggy summer air. The maidmechs rolled in as the seats emptied, ready to clear away bottles and other human debris.

"Osbourne, where are dead Vitruvians Archived?" Azad asked.

A pause. The hairs on Azad's neck stiffened, waiting for the computer's familiar, skin-warming response. Finally, Osbourne spoke in Azad's ear.

Vitruvians can have their neural imprint downloaded to the city's central processor after death, as regular Nabateans such as yourself do, Osbourne replied. Was there a veiled threat in that subtle reminder of Azad's mortality?

Notable Vitruvian travelers are Archived in the Library of Souls on Cerata.

Cerata. The Shadow Moon of Nabatea, a name that referenced both the satellite's limited hours of sunlight and the eccentrics who chose to make it home. Loners, troublemakers, criminals, artists and artisans. And an ancient building filled with the neural firings of dead Vitruvians. The Vitruvian who died under Azad's care today was Nenah VitruviaAxel3247 – her humanoid status, her home on the *Axel* spaceship and her ship's crew code, respectively. A traveler, one who explored the void beyond Nabatea. What was left of her would be on Cerata.

The crowds along Palmyra Street thinned as they flowed into tributary roads, returning to their homes in preparation for morning shifts. Azad strolled at a steady pace, hands in his pockets and eyes drawn to the night sky. Cerata hovered low, its deep crescent curved in a lopsided smile. Inviting him to seek and find.

★   ★   ★

The next morning, Osbourne informed Azad that he would be assigned the traffic control shift. He also provided three options for getting there. Instead, Azad bought a ticket to Cerata.

"You are now fifty minutes late to your shift," the processor's voice echoed inside his ear. An emotionless statement of fact, without chiding or threat. Azad ignored him.

"We're going on a trip, Osbourne," he said. "Just for a few days. Log a vacation request for me."

He wouldn't have a few days. While there was nothing illegal in Azad's impromptu visit to the shadow moon, Osbourne's algorithms would correctly calculate his pattern of behavior as a Problem and flag him accordingly. When he received the flag, Averro would certainly contact officials for help, possibly even Vitruvian authorities if a missed work shift and a random lunar visit alarmed him enough.

Azad's teeth rattled as the morning shuttle climbed through Nabatea's atmosphere. Supporting launch cables and the shuttle's internal counter-pressure made the ascent as smooth as scientifically possible, but any launch into space stressed the body. A young woman nearby vomited, her clammy head pressed into the back of her chair.

Cerata's surface, while fully terraformed, only had one town, which its inhabitants decided to locate on the sunless side of the moon. Its perpetual darkness wasn't the only way Cerata rebelled against its mother planet. After he disembarked the shuttle, Azad stood slack-jawed for several minutes, absorbing the dizzying assault on his senses. Spices and smoke greeted him along the main thoroughfare, flanked by thatched-roof houses and high torches that illuminated cracked, cobbled roads. The same smells found on Nabatea, of incense, cumin and dried figs, were heightened under the moon's dense atmosphere, watering Azad's eyes. A Ceratan merchant lifted a snake from a hissing pit. The sacred Vitruvian animal, handled so casually by an orthodox human. A chill ran down Azad's spine at the blasphemous sight. He *was* far from home.

Raised on a planet of straight lines and clear boundaries, Azad tensed at the winding pathways before him. Cerata's darkness, tempered by the glowing torches and blue light-tinged buildings, bothered him less. Nabatea City was most beautiful at night, and Cerata's patchwork of shadows soothed his rattled nerves.

The dense, jostling crowds also crackled with the moon's rebellious aura. Merchants hawked strange gadgets and exotic foods to passersby, dressed in a dizzying kaleidoscope of material and color. A young girl in opulent blue robes, anchored by elegant, pointed shoes, handed Azad a skewer of a thin delicacy coated in powdered sugar. He accepted it with a shy smile. The food was hot and sweet, warming his tongue. When he nodded his approval, the girl gestured him toward the stall. Osbourne kicked into gear, highlighting three baked items to choose from, but the girl hawked other options, dangling an assortment of colorful sweets. When Azad pointed at the pastries, the girl's eyes danced and she launched into a fierce haggling session that neither Azad nor Osbourne were prepared for.

Two older men who had presumably witnessed the exchange laughed as Azad stumbled away from the stall, sticky fingers clutching a small box of sweets. Behind them, a group of older men and women played backgammon before a captive audience, sipping a thick, fragrant beverage. They gossiped and debated, with no signs of Nabatea City's usual hierarchies at play. Azad found shelter under a tree, devouring the rest of his sweets. The familiar flavors calmed him, conjuring memories of Ledo and lazy summer afternoons, a time before work shifts and Problems.

Ledo. He clung to her name, an anchor on this strange moon. He had come here for her, and he wouldn't leave until he found answers. The thought warmed his chest with a surge of much-needed confidence.

A tall building rose above the thatched roofs, its angular peak protruding like a shard of broken glass. The Library of Souls. Odd on first thought, that the Vitruvians would place their deceased, their history, on a moon populated by rebels and outcasts. But Archiving was a subversive science. It didn't keep the dead alive, but it preserved their memories and knowledge for future generations to consume.

The meandering roads added deceptive distance to the library, and Azad panted as he pushed through the crowds. He turned down an alleyway, hoping for a shortcut.

Water splattered from a second-floor window. Azad barely dodged it, craning his neck to find a terrace covered with thick, moving vines. Azad recoiled but his skin tingled. Gardening in Nabatea was a highly regulated activity, critical to ensuring the right balance of oxygen and carbon dioxide within the planet's temperamental atmosphere. On barren Cerata, vines curled like sheltering snakes around copper railings and plants sprouted from windows, a pointless exercise due to the lack of sun, but a colorful indicator of wealth.

Something was wrong. The balconies and terraces across the alleyway were empty, but the air hung thick with an unannounced presence. A chill ran down his spine. His heart quickened.

The alleyway was empty, silent save for the distant cacophony of the main street. And closer to him, footsteps. Steady, purposeful, in time with his own. Azad's shoulders tensed, a prey's instinct under a phantom gaze.

He was being followed.

Chapter Two

Kezza

CALYPSO CORPORATE CAMPUS, MARS
2195 A.D. (1,209 YEARS PRIOR TO
NABATEAN SETTLEMENT)

Lockdown. The evacuation order blinked across the arena in blazing neon. Sirens followed. Perched on the arena's upper stage, Kezza crossed her arms and rolled her eyes.

Please evacuate now. This is not a drill. Remain calm.

Kezza sighed. She unstrapped herself from the harness. Her glittery heels creaked on the rickety stage steps as she descended from the rafters. Bai, one of the lead contortionists, handed her the remnants of her whiskey sour, compliments of an Earth-bound ambassador during intermission. She raised her glass in toast and he winked.

"Think we're going to die this time, Kez?" he asked.

"Everyone's going to fucking die if they keep cutting my act short," Kezza said with a grim smile. She'd been about to debut a new performance on the lyra, her favorite aerial apparatus, when the lockdown call came.

"Maybe the revolution's starting early," LaValle, the company's second contortionist, said to no one in particular. His eyes glowed through his black kohl liner. "Firing up the guillotines before the new ship gets here."

Kezza pressed her lips together to hold back a reply. She had her own plans for Mars's newest visitors, but the rest of the troupe didn't need to know them. She loved them, but they were horrible gossips and before long, all of Mars would know her darkest secrets. No, better to keep her mouth shut. For now.

Tugging at her fishnets, Kezza joined the line exiting the Coliseum. Her costume's black feathers scratched at her neck. In the crowd, you could tell the native Martians from the Earth visitors by their shoulders alone. The Earth folk carried the tension along their shorter bodies, arms rigid as they rushed to the exit. The Martians cracked jokes, their gaits relaxed, as they complained about their corporate overlords and their overzealous safety precautions.

On her way out, Kezza brushed her fingers against the copper lion statue beside the Coliseum's main doors. A tipsy gesture rooted in genuine affection for Mars's largest indoor space. Kezza endured a world of low ceilings and narrow tunnels framed in fluorescent light, but in the Coliseum, gliding across aerial silks and trapezes, she could fly.

"Everyone stay calm and exit in an orderly manner," an usher called out unnecessarily. The crowd, aside from the Earth people, exuded no panic. Just irritation at another disruption. The third alarm in seven days.

The crowd spilled into the main Atrium, where yawning windows separated Calypso Corporate Campus from the Martian atmosphere. No cracks or obvious signs of a breach, although a fierce dust storm outside whipped sand against the triple-paned glass. It hissed as it slid down the clear surface like a bubbling tide. Mother Nature, the saying went, played by simpler rules on Mars than on Earth. When in doubt, add wind.

The lockdowns, once an annual drill, became more popular after the announcement of the great civilizationist Barrett Juul's impending arrival on Mars. To Calypso, no less. Out of two equally corrupt, misery-laden corporate cities, he had chosen the one Kezza called home. His broadcast from Earth spread from Martian to Martian the way teenagers circulated gray market pornography. Kezza had listened to the recording countless times and would probably replay it again once she reached her quarters. In a speech like no other, the civilizationist promised an announcement when he reached Mars that would change their lives forever. Everyone had their own theories – a terraforming project, a new Martian settlement to rival Calypso and Palmcorps, even a technological advance that would enable the Mars-born to function in Earth's gravity, allowing a safe return. But almost everyone agreed that the announcement would be something wonderful. The first signs of much-needed hope.

It all sounded nice, but Kezza was a simple woman with simple needs – revenge.

Barrett Juul, with his big ideas, was the reason Kezza was born on this hellish rock. He was the reason her mum died young and brokenhearted. He needed to die in return. Killing the entire corporate board would be a nice bonus, if Kezza could manage it. She didn't know how yet, but she had free time between circus performances to figure it out.

The sirens continued their screeching. A security guard waved workers through the doors to their residential quarters. The smile crawling along his puffy face told Kezza what would happen before it began. She could almost see the thought balloon forming over his head, a cloud with her in the center. Her skin prickled. She walked without breaking pace, eyes trained ahead. As she stepped across the doorway, he grabbed her backside. A rough, unsparing grip, his untrimmed nails piercing her stockings. A stray finger probed further, sending a jolt of shock up her spine.

Kezza sucked in her breath. Her back tensed and she closed her eyes. In her mind, she swung around, a flurry of black hair, feathers and sinewy arms, landing an elbow on his jaw. Kezza could almost smell the imaginary blood that would erupt from his gums. He would reel from the sickening crunch of the blow, collapsing under a medley of kicks and punches. Roars of approval swelling around her. Others joining in on the assault, all slighted in their own way by Calypso Corporate Security. Aerialists sat at the bottom of the Martian social hierarchy, just above smugglers, junkies and accountants, but at least she wasn't a cop.

Kezza gritted her teeth, steadying herself. She passed through the door without breaking stride, her face a dignified mask. Now was not the time to get put in lockup. She wouldn't have to endure this forever. Kezza knew the game and intended to win in the final stages. Righteous anger is a currency here, her mother once said, like air and water. Save it up for something worthwhile.

Kezza would save it for Barrett Juul.

A loud bang cut through Kezza's stream of consciousness, its reverberations echoing along the narrow stairwell. Gasps and muttered curses followed. The wailing sirens reasserted themselves in Kezza's ears.

"Come on, keep moving!" the guard shouted above them. "Everyone to your quarters."

"Well, we might have an actual emergency this time," LaValle muttered.

While no one panicked, the line quickened pace. Dread coiled within Kezza like a tightly wound spring, one she longed to release with a single, raw scream. But she held it in, like everyone around her. She was Martian to the core, well-versed in bottling her misery. In the controlled confines of Calypso Corporate Campus, known not-so-affectionately as the Triple C, panic was an unaffordable luxury. An atmosphere breach, a pressure failure, a fire – all could be dealt with in some way. The threat localized, its effects minimized to an unfortunate few. But fear, a loss of faith in their collective survival, would destroy Calypso from within, a message repeated every hundred feet along the glowing Atrium screens. *Remain calm. Keep moving.*

Order prevailed – for the moment.

The stairs led down to the underground portion of the campus, where low-wage employees lived in one-room units, regardless of family size. Some called them the Catacombs, which Kezza found overdramatic. It was a corporate slum. Pigeon-gray grime smeared the stairwell's walls. A light flicked on and off about them, its dying bulb sizzling like candied bacon. The ever-present smell of raw sweat greeted Kezza's descent.

Something sharp dug into Kezza's knees. A small child gripped her legs with tiny hands, whimpering softly. She recognized his face through the trails of snot running down his nose. A boy, maybe five or six, who ran down the hallways on her floor for entertainment. Toyless and perhaps even parentless. She scooped him into her arms, raising the child's head over her shoulders, inviting someone, anyone, to claim him. The crowd continued to shuffle down the stairwell.

"Guess you're stuck with me for now," she murmured. The little boy snuffled in response, his breath sweet and milky.

Another loud bang echoed, followed by distant shouts. Kezza froze. The child tightened his grip around her neck. Tension spread through the stale air, the crowd shivering with a shared understanding that this lockdown was different. Something had happened.

Silence.

Then another bang. The energy in the stairwell shifted, a change in the air's vibrations, as composure gave way to panic. Sporadic screams rose through the crowd as it stampeded forward, deeper underground.

Warm bodies pressed against Kezza's back, tugging at her feathers, but she had nowhere to go. She lost balance, her pulse quickening at her throat. Hands shoved her from all directions. The child cried and pushed her away, his small nails clawing at Kezza's face. Her senses, dulled earlier by drink, came to life at the prospect of an imminent crushing. The tangy smell of sweat and fear filled her nostrils. She coughed, her throat burning. Her chest also burned with anger and she shoved back against the crushing bodies with an angry snarl. *No.* She would not get turned into a human pancake only weeks before Barrett Juul arrived. She had murderous plans to enact.

A loud crack cut through the noise. An electromagnetic stunner.

"Keep pace, idiots!" an authoritative voice yelled over the humming crowd. "No one needs to get crushed."

The pressure loosened around Kezza's chest as the crowd obeyed the command. Reaching the third level underground, she forced her way out of the stairwell. She gasped, lungs summoning recycled air. The child wriggled from her arms and darted around the corner. For a second, Kezza fought the urge to follow. The child had forced her to remain strong, to care for something other than herself, but in the end, she was on her own.

Running along the corridor, Kezza kicked off her high heels, cursing herself for not thinking of it before. Other Catacombs residents ran alongside her into their own rooms – quarrymen and women in dust-coated uniforms, Tier Three research assistants, parents yanking their children by their spindly arms. Kezza's bare feet slapped against the cool, grated floor. Graffiti lined the walls, crude slogans painted over official Triple C postings. Gang symbols, warnings to Corp informants. She spun to the left, skidding to a halt in front of a room marked *S5633* above its door. When she leveled her eye in front of the scanner, the door opened with an obedient click.

Welcome, Kezza Sayer, the screen read. She entered.

Kezza loathed her name. At the time she was born in Independent Wales, everyone's name had an affectionate abbreviation. Sharons were known as Shazza. Jasmines were Jazza. Michaels and Mackenzies became Mazza. But her mother skipped the pretense of a proper legal name and listed her screaming newborn as Kezza on the birth certificate. Short for Kerry, she explained.

It made no sense. Kerry had the same number of syllables as Kezza, the same expenditure of vocal energy. But few of her poor mother's decisions had made any sense.

Kezza rubbed her bare arms and closed her eyes. She strained her ears for a useful sound over the sirens. The hiss of tear gas. Screams. Even a chattering sound that could have been gunfire, although a shooting on Mars would be unprecedented. Calypso strictly controlled firearms for obvious reasons, although rumors existed of a secret stockpile in headquarters, in case gang activity turned political.

But the sounds never came. Nothing to reveal what was unfolding beyond her narrow walls.

Then, a high wail interrupted her thoughts. High enough to be heard over the sirens, a voice cried for help outside her room. Her stomach twisted into a cold knot. She pressed her forehead to the door and a square cleared to form a transparent window into the hallway. The child she had carried stood in front of her door, tearstained and alarmed.

Kezza sighed. Poor kid. It was never a good time to get lost in the Catacombs, but especially during a lockdown. She opened the door. The kid's eyes widened and he immediately ran down the hall.

"Hey, come back!" Kezza yelled.

A force struck her from the side, knocking her to the ground. Hands pressed down on her face, pushing her cheek into the chilled, grimy floor. A furious cry escaped her clenched teeth as another set of hands fumbled in her pockets, fishing out her tips from the last performance — free drink coupons, ration stamps, gift cards. Further down the hall, the kid disappeared around the corner.

Kezza spat on the ground. The little brat was part of the con to get Kezza to open her door. An apprentice thief to some older kids who were about to be taught some manners.

She'd been robbed before. Since most Martians stored their wages on their personal CALPal accounts, few carried tangible goods worth stealing. Kezza, a performer popular with new Earth arrivals ignorant of Martian currency, was one of the exceptions.

Kezza struggled against her attacker. The guard had been spared her wrath earlier, but these kids wouldn't get off so easily.

When the hands released her, she shot to her feet with a dancer's agility. The thieves were already sprinting down the corridor, hooting in triumph. A grown man and two teenagers, a boy and a girl. Kezza gave chase.

They ran up the emergency exit stairwell, triggering another alarm that drowned beneath the lockdown sirens. Kezza followed, panting but keeping pace. Blood pounded in her ears.

"Give me my shit!" she yelled.

"Get boiled, slut!" a gangly boy of about fifteen shouted back.

Little fucker. Boiling, the worst form of death on Mars. On a hostile landscape with limited inhabitants who struggled to reproduce, Calypso authorities reserved execution by boiling, essentially direct exposure to the Martian atmosphere, for extreme cases. Corporate treason being the most obvious, above murder, rape and embezzlement.

Kezza caught up with them at the top of the stairwell, grabbing her tormenter by the hair and slamming his head against the wall. He kicked backward and landed a blow directly on her shin. She winced, gripping her sides to steady herself against the burst of pain, but resumed the chase. One of the thieves cursed ahead of her. Kezza almost laughed. She was an aerialist, a line of work that earned her share of falls and bruises. A trio of Catacombs lowlifes with poor endurance wouldn't stop her.

"I fucked you once," the uglier one crowed. He meant it in the virtual sense. A digital replica of her face and body, down to every detail, existed within Calypso's Virtual Fantasies room. Everyone in the circus troupe had to accept this invasion of privacy in their contract, submitting themselves to a full body scan. Every leer she received on Calypso's corridors reminded her that anyone over the age of eighteen could rent a simulation of Kezza Sayer by the hour.

The remark had its desired effect. Kezza screamed a string of curses, raw fury pulsating in her bones. They passed through an empty engineering room and Kezza grabbed a wrench and hurled it at them. She missed, the metal clattering to the ground.

She snarled in frustration. The lockdown, the police, whatever was happening upstairs – none of it mattered. All that mattered were the three parasites in front of her, in desperate need of a lesson. She grabbed the wrench again.

They ran through the Greenery, a level below the Atrium, tearing through rows of crops on Earth-imported soil. Everything took on a yellowish tint underneath beams of artificial sunlight – stalks of sweetened corn, patches of chocolate-infused zucchini and sugared sweet potatoes. Calypso had made its original money through high-fructose corn syrup, so the evil geniuses in charge found a way to make anything sweet.

Kezza followed the thieves around a corner, cutting her hand on a stray husk of corn. Gritting her teeth, she swiveled around, keeping pace. Panting across the expansive room, she humored the idea of defecting to Palmcorps, if only to experience sugarless food.

They burst through the doors at the far end of the Greenery, trading its warm, muggy air for the deafening whine of machinery inside Calypso's waste disposal area. The unimaginatively named Waste Room. Sweet, pungent decay filled the high-ceilinged room, where mounds of trash crawled up its walls. Anything that couldn't be recycled was fed through pipes and airlocked chutes into the Martian desert, where it was burnt. Even corpses passed through its doors, for those who eschewed burial. Nothing on Calypso went to waste. But everyone, including Kezza, was disposable.

Ahead of her, the thieving trio slowed, thin bodies growing rigid. One pointed ahead at something on the ground.

Kezza skidded to a halt. A chill ran through her, making the frail hairs on her arms bristle against her costume's lace. Two long shapes stretched across the ground.

Human shapes.

The thieves spun around. Before Kezza could react, they barreled past her, knocking her to the ground.

Kezza scrambled to her feet, but the shock of the bodies on the floor had tempered her fury. She hesitated for a moment, torn between the instinct to continue the chase and her curiosity over the motionless figures.

With each step forward, dread sank deeper into the pit of Kezza's stomach. Her throat tightened. The disjointed shapes became a man and a woman, lying feet away from the airlock.

The woman was unmistakably dead. She bore the same glassy eyes as Kezza's mother when it had finally happened, the same stillness in her limbs. This woman's skin was a bruised purple, as though thousands of vessels had erupted across her body. A ring of blood swelled around her eyes, seeping down her cheeks.

Kezza squeezed her eyes shut, fighting back nausea, before opening them again. The man lay on his stomach, the back of his neck bearing the same discoloration. With his face hidden, he could have just been unconscious. She had to help him if that was the case, despite the very loud voice in her head screaming at her to run.

Kezza knelt beside him for a closer look, pulling on his shoulder. She turned him onto his back.

The man's eyes flew open, bloodshot red. Kezza jolted. He drew a sharp, desperate breath and coughed, spit and blood spraying like mist around him.

Kezza screamed. She swatted at the mist of blood on her face. The man shot from the ground with alarming strength and speed and landed on his feet. After scanning the room wildly, he knocked Kezza down. Pain shot through her wrists as she broke her fall. The man was gone, charging toward the Greenery.

Heart pounding, Kezza ran her hands over her body, checking for damage through pulsing waves of adrenaline. No obvious signs of injury. But what had happened to the dead woman and suddenly very alive man? What discolored their skin, tinged their eyes with blood? She held up her cut hand, the same one she used to turn the man around and then wiped his blood from her face. Terror gripped her. Was it contagious? More importantly, was she a complete idiot? She could have been beating those brats within an inch of their lives right now if she'd just turned around.

A loud crash echoed through the Waste Room. The man sprinted back toward her, eyes wild but trained on the airlocked door leading outside, into open Martian desert. Kezza's breath stopped.

"Are you crazy?" she yelled. "Stop! You don't have a suit on."

Reflexes took over. Kezza ran, skidding on a streak of trash stretched across the floor. She landed on her elbows as the man leapt over her like a gazelle. He charged at the exit and opened the first of two doors.

Kezza struggled to her feet. The emergency lock beckoned her across the room. She jumped over another pile of waste and ran at breakneck speed. She blinked as the burning stench of refuse reached her eyes. Nearing the lock, she slammed her hand down on the red button. It would trigger yet another alarm, but that mattered less than keeping the man inside.

Kezza ran back to the inner door's portal window. She'd reached the lock in time – the emergency control had secured both doors, effectively sealing the man in between them. Through the small, foggy window, he pounded at the outer door.

Watching the trapped man struggle, Kezza couldn't help but pity the crazy bastard. He had knocked her to the ground, true enough, but hadn't stolen from her, abused her, or insulted her as so many others had. Desperation consumed his every movement. She shouted through the window, hoping she could reason with him.

"Hey, calm down! You need help, you're sick. Come back inside and I'll take you to the med ward."

The man turned at the sound of her voice, a flicker of understanding in his eyes.

"Come on," Kezza encouraged. "Let's go together."

At those words, the man's face clenched, skin forming ripples across his forehead. The wildness returned to his eyes before sadness flickered across his face. His lips moved, and Kezza read the words. *I'm going home.*

And in a single, swift motion, the man hurtled the full weight of his body against the outer door. It burst open, falling into the sand. Kezza blinked, unwilling to believe her eyes. A sealed airlock door, falling like a domino. The man ran out.

Kezza gasped, pressing her hands to her face. Through a part in her fingers, she saw the man swing his clenched fists with military rigidity as he tore across the open landscape, without oxygen or protection from the predatory Martian atmosphere. A self-boiling in action. Several agonizing seconds passed but he didn't fall over or even slow down. He ran further into the desert, finally stumbling to his knees before he collapsed into a dark, twisting shape in the windswept dust.

Kezza froze. It was impossible. Coldness spread through her limbs, her breath fogging the window portal. A man, after rising from the near-dead, broke an airlocked door open and ran through open Martian atmosphere. She flexed her hands, now numb with adrenaline, and touched the door. It felt cold and real, but could she trust her own senses anymore?

The wail of the sirens, so continuous that she'd forgotten about them, reentered her ears. The ground swayed. The dead woman came back into focus on the floor.

Time to go.

Kezza sprinted out of the Waste Room, darting through rows of corn, when the familiar drumming of footsteps reached the Greenery. Holding her breath, she slid into a thick patch of cornstalks, every limb of her body still. She closed her eyes. As she opened them, a line of armed men rushed in single file, advancing into the Waste Room. Summoned, no doubt, by her pressing the emergency lock.

The last security guard disappeared around the corner. Kezza sprinted in the opposite direction, running as though a Terran wind carried her. She didn't look back. She didn't sharpen her ears for voices. She didn't stop running until she tumbled through the rear Catacombs stairwell.

The lockdown sirens finally ended their chorus, in what must have been a Calypso record. Kezza sank to her knees, pressing her head against the cold metal railing. She crouched there until her heart ceased its violent drumming.

Families spilled from their rooms in droves as Kezza walked numbly back to her own quarters, drawing curious stares. She trained her eyes ahead, clenched her injured hand, and hoped her appearance gave away nothing of the last hour. She reached her room with a relieved sob, slamming the door shut behind her.

She stared at her own reflection in the mirror, but the same sad face, wrapped in the same overworked body, stared back at her. Her gaze turned inward, scanning her body for signs of illness. Her heart skipped at every physical quirk, every itch and twinge of discomfort. She forced herself to breathe, to return to reality.

Maybe you'll be fine, she reassured her tense reflection.

But she wasn't fine. She'd found two corpses in the Waste Room. One sprang to life and made an impossible sprint across open Martian terrain, only to collapse into the sand. Was the incident tied to the lockdown? It had to be. The planet may have been large, but Calypso was a small place, too small for coincidences.

Outside of her room, the Catacombs returned to dingy normalcy. Voices trailed down the hallways, the sound of scuffles and excited chatter as another night descended over the city. Somewhere, her thieves were spending her hard-earned tip money.

To calm down, Kezza began her daily stretches. She wasn't as naturally flexible as most of the circus performers, so she had to work continuously to keep her body limber for her job's demands. Her hands, calloused from her hours on the lyra, pulled at her foot arches as she sank into a deep forward stretch. A familiar, pleasant ache ran through her hamstrings. Kezza held on to the pain as her mind drifted away from the inexplicable events at the Waste Room to the more important topic at hand – killing Barrett Juul.

She reached for the handheld radio on her nightstand and pressed play. Barrett Juul's clipped, Danish-accented baritone filled the room.

Good people of Mars, I reach out to you three months into the journey on Calypso One, the recording began. *Had I broadcast this message from Earth, they would not have allowed me to board, even with my reputation and credentials. You know who 'they' are, because you live on their terms, day in and out. They control the food you eat, how much water you drink and when you can bathe. You struggle on the paltry wages they give you, knowing that to try and earn more means risking a fine that will place your family in generations of debt.*

The rest of the troupe loved those opening lines, nodding vigorously around the radio when they first heard them. But Kezza scoffed. Barrett Juul was one of the people on every podcast and news channel advocating for Martian immigration – adding, of course, that corporations could lead the way. What did he think would happen when Calypso and Palmcorps claimed the first two authorized stretches of Martian territory? That they'd set up free ice cream stands and affordable housing?

But here is what they can't control: the reality that they need you more than you need them. That Mars, through the blood and sweat of your labor, belongs to you.

Tell that to Kezza's mother. Her dad worked for Calypso, when he wasn't drinking and being an all-around shitstain. He answered Barrett Juul's call and boarded the next ship to Mars, dragging Kezza's mum with him. But the high radiation voyage killed her dad that same year, and Mum would eventually follow.

I come here of my own accord, with a team of investors behind me. Since these investors own controlling shares in Calypso and the Obscura station, the board has no choice but to host me. I don't wish to disrupt the system in place on Calypso Corporate Campus for those who wish to perpetuate it. But for those of you who feel crushed under its heel, who can't bear another day under its narrow domes, I speak to you: I offer an alternative. I aim to recruit you for something that will alter the course of human history. On Earth, we speak of the crooked axis of humanity. History repeating itself again and again. With your help, let's break free from its orbit and carve out a new trajectory into the stars.

Those closing remarks impressed many Martians, but Kezza could read between the lines. Juul didn't want to disrupt the status quo on Mars too much – rich and powerful men rarely did – but he wanted to dupe people into some new vanity project of his. A rival corporate city. No doubt it would make him richer and probably kill a lot more people from radiation sickness.

But Kezza could play along. She would do anything – seduce him, manipulate him, dive headfirst into a vat of sugar – if it meant getting close to Juul and finding her moment to strike.

But first, sleep.

Exhausted, Kezza finally peeled off her costume and collapsed onto her coffin-sized bed. Immediately, the timer kicked in on a nearby screen, warning her of the seven-hour sleep limit. Another screen lit up on the ceiling, projecting Calypso-approved images – running water, smiling children, the sun rising over Martian hills. Hints of Earth, but nothing too explicit. Nothing to fuel Kezza's longing for animals and open, green places.

Shimmering costumes hung from her closet, while her own clothes were packed in a single drawer in her nightstand. If Kezza died, Calypso authorities would clean her room out in less than an hour. Half of what she owned really belonged to the circus – objects to make her thinner, prettier, a more functional ornament for the masses. Borrowed objects for a borrowed existence, ones that would be handed off to another dancer before the Waste Room finished charring her bones into ash.

In the seconds before she drifted into sleep, Kezza drowned in the echoes of the day's sensations – ears ringing from the sirens' wail, the stench of garbage bitter in her throat, empty promises from a distant stranger. And the silhouette of the man, jerking and crawling like a spider in the open Martian air, danced behind her closed eyes.

Chapter Three
Azad

CERATA, SATELLITE MOON OF NABATEA
YEAR OF SETTLEMENT 1208

Azad began to run. The footsteps matched his quickened pace. His vision heightened, giving edges to the alley's dark shapes. His heartbeat punched through the stillness. Even his sense of smell sharpened, filling his nostrils with smoke and ripe figs from the now–distant main road.

Osbourne chimed in.

Your neurochemical responses suggest you are in a fight-or-flight situation. Would you like to:

Face your pursuer and clear any misunderstanding?

Run?

Turn around and attack? Note that if the action is not determined to be justifiable self-defense, you risk prosecution under the Oasis from Violence Act, Nabatean Code 133-1772.

"Not now, Osbourne," he muttered under his breath. Nabatean choices of three would not help him here, in a place with few rules to speak of. Had he been reported missing already? Or had he drawn the wrong kind of attention on the main road?

Forcing down panic, he clenched his fists and spun around to face his pursuer. A tall shape darted through a side door. The figure moved too fast to reveal a face, but the light caught a tattooed snake, red and black, coiled around the person's exposed chest. Azad shuddered. A Vitruvian. That changed everything. Even if he could catch them, and he couldn't, he'd be no match for a Vitruvian.

Azad stumbled in the alleyway, disoriented and struggling to control his fluttering heart. Was this related to Nenah, the Vitruvian woman who died on his table? Had he attracted negative attention for his defiance while trying to save her, a red flag exacerbated by her cryptic final words? Nabateans had been charged, even expelled from the city, for far less.

The Library of Souls towered overhead. Thick, graying condensation smeared across its highest windows, concealing the building's secrets.

This was it. This was his greatest chance to learn what happened to Ledo. A quote from Barrett Juul emerged from some long-forgotten lesson: *If not now, when?* With a deep breath, he strode into the bustling street toward the library.

Though the main librarian greeted Azad with some curiosity, likely used to dealing with Vitruvians and eccentric locals rather than soft-faced, nervous people from the main planet, she directed him down a cave-like hallway, a tunnel with walls that glowed an effervescent blue, into the main Archive room.

Azad gasped, prompting a subtle smile from the librarian before she disappeared around a corner. From the inside, the main library stretched upward like a giant cylinder. Stone staircases twisted around its walls. A small desk with a cozy lamp and a spherical monitor sat in the center of the room, a gesture to tradition that went unused, as there were no books or bookshelves to speak of. Instead, tens of thousands of dark plaques covered the rounded walls, a mosaic of black and white from the base to the sunless roof.

Azad approached the wall, raising a shaking hand toward a plaque at his eye level. His fingers brushed against its smooth, cold surface. Immediately, the blackness turned cloudy and dissolved, revealing a name.

OfPalmyra, Jae. Archived YOS 52.

The man or woman, Jae, had passed away only fifty-two years after the settlement of Nabatea. He hadn't come for a history lesson, but this was too interesting to pass up. Azad's fingers pulled at the space below the plaque.

The plaque drew away from the wall, exposing a long drawer behind it. His hand dropped in time with his stomach at the sight of a human head, the color of chalk and cracked in various places, inside the drawer.

Azad pressed his clammy forehead against the wall, sucking in deep breaths. Though he'd seen bodies at the hospital before, they'd been freshly deceased. There was nothing natural about this detached head. Both ancient and lifelike, its bones emerged behind tears of flesh but the features were otherwise intact. He longed, strangely, to see the androgynous person's eyes, but the Archive Band covered them like a slipped crown.

He spun around at a sudden whirring noise. The sphere on the desk had come to life, rotating with climbing speed. In its center, shapes twisted and shifted like a flag caught in the wind. Up close, they formed the familiar, rosy tones of Nabatea City, interspersed with unfamiliar faces and buildings.

The cognitive imprint from the deceased settler. Not memories, exactly. Certainly not a soul. There was nothing personal in the imprint, no evidence of love or suffering – only places, people, moments.

Azad sensed her before she came into view. Motion caught his eye, and he looked up to find an elderly woman descending one of the winding stairways. How he had missed her when first entering the room, Azad did not know. She took slow, cautious steps, a careful eye trained on Azad. Her shock of white hair extended in every direction like a wreath, in sharp contrast with her dark, weathered skin.

Azad extended a hand to help her down the last step. Whoever she was, good manners never went out of style and Azad always respected his elders. The woman nodded to him in a subtle gesture of gratitude, her wide mouth arched in a smile. Her long dress, the color of dried grass and patterned with palm trees, suggested a sweet, senior retired Nabatean on a vacation, but something about her gave Azad pause. A stern regality in her eyes.

"A lovely place, isn't it?" Her voice was low and rough like gravel.

Lovely was not how Azad would have described a dark room full of decapitated heads, but he nodded.

"So much history," he said, earning an approving nod from the smiling woman. "It's incredible to think about all of these lives that came before us."

"Are you looking for an ancestor, dear?"

"Something like that," Azad said, unwilling to offer specifics to a stranger, kind and harmless as she seemed. A thought struck him. Perhaps the Vitruvian patient, Nenah, had been placed outside of the main Archive room, given the sensitive nature of her death.

"Are all of the Archived souls in this room?" he asked the old woman.

"All except the Vitruvians," she replied. "They're in a private area, open to select Vitruvians only. Were you looking for someone in particular?" She frowned.

Azad's heart sank. Of course it wouldn't be as easy as strolling into the library, examining the Vitruvian woman's Archive and finding Ledo's now-adult face staring back at him. Had he really expected as much? He recalled the contempt in the officials' eyes, the speed with which they wheeled their fallen comrade from the hospital. They would never place a Vitruvian mind open for public consumption, for the masses to mine for insight.

Harsh, echoing voices erupted from the library's entrance. An argument. Azad's skin prickled with apprehension.

"I'd better go," he said to the old woman, but her attention was fixed on the main door, her round frame rigid and alert. She clenched one fist; the other hand crept into her pocket.

A tall man burst through the front entrance. He was wiry but muscular. His gait managed to be both swaggering and feminine in equal measure, an aesthetic mirrored in his black, skintight pants and an open jacket. The room's glow glinted off the shine of his bald head, his strong features offset by an artfully pomaded mustache.

"Found it, Zelle!" he said, shaking a small object in his gloved hand. "Watched enough to confirm our suspicions. Our recently departed friend came from the *Axel*."

The woman named Zelle shot him a warning look, tilting her head in an open, unsubtle gesture at Azad. But Azad stared at the spherical shape rolling between the man's fingers, a swirling orb with ghostly faces in its center.

"Is that from the Vitruvian Archives?" he asked the man. "How did you get it?"

The man and the woman gaped at him as though he'd been Blanked.

"What do you want with Vitruvian brains, *hadir*?" the man asked.

Whatever *hadir* meant, it wasn't a title of respect. But no matter. The man's words rattled in Azad's ears. *Recently departed. On the Axel*, the interstellar ship that formed part of the Vitruvian's, *his* dead Vitruvian's, name. Too many coincidences to be dismissed. Azad rounded on the woman named Zelle.

"Is that Nenah from the *Axel* ship?" he asked in a low voice. Footsteps swelled from the hallway and urgency gripped him. Someone was coming. "She died on my table in Nabatea hospital yesterday. She knows someone I lost a long time ago."

Amusement drained from the woman's face. Her brows tightened over olive green eyes, surveying him with newfound suspicion. Then, her eyes flickered and widened with surprise. Recognition.

"Who are you?" Zelle whispered.

Azad paled. He looked just like his sister. Had this Zelle woman met Ledo?

But before he could answer, a heavy thud echoed from the library's entrance.

"Company," the mustached man said, twisting to peer over Azad's shoulder.

It happened in a matter of seconds. The man shot forward, reaching the door faster than Azad could turn his head. The main door burst open with a loud thud, revealing at least ten guards outside. Orthodox rather than Vitruvian, with matching uniforms and slow reflexes. Weapons flashed in their hands. With a single, powerful kick, Zelle's companion sent the door back into its hinges. Shouts of surprise and curses erupted from the other side. The man crawled in an upward arc along the wall like a spider and yanked a curtain rod from its hinges with one arm.

Azad's jaw dropped. He knew about Vitruvian strength and dexterity, but had never seen it put to such effective use. Less impressed, Zelle stamped her foot.

"Hurry, Feisal, we don't have all day!"

The guards outside pushed and banged against the door.

"You're under arrest!"

"Zelle of Nabatea, come with us quietly!"

Azad exhaled loudly. They weren't after him. But he was here, in a room with a pair of wanted criminals, and that was enough to get him arrested as well. And whoever these people were, Zelle and Feisal, they knew something about the Vitruvian woman who knew Ledo. If he wanted answers, he had to cast in his fate with theirs.

"Guards of the Shadow Moon, come and try!" the man named Feisal cackled after wedging the rod into the door handle.

"We'll go out the back," Zelle said, businesslike.

"Why do you want Nenah's memories?" Azad asked. Zelle ignored him, gesturing at Feisal.

But for once, Azad would not be ignored. For the second time in two days, a stranger looked at him with recognition. This woman Zelle may have been a fugitive, but she knew Ledo and unlike Nenah, she was alive. Abandoning all caution, Azad stepped in front of Zelle, blocking her path to the stairway.

"Let me come with you," Azad said.

"Go home."

"You recognized my face. You know Ledo, don't you?"

As Feisal ran toward them, a Vitruvian snake tattoo flashed across his pale chest through his unzipped black jacket. Azad's stomach knotted at the familiar red and black pattern.

"It was you," Azad said, raising his voice. He trailed behind Feisal and Zelle as they climbed the stone stairs. "You followed me outside the library."

"Clever little city-boy," Feisal called over his shoulder, sneering. "But maybe that means it's not smart to follow us. We're dangerous folk, *hadir*. Are you trying to become a hostage? Would anyone care enough to save you?"

"I said I was coming with you," Azad said, huffing as he climbed behind them. He struggled to keep pace with the Vitruvian and even Zelle, who had gathered her patterned dress in bunches and ascended in light, airless steps.

Zelle stopped halfway up the stairway. She pushed on a plaqueless gap in the wall and it gave, revealing a hidden door. Azad gasped, sweat streaking down his brows. Below them, the guards had broken the main door apart and crawled over splintered wood into the library. The trio slipped through the door before the first stunner shot fired.

They spilled into another set of glowing, cave-like tunnels. Feisal lowered his head to avoid its curved, rock ceiling. Ahead, the tunnel forked in three directions.

"Which way?" Azad said.

Osbourne, unsettlingly quiet since their arrival in the library, chimed in, awakened by the simplicity of the question.

You appear to have three pathways, Azad. Do you want to proceed (choose one):

To the right (no map available – end point unknown)?

To the left (no map available – end point unknown)?

Through the center (no map available – end point unknown)?

"That doesn't help, Osbourne," Azad said in a low moan.

"You're not talking to one of those Juul-cursed brain-scramblers, are you?" Feisal spat. "Run back home, *hadir*."

"Take me with you!"

"Captain, let me kick a hole in him."

Ignoring both men, Zelle reached into the pocket of her voluminous dress and pulled out a strange device. It resembled a camera, the kind placed on Nabatean walkways and shuttle ticket stops, but this was no ordinary camera. Silver and sleek, its lens projected out like a funnel cloud, its center unnaturally black – purest black, the kind of black seen only when there's no light to absorb.

"Let's see where trouble's waiting," Zelle murmured.

She pointed the device into the forked intersection and adjusted the dials. Feisal stood back. The device whirred in soft tones and the air around them shivered, a sensation that made Azad dizzy.

Azad's jaw dropped. Armed guards charged through the leftmost tunnel, running backward. Like a film playing in reverse, they backed into the central pathway. They ignored the three figures standing in the fork, and in an instant, Azad understood. The guards had soft outlines and a transparent sheen because they were not really there. At least, not at present.

After several seconds, more guards passed in reverse into the central pathway, Vitruvians in white uniform.

Zelle switched the device off with a grim but satisfied smile.

"Quickest way out's in the middle," Feisal said. "They're still there. Think I can take them, fearless leader?"

"Too risky," Zelle said. "We go right. Alert Nawalle to get the ship ready."

Stunned, Azad stumbled on shaky knees as he trailed them down the right tunnel. What had he just witnessed?

Azad's lungs burned from the effort of keeping up with Zelle and Feisal. His eyes trained on Feisal's swinging jacket, the sphere bunched in his pocket. His best chance at finding Ledo and her fate. The Vitruvian shot him a scowl but tolerated his presence the way one would tolerate a child tugging one's arm, begging for sweets.

Footsteps echoed behind them from the tunnel fork. Azad's muscles seized with adrenaline. The guards. No doubt they would split up along the tunnels, but some would find them.

"Up ahead!" Feisal said, his voice free of exertion. "Through that window."

There was indeed a window, the first one Azad had seen inside the library. A beautiful pattern of swirling, multicolored glass that Feisal swiftly put his fist through.

"Nawalle, get lined up along the aft side!" Zelle barked into her shoulder.

"What about the *hadir*? Do we cut him loose?" Feisal asked Zelle.

Zelle rounded on him, looking ready to strike. Even the tall, powerful Vitruvian recoiled.

"Do you not recognize him?" she asked. "Look at him!"

Feisal turned to Azad, his kohl-lined eyes widening with realization. He sighed, rolling his eyes to the heavens.

"There they are!"

Shouts echoed and boots thundered against the rocky floor. A rushing sensation whipped past Azad's ear. A stunner. He had received basic training on how to use one during an ill-fated security shift, enough to know he didn't want to be on its receiving end.

Zelle crawled through the window, bunching her skirts, and fell into the open air. Azad's heart stilled and an invisible icy hand plunged into his stomach. They would have to jump.

"You're next," Feisal said. He leapt between Azad and the oncoming guards, twitching but not falling under a stunner blast. He absorbed a second hit with ease.

Azad's knees locked. With an imperceptible gesture, he shook his head. He couldn't do it. Groaning, Feisal shoved him against the window and Azad's body moved into action, even as his mind kept screaming at him to stop. Osbourne, once again, was silent.

Azad climbed through the window, gritting his teeth as broken glass scraped his elbows. He paused, disoriented by the dark, before remembering that he was on the Shadow Moon, and night and day meant nothing here.

"Out!" a voice yelled, and with a harsh push against his back, Azad was in the air, flailing for something solid to grab. Before he could scream, a solid, gray shape rushed at him and he landed on top of it with a sickening thud. Pain exploded across his left side. Bursts of light danced before him and an engine screamed in his ears. His vision narrowed and he struggled against it until a pair of soft hands found his arms, and he surrendered to the encroaching dark.

Chapter Four

Kezza

CALYPSO CORPORATE CAMPUS, MARS
2195 A.D.

The silence of the authorities after the lockdown spoke volumes. No mention of a corpse in the Waste Room or another fresh body outside. No explanation for the strange bangs that had sent the Catacombs into a panic. Something sinister lurked behind the lockdown, beyond the usual drills and gang disturbances. A secret the authorities couldn't even develop a lie to conceal. Juul's arrival loomed over the campus like a dense fog, wafting into every conversation. Everyone drew a connection between the two events, however tenuous. Tension crackled through the stale, recycled air of the Triple C.

For Kezza, the days dissolved together in a liquid haze. Her waking days were consumed with circus rehearsals, but in her dreams, she returned to the chase across the Greenery, the man rising from near-death before surrendering his life to the Martian terrain. But she shrugged those dreams away every morning. Barrett Juul was her top priority. She had a civilizationist to assassinate.

Then came her monthly health checkup.

"You're putting on more muscle than expected for your protein intake," the doctor muttered, sifting through her vitals. An older man with long white hair slicked back like a cockatoo, he abandoned his 3D scanners and gripped her arms, as though he could probe her flesh for some secret the machines couldn't reveal. He squinted his gray eyes into narrow slits.

"Run full diagnostics," he said. His breath carried the faintest whiff of alcohol. Kezza coughed. "Transmit to my CALPal."

Underneath his pale skin, text appeared. Kezza shivered. Most Martian residents had opted to have their personal handheld devices, named CALPals – what they used to communicate, purchase and store corporate credits – embedded underneath the skin of their arms like a chip. Protection from loss and theft, the ad campaigns reassured. Though the screens were paper-thin and the process reportedly painless, Kezza balked at the thought of turning her arm into a computer monitor. Not an attractive look for a dancer, she figured, and she liked her own CALPal, a hand-sized computer shaped like a fox's head. The closest she would ever come to seeing wildlife on Mars.

"Yes," the doctor said, tilting his wrist. "Far too much muscle, and it's everywhere. Legs, torso, arms." He shuddered, as though she were growing a tail.

"Not sure if you've heard, but it takes some strength to do aerials," Kezza shot back. "Give my lyra a try sometime if you don't believe me."

The doctor sniffed. "Too much muscle," he said with an air that shut down any further debate.

"Great news, Kezza, you can get a break from the trapeze and become our circus's strong man," a deep voice said teasingly across the medical room's partition. The Martian Circus's contortionist, LaValle, lay back as a small army of physical therapy medmechs went to work on his overstrained ligaments.

"Look, I've been following the diet and exercise regimen," Kezza said to the doctor. Her throat tickled, and she fought the urge to hack directly into his smug face.

"I'm aware," the doctor said. "You know that MyHealth chip in your shoulder can read everything you consume down to the micronutrient level. Your eating habits are no secret from me. And how long have you had that cough?"

Kezza gasped for air after a violent burst of coughing, thumping on her chest with her open hand.

"It's been on and off for the last few weeks," Kezza admitted, throat raspy. The coughing came in fits, the only sign of trouble after the incident in the Waste Room.

The doctor shook his head.

"The cough worries me," he said without conviction. "But not as much as the weight gain. Your job requires you to be lightweight, Ms. Sayer. Keep putting on that muscle and you might as well be at a circus act on Earth, crashing to the ground at the slightest imbalance. I'm going to adjust your diet, take out some of those powdered eggs. The smoothies are fine. And more cardio, less strength training. In fact, no strength training for three weeks. You get enough grabbing on to those ropes and ribbons."

"Can she still drink alcohol?" LaValle called over the curtain, voice laced with ironic gravity. The doctor pursed his lips, considering the question.

"Why not?" the doctor said. "As long as you don't eat more to absorb it. In fact, a few rough mornings over the toilet might help keep the calories to an acceptable minimum."

Kezza's mouth twitched in a scowl, but she nodded. It could have been worse. In the past, the Calorie Police would take everything enjoyable out of her diet before big shows. At least she'd keep her alcohol and have to spend less time on push-ups and shoulder presses.

But the doctor, and the circus overlords who hired them, were wrong. She could do incredible things on the trapeze, the lyra and silks if they let her get stronger. The new routines she choreographed in her mind, with their dizzying climbs and dazzling drops, could become a full reality with enough practice and strength. But no – she had to look a certain way, keep her arms slim enough and her proportions hourglass enough for the Earthly gaze.

His medical duties fulfilled, the doctor shook Kezza's hand, flattened his spiky mane and moved on to the next patient, another costumed dancer strapped to the metabolism machine like a prisoner on the rack.

Her monthly torture complete, Kezza joined the other performers on the far end of the Atrium, at a dive bar popular with ore mining crews. A shift had just ended, the smell of rust and sweat overpowering the cramped, dimly lit room. Men and women in bright blue suits, designed to stick out in their clay-red surroundings, sat in clusters with foamy beers. Kezza ordered a vodka, straight – anything else was guaranteed to be poisoned with unnecessary sugar. The Ukrainian-based miners' guild had successfully lobbied to keep their traditional beverage sucrose-free.

"Have you heard who's coming with Juul *only seven days from now?*" LaValle asked the group with a confidential smile.

Kezza smiled back. Transporters arrived from Earth every opposition, when Mars and Earth orbited closest to each other around the sun, bringing new colonists, temporary residents and whatever cargo fit in between. The next transporter, the flagship *Calypso One*, would dock above Calypso next week.

"Someone obscenely rich, or I don't care," said Sergei, a male acrobat with gold teeth. He'd spent a month's salary to plate them after reading about the trend in an Earth-smuggled magazine, hoping to impress wealthy visitors. As soon as a fashion arrived in Mars, however, it was guaranteed to be obsolete on Earth. Fashion was fickle enough without the added lag of space travel.

"Word is that a bigwig astrophysicist is coming to check out the Obscura over some new breakthrough," the contortionist continued, winking at Kezza. Within the competitive and drama-prone circus troupe, LaValle was her closest friend. "None other than Dr. Hamza, the mother of our civilizationist savior, Barrett Juul. It's a family affair. Wonder what kind of breakthrough she found."

Kezza buried her startled expression in her glass, letting the vodka burn her throat. His mother was coming to Mars with him? The reality of the situation struck her like a bucket of icy water to the face. Could she kill a man in front of his mummy? Even life-destroying billionaire vultures had families. Her own mother's face, hollowed out from chemo, leapt into her mind's eye and she put down her glass with a cold smile. Yes. Yes, she could.

"What's a civilizationist, anyway?" asked Jen, the small, spiky-haired artificial-fire dancer. Since real fire proved a serious hazard on Mars, the fire dancers used harmless artificial flames, making them the dullest, most useless portion of the circus's act. Jen was all right, though.

"Do I look like I know or care?" LaValle retorted. "I guess someone who studies civilizations."

"They design them," Kezza said, drawing surprised looks around the table. "Like urban planners, but instead of designing cities, they design societies. They create social institutions and cultures. It came about after those horrible wars in the Levant and the Korea famine, when they basically had to restart entire nations from scratch, after refugees started going back home to the rubble."

Kezza did her homework on the things that mattered. She had been a serious student before her mother's diagnosis, displaying an aptitude for patterns and spatial awareness, qualities that could have fast-tracked her into a Tier Two position. A boring desk job in engineering or terrain-work. But the classroom suffocated her, her mother's illness choked the ambition out of her, and when she wandered into the half-finished Coliseum on a lonely day, watching the newly formed circus practice pirouettes under Martian gravity, Kezza knew her calling.

"But why come here?" The shiny-toothed Sergei shook Kezza back into the dim, smoky present. "He's got plenty of work on Earth. What does he want with us low-grav, light-boned Corpslaves? Think it's true he means to take over Calypso?"

"Don't see how he could make it shittier," Jen sneered.

They drank in silence, unable to expand on that last sentiment. Kezza frowned. Whatever Juul had planned, he wouldn't get far. She would see to that.

"Immigrants, though," Jen added, cheerier. "It's always fun to see the new arrivals."

"Don't get too excited," LaValle's voice cut in. "That ship will have two interesting people, and a whole host of indentured Corpslaves and duped Earth assholes looking to atone for their credit debt."

Unlike the Lunar colony, Mars had little in the way of tourists, given the two-year journey from Earth. People came to Mars to stay and work.

The exceptions to this rule were high-ranking government officials and thinkers keen to observe life on Mars, and Calypso Tier Two workers who used a temporary contract Martian assignment to escape troubles at home.

A lump formed in Kezza's throat while her friends bickered over their beers. Should she confide her plans to any of them – LaValle, maybe? No one, she was sure, would report her. The circus stayed together, tight-knit by necessity on a world that looked down on them. But she wouldn't let them go down with her. Whatever happened in the aftermath of her message to the powers on Mars, she needed the circus, her people, to carry on.

As the circus troupe lapsed into thoughtful silence, a trio of Tier Twos strolled into the bar. Two men and a woman dressed in paper-crisp suits. Recent arrivals from Earth, likely from the last opposition twenty-one months ago. Their body language gave them away. The way they threw their heads back as they laughed and swung their shoulders freely, as though air and space were infinite commodities. Kezza's shoulders tightened and LaValle tutted under his breath.

"Dancers!" one of the men shouted, predictably. "The great Martian Circus. Weird to see y'all without your getup on."

"It'd be weird if we walked around in tights and feathers all day," Sergei replied, raising his glass in a polite, perfunctory toast that indicated, "It was nice to meet you. Now, fuck off."

A second man pulled up a chair next to Kezza. They had started their night elsewhere; alcohol polluted his breath, already heavy from the exertion of pulling up a chair.

"You have a nice body," he said to Kezza. "Tiny Martian bones. You born here, honey?" The unfolding scene drew eyes around the bar.

Kezza nodded, tipping her glass back to bury her face again within its foggy sphere. She had emigrated at the age of three, technically, but the musculoskeletal effect was the same as if she had been born Martian and she had no desire to prolong the conversation with specifics, and this drunk creep cared even less about the science. The man's eyes remained fixed on her and she felt, rather than saw, his gaze harden with annoyance.

"Too bad about your face, though."

The uneasy silence spread across the table. Kezza's knuckles whitened where she gripped the glass. A tale as old as time. They always called her beautiful until she rejected them, then her flaws multiplied.

"Don't you have Tier Two bars where you can enjoy your overpriced drinks?" LaValle said, his conversational tone edged with impatience.

"We want to mingle," the Tier Two woman said, casting an appreciative glance at Jen, the fire dancer. Kezza had learned from experience that Tier Two women could be worse than their male counterparts, eager to prove themselves as something separate from lowlifes like Kezza. Someone worthy of approval. Not a collection of body parts with an inadequate face.

Kezza closed her eyes and imagined hurling the spoiled, drunk man-toddler one-handed across the room, faster than his 'friends' could drop their jaws. Chasing those thieves weeks ago left her restless for justice, an itch not quite scratched. Her breath shallowed.

"If you were nicer, I could pay to get your eyelids fixed," the drunk man continued, his breath hot on Kezza's neck. "Everyone has lid implants back home now. We could even shave that long chin down. Reduce your friction in the air."

Anger bubbled inside Kezza like a tangible substance, burning her throat. Her mixed Welsh and Korean heritage had gifted her with unfashionable monolids, a feature Kezza had been pressured to correct through surgery starting her first day at the circus. Repeatedly, she refused the racist request.

The other Tier Twos laughed, but the room thickened with tension. Even the ore workers, who normally shunned the circus performers, looked ready to intercede on Kezza's behalf. She didn't work fourteen-hour shifts operating machinery in a terrain suit, but she was still Martian, one who lived in the Catacombs, shared their water rations and grimy toilets. A man with a weathered face stood up, clenched fists ready at his sides.

"Time to go," the miner said. "You can bother these people after the show, like everyone else. Leave them to their drinks."

"Come on, can't we unwind like the rest of you scroungers?" the other man said, breaking his drunken silence. As he spoke, he squeezed Kezza's shoulder.

Something inside Kezza broke free, like a rubber band holding her together had snapped. With one hand, she grabbed his sweaty wrist and shot from her chair, swinging her leg around. An ice dancer's move, her body dipping and her foot orbiting to land directly on the man's face. A crunch followed, his hard nose collapsing under the force of her kick.

A scream cut through her ringing ears. Her pulse pounded at her neck, sending a strengthening heat through her body.

The man was still upright. She kicked again, both feet coming off the ground, the force of the blow sending the man backward into the nearest table. Motion drew her eye toward the drunk who offered to alter her face and she aimed another kick at his jugular.

Despite being saturated with alcohol, the man dipped successfully out of her way. Kezza's foot passed over him, inertia carrying it to the wall, where it landed with a thud and tore a gaping hole through the plaster.

Peripheral sound returned, as though she had come up from underwater. Shouts, cries of alarm, scraping chairs. Scuffles erupted around her, the remaining Tier Two woman dragged by several miners out of the dark room. LaValle hovering in front of Kezza, his mouth moving but the words scrambled. And over his shoulder, the evidence of her fury. The wall plaster torn open like a wound, exposing Calypso's intestines – pipes, air ducts, insulation, alarming in their bare frailty. The first man she attacked moaned against the collapsed table, clutching his bloodied face with shaking fingers. Blood gushed from his battered nose.

The circus troupe surrounded her, nudging her toward the door and speaking in urgent tones over each other. Through the haze, Kezza understood. Security would arrive soon. She had a window to escape, when everyone in the bar could feign ignorance.

She ran toward the Catacombs, swaying and disoriented as she stepped into the brightly lit Atrium. She teetered slightly, either from adrenaline, alcohol or general shock at what had just transpired. How had she managed to knock a full-sized man across a room and open a wall? Her bones, as the Tier Twos had helpfully reminded her, were of Martian density, her frame diminutive even by Martian standards. Until recently.

She doubled over inside the stairwell, retching. Her lungs burned and her throat spasmed with each coughing fit. When it subsided at last, Kezza froze.

Something black, like watery tar, covered the hand she had coughed into. It dangled across her shaking fingers. She spat, leaving another streak of the black substance on a step, where it seeped through the grating to join the rest of the grime.

What was happening to her?

Advancing through the Catacombs on shaking legs, Kezza finally reached her quarters, only to freeze at the entrance. A message in ghost-white paint ran in a childish scrawl across her door.

TRAITOR. CORP WHORE.

Kezza cursed. Apparently, the thieves she chased into the Greenery were also vandals with a grudge. But no matter. This was small potatoes compared to what had just happened in the bar. On the spectrum of enemies, disgruntled Tier Twos posed a more immediate, existential danger than an underfed Catacombs gang. And then there was the black tar coming out of her mouth.

Despite this, Kezza's wrist shook as she attempted to wipe away the words. When they failed to smudge, she barreled through the door, not even bothering to confirm she was alone before collapsing onto her bed.

★   ★   ★

Kezza woke with ringing ears. She twisted beneath her sheets, untangling herself from a tight fetal position. Her dry tongue stuck like tape to the roof of her mouth. And a dull, persistent ache throbbed in her right foot.

The tavern. She ran her hand along her foot. The skin around her ankle was peeling where she had struck the wall. A low, fearful moan escaped her lips. The clock on her wrap-screen showed eleven p.m. How had she not been arrested yet?

Kezza studied her reflection in the mirror. Black eyeliner had pooled around her lower lids, adding even more weight to her already wide, downcast eyes. Her strawberry-toned lipstick had smudged and faded.

Her body looked different. The doctor, for once, was right. The transformation was subtle, but her spindly arms had acquired the gentle curve of strong triceps, hard like brittle branches, while her legs had thickened with new muscle.

The dead woman loomed in her mind, wrapped in bruised skin. If Kezza had contracted whatever the couple carried, why was she stronger, more energetic than ever?

She couldn't be sick. The woman on the floor had blood leaking from her eyes. Weeks had passed since then, with only a cough to show for it – a cough that now conjured black liquid, thick in her throat. An especially frightening symptom. Plenty of foul things lurked in the Catacombs, but no one coughed up tar, not even the miners. Or did they?

Kezza's mouth twisted in a grimace. She wouldn't tell the doctor about that latest development. She couldn't. At best, he would dismiss it, as he'd done earlier, and at worst, he'd pull her from the show and off her lyra, the only thing that gave her joy.

Unable to sleep, Kezza wandered to the prayer room next to the Atrium. The *Isha* night prayers had long ended, but stragglers remained, ore crews newly returned from their shifts. Her casual T-shirt and baggy sweatpants drew stares from the more conservative congregants, but the Imam greeted her with a raised hand and no one voiced their objections aloud. The faithful had grown accustomed to the vodka-drinking, fishnet-wearing trapeze dancer who liked to pray, so they indulged her visits with a mixture of bemusement and warmth. Kezza sat next to a young couple – on Mars, there was no space for gender-segregated prayer rooms – and knelt, turning her head to each side before pressing her forehead to the cold ground.

The motions of prayer calmed her. While others gave themselves up to God, Kezza used the time to process the day's events. And she had a lot to process. A tavern fight, a possibly deadly cough, and on top of it all, the murder of a civilizationist to plan.

Every time she sank to the floor, her eyes turned to the door, waiting for security to burst through and drag her away in cuffs. But she finished a full prayer cycle unmolested. In the silence, the reason came to her.

The man she struck must still be unconscious. The tavern-goers vouched for her and the other Tier Twos chose silence out of self-preservation, eager to finish their tours on Mars without further incident. But the man she incapacitated would recover in a medical ward deep in the Bokambe sector, and when he did, he would identify her.

Kezza thanked the Imam with a subtle nod before wandering outside. The Atrium was alight with night activity. Past the Atrium, crooked signs and neon lights indicated rows of shops and supply hubs. The commissary, repair shops, clothing stores for the wealthy, and swap meets for everyone else. On the far end, at the base of the Observation Deck stairway, lay the Virtual Fantasies room. A line of mostly men always existed outside its glowing, lurid doors, no matter the hour, earning Kezza a gauntlet of leers as she passed. An advertisement from the window caught her eye – a digital replica of Barrett Juul, available by the hour. Kezza let out a disgusted snort. He was a good-looking guy, sure, but could the people of Calypso have a little self-restraint?

After prayer, or at least the ritual of prayer, Kezza always gravitated to the Observation Deck, Calypso's highest point. Above her, night stars shimmered like dust, and ahead, acres of Mars stretched before her. The Arabia Terra desert carried a quiet beauty, as deserts back on Earth must have, a rolling red landscape punctuated with the high ridges of craters and streaks of light sand carried by canyon winds.

Kezza scanned the dark horizon, searching for the distant glint of Palmcorps Corporate Campus. *I'm going home*, the dead man said to her. Did he mean Palmcorps, the only other outpost of civilization on Mars? The rival corporate city? What kind of a home did he have there, to be worth a desperate flight across a hostile world?

An impulse seized Kezza. She gripped one of the thin, arched metal columns that ribbed around the Observation Deck's dome. With a low grunt, she pulled herself up and began to climb.

It was effortless. Her feet barely grazed the column as her upper body did most of the work, climbing higher and higher toward the top of the dome. As an aerialist, she was already strong, but not like this. Not before.

A shiver ran through her body. She wrapped her arms and legs around the column. The floor of the deck shone far beneath her and through the glass windows, the Martian landscape stretched before her, a deep red under the night sky. The high ridges of the Arabia Terra craters rose along the terrain like raised scars.

The man who died was unnaturally strong, too. He'd kicked an airlocked door open like it was made of plywood. Whatever gave him that strength, he seemed to have passed along to Kezza when he coughed blood in her face. It was the only explanation that made sense.

Kezza closed her eyes as blood rushed through her ears. She was changing. Something was happening to her, to her body and perhaps to her mind. If she could kick walls and doors apart, what else could she do? Killing Barrett Juul might be easier than she'd originally envisioned – provided she could stay out of trouble until he arrived.

Her lips parted in a smile. Tears slid down her cheeks. When she opened her eyes again, a new wave of vehicles began their trek across the desert toward the red, blurry horizon. The next mining shift; they never stopped. Waves of emotion struck her like surges in a sandstorm and she let them come – terror, grief, fury and triumph. Whether this change inside her was a gift or a curse, she would use it to her advantage. She'd strike back at Juul and the system he created.

Chapter Five
Azad

NABATEAN ORBIT
YEAR OF SETTLEMENT 1208

Azad opened his eyes and closed them again, wincing at the hollow pain in the back of his head. Sounds reverberated in his ears, distant and thick like oil. He lay on a hard surface, a dull ache throbbing down his spine. When he pulled himself upright, his forehead struck another hard thing, something cold and metallic, making him groan and sink back. Pain on both sides of his head gripped him like a vise.

"Nawalle, your patient awakens!" a familiar male voice said.

Through his blurred vision, a dark shape emerged. It hovered over him, reaching forward until a cool finger touched his face and drew back an eyelid.

"Where – what happened?" Azad asked, before memory returned to him in static bursts. Ledo. Cerata. The Library of Souls. A man and a woman running down a tunnel. And the terror of falling, until something came between himself and the ground. Something hard, and therefore not much better than the ground.

"Take it easy." This voice was female, matter-of-fact. "You're on a ship. The *Magreb*. You're safe but don't—"

Azad rose again, bumping his head against the same metal barrier.

"Move," she finished.

"You appear to be confined in a small space," the male voice said in a clipped, mocking tone, bearing an uncanny resemblance to Osbourne. "Do you want to (choose one):

Bash your thick skull against the wall again?

Use what remains of your brain and ask why you're here?

Attempt a getaway and give me an excuse to knock you out again?"

The source of the voice came into focus. Feisal stretched across a bench, an elegant, stringed musical instrument in his lap. The snake tattoo, so real it could have been a pet resting across his chest, peered out behind a red velvet jacket.

Azad bristled but struggled for a retort through the pounding in his head.

"Be nice, Feisal," the young woman called Nawalle said. She inspected Azad with calm assurance, the corners of her lips upturned in the barest of smiles. She pulled her curly, dark hair back in a practical ponytail, revealing a square face with blunt, strong features. Her gray mechanic's uniform had been splattered with layers of engine grease.

"I just don't understand why we picked up this *hadir*. I don't care who he's related to, he's not her."

"You keep calling me that," Azad said, his face heating. "And I know it's not a compliment. My name is Azad."

"It means you're one of the sedentary," Feisal said without looking up. He strummed his instrument and a beautiful, simple melody filled the air. "You live like a piece of plankton in a terraformed bubble on Nabatea, with a fake community chosen for you and a computer in your ear, telling you exactly when you can eat, shit and sleep. You settle for three options at a time instead of endless possibility, and that, Azad, makes you a *hadir*."

The words stung, his thirty years of life so succinctly summarized far from the cheerful vacuum of Nabatea City. "I can't help being Nabatean," Azad said in a low voice.

"This one's orthodox as well, but she doesn't live like a slave," Feisal retorted, gesturing over at Nawalle.

"I don't like that word," Nawalle said with an edge. "Orthodox. It came from the Vitruvians, to mark us as different. Like we're something outdated and lesser. I didn't choose it for myself."

"It's just a descriptor, and an accurate one," Feisal said mildly. "Just like I'm a Vitruvian, Zelle is a ship captain and this blank-eyed fool is a *hadir.* We're about to make the wormhole passage. We don't have time for amateurs who had a boring day on their shift and think they want to play cosmic nomad. I don't see why we're taking him."

"It's not even a question, Feisal, look at him!" Nawalle said, pointing a finger between Azad's eyes. "Sorry," she added with a smile. "I'm just excited to meet Ledo's brother. You are her brother, right? You look just like her."

At that familiar phrase, Azad straightened his back, although he had the sense not to hit his head again.

"You know Ledo?" he asked. He grinned, heart quickening.

Nawalle nodded with the faintest of smiles. "Very well."

Azad's heart danced in his chest. He'd been right. The flight to Cerata, missing his shift, running from armed police – they had been for a purpose, leading him to this strange ship with an even stranger crew. His sister was alive. "Do you know where she is?"

A cloud passed over Nawalle's face, eyes darkening behind long lashes. After a moment, she shook her head.

"She was part of our crew," Feisal said in explanation. "For a couple years. Good worker, took to the research."

"She lived on this ship?" Azad asked in amazement.

Feisal dug his hands into a bowl of freeze-dried grapes. He let one float in the low-gravity air and caught it with his mouth. Noting Azad's stare, he continued with a smirk.

"Until about twenty Sols ago," he said. "Left us to do some contract work for the *Axel* ship, one of the largest Vitruvian exploratory vessels. Impatient, that one. Anyway, no sign of her since. We liked her. She got a better version of your face, and the gluttony gene that afflicts you – I see you eyeing my grapes, little Nabatean – obviously missed her. Brave. Smart. Very close to Nawalle."

Nawalle's face tightened with something more than closeness. Love swirled in her sad, liquid eyes, but her mouth hardened into a thin line.

"She barely said goodbye," she said. "Met a persuasive Vitruvian in a Cerata tavern, scouting for Nabatean recruits for an expedition on the

Axel. Had a contract and everything. That was the first sign something was wrong. They never give contracts to non–Vitruvians unless it's something no one in their right mind would sign up for. Ledo kept forgetting that most Vitruvians aren't like Feisal, they don't see us as their equals. We're lab rats for their interstellar games if we haven't tied ourselves to the Nabatean labor system."

Azad's eyes narrowed. From his limited interactions, Feisal didn't see them as equals, even though he respected his crewmates, but Azad wouldn't press the point. The elation at hearing about Ledo dampened as Nawalle's words sunk in. He shivered.

"She could be in danger, then," Azad said, his breath suddenly shallow. "We have to look for her."

"We?" Feisal asked in a voice rich with malicious glee. "You think that chasing us through a library and falling on a ship makes you part of this crew? You're a stowaway until the captain says otherwise, *hadir*, and as her first mate, I'm going to advocate putting you and your little brain chip companion out the airlock."

Azad swallowed. He had no illusions that the Vitruvian could watch him suffocate without batting a kohled eye.

"Oh hush, Feisal," Nawalle said, her tone soothing. "We want to find Ledo as well, Azad, but there's bigger things underway. I can't say more without the captain here. But she's tough, our Ledo. She has to be, with all of the trouble she keeps finding."

Azad's heart sank. But was it that surprising? Ledo had abandoned him without a farewell, in search of bright, distant objects. Years later, she had done the same again, to others who cared about her.

As though reading his mind, Nawalle nodded at him.

"I think she loves us, in her way," she said. "At least, that's what I want to think, that we're not just rungs in a ladder she wants to keep climbing to Juul-knows-where. But she's always chasing something. Looking for something better, or failing that, something different."

Feisal filled the ensuing silence with his instrument, a long type of oud with two sets of strings. He played a complex and haunting melody, rising and falling like waves against a dark, distant shore. Azad sank back, heavy with melancholy, the oud's strings reverberating in corners of his heart he never knew existed.

"What song is that?" he asked.

"Feisal just plays," Nawalle said. "He loves music, but never plays the same thing twice."

"You improvised that?" Azad asked in disbelief. "Can all Vitruvians do that?"

"No," Feisal said, closing his eyes. He seemed sedated by his own chords. "Just like not all of your kind can fly shuttles."

Breaking from the melody's trance, Azad remembered the sphere that Feisal and Zelle took from the library.

"You said Ledo was recruited by the *Axel* ship," he said slowly. "I went to Cerata because my Vitruvian patient recognized me as Ledo's brother before she died. According to her name at death, she was also on the *Axel*. We're all following the same trail."

"You're right about that," Nawalle said. "Cerata isn't just a rock for oddballs. It's a waystation for space travelers and we untethered Nabateans share information with each other, watch Vitruvian alpha-vessel movements. Wormhole traffic showed that a small crew had passed the Emigrant's Wormhole from the mother system back to Nabatea on one of the *Axel*'s ancillary shuttles. Meaning, a part of the crew left the ship for some reason. It seems the shuttle crashed somewhere outside of the city, but the Vitruvians cleaned up the evidence. Your patient is the only one that's been seen alive."

Azad exhaled. A crew evacuated the *Axel*. Ledo might be among them. But why had only Nenah reached the hospital?

"What happened in the hospital was unlike anything I've ever seen," Azad said, his voice tightening at the memory. "It shouldn't have been possible. Her insides liquified before my eyes. She suffocated with black tar pouring from her mouth. But the medmechs couldn't find a cause. Not even a sign of foreign infection."

Nawalle gasped. Feisal stopped playing his oud, looking at Azad for the first time on the ship with narrowed, uneasy eyes.

"Somehow, she made it to the hospital in that state," Nawalle said with a shake of her head. "But how could that have happened? She left the *Axel* and passed through the Emigrant's Wormhole in a little shuttle. What was so bad that she had to leave the station?"

A lump formed in Azad's throat.

"But Ledo could still be there! Where's the *Axel* now?"

"No one knows," a voice boomed across the room. Zelle stood at the narrow doorway. Though a small figure, even in the narrow confines of the ship, her presence filled the room. Her grandmotherly dress in the Library of Souls was gone, replaced by unglamorous but practical olive-green overalls, a captain's insignia across her heart. She held her white hair together with thick braids, pulled into an elegant bun atop her head.

"The *Axel* could still be in the mother system, as the Archive from the library hinted," Zelle continued. "But before I go any further, Azad of Nabatea, I want to be clear on one thing. Our primary goal is not to find Ledo. Make no mistake, we'll search and we'll try to find her – she was one of our crew. But we have broader aims than a rescue mission and if you're going to join this operation, you must understand that above all else."

For the first time since Azad regained consciousness, the ship itself came into focus. Though freshly painted, caulking lined the wall's corners, evidence of damage fixed several times over. Thin cracks snaked along the overhead pipes. A ship held together by capable hands, running in spite of itself. This was not a Vitruvian alpha-vessel. They must have been in the main body of the ship, where rotational gravity took effect instead of the linear gravity used on larger, more powerful ships. The room was curved, with a long cylinder in its center, glowing with pale light. Azad had fallen, literally, onto a ship of outcasts with an agenda that even Osbourne could not help him untangle.

Osbourne. His computer had been uncharacteristically quiet, given the circumstances. Azad also realized that he had been talking to the crew from inside a metallic box with one side open. He must have banged his head along its walls when he first regained consciousness.

"Why am I in this thing?" Azad asked, addressing Zelle. "And why isn't my processor working?"

Zelle smiled as though he were a star pupil who had asked a particularly insightful question.

"Well, you certainly have your sister's talent for drawing connections," she said, tilting her head at Feisal, who grunted. "The casing prevents that device in your neck from transmitting signals and acting as a beacon. You are being searched for now, after the incident at the library. This keeps us from being followed, until we remove it."

"Remove Osbourne?" Azad asked in a small voice. His shoulders slumped the way they used to when he was a child in Township, being punished for some minor infraction.

"It's a non-negotiable condition to remain on my ship," Zelle said.

"But we wanted to give you the chance to decide first," Nawalle said.

"And if I refuse?" Azad asked, though he guessed at the answer.

"Then you go home," Zelle said. "But your choice to follow us in the library may be a hard one to explain back on Nabatea. We're not popular with the authorities there."

Fear twisted a tight knot in Azad's stomach. Would the authorities Blank him if he returned? Aside from this solitary incident, he boasted a spotless record. But more importantly, did he want to return, with Ledo in possible danger?

"Are we forgetting the option where we don't give the *hadir* an option?" Feisal said, looking up from his oud. "What does it matter if he's Ledo's brother? This isn't Nabatea City. We don't hire crew based on nepotism. If we're too nice and civilized to airlock him, we can drop him back on the Shadow Moon and let the authorities deal with him."

Ignoring Nawalle's sputter of outrage, Zelle turned to Azad with a thoughtful gaze. Azad waited with polite silence; he couldn't add anything to his case that this woman didn't already know.

"We need another crew member," Zelle said slowly. "His profile indicates medical training, which we will undoubtedly need. And if he's willing to leave everything in Nabatea to find his sister, I suspect he belongs here more than even he realizes."

Zelle smiled and Azad lowered his gaze, overcome with emotion. In the last hour, he had learned that Ledo still lived and that he stood among her crew, the closest she had to family. And she needed him more than ever.

As though reading his mind, Zelle spoke again. "We'll find Ledo, if we can. But as I said, we have important work to do and I'll welcome you on my crew, provided you understand my rules."

Azad's trembling fingers traced the back of his neck until he found Osbourne's faint outline, his skin warming under his touch. The chip had been inserted on his thirteenth Sol day, the day of his induction into adult life on Nabatea. It had become a part of him, as much as an ear or a knee. A confidante and advisor, even a friend in those dark days after Ledo left.

Facing Zelle, her eyes cool like charcoal, he nodded.

Zelle's face relaxed, warmth returning to her eyes. She nodded at Nawalle, who approached Azad, beaming.

"So you worked as a doctor?" Nawalle asked. She thumbed through a box of small, unnervingly sharp-looking instruments.

"I do – I did – one of my shifts. I also did traffic control, gardening, and cosmetics consulting."

"Well, if anyone needs a new face or a flower arrangement, we'll know where to go," Zelle said drily, leaning back with folded hands. "But I have no doubt that you're adaptable and can learn additional skills in no time. Nawalle keeps this ship running and I'm sure she'll welcome a second set of hands."

"Captain, I can't function *without* more hands," Nawalle chimed in. "Ledo and I kept the engine going."

Feisal snorted but held back whatever innuendo lay at the tip of his tongue.

"And what exactly do you do on this ship?" Azad asked. Talking helped keep his heartbeat regular as he braced for whatever Nawalle was about to do. "Are you explorers, merchants…smugglers?"

Zelle smiled broadly, as though she had been waiting for that question. The question had apparently sealed the agreement; Nawalle joined Azad in the metallic box, armed with a long syringe and an even more alarming scalpel. She squeezed around him as he sat upright and cross-legged, so close that her breath warmed the back of his head. Their heads grazed the top of the box and Nawalle's legs straddled Azad after she made her way directly behind him.

"Lean your head forward," she whispered. "I wish we could do this on a proper medical table, but I can't risk you stepping out of here and sending a signal."

Azad nodded, his throat dry and pulse quickening at the anticipation of something that was sure to be invasive and deeply uncomfortable.

Zelle clasped her hands, pacing in front of the box. The bangles on her wrist clinked as she spoke. "We are doing the real version of my one true passion on Nabatea," she began, her voice rising. "Without censorship or pretense. We smuggle and trade as a means to an end, but our end is unique amongst all the ships in this great system. We explore and study the past."

"The past?" Azad asked. His brow knotted in confusion. "Why?"

Feisal shot to his feet, tossing his oud aside.

"You undersell us to this chip-infested *hadir*, Captain," he said. "We don't just look into the past. We aren't passive students. We are truth-seekers, archaeologists of antiquity and wranglers of time. We shake the tapestry of humanity's story through the stars and see what falls out. We are what the authorities fear, because we dare to look back instead of just exist in the moment, like plants or asps. We know that looking back is the only way, *hadir*, to know how to move forward." His breath slightly heavier, he sank back into his seat, reclaiming his oud.

"In other words, we're historians," Zelle finished with an amused arch of her brow.

Azad blinked, more confused than ever.

"Historians? You mean like people who sit in the Nabatea Library and read about the founding years?" Azad tried to ignore Nawalle, who applied something damp to the back of his neck. He clenched his fists so hard, his calloused knuckles ached.

"Yes, but as more than a pastime," Zelle said. "It's a strange concept, I know, but believe it or not, it was once a credible, legitimate profession for our ancestors in the mother system. Nabateans are told to look forward, never back to where we came from. But even Barrett Juul was a historian of sorts. He modeled the aesthetics and structure of the planet on an ancient civilization on Earth, ancient even for his own time. They were even called the Nabateans, too."

"How have I never heard this?" Azad asked, wincing as a thin needle entered the tense skin between his neck and shoulder.

"Just numbing you up," Nawalle said gently.

Feisal snorted, leaping to his feet again in a swift, catlike move. The Vitruvian's sudden movements were going to give Azad a headache, beyond whatever Nawalle was about to inflict with her scalpel.

"You don't know our origins by design, *hadir*," he said. "The people who run that planet don't want anyone digging too deep into who we are and how we got here. They like their myths, of course. Heroic Barrett Juul, foreseeing disaster on Mars, leading a ragtag band of survivors to a better world. The mother of the first Vitruvians, loyal at his side. But myths are like dust – formed from something solid and real, but fragments of the truth, liable to slip through your fingers and settle where the wind carries them. Real historians examine the good and the bad, and everything in between."

Azad's neck numbed, his ears tingling with peripheral sensation. In the corner of his eye, Nawalle traced her finger along the scalpel, testing its sharpness, and he forced his attention back on Zelle and Feisal.

"I was like you once," Zelle said to Azad. "Living in a controlled neighborhood in the Nabatean farm district. Every day interchangeable from the last. But I became restless, asking questions about things that weren't supposed to matter. But they did. I went to the Nabatea City Archive building whenever I wasn't on shift – notice how they placed our history records on the edge of the city, surrounded by grass and crops? Hidden and pushed aside. I studied every memory recording and chronicle of the early days of colonized Nabatea and even before then, the Great Escape across the stars. But I knew where the real information lay – in the Library of Souls on the Shadow Moon. I realized then that the city life wasn't for me."

Azad yelped. Pain cut through the numbness on his neck, the sharp scent of blood flooding his nostrils. His chest fluttered in panic.

"I'm a doctor," Azad gasped. "There has to be a better way of doing this. Oh! It stings."

"You have to be conscious," Nawalle said. She pushed deeper into the back of his neck, her fingers light, but the scalpel sharp.

"I scoured the Library of Souls day in and out," Zelle continued, and Azad strained to refocus back to her voice. Anything to take his mind off the pain. "What I found was not as interesting as what I didn't find. No explanation for *why* the Martian colony collapsed. No clear indicator of why the emigrants left when they did. We learn in Township how terrible life was on the mother system, all of the poverty and exploitation and despair, but the specifics are surprisingly few."

Heat spread across Azad's temples, pushing beads of sweat down his face. It was more than physical pain. A buzzing sensation swelled in his ears, accompanied by a rising panic that drowned out Zelle's monologue. Osbourne, resisting.

"Wait," Azad said to Nawalle in a thick voice. "He's not ready, he's afraid."

"It's a survival mechanism," Nawalle said. Her wrist twisted behind him and he cried out at the sudden burst of pain. "It's just a computer networked into your entire community. It's not dying, and it has no sense of what death even is. Just relax and don't fight me."

A metallic taste filled Azad's mouth. Blood pounded in his ears and he closed his eyes, dizziness twisting his vision. He would faint at any second.

And with a final tug, the chip that had been a part of him for nearly twenty years came loose. Azad exhaled as Nawalle pulled it away, a thick stew of relief and sorrow bubbling inside him. Nawalle pressed gauze onto the back of his neck. A rush of heat followed. A targeted microfiber blowtorch, designed to burn fragile capillaries.

"Free at last, *hadir*," Feisal said quietly, strumming the oud. The gruesome procedure had not earned Azad a respectful title, but at least something softened in the Vitruvian's voice.

"You're free to move," Nawalle said.

Wincing, Azad crawled out of the metal enclosure, pressing down the gauze. Nawalle followed him and placed the bloody chip, businesslike, into a nearby metal tray. She flexed her hands and admired her handiwork.

With shaking breath, Azad faced Zelle. Despite the trauma of Osbourne's removal, he'd heard and absorbed her every word. How she became a historian. All that had been left out of the Archives. The great mystery she had made her life's mission to solve.

"So your goal in all of this is to find out what really happened on ancient Mars?" he asked. "What makes you think it was any different from what the stories said? Barrett Juul came to Mars to find a failed society, just like Earth. He led a wave of emigrants off the planet and they founded Nabatea."

"*A man made of fire and a woman born of air*," Feisal quoted the Township pledge all Nabatean children learned in a mocking, singsong voice.

"As historians, we know that history is written by the victors," Zelle said. "In every past war on the home planet, our ancestors wrote the version of the story they wanted told. I searched for evidence of what happened on Mars, but everyone who came to Nabatea in those first years of settlement had been part of the group that escaped, and therefore had a bias and possibly limited information. Little is said in the Archives about why they left when they did. Maybe they didn't want to say, maybe they didn't want to look back on all they left behind. In short, we lacked objective, balanced sources."

"But then there's no way—"

"Until now."

Zelle nodded at Nawalle, who activated the room's holo-screen with a flick of her wrists. The display monitor came to life and Zelle pulled a small orb from her pocket.

Azad stilled. The Archive from the Library of Souls. The Vitruvian woman's memories.

"It takes a long time to unpack a full Archive Band," Zelle said. "Months of decrypting to extract specific memories. All we have now are recollections of ship schematics and last coordinates for the *Axel* station, which place it in Martian orbit. And a few tangible memories, her more recent ones."

The monitor cut to a view of a ship breaking through atmosphere, the red patchwork of Nabatea City spinning below. Azad's stomach twisted.

The crash. Furious, black smoke flooded the holo-screen's display, so vivid Azad could almost taste it in his mouth. This was Nenah's shuttle returning to Nabatea. But no sign of Ledo. He allowed himself a small exhale of relief.

The insides of a large vessel followed, Vitruvians lying across the floor.

"They look dead," Azad whispered, pulse quickening. Relief flickered in his chest, again, when he failed to spot Ledo among the prone bodies.

The monitor switched to Nenah's next memory. A small room with white walls and shelves of supplies, a red landscape peering through a round window, redder than Nabatea. A curve of a blade, blood spurting from a man's throat. And a face, calm and appraising. A face he had never forgotten, thinner but with that same smile in her eyes, looking back at him.

Azad nearly cried out. *Ledo.*

"She knew Ledo," he said.

Feisal nodded.

"The memories are foggy, blurred around the edges," he said. "Probably because she was ill at the time and died before her memories could be fully processed. If her brain was damaged, we may never extract everything she saw."

"But she was with Ledo before she left the system," Azad said. "So Ledo could still be on Mars somewhere, or on the *Axel* ship, alive." Dizziness attacked Azad with renewed vigor. The Vitruvian's other memories carried horrible snippets of time – the sliced throat, the room of bodies on the floor. What had Ledo seen? What had been done to her?

"The *Axel* ship seems the most likely possibility," Zelle said. "Given that we received an encrypted recording from the vessel six Sols after Ledo left us."

"A recording?"

Nawalle smiled, excitement brimming in her dark eyes. "It had to be her, Azad – Ledo sent us a message from the *Axel*."

The holo-screen loaded again, displaying two-dimensional footage in the center of the room, crude compared to Nenah's flashes of memory. Through the grainy image, a woman stared out at them, though her eyes shifted sideways with the frequency of someone bracing to be interrupted. She had a long face, and gray eyes heavy with sadness.

The woman spoke in a low, urgent voice.

If anyone finds this, I'll be dead, hopefully on my own terms. I don't have much time in any case. This is my confession, but even with…even with nothing to lose, I'm still afraid. I'm afraid of Barrett Juul. I was wrong about him and maybe by the time someone sees this, you'll all realize it as well. I have to do this. They'll kill me if I don't do it first. I don't want to die, but I…I can't let them use me to create something terrible. A world just as bad as the one we left behind on Calypso and Palmcorps.

"Calypso? What's a—?" Azad began before Zelle silenced him with a stern look. The woman's voice cracked and she lowered her head, battling for composure. When she raised it again, her features fixed in a performer's mask. A look heavy with defeat and determination, from someone with nothing left to lose.

Whoever finds this, whatever kind of life you've been dealt, I hope it's a free one. I hope Nabatea is everything we hoped for. I hope nothing holds you back. It's all I wanted and why this is all my fault. Everything's fallen apart, because I wanted something and didn't count the cost. If Nabatea failed, then I hope you can forgive me.

The woman spun around and the screen turned to static.

Nawalle turned off the holo-screen. The silence that followed weighed down on them, heavier than the gravity keeping them in their seats.

"That was a message from a Martian on the *Calypso One* ship's voyage, dated 2195 A.D., the mother system's calendar," Zelle said. "The same year that Juul and the first emigrants left Mars for Nabatea."

Azad opened his mouth to speak, but a dam of questions flooded his mind and he struggled for the right one to ask first.

"We don't know who this woman is or what happened to her," Zelle said. "But this message – if it is a true record, found by the *Axel* vessel – is the first evidence of what *really* happened on the final days of the Martian colony. We have been told that the Great Escape involved a small fraction of the population, escaping a society that fell apart decades later, alongside Earth's collapse. This woman's testimony contradicts that assumption, saying that they left a planet in the throes of disaster. *Everything's fallen apart*, she said. But how? And notice she mentioned a place called Palmcorps. We know of Calypso, the corporate city Juul liberated. But what is Palmcorps? We have no record of such a place existing. Why is that? And why does she fear Barrett Juul?"

Feisal stood, swinging his arms in a delicate motion and tracing his fingers at the spot where the woman appeared.

"And to take us into present-day concerns," he said. "Why is this recording on the *Axel*, and what does it have to do with the ship's present location on Mars? Did they discover it and decide to investigate it, like we plan to do?"

The back of Azad's neck throbbed and his head ached for Osbourne's comforting voice, always ready with an answer, delivered in threes. An existence starved of mystery. One far removed from this new reality of questions and secrets.

"So you want to use this…history, to find out what happened on Mars?" Azad asked.

"Got it right the first time, *hadir*," Feisal said.

"How?"

"Vitruvian magic," Feisal replied with a sharp, wicked grin.

"Enough, Feisal," Nawalle said with a note of warning. "Let him get some sleep. We could all use some rest."

Nawalle's last words barely registered in Azad's ears before a heaviness overcame him. Nawalle led Azad to his new quarters. His limbs, his head, his very eyelids sank as though the gravity in the room had increased tenfold. With a faint sigh, he leaned back, closed his eyes and surrendered to blissful sleep.

★   ★   ★

Azad woke the next day (assuming days meant anything in space) with a faint ache in the back of his neck and a bruise where he'd fallen on the ship, but was otherwise no worse for wear. He rose from his sleeping cot near the engine room and traversed the hallway on wobbling legs, extending his arms to balance himself. When Osbourne failed to list out his breakfast options, Azad ached in a different way. Osbourne had been a companion, a family member for all of his adult life – the fact that he was a computer program was incidental. He'd been there for Azad every day, and that meant something, even if giving him up was a worthwhile price to find Ledo.

"Sleeping beauty awakens," Feisal crowed in the galley room. Zelle gestured Azad to sit beside her and offered him a plate.

"We have to move," Zelle said to him. "But we have time for answers. I wouldn't expect anyone to join my crew without fully understanding what we're doing. What we're dealing with."

After a muted breakfast of oatmeal and manaqish with za'atar, Azad followed the crew down a narrow ladder to the ship's lower level. Whistling pipes and machinery fought for space along the narrow quarters. The ship's engine grumbled below them, sending vibrations through Azad's feet. As he stepped away from the ladder, however, all his senses trained on a machine in the center of the room, separate and isolated from the general noise and clutter. Sleek and familiar, with a funnel-shaped lens protruding from a silver box.

"This is that strange camera you used back in the Library of Souls," Azad said in a soft voice, drawing closer. "Only it's—"

"Larger," Zelle finished. Pride crept into her voice. "And far more powerful. What you saw in the library was the prototype Feisal constructed. But this is what we'll use on Mars."

"Mars? But there's nothing left on Mars."

"There are many things left on Mars," Zelle said. "And even more that once were. Things that linger and leave a quantum imprint. Particles and waves, rearranged."

The lens pulled at Azad's gaze like a black hole feasting on light. Unable to turn away, he inched closer to its unblinking eye. The darkness at the center was absolute. The kind of darkness that looked ready to swallow Azad whole if he came too close, every color within him dissolved into nothing.

"Stay back," Nawalle said.

Her voice broke through Azad's trance. Zelle surveyed him with careful eyes.

"What is this thing?" he asked, barely above a whisper.

"The first and only quantum historical projector," Zelle said. "With careful configuration, you can set it to a specific time in the past and see a basic, admittedly crude, reflection of what occurred in that segment of space-time. Movement. People. Places as they once were."

Zelle's words ran through Azad's ears like voltage, rooting him where he stood.

"It's impossible," Azad said. A machine that showed the past; the very concept was absurd.

"Says the illustrious gardener-doctor-assistant-traffic controller," Feisal said. "Everything is a probability until it's not, *hadir*. A wave collapses into particle form only when it is observed. That fateful, conscious-driven act gives it a specific place to be at a specific point in time. All my machine does is track that point in time and recreate how particles and mass were arranged in that moment. A reenactment of the instant Schrödinger's box is opened and the cat blinks back."

"The cat?" Azad asked in a soft, dazed voice.

"It's a quantum thought experiment used by our ancestors on Earth," Feisal said with a trace of smugness. "Their knowledge was…imperfect, but they understood the probability concept. If you place a cat in a box, the orthodox scientist Schrödinger said, the cat could simultaneously be alive and dead until someone lifted the lid. It was meant to be a paradox, but that's what we're doing, *hadir*. We're going to observe the moment when the box opened and reality happened, over a thousand years ago."

Azad shook his head. It was ridiculous. And yet, his mind roamed back through the library's serpentine tunnels, when the miniature device spat out the grainy image of figures running backward and forward again. People fully formed but not entirely there, oblivious to their presence.

He nodded but took a careful step away from the machine.

"They looked so real back at the library," he said. "When you… reenacted what had happened before."

"The further back you go, the less clear the image becomes," Nawalle said, her voice rising in excitement. "That was only a matter of hours, we're talking over a thousand years when we go back to Mars, when it had life. But you can still view the past as it occurred. We tested it near the Sulpherlands, back during the fifth Year of Settlement. We could see them, Azad. It was incredible. Crews at work, in their old-fashioned clothes, building Nabatea side by side with their mechs."

"Can it see into the future?" Azad asked with a surge of excitement. Feisal snorted.

"The future is still probability," Feisal said. "Until there's observation, there's no wave function collapse, and therefore nothing for us to read. So the answer is no, *hadir*. We're not magicians."

But close enough. Azad let out a low whistle. His hands tingled with a low current of adrenaline. From what Nawalle described, they did not enter a different time, one they could tamper with, but could witness the past, exactly as it occurred, from the safety of the present. Not time travel, but the next best thing.

And considerably less dangerous than real time travel, where someone could interact with the past, change it. Azad's head spun with possibility.

Nawalle continued her cheerful recollections about the fifth Year of Settlement but her voice grew distant. The device in the center of the room tugged at Azad again, drawing his gaze but releasing something deeper, a sense of infinite possibility that felt as alien as the distant stars. A way to see the past, to witness the long-dead walk again.

"What's it called?" Azad asked in a hushed voice.

An uncomfortable pause followed.

Finally, Nawalle rolled her eyes. "Barry."

"Barry?" Azad blinked.

"We let Feisal name it, since he invented it," Nawalle said with dull resignation.

"It looked like a Barry," Feisal said with a shrug and barely concealed glee. "The Archives show three Barrys on the Great Escape roster. Why shouldn't my machine have an old-fashioned name?"

"Because it's ridiculous!" Nawalle snapped.

"It's perfect, and you all know it. It even sounds short for Barrett Juul, our precious, almighty founder."

Azad winced at the blasphemous sarcasm, but he was the only one.

"Enough," Zelle said. "We have a course to set."

Nawalle stood with folded arms, as though waiting for another question, an anxious remark or protest, but Azad nodded his assent and followed Feisal up the ladder. For the first time since the Vitruvian woman burst through the hospital doors, hope overcame his doubts. He would go to Mars, cross its ancient terrain and learn what others couldn't even guess. And despite Zelle's warnings about the crew's mission, Azad would find Ledo or know her fate. She journeyed on the *Axel* to the mother system. And now, at long last, he would follow.

Chapter Six
Kezza

CALYPSO CORPORATE CAMPUS, MARS
2195 A.D.

The arrival of new Martian immigrants every two years drew a reliable crowd at the docking bay. The transport ship itself, *Calypso One*, hovered in geostationary orbit while shuttles brought down passengers in waves. The wealthy always disembarked first, wobbling and shell-shocked as they placed their feet on solid ground for the first time in six months. Kezza never understood it. *Calypso One* generated a gravity that matched that of Mars, one less adjustment for Earth migrants to make upon landing, but they always stumbled on that first step. A fitting metaphor for their idiotic decision to leave Earth.

Acclimation to life on Mars took on many phases. The initial excitement upon arriving dulled any discomfort with Calypso's confined spaces but before long, cabin fever sharpened. New arrivals started to miss the open skies, the crispness of fresh air. After several agonizing months, most adjusted, although there'd been at least one hundred cases in Martian history of crazed settlers choosing suicide by airlock. Self-boiling, something no self-respecting Martian would do. Transport mechs had the honor of dragging their corpses inside.

Kezza stood at the periphery of the crowd with folded arms. Her nails dug into her skin. Excited chatter and the scent of cheap coffee filled the dour room's yawning walls. She arrived several hours before the first shuttle's scheduled disembarkation only to find the rest of Calypso had beaten her to the punch. Ore miners, botanists, mechanics, cleaners, even

Tier Twos – all jostled for space and a clear line of vision toward the first class disembarkment ramp. Juul, surely, would arrive in the initial wave. Calypso authorities prepared accordingly – armed, masked security goons lined the unloading area, forcing the front row to peer over their shoulders for a glimpse of newly arrived friends and family from Earth.

And Barrett Juul. Because that was why most of these people were here.

Kezza chewed her lip, drawing a tangy taste of blood. She tasted blood when she coughed as well, which was more often. But she couldn't let that consume her. That only made her task of taking care of Barrett Juul more urgent.

With everything that had happened, she hadn't had full time to plan his murder. But she had ideas. It needed to be public and dramatic. One of her performances would be ideal. A part of her hoped to escape – to steal a spacesuit and all-terrain vehicle and seek sanctuary in Palmcorps, the corporate city on the other side of Mars – but that wasn't realistic. Calypso only had so many hiding places, and Palmcorps wouldn't exactly welcome her, even if they felt spurned by Barrett Juul. No, she needed to be prepared to be carried away in cuffs, raising a triumphant fist before a stunned crowd.

But how to actually kill him? Since she was planning to break into the Bokambe complex anyway, to learn more about what happened to that couple in the Waste Room, maybe she could steal some deadly poison. Get close and plunge a syringe into his heart.

But she had other weapons already. Her feet, mainly. She'd gotten strong, strong enough to kick a hole into a fucking wall. She put a man in intensive care. A single, well-placed kick to Juul's jugular would remove him from the conscious plane of existence.

Her mouth twitched in a cold smile. An officer scowled at Kezza through the narrow slits of his balaclava, as though in warning. They had come prepared, no doubt expecting a stampede over the great civilizationist's arrival. Kezza scowled back.

She craned her neck over the rows of Martians awaiting loved ones, signs in hand. With each wave of new passengers disembarking from the shuttle, clusters broke away and ran into the arms of spouses, relatives and friends. Hugs, laughter, tears of joy accompanied each reunion. Some raised their new CALPals to record the moment, while others opted for more dramatic gestures, bending down to kiss the floor. Kezza's mouth stretched in a faint smirk. The reality of Mars would hit these doe-eyed arrivals soon enough.

A woman crossed the arrival gate with a girl, no older than five, clutching her hand. The girl clung to her mother's side, legs wobbling like a wooden marionette's. The smile left Kezza's face and a pang seized her chest. When she'd arrived on Calypso over twenty years ago, a similar age and size, no one greeted her on the gangway. When the little girl met Kezza's eyes, Kezza smiled back. The girl gaped, vacant and unblinking, before her mother tugged her forward to the processing queue.

Whispers rose around Kezza; random eyes darted in her direction. Word of her fight at the Atrium bar had spread across the Catacombs, inviting even more scrutiny in a city already too small for comfort. Even the guards eyed her with surprising wariness.

Despite her sudden notoriety, no charges had been pressed against her. Not yet. The Tier Two man she'd knocked across the room remained unconscious and his companions had kept silent, likely fearing retaliation. A sensible strategy for temporary Martian residents, to finish their two-year detail and return to Earth without facing Catacombs justice. Kezza hoped that her newly fearsome reputation extended to the gang that had defiled her front door, which she cleaned after a rigorous half day of scrubbing. The effort had burned two hundred and thirty-seven calories, which earned her a free smoothie on her CALPal.

The air around them crackled with impatience. A chant of "Juul" broke out on the other side of the crowd, rising as helmeted guards nudged the first row back.

New migrants, now at the Tier Three level, gathered at the far end of the docking bay, lining up for processing. Suddenly, a man broke away from the shuffling crowd and climbed an elevated platform. Curiosity swelled when the guards did nothing to stop him.

Kezza's heart fluttered. It was him. It had to be. A cold sensation snaked down her spine.

"Ladies and gentlemen of Calypso Corporate Campus, come closer," the man said in a ringing voice made for theater. The crowd obeyed, inching toward the platform. "Don't be alarmed, I simply have an announcement. I was offered the opportunity to exit the ship first, with a small group of wealthy travelers who receive special treatment upon arrival and subsequently live different lives on this colony. I chose not to do that, because first and foremost, I am here because of you. I am here for you."

Murmurs swelled from the crowd, filling the air like smoke. The line of security guards tightened, locked shoulder to shoulder. New arrivals and locals alike pressed together, craning necks toward the man's perch. Kezza almost laughed. Were they still doubting what every cell in her body was screaming at her? This was Juul. He matched all the pictures and videos that had been circulating around the city, though a little more pale and haggard. The civilizationist smiled, and Kezza couldn't resist smiling back. He was magnetic. He drew every eye in the room with ease. But he was also a vampire, here to drain them dry – unless Kezza could stop him.

"I am Barrett Juul of Earth," he said. "With dedicated colleagues back home, I have rebuilt societies undone by war, famine and flooding. My work was cut out for me, but you know that – all of you left Earth for a reason. A chance to create something better. To draw from our common history and origins but not be bound by them."

In person, Juul's slight frame was at odds with the deep, authoritative voice on his broadcast. Medium height, with a long, hawkish nose and soft features partially concealed under a trimmed beard, he was attractive in an unconventional way. But his voice, a smooth, Danish-accented baritone, carried such assurance and authority that his presence enveloped the crowd like warm honey. Even Kezza, who loathed any physical contact with strangers, moved closer.

Juul raised both hands up to his ear level, fingers pointing to the high ceiling. His mouth curled into a conspiratorial smile.

"The Martian experiment has failed. Everyone knows it, from the highest Tier to the lowest shifter, but no one says it aloud. It may be a success for shareholders on Earth, but it has crushed those who toil under its demands."

Silence greeted his words. Several heads in front of Kezza rotated around like gears in a machine, exchanging nervous glances with their neighbors. The hairs on Kezza's neck prickled to hear her thoughts being articulated so simply and directly, while the hated Calypso Security detail stood helplessly by. She imagined, with a pulse of cold satisfaction, the Corpsboard squirming from some fogged window above the docking bay.

"I know how the ordinary Martian suffers," Juul continued, apparently undeterred by the subdued reaction. "You live under harsh conditions, crammed like sardines in a hostile environment. You are pioneers on the furthest boundaries of human expansion into space, but you are still human. Human nature remains constant, even when its tendrils sink into alien ground."

"It's a prison!" an old woman interjected, which unleashed a dam of assenting shouts.

"We're trapped here!"

"It's Hell without the heat."

"I work eighteen-hour shifts in the Terra! No overtime!"

Juul lifted his hands again in acknowledgment and the crowd simmered, a stew of indignant muttering.

"The conditions you live under here have not gone unnoticed by me and others from Earth," he said, amused eyes sliding to his right, where a row of Calypso Security took formation. "Changes are coming."

The crowd's energy surged at those words, moved from cautious hope into something stronger, angrier. A desire to fight back. Kezza clenched her fists, the crowd's energy warming her veins. A thousand, long-buried emotions swelled within her at once, a lifetime of abuse and indignation laid bare by Juul's speech. Her fists clenched. All the rage she had directed at him rose like smoke in the air, spreading across the room – finding the Board, the police, the entire system that had killed her mother. She followed his eyes as they danced across the crowd, alight with purpose.

For once, she was the captive audience, rather than the performer. A willing captive. She blinked and drew in a sharp breath. No. She couldn't be swayed that easily by pretty words. Juul was a liar. He was telling the crowd what they wanted to hear, but he was a part of that same system he condemned. He fed off it. A memory of Kezza's mother returned to her, grounded her – a wilting woman wreathed in tubes and IV drips.

An elderly man in a miner's suit raised his fist, standing as straight as his crooked back would allow, and shouted Juul's name. Others followed, picking up the chant.

Juul. Juul. Juul.

He'd done it – seduced the crowd. He'd almost seduced Kezza; he was that good. But not good enough.

The Corpsboard. They didn't show themselves, of course, but the second wave of security that spilled into the docking bay confirmed their presence. They'd seen enough. The crowd reeled as though they had been collectively slapped, shouts of outrage rising into the air.

"No violence!" Juul's voice rose through the din, but no one heeded him, least of all Calypso Security. The first swinging club struck at the elderly miner who started the chant. Kezza's breath stopped at the sound of frail bones cracking. He fell to the ground and the crowd howled. Scuffles broke out across the front line, screams rose from the back.

The familiar lockdown sirens wailed. Juul waved his arms in an appeal for calm, but two masked goons arrived at his side, pulling him toward the docking bay's exit. An escort to safety, but the crowd saw an attempted arrest underway. The chants swelled, escalating as the guards pushed Juul through the crowd. Another wave of frozen-faced *Calypso One* passengers stepped off the shuttle into a scene of chaos, looking ready to retreat back onto the ship.

Security goons swung their clubs and unleashed their tasers. Bodies scattered and fell. Anger coursed through Kezza's limbs, propelling her forward. Behind one of those masked faces was, in all likelihood, the guard who had grabbed her weeks ago. Another thug with a badge, hiding his face while he wielded his baton.

But she held back. Through her fury, her mind spun with new calculations. Her tavern fight had earned her unwanted attention. And now, the man she wanted to kill had become, in a matter of minutes, the most popular man on Mars. Her mission had just gotten harder.

Under the cover of the crowd, she ran along the docking bay's perimeter, in the direction of the restricted loading area.

Kezza crossed through a narrow archway into the smaller bay area, where mechs loaded fresh supplies and fuel into the *Calypso One* shuttles.

On the ground, Kezza lacked the grace she possessed in the air but could still move with fast, light feet. The machines that handled cargo could detect Kezza when she ran in the open but lacked the cognitive ability to question why she was there. Calypso authorities, fearful of making their robots too intelligent on a foreign planet where they had the outdoor advantage, left security and law enforcement functions to human guards. Guards that were now occupied with a riot.

On cue, an armed man burst through a set of double doors and Kezza slid sideways behind a box. She held her breath. On the other side, the guard barked unnecessary instructions at the mechs, who continued their pre-programmed tasks, before running toward the docking bay. Kezza jumped and gripped the side of the loading shuttle with the tips of her fingers, pulling herself up. Just like the trapeze, only in this case, her goal was to avoid attracting attention. On Martian gravity, a jump already carried more lift than it would on Earth, but Kezza left the ground with a notable burst of strength. Just as she had done in the tavern.

She shimmied along the cargo shuttle's rear-facing side, sliding her feet across a narrow ridge where metal parts had been welded together, her fingers wedged inside a similar groove above her head. Supported by this narrow grip, she inched sideways, shielding herself from view. Once hidden, she peered around the ship's corner, where the mechs continued to unload crates from *Calypso One*. Kezza chewed her lower lip. She'd snuck into an unauthorized area to witness boxes move. Would she find anything useful here, or had she taken a risk for nothing?

A line of men and women in black jumpsuits filed out of the shuttle. Kezza's mouth curled into a smile. Her instincts had been right, after all. The last of *Calypso One's* human cargo, hidden from public view. They shuffled down the ramp, close together with shoulders hunched. The smell of stale sweat steamed the air. A set of yellow numbers ran across the back of each jumpsuit. Convicts. Sent to Mars in indentured servitude for their Earthly crimes, to perform the labor that even the non-unionized ore miners wouldn't touch. Unloaded from *Calypso One* with boxes of condensed sugar and electronics.

The guards shoved the prisoners toward a large set of double doors. Kezza's heart leapt at the red sign over the entrance – the Bokambe sector. The center of scientific research, high-level security and all manner of restricted activity on the Triple C. The place where her superhuman friend from the Waste Room must have escaped from.

She peered further around the corner, her knuckles white against the box's side. She'd have to be quick to run inside with the prisoners. But no, she'd be seen – if not immediately, soon enough as she wandered Bokambe's hallways. Kezza sighed. So close to Mars's best kept secrets, yet so far.

Something dark and fast caught the corner of her eye. Across the docking bay, a figure in a convict's black jumpsuit darted behind a row of crates waiting to be loaded. The prisoner crouched low, casting frequent glances at the guards.

A loose convict. Where were they going? And more importantly, did they know anything useful?

Kezza sidled across the shuttle. When she reached the edge, she dropped down and ran between the crates toward the lone convict. She held her breath, silently praying that no one would see, that the guards would remain distracted in the docking bay.

Kezza slid up to the last row of crates. Up close, the figure turned out to be a man – small, middle-aged, with a bald patch at the top of his head wreathed in stringy black hair. She scanned his loose-fitting jumpsuit for the telltale bulge of a hidden weapon, but found none. Her legs tensed at the memory of her forceful kick in the Atrium. She wasn't helpless. She could even be dangerous.

Kezza struck quickly. By the time he turned in her direction, she was a foot away, fingers pressed to her lips. His mouth parted to scream but she clamped a hand across his face, the force pushing him back against the crate. A whistled shriek escaped from his clenched teeth.

"Quiet," she said with hushed menace. "I'm not Corp. What are you doing here?"

The man fell to his knees. "Please," he whimpered. "Leave me alone. I just want to get out of here."

His short, stocky frame suggested a later-life Earth migrant. Taking in his watery eyes and soft, doughy hands, the hands of a pampered office worker unaccustomed to blisters or radiation burns, Kezza arched a curious brow. Nothing about this man suggested a hardened criminal laborer.

"Did you come here with them?" she asked in a low whisper, tilting her head toward the convicts. The man shook his head, wetting his lips.

"I've been here three years," he said. "Medical research. I need to get off this planet and this is the only way. Please, don't scream and don't report me. I'll do anything."

"You're a Tier Two," Kezza said, taking a step back. A highly skilled white collar worker, sneaking around crates to smuggle himself off Mars. This was getting more interesting by the nanosecond.

"Tier One," the man said. Kezza's eyes widened. "Not that it matters. I got all the access but not the Tier One credit pay. But they're going to downgrade me. I've seen too much. They'll make me work with them." He gestured toward the door, where the last convict had passed through.

Kezza's heart quickened. *I've seen too much.* "What have you seen? That lockdown...did something happen in Bokambe they're keeping secret?"

Still on his knees, the man moaned, shifting his weight from side to side like he wanted nothing more than to leap out the nearest airlock.

Kezza leaned ominously forward and the man shrank back.

"Please, I'm running out of time, they'll finish loading soon."

"What do you know?" Kezza asked again, letting the menace creep into her voice. "Tell me, and I'll let you pass without causing a scene." If Kezza knew one thing, it was how to create a scene.

"Listen, I can't say, only that it's not safe here. They found something in the desert. The T-terra. And they're sending prisoners to explore it. I was in the observation room when the last wave came back. Terrible... their faces..." The man shuddered from shoulders to knees, face clenched as if to hold back tears.

"Found something in Arabia Terra?" Kezza asked, irritated. "What does that mean?"

"Don't ask me, I didn't get sent there," he said in a rush. "They dug up something in one of the craters. Miners came back from the crater... sick. Not just sick...different."

The room spun. Kezza leaned against the crate, absorbing the Tier One's words. The stretch of desert between the two corporate campuses, Arabia Terra, remained hotly contested real estate, thanks to its abundance of hidden ore. No surprise that prisoners would become canaries in an ore mine when something inexplicable was discovered there. But Arabia Terra had been mined for decades. What existed there that hadn't yet been unearthed? And how could something on lifeless Mars make anyone sick?

Kezza swallowed. The bodies in the Waste Room. The dead woman, and the man who ran through the airlock. The pieces fell together in Kezza's mind with such speed that she reeled. They'd been part of that group of contaminated prisoners, forced into the desert. And then they escaped Bokambe, triggering the lockdown.

And then Kezza found them. The man coughed in her fucking face. A week ago, she'd been grateful, even joyful, for the strength she'd gained from that close encounter. But clearly, the power had come at a price for others.

Kezza trembled. "Have they all died? The prisoners?"

"I don't know," the man said with a low moan. "And I don't care. Please, let me go."

"Or what, you'll scream?" Kezza asked with a sneer.

It happened in slow motion. His small, cigarette-stained teeth bared and his hands shot toward her neck. Kezza moved effortlessly out of the way. Propelled by inertia, he stumbled forward and she brought her fist down on his back. He landed on the hard floor with a painful thud.

"My back," he gasped as Kezza knelt over him, pressing a knee against his collarbone. "How did...?"

"I've been feeling stronger lately," Kezza said. "Ever since I met some interesting people during the lockdown. They sound like they might have been friends of yours. So I'm going to ask you again...have all the prisoners died?"

His eyes became black orbs watery with fear. "As far as I know...yes. Some got strong like you. But then their bodies fell apart. They all died."

Blood pounded in Kezza's ears. Everything felt light and distant, as though she were about to float up to the ceiling. The trembling man beneath her anchored her to the ground, his pulse hammering underneath his sweaty neck.

"Give me your badge, your CALPal and any other identification you have," Kezza said. She spoke in a flat monotone. She didn't know why it mattered, but instinct propelled her forward. "Hand it over, and I'll let you go on your way."

The man blinked. "You want my identity?" His eyes widened.

"You won't need it if you make it back to Earth," Kezza pointed out, her tongue now fuzzy like cotton. "And they might not notice you missing as quickly if someone is swiping and purchasing with your CALPal."

The man acquiesced. He was on the floor, and Kezza, the dying, infected woman, probably looked crazier than ever.

Kezza fiddled with the CALPal as the man stumbled onto the loading ramp. He'd make it back to Earth, which was more than Kezza would ever do. She gave a bitter salute to Alan Schulz, ID# 32771.

★　　★　　★

Stars glittered over the Observation Deck, as beautiful as it was haunting. Kezza rarely paid much attention to the glass ceiling when she performed there, too focused on her upcoming routines. But the world had spun off its axis in the last few days and she was adrift, stripped of her plans and schemes. As she did her warm-up exercises, a single word rattled between her ears, a slow drumbeat.

Dying. Dying. She was dying.

Mars had won. This planet, with its broken system, would kill her just like it had her mother. Would she suffer like her mother as well? In those last weeks, the weeks that felt like years, Mum had begged for more morphine in pitiful wails. She didn't get it, of course. It had to be rationed for the Tier Ones and Twos.

Kezza coughed, her ribs aching against the vise that was her red corset. Her lace-gloved hands dropped to her thighs as she tugged at her fishnet stockings. She had been trussed up like a turkey for an impromptu performance, scheduled for the new Tier One arrivals.

Barrett Juul chief among them.

Kezza peered through the curtain. Juul sat in the center of a plush, teal sofa. He pressed his knees together like a shy schoolchild, fingers interlaced. Around him, the fifteen-strong Corpsboard were locked in a tempest of rapid-fire conversation and drink refills. Every sentence was thick with subtext and ulterior motive, every interaction a power play. The Corpsboard members who weren't speaking to Juul spoke around him, raising their voices at the opportune moment and tipping their ears in his direction, drinking in his small talk. No doubt they were angered by his fiery rhetoric against the Corpsboard but knew better than to be outwardly hostile to a visitor with his power and money. They would play the game, and hope his speech was just theater for the masses.

Rage bubbled, hot and thick, through her veins. Her fingers curled into clenched fists. In minutes, she would be on the Observation Deck's small stage, feet away from Juul. And all her ideas of escape, of avoiding punishment, no longer mattered. She'd be dead anyway.

Kezza was the last of the circus troupe to line up behind stage, coughing. Sergei the acrobat bounced on his heels like an excited teenager, gold teeth flashing as he peered through the curtain.

"They're all here," he whispered. "Juul, his scientist mother, Earth investors, the Corpsboard themselves! Enough money in that room to buy China and all its satellite states." He shivered in apparent ecstasy.

"You're not becoming a trophy husband, Serg, no matter how many times you bat your eyelashes at those fuckers," Jen said icily. "Least of all, Barrett Juul."

"The hero of the people, now partying with the Corpsboard," LaValle chimed in with a dry chuckle. "Apparently, thirty people were arrested today, thanks to him. Kezza, what's wrong? You look white as a sheet."

"I'm fine," Kezza rasped. She powdered her hands and bounced on her heels, only to double up again in a fit of coughs. LaValle squeezed her shoulder, his face tight with concern.

"You can't go on like that," their manager, Eddie, said. "Barrett Juul didn't travel all this way to have an aerialist spray phlegm in his face."

"I can hold it together," Kezza snapped, while she filed in the back of her mind that coughing in Juul's face would be a subtle way to take him out. But she didn't want a slow decline in a faraway hospital bed. She wanted to watch the lights leave his eyes.

But Eddie shook his head. "You're out. This is not negotiable. Lucie, you'll take Kezza's place tonight on the lyra and silks."

Kezza glowered and ripped her gloves off, tearing the lace in the process. A ripple of laughter broke through the curtain. Through the slit in the red velvet, Juul whispered to an older woman who must have been his mother, the famous Dr. Saadia Hamza. A Corpsboard member on his other side downed his cocktail and let out a high-pitched giggle.

Kezza burst through the curtains. The lights had just dimmed for the show, so curious but excited eyes turned to her, expecting her to be part of the act. But she retched, stumbling to one side as another coughing fit consumed her. Eddie yelled something behind her, something she couldn't hear through the high-pitched ringing in her ears. Her surroundings blurred, taking on red-tinted edges.

A hand closed around her arm and she shook it away. She leapt in a graceful, powerful arc, rotating mid-air and earning several gasps in the process. The group applauded when she landed with an aerialist's grace only inches away from Juul. She knelt at his feet, her kohled eyes rising to meet his. He sat upright, the corner of his mouth twisted in a polite but bewildered smile. The smile waned as she rose to her feet. Her fists balled, she leaned backward, ready to raise her leg in a well-placed kick to his heart. She wished she had remembered to grab something sharp, but she couldn't turn back time. She had her body, her feet and fists, and that was enough. Her eyes must have betrayed her, because Juul's eyes widened in unmistakable fear.

"Kezza, no!"

Strong hands gripped her arms from behind, pushing her to the ground as another coughing fit seized her. Her hands tingled from the force of her coughing, from the lack of air in her lungs, and her head spun with dizziness.

She managed a cry of frustration before Barrett Juul became a blur in her waning vision.

★　★　★

A loud, monotonous beeping rang in Kezza's ears. She forced her eyelids open, wincing under the glare of bright, fluorescent lights. Her head pounded in agony and her neck ached as she craned from side to side. Her toes wriggled under a stiff cotton blanket. She was in the medical ward, lying on a hospital bed. The beeping came from a monitor next to her, the sound pounding at her tender skull.

"Why did you try to kill me?"

The soft, accented voice cut through Kezza's headache. Barrett Juul sat to her left. His posture and face were relaxed. The only hint of fear was in his dark, wary eyes.

Kezza massaged her neck. "I didn't try to kill you," she said. "I'm sick with something and made some bad decisions, coming out to meet you."

His mouth twitched. "I saw that look in your eyes," Juul said. "You looked at me like I'd murdered your whole family. Like you hated me. Why, Kezza?"

So someone had given him her name. She squeezed her eyes shut, trying to push the burning tears away. But they came. She gulped and shuddered. Barrett Juul sat in silence, like a professor patiently waiting for a student to raise their hand, while Kezza cried.

Finally, Kezza broke the silence.

"I don't have to explain myself to you," she said. "You're safe and I'm in custody. You can leave this room and forget this all happened. Carry on with your life and live your dream of destroying Mars."

Juul's brows climbed up his forehead. But then his face broke into a careful smile.

"You're not in custody," he said. "After you fainted, security wanted to arrest you for disruption and argued about your 'past behavior', though they didn't give details. But I asked them to drop any and all charges. That you seemed feverish and confused but clearly meant no harm."

Now it was Kezza's turn to register surprise.

"Now why would you do that?" she asked. "You knew that wasn't true."

"I'm curious about you," he said simply. "I want to get to know this place and the people who live here. In my line of work, you meet a lot of people and develop a sense of the ones who can help you. You're an aerialist in a Martian circus. That's interesting enough. You ran out to attack me, faster than I've seen anyone move before, and now you accuse me of trying to destroy Mars. I sense you're a better indicator of the pulse of life here in Calypso than those pampered clowns on the Corpsboard."

Kezza managed a snort. "No one sees me as a representative of the average Martian," she said. "If you want that, go talk to one of the thousands of ore miners in the Catacombs. They won't try to punch a hole in your rib cage either."

Juul laughed. "I didn't say I wanted to get to know you because you're the average Martian," he said. "If anything, you're something else entirely. One of those who moves the needle forward. A rock in the middle of the current that directs water down a new stream."

"Maybe you just think I'm pretty," Kezza said in a syrupy, mocking tone.

A pink tint spread across Juul's cheeks but his voice was firm when he replied.

"You say I want to destroy Mars," he said. "In a way, you're right. But in truth, I want to do so much more than try to change the broken system here. I want to break you all free of Mars."

Kezza's eyes narrowed. Juul was being deliberately vague, trying to pull questions out of her, but she wouldn't take his bait. She rose from the bed and began yanking off wires and sensory pads. Juul winced as she tugged the IV out of her vein. The damned beeping finally stopped.

"You know, you're the reason I'm in this shithole city on this shithole planet," she said, rubbing her arm. "One of your famous speeches convinced my dad to drag us out here. And now this is where I'll die." She coughed violently for dramatic effect.

Juul stood up, extending a hand to her. The warmth in his face dissolved, replaced by something oddly intense, and urgent.

"Do you want to leave Mars?" he asked.

"It doesn't matter what I want," Kezza retorted. "It's not possible. I can't go back to Earth. The gravity would be torture."

Juul shook his head. "You can leave Mars tonight. Let me make things up to you. Let me show you what's possible."

Chapter Seven
Azad

NABATEAN ORBIT
YEAR OF SETTLEMENT 1208

While the crew slept, Azad did pull-ups in the *Magreb*'s long corridors. He relished the quiet of resting hours, just the occasional rattle from the pipes and the sound of his own labored breathing. Heat coursed through his shoulders as he pulled his body upward. Sweat stung his eyes. Azad gritted his teeth in satisfaction. He was getting stronger each day. Even Feisal grudgingly noted that he couldn't call Azad 'soft' anymore.

But Azad wasn't doing it to prove a point to Feisal, or the rest of the crew. He wanted to be useful on the ship, of course, but more importantly, he needed to be in a state to help Ledo when she needed him. Whatever trouble she was in, he'd be ready.

A loud clang reverberated through the corridor when Azad dropped to the ground. In the galley, he heated a fresh pot of coffee and activated the recording of the Vitruvian woman's Archive. Through the silent hologram, Ledo blinked back at him with her small smile. Azad's throat tightened. He sipped his coffee and smiled back at Ledo's frozen image, as though they were enjoying a quiet moment together in Nabatea City before starting their work shifts.

Then, he began the second part of his morning ritual – his deep study of the Martian woman. He kept the volume of the recording low so the woman's quavering voice wouldn't wake the rest of the crew.

If anyone finds this, I'll be dead, hopefully on my own terms. I don't have much time in any case.

Azad's eyes narrowed as he paused and replayed the footage. The woman was short, as most ancient humans were, but there was something Vitruvian about her. The way she commanded the space she occupied. The coiled energy she carried in her broad shoulders and bouncing heels. Powerful, despite the frailty in her dark, sad eyes. Defiant even in defeat.

Who was she? And what did she mean to Ledo, assuming that Ledo transmitted this recording? At first, Azad didn't care about historical mysteries and why his ancestors left Mars – that was a long time ago, and wouldn't change anything about Nabatea now. That was Zelle's quest. But understanding this woman felt connected, in a way, to knowing Ledo. The harsh truth gnawing at Azad was that he knew very little about his sister – the adult woman who lived a life so different from his. She was a collection of childhood memories, tinged with his own anxieties about why she'd left him behind on her journey into the stars. Being on this ship, joining her old crew and studying this ancient Martian woman were his small, tentative steps to understanding the sister he missed so terribly.

"Got any extra caffeine for me?"

Azad jolted. Nawalle greeted him with a lazy smile and an even lazier wave. She tightened her robe around her waist and grabbed a chipped coffee mug decorated with Vitruvian snakes.

"Sorry if I was too loud," Azad began, before the words dissolved in his mouth. His face flushed as his eyes darted to the frozen image of Ledo and the still-moving footage of the Martian woman.

"You weren't," Nawalle said. Her fingers tapped against the mug while she waited for the coffee to cool. "The engines don't sleep, so I don't get much rest either. Any new insights into our friend?" She nodded at the woman.

"Nothing we haven't talked about already," Azad said, but as he spoke, a tingling sensation spread from his spine. In the grainy footage, the woman fidgeted with her collar, her fingers reaching for something beneath her jacket.

Azad raised his hand to pause the footage, then spread his palms out to zoom in on the woman's chest.

A badge, underneath her jacket.

"Feisal!" Nawalle barked.

An hour and several cups of coffee later, Feisal had run full forensics on the footage, grabbing every possible angle on the half-hidden badge and sharpening the resolution.

"I've got words," he said. The Vitruvian leaned back with a smug, satisfied smile.

"It's gibberish," Azad countered. "The lettering doesn't make sense."

"That's because it's over a thousand years old, wise one, and different lettering from what we use now," Feisal said with glowing eyes. "Luckily, historians don't live with the limited knowledge of the present, so we can translate the wording."

Zelle sighed but said nothing as Feisal and Nawalle went to work on the translation.

"It makes no sense," Feisal said. "It doesn't mean anything in English, Chinese, or any of the other old languages."

But before Azad could gloat, Nawalle laughed.

"That's because it's an identification badge," she said. "It has her name on it. And it's a weird one."

A name. The skin on Azad's arms prickled. Zelle leaned forward, her dark eyes alight.

"Her name," she said, "is Kezza Sayer."

Chapter Eight

Kezza

CALYPSO CORPORATE CAMPUS, MARS
2195 A.D.

Kezza shrieked. Her brain rattled inside her skull as the shuttle to the Obscura station lifted off. The force of liftoff was overwhelming, and exhilarating, like nothing else she'd experienced. Next to her, Barrett Juul laughed.

"Aren't you an aerialist?" he crowed. "You can't be afraid of heights!"

Not remotely. A faint resurgence of murderous intent warmed Kezza's chest at the sound of Juul's giggling. But this wasn't about heights. The city of Calypso shrunk beneath her through the small port window, an elaborate pattern of white buildings against the burnt Martian landscape. And above her, endless space.

For the first time since she was a toddler, she was off Mars.

The shuttle slowed as it prepared to dock on the Obscura and Kezza's heartbeat slowed with it. Adrenaline fading, her lips cracked into a smile. It suddenly felt very, very good to be off the planet. Her eyes met Juul's and her grin widened, turned mischievous. She still had a plan for Barrett Juul. But she was willing to be surprised, to let the course of her revenge take a more winding path.

The airlocked door opened to the Obscura's control room, which was, if Kezza were honest, a little underwhelming. Lots of buttons, colorless walls and monitors. But the zero gravity of the station was a joy; Kezza somersaulted into the main room with easy grace. Years of dizzying spins on the lyra had more than prepared her for this moment.

The team of scientists inside the control room barely glanced up from their monitors at the sight of Barrett Juul and a twirling woman in red sequins. But the air rushed out of Kezza's lungs when they approached the window that spanned the station's side. Mars glowed beneath them under the emerging sunlight, beautiful, as most things were, from a distance. Free of its dusty storm clouds, stars and worlds glimmered around them like scattered diamonds over a black cloak. And in the distance, one shone just a little brighter than the others.

"That's it," Juul said, pointing. "Earth."

A lump tightened in Kezza's throat. She had been born there, drew her first breaths on that rock. So tantalizingly close, yet forever out of reach.

"Do you miss it?" Kezza asked.

"Not a bit." Juul bit his lip, smoothing his hair back. He turned to Kezza. "Do you dream of Earth? Do you remember it at all?"

"Not much," Kezza admitted. "But I dream of it every day. Everyone stuck on Calypso does. A place where you can breathe unrecycled air and dig your toes in the natural ground without your blood boiling out of your eye sockets. Sounds like paradise to me."

"And there are people on Earth living in slums or dying in refugee camps, who dream of an exotic red world where they can breathe without stepping on ten people," Juul said, not unkindly. "We all want what we can't have."

"Says the man with all the choices in the world," Kezza retorted. "When you get tired of your little Martian visit – whatever you're planning here, taking advantage of all these poor, stupid, gullible people, you'll be able to fly back to Earth and recover in one of your forty mansions. So maybe you're not the best person to talk about perspective."

Juul stared back at Kezza, his normally mild-mannered features stunned. Kezza wet her lips, silently kicking herself. She had overplayed her hand, let her emotions get the best of her. With a shuddering sigh, she tried to recover.

"Thank you for taking me up here," she said. "Really – I appreciate it. It just brings up a lot of complicated feelings. Reminds me of the choices that have been closed off to me."

Juul's face relaxed, though a trace of wariness lingered in his eyes.

"Choice is a complicated thing," he said. "Too little of it, as you've articulated, and we feel stifled and restless. Too much, however, and we become paralyzed with our abundance of options. An old academic concept, the paradox of choice. It used to be thought that seven was the optimal number of choices, but I believe that most decisions, big and small, are best simplified to three. I applied that system to a village chain in the Bekaa Valley, with wonderful results."

"You limit people." Unease seeped through Kezza's mild intoxication. She'd had a couple of vodka cranberries before her failed assassination attempt, and the effects lingered.

"And why not? Some of the happiest people I've met on Earth lived in the poorest places, overcrowded and lacking in luxury. And yet they found contentment and purpose to their lives, unlike the neurotic messes you encounter in Dubai, Toronto and Tokyo. There are limits, of course. Safety and basic necessities must be met, to allow someone the psychological space to be happy. That's the problem with Earth – the lack of safety, the basic struggle for many to survive. Dr. Hamza, my incredible mother, came from Lebanon, after the 2056 Treaty Collapse. Watched militants tie her uncle between two cars and rip him in half as they drove in opposing directions! Lived in fear of the same or worse happening to her, before she escaped to Copenhagen. When I worked on the team that repaired Lebanon after the disintegration, however, many of them wanted to arrogantly impose a Western model on a culture that had no need for it. Introducing the culture of Me and More, of capitalist greed, would have been a disaster. Lebanon responded favorably to the Choice of Three model, despite much early skepticism."

"I understand that logic when it applies to objects," Kezza said slowly, shivering at the thought of a screaming man torn into bloody pieces. "Toasters, televisions, peanut butter or whatever else you have over there. But to apply limited choice to what you do each day? Who you spend time with? Who you love?"

"Even that. As shocking as that may sound, it is empirically a better way to live."

"Three choices for everything," Kezza said with a bemused twitch in her mouth. Her dark hair spread like rivulets of ink in the zero gravity. "Ok, life coach – or should I say society coach? What options do you have for me?"

Her tone was flirtatious. Juul picked it up immediately, matching her.

"Well, Ms. Sayer," he said. "You can, one, get back on the shuttle down to Calypso and go to bed, dreaming of Earth again. Two, you can stare at Earth a little longer, until the wanting of something else leaves a dull ache in your heart. Or three, you can learn some secrets. What I plan to do on Mars."

An odd, tingling sensation radiated from Kezza's chest. Wherever she was expecting this odd, pseudo-date to go, this wasn't it. Her throat was suddenly dry, and she wished she'd brought another drink up to the Obscura.

Did she care what Juul planned to do on Mars?

Yes, oddly enough. At best, it would make her feel better about killing him. At worst, if it was a half-decent idea, she'd share it with LaValle and the rest of the troupe. A lot of people put serious trust and money into Juul's ideas.

Kezza grinned. "You made it easy for me," she said. "Martians trade in secrets. But you've already said on your broadcast that you want to recruit Martians for something. Was that the truth?"

In answer, Juul beckoned her toward the researchers hard at work over their machines.

"Did you know this station features a telescope designed to search for habitable planets?" he asked. "My mother's initiative, along with other sponsors, of course. We're here now because we've found one."

"Another planet?" Kezza frowned. Her brain began to assemble the pieces together, pieces in different colors and shapes than she expected.

"Yes."

"To live on?" she pressed. Her mouth had gone dry.

"That's what a habitable planet entails," Juul said.

"Who would live on this planet?" Kezza knew the answer now – the pieces all but assembled – but she needed to hear it from his own mouth.

"Any Martian who wants to join me," Juul said.

Kezza gripped the nearest rail, the zero gravity suddenly overwhelming. The tingling sensation spread down to her clammy palms. Juul did not come to Mars to terraform the planet or set up his own city. He came with the intent to leave. To start not just a new civilization, but a new *planet*. And he would recruit Martians for the task.

After a moment's pause, the first question solidified in Kezza's mind. "How far is it?"

"About one hundred and ten light years away."

Kezza scoffed. "That's quite a distance."

"Is it?" Juul asked, an amused twinkle in his eyes.

But Kezza persisted. "For human space travel, of course it is. I studied the logistics of interstellar travel theory in school. We can only travel at a twentieth of the speed of light, not to mention dealing with sustaining long-term space flight, having supplies and radiation protection. You're asking people to live out their lives, and their children's lives, traveling through space."

Juul's grin was knowing, as though he'd expected her reply. He nodded at the Obscura's workers and lowered his voice.

"This station does more than point a telescope into deep space," he said. "My mother leads a research initiative into more economical means of space travel. Let's just say we've found a shortcut."

"A shortcut?" Kezza raised a brow. "Like a wormhole?"

"Right on the first guess."

"But those are theoretical," she countered. "Unless…you've either discovered one, or discovered a way to construct your own wormhole."

Juul laughed. "Why aren't you working up here, Kezza? You're sharp. You must be the most underemployed person on Calypso."

"Don't be so sure," Kezza said. "This planet. We'd get there in our lifetimes?"

"The voyage should take a little over a year once we pass through the wormhole, based on Dr. Hamza's projections."

"And the air on this planet is…breathable?"

"You will live in an oxygen-rich, open atmosphere. No more confinement."

The room spun in a way that had nothing to do with the lack of gravity. Kezza had been holding her breath while Juul spoke. She closed her eyes, suddenly drunk with the possibilities. Was it really attainable? Or was this just a billionaire's ego trip at work?

"What do you think?" Juul's baritone cut through Kezza's thoughts.

Kezza swallowed, but managed a composed, careful smile.

"What does the Corpsboard think of you trying to recruit their entire labor force to another planet?" she asked. "Or is this a Calypso venture you're planning?"

Juul's face darkened.

"There is nothing, and I mean nothing, in this corrupt corporate city that I want to replicate in a new world," he said with surprising passion. "Kezza, I know you don't fully trust me. You think I'm here to make things worse, to meddle in things I don't understand. And I admit that I don't understand everything – that's why I need you, Kezza, to learn about this world. But I know some things. My mother was a refugee – she went through hell to give me a future and all of my work is in service of her dreams. This is the end goal – the apex of our vision. To leave all that is broken in humanity behind and start again, somewhere very far away."

Kezza shivered. She actually, fucking *shivered*. What was wrong with her? Hours ago, she had every plan to snap the man's windpipe with a well-placed kick, and now, with his words pouring like sweet, A-grade Calypso honey in her ear, she was ready to become his first recruit.

But his vision spoke to something deep within her, an old ache in the deepest chambers of her heart that she had long numbed away. She'd always expected to die on this planet, never seeing beyond Calypso's walls. Earth was forever closed to her, thanks to Martian gravity. Tonight, she'd been presented with another possibility – living somewhere else. Somewhere far away from Calypso, with its Corpsboard and Catacombs and calorie rations.

Maybe it was a crazy dream. But Kezza always had a streak of crazy running through her. It was why she joined the circus and glided through the air every night, instead of sitting at a desk writing code. It was why she chased after those thieves during the lockdown and approached the body lying in the Waste Room. Hell, it was why she planned to be Calypso's first assassin, until right now.

If Juul's plan failed, she could change course again. It's what she did – adapt and survive.

"I'm in," Kezza said. "What do you want me to do?"

But before Juul could answer, Kezza doubled over in a fit of coughing.

"Kezza? Are you all right?"

Even the workers at the monitors turned around, then exchanged alarmed looks, when Kezza coughed and retched, her knuckles white as she gripped her knees. Her ears rang from the force of her coughing; her lungs burned as they became starved of air.

Juul glided to her side, holding one of her arms as she doubled over, her body rising. His eyes widened in shock and horror.

A streak of hot blood erupted from her mouth, leaving small, bright red spheres in the air. They floated, a miniature, macabre solar system, until a crying Kezza swiped them away.

Chapter Nine

Azad

EMIGRANT'S WORMHOLE, JUULIAN SOLAR SYSTEM
YEAR OF SETTLEMENT 1208

In the weeks it took to reach the Emigrant's Wormhole, located on the far edge of the Juulian solar system, Azad familiarized himself with anything the crew would show him. He embraced ship life like a child in Township, eager to pass any test placed before him.

The *Magreb*'s sick bay spanned the length of Azad's closet at home in Khazneh and he treated it with the same level of care, scrubbing its floors and shelves until his thinning face gleamed back at him. Many of the medications, including gravity-adjustment pills, anti-radiation tablets and nutritional supplements, had long expired, likely procured during smuggling runs on Cerata. The surgical equipment, however, shone with evident non-use. The triage machine whirred to life after several taps and Azad grinned, running his hands along its smooth edges. Not a medmech in sight. When injury came – and Azad had little doubt that it would – he would be the one to administer the healing.

On the morning of the planned passage through the wormhole, Azad woke with his fists clenched against his chest. He dreamed of quantum foam as though it were a tangible substance, not unlike the bubbling, hissing fields of the Sulpherlands. It was through measuring space-time at the quantum level, Nawalle had explained with formidable patience, that their ancestors were able to create a traversable wormhole from the tiny wormholes that could appear and disappear on the quantum scale, via manipulation of dark energy. Their ancestors made an incredible scientific leap given the time they lived in, when space travel had taken a back seat to environmental problems on Earth.

"In the end, they were right to think big, and take the risk that they did," Zelle said. "Earth, according to the Archives, was woefully overpopulated, with terrible displacement caused by rapid climate shifts. Many fled to Mars for work and stability, but undoubtedly found a new set of problems when they got there. Barrett Juul and his mother, Saadia Hamza, it seems, exploited that desperation to orchestrate the most incredible migration in human history."

Feisal strummed his oud. His melodies drowned out the voice of the ancient Martian woman, Kezza Sayer, whose recording they rewatched on the kitchen's hologram screen. Zelle bent over the table, peering into the woman's pale, frightened face for some new insight. She had been playing the mysterious footage all morning on a continuous loop, muttering the woman's words at the end of each session.

"...*create something terrible.*"

"No offense, Captain, but if I have to hear that deathbed speech one more time, I'm going to create something terrible on this oud and play it until your ears bleed," Feisal said, eyes closed.

"You couldn't create a bad melody if you tried," Zelle said. "And don't interrupt a historian with a precious historical record in her hands."

"Have some compassion, Feisal," Nawalle said. She pulled her curly hair into a ponytail, fingers black with engine grease. "Those could have been her final words."

"Why did she have to make them so Juul-damned cryptic?" Feisal said with a theatrical roll of his eyes. "She would have done us all a favor, me above all, if she just rattled off everything that was bothering her about Juul and the journey."

"It likely wasn't safe," Zelle said. "Or she wasn't thinking clearly. The more I look at her, the more I see someone who is unwell. Medically ill, I mean. Look how red her eyes are. Look at her skin."

"We had some pale ancestors," Feisal noted. "She definitely could have used some Nabatean sun, if she only knew what awaited her."

Azad let out an involuntary laugh and Feisal glowered.

"She was unwell," Zelle said. "In body, and perhaps in mind as well. Whatever was wrong with her, she looked desperate."

Azad remained silent under Feisal's cold glare, but shared Zelle's assessment. The red corners of the woman's eyes resembled Nenah's in the Nabatean hospital, before blood seeped from their corners. The more distressing comparison in his mind, however, was between the troubled young woman and Ledo. They did not look alike, exactly, aside from their black hair. Ledo's skin was darker, her face heart-shaped, where this woman's was narrow and heavy with sadness. But he struggled not to imagine Ledo in a similar, desperate state as this woman, far from home and starved of options.

"Twenty Ceratan minutes until contact," a disembodied voice boomed overhead. The ship, the *Magreb*, used its communication system as a warning.

"Does she mean the wormhole?" Azad asked in a small voice. His insides clenched, an unpleasant burning sensation crawling up his throat.

"She does," Nawalle said cheerfully. "Time to prepare."

"Nap time, travelers!" Feisal said, putting his oud away with particular care. He grabbed Nawalle's hands and twirled her down the narrow corridor in an artful pirouette. His shiny, bald head grazed the low ceiling. Nawalle laughed, but Azad failed to muster a smile. Twenty minutes until every molecule on the ship passed through a bend in space-time and the crew acted as though they were heading for afternoon coffee.

"We'll need to get into the resting pods at the base of the ship," Zelle said by way of calmer explanation, strolling alongside Azad. "We'll be unconscious for the next few hours and saturated with gravity-equalizing chemicals while we pass through the Emigrant's Wormhole, and trust me, you'll want to be. The *Magreb* has a set course, and she'll steer us on the other side as we wake up."

"The Emigrant's Wormhole?" Azad asked. His mouth soured with bile. "Doesn't that put us further from Mars within the mother system? Isn't there a closer one that opens near, what's the name, Jupiter?"

"It does indeed. That one is closer, but also more trafficked by Vitruvian power ships, and actively maintained by Nabatean authorities.

Our path will mirror the Great Escape taken by Barrett Juul and the first human emigrants to Nabatea. We can slip into the mother system the quieter way, because that wormhole was not kept stable and supported after its original threading by our Martian ancestors."

"But...couldn't it collapse at any moment and destroy the ship?" Azad asked, his shoulders jerking involuntarily.

"It could," Zelle mused. "But if it does, we'll already be unconscious and won't know the difference."

The thought gave Azad little comfort. But as they reached the ship's sleeping quarters, the crew climbed without hesitation into their resting pods and Azad followed, forcing down the tremors of terror that seized his body. His stomach flipped the way it might if he were pushed over a ledge, which in a sense, he was – all of them, about to hurtle through a mysterious, bending tear in the universe's complex fabric and hope to come out in one piece on the other side.

"You're in Ledo's bed," Nawalle said cheerfully from her own recliner, giving him a reassuring smile.

"I'm switching us all off!" Feisal barked, businesslike. "See you across the stars, kids!"

"Do you think she's still out there?" Azad asked Nawalle, both now lying on their backs but facing each other across the room.

Nawalle opened her mouth but her face became a blur, like a raindrop on a painting, and whatever she said, the words turned to water in Azad's ears.

Chapter Ten

Kezza

CALYPSO CORPORATE CAMPUS, MARS
2195 A.D.

"Drink."

Kezza's lips trembled as she brought Juul's Earth-imported tea to her lips. She shuddered at the bitter taste, but it calmed her throat. The rusty taste of blood lingered on her tongue. Kezza barely recalled the journey back down to Mars from the Obscura, only that it was easier going down than up.

Now, she sat cross-legged on a plush pillow, surrounded by soft orange lights and ornate carpets. Juul's guest quarters on Calypso. The room was the size of at least three standard family apartments in the Catacombs. Juul sat on an ottoman near Kezza, staring at her as though she'd grown a second head. Behind him, a regal, elegant woman with long, chestnut hair walked into the room. Dr. Saadia Hamza, his mother. She wore a pantsuit and a curious expression as she pulled up her own seat near Kezza.

"Do you need medical attention, dear?" she asked in a low, melodic voice.

"Not a bit," Kezza replied. "I've had this cough for some time now. The circus doctor's got a plan for me." A diet of powdered Greek yogurt and sweet soy broth to help her lose weight, but they didn't need the details.

"The circus doctor." Juul nodded and pressed his lips together. "What does he say about a sick person who can bend metal rails?"

Silence followed. Kezza frowned, scratching the corners of her memory before it came back to her – Juul ushering her into the shuttle, her legs flailing and her body racking with coughs. Her hand reaching, desperately, for support in the anchorless world of zero gravity. The way the steel bar along the shuttle's door bent like a pretzel under her grip.

Kezza sighed and rubbed her temples.

"It was like something from a comic book," Juul said in a shaky voice. "It was unnatural."

"It's been a wild month in the Triple C," Kezza agreed with a wry smile. "Now, I'll let you in on my secrets."

Kezza told him everything that happened from the Waste Room onward. Why not? If she was going to plot a Martian revolution with the man, she might as well arm him with some useful information. It also felt good to tell someone what had been happening to her. LaValle and the circus troupe hadn't gotten the full story, lest it put them in some kind of danger with the Corpsboard. Juul mattered less.

Barrett Juul and Dr. Hamza listened in rapt silence until the end, although both visibly reacted when Kezza described the two bodies in the Waste Room.

"Were they Calypso employees?" Dr. Hamza asked.

Kezza frowned. An odd question. "Who else would they be?"

"Palmcorps," Dr. Hamza said with a knowing glance at Juul. "Barrett, are you thinking what I'm thinking?"

"I am," Juul said before turning to Kezza. "We've been in touch with allies in Palmcorps across the desert. That city is far more organized and ready for revolution than Calypso, which is why we started here – to stoke new fires. They lost two miners in the Arabia Terra desert, who ventured into an area where Calypso mining was active. There was speculation they may have been detained by Calypso. A married couple active in Palmcorps resistance."

Kezza's hand flew to her pounding heart. The man with the desperate eyes had mouthed that he was going home. He had been trying to return to Palmcorps.

With shaking hands, Kezza reached into her back pocket and pulled out the CALPal device she'd procured from Alan Schulz, the man who was hopefully on his way back to Earth, hiding in the cargo bay.

"That Tier One said that they found something in a crater in the desert," she said. "Something that was making people sick. That's what I have. Something that makes people deadly ill, but also very strong. That man ran out into open Martian atmosphere and survived way longer than he should have. I don't know what that means for me. I'm also getting stronger – I think I can even see better than before – but the cough's also getting worse. Maybe he's got something we can use. I've been meaning to look at his computer to see if there are some clues, but I've…I've been afraid." Her voice cracked. Vulnerable Kezza was her least favorite version of herself, but Kezza relaxed as Dr. Hamza rubbed her shoulder and spoke to her in a soft purr.

"I'll look through it," she said. With deft fingers, she swiped Alan's badge against the CALPal and her brows formed a dark shadow over her eyes as she began her search. Barrett Juul sat in silence while his mother went to work. Kezza, unable to sit still, began practicing handstands, doing her best impressions of LaValle's more difficult contortions.

The circus. The only thing that gave her joy on Calypso. What would become of it if Juul's crazy scheme became reality? Would her comrades in the troupe join his journey across the stars? Would there be a place for entertainers in the civilizationist's new world?

"Oh!" Dr. Hamza clasped a hand to her mouth. Color drained from her face, leaving her skin the hue of sour milk.

Kezza and Juul gathered around the doctor, looking over her shoulder. Dr. Hamza had frozen a thirty-four-seconds-long video. It previewed a blurry figure on the floor, but something about the image suggested the horrors it might carry.

"What is that?" Juul whispered.

She clicked replay.

Wails erupted from the CALPal's speakers. On the screen, the camera jumped around a sterile room, a laboratory of some kind, where a team of men and women lay in varying states of collapse on the floor behind a glass door. Some clawed at their throats, their screams tempered by fluids seeping down their chins, while others spasmed in silence.

Kezza clapped a hand over her mouth, forcing back a cry of her own. Her hands shook. Juul cursed, spinning around before returning to his place over Dr. Hamza's shoulder. Even through the blurry footage, she could make out the trademark purple blotches across their exposed skin and the streaks of red leaking from their eyes.

They had the same illness as the man in the Waste Room.

What Kezza had.

With trembling fingers, Kezza scratched at her arms. How soon would it be before she erupted in purple blotches and cried blood? She nearly doubled over from a dizzying wave of nausea.

Alan Schulz's voice cut through the horror.

"All of them came back from field work in Arabia Terra…all with the same symptoms," he narrated. "The onset was sudden, the decline rapid. Three died yesterday, and this group looks ready to follow suit. It appears to be contagious by close, prolonged proximity and through fluids. All are being kept in isolation at present, after all of our treatments failed."

One figure on the floor crawled forward. A man whose eyes bulged even as they bled. The eyes met the camera, alight with fury. He lunged upright in a shocking burst of strength, the same way Kezza performed her opening leap on the trapeze. His fist swung at the glass door, scattering shards across the floor. New screams followed, louder and healthier, as he burst through the shattered glass and struck at something beyond the camera's line of vision. The shaking camera turned to the floor before going black.

The silence that followed thickened like fog around them. Blood pounded in Kezza's ears and her heart hammered in her chest. She was going to faint, she couldn't breathe, she…

"Kezza." Juul grabbed her shoulders and through her panic, she dug her nails into his wrists. "We're going to stop this. We're going to expose this. And we will find a way to treat this sickness. Kezza, listen! You're going to be ok."

Kezza gulped for air. How was this possible? Only days ago, she'd climbed to the top of the Observation Deck, strong and invincible, and here she was, recoiling with Death's cold breath on her neck. She had been ready to murder Juul for his part in her broken life – now she clung to him for dear life, as though he were an anchor in a storm.

Kezza closed her eyes. She drew inward, drowning out the sound of Juul's reassurances, of Dr. Hamza's schemes and the screams of the dying on Alan Schulz's device. She felt the blood flowing through her arms, her calves and back, and felt the strength in her limbs. She inhaled, noting how long she could hold her breath and how she could detect the subtle smells in the room, of perfume and leather and recycled Martian air.

She was vulnerable, yes. But she was also powerful, evolving in ways that no one could understand. It was that side that mattered now, bolstered by all the internal strength she had in her. She'd held her mother's hand while she rotted away from radiation sickness. She'd endured bruised bones and torn muscles from her years of training at the circus.

She would not die on Mars. She would survive this.

"Kezza?" Juul spoke again.

Kezza cleared her throat and wiped her eyes.

"Forward the video to my CALPal," she said. "I'm going to start spreading the word around the Catacombs. You contact your friends in Palmcorps – get them ready. We're going to storm the Bokambe complex, find anything useful we can, and then burn this place to the fucking ground."

Part Two

Anointed in Starlight

Evolution is generally seen by the unenlightened as the linear progression of a single species, but many forget that there are frequent forks in the road. We share much of our DNA with chimpanzees. Our cousins the Neanderthals once walked among our humanoid ancestors. It is fitting, therefore, that on the way through the stars to our new home, humanity would find itself at another fork as a new mutation revealed itself among those born on the journey. The word 'mutation' carries a negative connotation, but the emergence of the Vitruvian race is anything but — a people kissed by starlight, made in the depths of space and better adapted to explore and survive in it.

As a result, the new society we forged on Nabatea had to recognize this clear distinction. We recognize our common humanity and our equality, but we are fundamentally different and must be treated as such. The unevolved among us followed the societal model I had constructed for Nabatea, to avoid the disasters of the mother system, and this newer, stronger variation of human found themselves with no past to avoid — a chance at something brave and new.

From **The Teachings and Sayings of Barrett Juul, Founder of Nabatea**

If a wind blows, ride it
Arabic proverb

Chapter Eleven
Azad

MOTHER SYSTEM, NEAR MARS
YEAR OF SETTLEMENT 1208

A tempest churned in Azad's stomach. Everything inside him felt out of place, as though he were a toy a child had taken apart and tried to reassemble again. He lurched sideways and vomited onto the floor.

"Our *hadir* awakens," a familiar voice called.

"I thought I was one of you now," Azad replied, sitting upright with a shiver. The ship's familiar chill greeted his clammy forehead. "Did we... make it?"

Feisal didn't dignify the question with its obvious response, but Nawalle passed them with a wrench in hand.

"We made it!" she said. She patted the *Magreb*'s walls affectionately. "The Emigrant's Wormhole held for another day. We're in the mother system."

Azad stumbled up to the flight deck and found Zelle at the controls. He followed her gaze out the front window.

The view did nothing to calm his stormy insides. Gone were the familiar curve of Cerata, the looming presence of the Sun. Stars blinked back at him in a foreign pattern, lacking the rich swirls of amethyst and gold that filled up the sky on the dark outskirts of Nabatea City. One star stood above the others, a fierce, blinding ball.

"The mother system's sun," Zelle said in a calm voice. Her gaze was fixed on the star. "A sight I've waited a lifetime to see."

Azad struggled for a response, but found nothing that captured the haunting beauty before him and what it meant. His pulse quickened at his throat.

"Get Feisal up here," Zelle said. "We're near an asteroid belt and need to track in-range objects that might give the *Magreb* trouble."

Azad tore his eyes away from the sun. His legs shook as he descended the steps from the deck. His surroundings pulsed with their own energy, as though the walls were closing in on him by fractions of an inch. Everything turned foggy and distant. His vision narrowed. The first stages of a panic attack took shape. It was too much, all of it. Azad had traversed a fold in space-time, everything and everyone he knew an unfathomable distance away. Osbourne lay dismembered in a waste box, leaving him at the mercy of a strange crew, and Ledo – lost, untethered Ledo – wandered somewhere in the infinite space before them.

The floor rushed at him before he could break his fall.

★　　★　　★

"I warned her against bringing the *hadir*."

"He'll be fine, Feisal, he just had a shock. Traversing a wormhole can do that. Some people don't talk for a whole day after." Nawalle's voice, mild and scolding.

"He's spring, too spring to be useful in any way. Unless Zelle has plans for him she won't share with us, which I'll admit is possible. A hostage exchange with the *Axel*, perhaps?"

"Of course not!"

Azad sat up, suppressing the urge to vomit again. Feisal's words bit him like the ship's cold air. His shipmates were both sitting, surveying him while he remained cross-legged on the cold floor.

"If you're going to keep insulting me, then you might as well send me to the *Axel*," Azad said, with a bite that made both Feisal and Nawalle's eyes widen. "I'm getting tired of it. I just left Nabatea City and now I'm across the galaxy, about to step on our mother planet. Haven't I proven I'm not one of the sedentary? At least on the *Axel*, the Vitruvians don't pretend to be our allies."

"I don't pretend anything, *ha*—" Feisal caught himself, eyes flashing. "I serve a Nabatean captain without hesitation or shame, while you—"

"So you think you can say what you like to me," Azad snapped. Maybe it was the renewed blood pressure after his faint, but Azad had never felt clearer in mind, heat coursing across his face. "Because I'm not the perfect, rebellious Nabatean – one who acts like a Vitruvian – I'm not one you have to respect. If you were so different from the rest of your kind, I wouldn't have to earn it."

For the first time, Feisal didn't have a retort at the ready. Pressing his lips together under his curled mustache, the Vitruvian stole a glance at Nawalle, who shrugged with casual indifference. But when she met Azad's eyes, a smile lurked in the corners of her face.

"Any problems here?" Zelle's light footsteps along the walkway announced her arrival.

Azad cleared his throat.

"I'm fine, it's just…feeling sick after waking up…"

"Imagine how the first emigrants felt traversing this wormhole after leaving Mars," Zelle chimed in as she pulled up a chair. Given that the entire crew sat together in the living quarters, they must have passed the asteroid belt by now. Meaning that Azad had been unconscious for more than a few, fleeting minutes. He rose to his feet with some effort,

"They were awake," Azad said, recalling early lessons at Township. "Thanks to Juul's breakthrough in quantum foam theory. But they were still ignorant of what would actually happen when they passed through."

"Very good," Zelle said with a serene smile. If the captain had sensed the tension lingering in the room, she chose to ignore it. "Only it wasn't Barrett Juul himself who discovered it. It was his mother, Dr. Saadia Hamza, and her team who made the discovery on the Obscura station, which we'll be passing on the way to Mars."

Azad frowned, turning to Nawalle for confirmation. She nodded vehemently.

"She learned that fact by combing through settlement data in the Library of Souls," Nawalle said with a nod to Zelle. "One of the first things that got her in trouble."

"Of course, our history gives Juul credit for everything," Zelle said. "He designed society on Nabatea, it's true, but he was a civilizationist, not a super-human. Not even a Vitruvian. The way we tell it, you'd think he could conjure a black hole with a snap of his fingers!"

Azad absorbed her words with a dazed nod. He didn't doubt her. Removed from the showy brilliance of Nabatea City, his old life seemed less real, a mirage held in place by ideas repeated over and over. Despair spread through his memories like a poison, infecting everything he had once learned and accepted without question. How many of his childhood stories were lies? And why had he never questioned them?

The passing weeks en route to Mars only strengthened this sense of distance from his old life. Azad took over doctoring duties, checking each crew member every few days to monitor bone density, vision and radiation levels. Without mechs to do the work for him, Azad performed his role with zeal. He assisted Nawalle with the mechanics and maintenance of the ship, monitoring the life supply backups. They also adjusted the rotational gravity mechanism every month, modifying the centrifuge to gradually acclimate them from Nabatean to Martian gravity.

"They're not that far apart," Nawalle explained over mealtime. "That's part of why Nabatea was chosen, for its similar gravity to Mars. Earth and Mars are more extreme. But adjusting is always good practice, because trust me, you'll feel the difference."

"Speaking of Earth," Azad began, "why not travel to Earth and use the device – um, Barry – there as well?"

"A few reasons, my inquisitive friend," Feisal said between mouthfuls of starch-compressed manaqish. The Vitruvian had made an effort to stop calling Azad *hadir*. "One, Earth is a mess at present. Churning, filthy oceans, foul air, stretches of wasteland that would make the Sulpherlands look like the Dusharan Gardens of Paradise. It's traversable but takes some planning. Not only do you have to land there in one piece through all the toxic storms, you have to dodge Vitruvian vessels, who *do* explore Earth frequently enough. Two, it's not as historically interesting in terms of understanding how Nabatea came to be, and we're historians. It's the more popular destination with pilgrims and wanderers like *us*—" his tone made it clear that Azad was not included in that statement, "—who want to see the mother planet and try to find some of our surviving ancestors, as if anything there could survive. But we're here for facts and truth, not adventure. We're children of Mars in the end, not Earth. And remember that sister you're all concerned with finding? Ledo may or may not be on Mars, but we know she's not wandering around Earth."

Feisal put down his fork with a dramatic flourish, wiping his mustache with the edge of his napkin. Azad gritted his teeth but refused to take the bait. After answering back to the Vitruvian, who *was* the ship's first mate, he needed to pick his battles. A subtle shift had happened between them after their altercation. Since then, the Vitruvian alternated between grudging concessions of respect and renewed insults, as though he were struggling to find a new balance of power between them.

"And also," Nawalle said with a barely contained smile, "Barry isn't advanced enough to read historical quantum signatures on Earth yet."

"I'll get there!" Feisal barked as Nawalle cackled. "Too much clutter on that hyperactive planet. Too much consciousness, between the plants, the organisms of varying shapes and sizes, and all the Juul-cursed people over the centuries. Mars is quieter, its conscious imprint simpler. But my other points still stand!"

Any lingering tension evaporated, however, as Feisal pulled out his oud after dinner. He played a joyful, energetic melody that even Azad could not resist dancing to. He linked arms with a laughing Nawalle, spinning around the narrow room while Zelle clapped her hands in time to the music. Zelle then performed a dance of her own while Azad took ownership of a Dusharan drum. While machines could generate music, no self-respecting Nabatean would let one keep rhythm, as nothing was more human than a song's beating pulse. Azad closed his eyes as his wrist struck the drum's canvas, its energy flowing through his limbs.

As the night progressed, the tempo of Feisal's songs slowed, melancholy seeping into his chords. They sat in a circle, Nawalle's head on Zelle's shoulder, a small crew of historians locked together in the present. Warmth flooded Azad's heart. For the first time since he bought that fateful ticket to Cerata, he felt a sense of security, and had to resist the urge to devolve into the Khazneh district's ceremonies – the daily recaps, the discussion of Problems. Those days were over. But this was something better. They had Problems, without doubt, and the expected tensions, but also something he had never felt before – a sense of kinship vibrating in the air between them, of minds tuned to the same frequency.

On his way to the sleeping quarters, Azad caught his reflection in the lone mirror on the *Magreb*. With his hair shaved close to his head, easier to maintain in space travel, his face took on a gaunt, weathered quality. The stubbled head, combined with his leaner frame, transformed him into someone he would have crossed the street to avoid back on Nabatea City. An outcast, one of the Blanked. A lost soul, rejecting or rejected by the perfect system Barrett Juul created. His reflection blinked back through the mirror, an uneasy mixture of hardness and fear in his eyes.

"I'm glad you're here," a soft voice said behind him.

Azad spun around to face Nawalle. She smiled lazily, still under the sedating spell of Feisal's music.

"Because I look like Ledo?" he asked. Not an accusation, but an acknowledgment of his place on the ship.

"Because you're kind," she said. "You still care about her, even though she left you. You gave up everything for her."

"I'm not sure what I gave up, to be honest," Azad said, his throat tightening as the words rushed out of him. The night's melodies, exuberant and sad, swam together in his head like honey in a teacup, clouding everything. Did he truly belong here? Could he return to his old life again?

Feisal sauntered past them in the corridor, slapping Azad's shoulder. Azad buckled under the Vitruvian's casual strength.

"Sleep it off, *hadir*," he said. "We'll be on Martian soil tomorrow."

★   ★   ★

The Obscura spun a slow lutz before them, an ancient relic not yet forgotten. As the *Magreb* passed the small, ghostlike station, colorful flags lined its frame, their tattered threads frozen by deep space. One stood out – the curve of a red snake on a yellow flag.

"Vitruvian explorer ships leaving their mark," Nawalle said to Azad in explanation. "Everyone who travels here visits the Obscura. It's how it all began, when you think about it."

Goosebumps covered Azad's arms. Shaped like a giant, rotating cone with a disc cutting into its center, the telescope at its head had first detected the planet of Nabatea over a thousand years ago. On the other end, the station had experimented with dark energy, leading to the creation of the Emigrant's Wormhole. Everyone Azad knew, every Nabatean, owed their existence to the minds behind this hunk of metal.

"Object within radar," Feisal barked. Azad's gaze snapped from the Obscura to the Vitruvian, who sat hunched over the scanner.

"Vitruvian vessel?" Zelle asked, stepping up to the control area. She leaned over Feisal's shoulder.

"Too small," Feisal said. "Looks like an ancillary shuttle or recon. But if they're buzzing around here, a bigger ship must be within drive range."

All eyes went to Zelle. Her face tensed, the pressure of a quick decision playing out across her features.

"Land us near Calypso as discreetly as you can," she said. "Hopefully, they haven't been paying attention to their radar. We're not here to fight or flee."

Azad doubted that a Vitruvian vessel would ignore their radar. But if Feisal objected, he didn't show it. With a quick nod, he gestured them toward the back of the ship. *Time to strap in.*

The *Magreb* shook and rattled at the breach into Martian atmosphere. Azad's teeth chattered, whether from the pressure or sheer terror as flames licked at the port window above his seat, he did not know. The landing on Cerata, a smaller object with less gravity, had been seamless in comparison.

Nearby, Nawalle let out a delighted shriek as the ship slowed into its descent. Zelle gripped the sides of her seat harness but her eyelids lowered heavily, as though lost in Dusharan prayer. Azad never prayed, but with the ship shuddering around him like it might split in half any moment, he considered it.

From the shaky view out of the side window, the landscape of Mars unfolded below them, wrinkled with red hills. An old world, its creases rich with secrets. For a second, Azad forgot his terror. Mars, home of his ancestors. Tears pooled in his eyes, shaken out by the vibrating ship.

"Welcome to the mother planet," Feisal shouted from the control room. "We're right at the doorstep of Calypso Corporate Campus. About a mile away."

The *Magreb* landed in the shadow of a steep hill, partially concealed to any overhead scanners. Partially.

"Why are we starting in Calypso?" Azad asked Zelle as they suited up. "Wouldn't it be more interesting to investigate this other city, Palmcorps?"

"All in good time, Azad," Zelle said. "We don't know exactly where it is on Mars, for one thing. And there's much to learn from understanding what happened here on Calypso, tracing from what we do know. If both human outposts were destroyed in quick succession, the causes may be related."

Azad nodded in agreement and assembled his suit in silence. He had worn an atmosphere suit once before, but that had been on a guided tour over the Sulpherlands in the un-terraformed half of Nabatea. The lack of oxygen beyond the *Magreb*'s doors unsettled him far more than bubbling pools of sulfuric acid.

The doors opened. Red dust whipped around their boots and slid back down the ramp, beckoning them out to the hazy landscape.

The clay-red earth and distant, jagged mountains resembled Nabatea, but the similarities ended there. Azad's chest tightened under the weight of this still, lifeless world. A wind gust passed by, but there were no palm trees that rustled against it, no scents of freshly baked turmeric bread and spiced cakes for the breeze to carry. Nabatea was light years away, literally and figuratively.

Surrounded by lifeless rock and dust, Azad had never felt more alive.

"Let's move, team," Zelle's voice intoned through Azad's headset. "The ruins are directly ahead. Feisal, can you direct Barry?"

"Barry can direct himself," Feisal replied with glee. The edges of his pomaded mustache brushed against his vizor. Behind him, the machine rolled forward on compact wheels.

They advanced into their ancestral terrain, ghosts of the past emerging through the thick haze. The domes of Calypso Corporate Campus loomed ahead, cracked like shells. Fragments of white tunnels connected the weathered domes. Away from the city, graves clustered in the distance, jutting from the red ground like half-buried fingernails.

Other traces of life or signs of Calypso's demise had been swept away by weather and time. Sadness and a strange sense of pride warred within Azad; for all of early humanity's accomplishments on Mars, only this ghostly skeleton remained. And yet a fraction of those embattled Martians had survived, even evolved, during their exodus.

And now, their descendants had come home.

Is this why you left, Ledo? Were you chasing this place, this feeling, before you even knew where to find it? Azad's mouth twitched in a faint smile. In this rare moment, he truly understood her.

"Look, there's something ahead," Nawalle said, pointing.

Four posts jutted from the sand, connected by tape like a crime scene. The crew paused, absorbing this evidence of recent human activity.

"Guess the *Axel*'s Vitruvians have been doing their own exploring," Nawalle muttered.

As they neared the squared-off stretch of sand, dread seized Azad's heart, quickening his breath. A shape took form amid the red earth and rocks, long and stretched in several directions. He knew it by size, and by its unnatural stillness.

A body.

More accurately, a dried out, mummified corpse, the size of a small adult or large child. Dry, colorless skin stretched across bones, cracked in places from the cold. The mouth hung open, revealing a full set of teeth. Tatters of fabric clung to its joints, rustling fitfully in the wind. Wind had shifted the body into unnatural contortions, but it remained remarkably preserved without heat and bacteria to feed the decaying process. On Nabatea, nothing would survive this long.

Nawalle muttered under her breath, familiar lines from the Dusharan funeral rites. Feisal dropped to one knee to examine the dead Martian from a respectful distance.

"Doctor?" Zelle said, her brows arching behind her vizor. "Care to date our poor friend?"

Azad ran back to the ship as fast as his suit would allow, and returned with an Autopsy-Scanner. A coppery taste welled inside his mouth and he swallowed back his discomfort. He ran the laser scanner over the corpse.

"A male," Azad began. "Around thirty to thirty-five years old when he passed away. No fractures, strong bone density. He…died on site, not before."

"So not an upended grave or a makeshift burial," Feisal muttered. "An execution, perhaps?"

"He's far from the livable campus," Azad said. The scanner gave him confidence, a willingness to contradict the Vitruvian in their midst. "If they were to shoot him or send him out to die, why do it so far out into the Martian desert? Why not just execute him within Calypso? There were no Vitruvians at this point, so they would have needed a vehicle to take him this far in the open desert."

A tense silence followed his words.

"Let's see what happened," Zelle said. "Feisal, set Barry back one thousand, two hundred and nine Martian years. Get it three Sols before the known Exodus date."

Feisal adjusted dials, entering data into the monitor. Despite himself, Azad had to marvel at the machine's precision, calculating a timeframe to the exact date so long ago, accounting for variations in planetary rotations and day durations. His own head spun at the math, his least favorite subject in Township.

A series of ventilators at Barry's base roared to life, spitting sand into the air around them.

"Careful, don't disturb the body!" Nawalle said heatedly. She had stopped praying but hovered protectively in front of the corpse.

"I'll keep that in mind, while I convert quantum wave function breakdowns into a macro-visualization of the past!" Feisal yelled over the groaning machine. The lens turned from black to yellowy white, glowing like a distant sun.

And in front of them, a blurred image took shape where the skeleton rested. On top of the present scattering of bones, a human body lay, partially covered in sand. Even through the shimmering, blurring mirage, the corpse showed signs of mummification, of skin shrinking as the blood dried away. The image vanished, only to appear again seconds later.

"How are we seeing it?" Azad asked. "I thought someone had to observe a moment for Barry to record it. There's only a dead person, with no one around back then to watch him."

Feisal grunted, a low sound tinged with grudging respect.

"If our friend was truly unobserved, we wouldn't be able to see what we're seeing," Feisal answered. "But that city had cameras pointed outside. People glancing out its windows, even if they didn't notice a corpse in the sand far away. It doesn't have to be direct observation – just observation."

"Go back earlier," Zelle said.

Feisal toggled the machine's settings and the ghostly corpse flickered before their eyes. It remained there, unmoving, but a shadow passed over it repeatedly as the sun rose and fell and wind shifted sand around it, revealing and concealing its frame. Azad gasped. They were rewinding back in time, spanning the days and weeks when this corpse lay here.

"Wait, there!" Nawalle cried. "Stop, go back."

And there it was. The corpse rose backward as though invisible strings pulled at its limbs, before it ran in reverse toward the Calypso site. Feisal paused the image, adjusting a dial. The scene then unfolded forward in time, like an old cinema reel that had been rewound and played back. This time, the man sprinted forward with a strong, militaristic gait before he collapsed in phases. A leg buckling, a shoulder dropping, a slump to his knees. The man toppled over, shuddering and gasping for the oxygen that wasn't there.

I'm witnessing a person die, Azad thought. His second death, after the Vitruvian woman on his table, but despite over a thousand years between them, their final moments carried the same dizzying intimacy.

"Why did he run?" Nawalle asked, breaking the silence. "Why run into a certain, horrible death?"

"And how did he survive that long?" Azad added. He cleared his throat, his mouth dry. "He made it at least two hundred meters away from the interior." He pointed toward Calypso's ruins, where Barry revealed the shell of an airlocked door.

"Only a Vitruvian could have functioned that long without oxygen and atmospheric pressure," Nawalle said.

"Oh, we can last far longer than that one did, but it wouldn't be pretty or pleasant," Feisal said. "That's what makes this interesting. More durable than a regular human, not quite a Vitruvian. Or at least, a Vitruvian at present."

Silence followed, interrupted only by Azad's breathing. Barry's engine sank into a low hum. They formed a circle around the skeleton.

"You think this person might be some early kind of Vitruvian, Feisal?" Zelle asked with interest.

"Not just me, Captain. Looks like the Vitruvians on the *Axel* ship might have had the same idea. Look – someone recently added that little fence and tape around our friend here. He's been examined, had all the sand covering him brushed away. The *Axel*'s interested in him for a reason."

"But that doesn't make sense," Azad said. "The Vitruvians came into being on the journey to Nabatea, not *before* it. They evolved during space travel – hence, kissed by starlight."

"That is the story," Zelle agreed. "But this is evidence of something else. What if the Vitruvians had an earlier origin? It's possible that if they're a genetic deviation from early humans, that mutation evolved over generations. If that's true, what we're looking at is an earlier Vitruvian – different from the orthodox but not as adaptable as Vitruvians have evolved to be now."

"So the story is a lie," Azad breathed.

"Or a natural evolution of the truth, assuming our theory is even correct. This is very scant evidence. But to the earlier question – why did he run out? Let's see if he was alone and what might have made him run. Feisal, if you'll bring Barry closer to the ruins."

"Come along, Barry," Feisal said. He hummed a catchy melody as they marched to the remnants of Calypso.

Ahead of them, the first hollowed-out structure jutted out from the main Calypso site. Its ceiling had caved in.

"What's this?" Azad whispered.

"According to our schematics…a processing area called the Waste Room," Nawalle said. "Where they pushed out anything they couldn't recycle."

Feisal fired up Barry again, setting it to the same time as the man's moment of death. Azad stood back, averting his eyes from the lens. Barry came to life again, filling in the cracked walls and crumbled spaces around them, giving the Waste Room an interior, with floors and equipment as far as its range would allow.

"Look!" Nawalle cried.

On the other side of the airlock, a lone figure emerged, its face wreathed in blowing sand. A woman peered through the portal window as the man began his sprint across the desert.

Zelle advanced, leaning forward to inspect the face. Nawalle gasped. Azad squinted, peering closer. His eyes widened in disbelief.

"It's her," Nawalle said. "Isn't it, Zelle? The woman from the recording."

Azad's jaw fell. It was her. Kezza Sayer.

"We can reasonably deduce as much," Zelle muttered, but her eyes shone like lit fuses through her vizor. "Our friend from the past seems to have been in the thick of things."

The ghostly image of the woman pulled back from the door, shoulders slumped in defeat. Through the glass and shimmering sand, her hooded eyes were heavy with sadness and shock.

On the other side of the door, another figure lay at a safe distance from Kezza Sayer. A corpse, arms set at an unnatural angle, face slack in death. Though hard to discern through Barry's projector, the body showed signs of discoloration and injury.

"Who's that?" Nawalle muttered.

"Our friend from the recording doesn't seem inclined to pay her mind," Feisal noted. "Someone dead and not important to her. Maybe someone she disposed of? Before the other one escaped?"

Azad shook his head, a gesture no one could see behind his vizor. She wouldn't do that. He had no proof, just a belief that Kezza, whoever she was, was not a killer.

Tearing herself from the window, Kezza ran up the Waste Room's stairs, disappearing out of Barry's range.

After several minutes, new figures appeared. Figures with features obscured by armor, weapons cradled in their arms. They approached the dead woman on the floor, keeping a generous distance. A primitive mech rolled in after them, dragging the corpse away.

"What's going on?" Azad muttered.

"Only one way to find out," Zelle said. "We follow her. We follow them."

★   ★   ★

They wandered the ruins, stepping over mangled piles of flayed metal and plastics. Nothing had rusted, with no oxygen around them, but harsh winds and radiation had left their mark. From time to time, Azad's pulse surged at the sight of shapes that resembled bones or a damaged skull, but aside from the lone corpse outside the campus and the distant gravestones, no other traces of life survived. Azad knelt and picked up a device in the sand. A wrench, heavy in his hands and no different from the ones Nawalle used on the *Magreb*. His throat tightened.

Feisal trudged in the rear, cursing softly as Barry rolled across the ground with wheezing wheels.

"Have the schematics come back from the *Magreb* yet?" Zelle asked over her shoulder.

"Still downloading," he replied with a strained voice. He ran a suited arm over Barry's side, as if to shield the machine from the demands imposed upon it. "He's transmitting recordings to the *Magreb*, recharging dark energy and following us through a ghost town. He needs some recovery time before we send him on a multi-Sol goose chase to follow our dead Martian friends."

"How long?"

"Tomorrow, ideally."

Zelle sighed, a single breath that echoed in each of their audio transmitters.

"Before we retire him for the day," she said, "let's get one more recording in here. I want to see this room, exactly thirty Sols before emigration day."

They stood under the largest dome. Its top had cracked open, dim sunlight pouring through its jagged edges. Rising platforms framed the circular room, filled with battered seats that formed a semicircle around the center.

An arena. Just like the Khazneh Arena on Nabatea, except it would have been indoors. Joy and sadness battled within Azad at this mirror of home, an ancient place where humans sat together and experienced the thrill of something bigger than themselves. He blinked back tears, unable to wipe them away through his environment suit.

"Here we go!" Feisal yelled.

Barry whirred to life again, the lens tilting up toward the upper half of the arena. The cracks between broken platforms filled, the dome above them now whole. Spectators filled the seats, human figures standing and shifting and applauding. Every face turned to the arena's center.

And in the middle of the stage, a lone figure spun in the air, circling on a bar hanging from the highest point of the dome. Her, again. Wherever they explored, the ancient woman followed. She crouched on the spinning trapeze, arms extending outward as she leaned forward, bending her knees. After a pause, she leapt into the air, her body long and taut with extension, before reaching out to catch another bar mid-air.

The machine captured only the ghost of the moment, with sight and no sound, but Azad knew the arena had exploded with rapturous applause.

Chapter Twelve

Kezza

CALYPSO CORPORATE CAMPUS, MARS
2195 A.D.

Kezza let go. Even after countless hours of practice and hardened muscle memory, the moment of release never got easier. That split second of fear as her feet left the bar and nothing stood between her and the paltry net only feet off the ground. Gravity blinked in that millisecond, as though surprised at what she had done, before pulling her down in a slow arc. She remembered herself and her hands stretched like spiders in front of her and curled around the waiting trapeze. She gripped the bar.

Her body swung in a graceful arc and the Coliseum erupted. Kezza pumped her fist in triumph. The audience liked those little moments where she followed an inhuman feat with a very human celebration. It was also a signal to her comrades in the troupe – security was moving in.

They all knew it was coming. Ever since the shocking video started circulating through the Catacombs of people retching and dying in the Bokambe sector, tension had been building. The miners went on strike on day three, demanding an explanation. Several demonstrations had broken out at the main gates to the medical center, though they were quickly dispersed. Even Tier Twos began speaking out on Calypso's online forums, noting the exploitation of prisoners serving out sentences and the many forms of corporate indentured servitude.

It was all nice and good, but all successful revolutions needed a match – the spark that would ignite the fire. Calypso authorities had muzzled

Juul and Dr. Hamza – they were allowed at public events, like the circus, but couldn't make any speeches. Calypso Security was knocking on doors and monitoring chatter, trying to find the source of the link – and while no one had traced it to Kezza yet, rumors persisted that it had started with the Martian Circus. The troupe had gone from ridiculed pariahs to sexy, subversive revolutionaries practically overnight. Attendance at the matinees and evening shows had skyrocketed, and the troupe had all injected subtle and not-so-subtle gestures in their performances to bolster the perception of their involvement.

Shadows emerged on the upper stage. Kezza continued to spin, gliding from the trapeze bar to the long, vertical aerial silks hanging throughout the stage. As she twisted and traversed them with practiced, muscled arms, the shapes behind the stage took form. Two security guards, arms crossed and stunners in their holsters, waiting for her act to end. After her final routine on her lyra, they would take her.

Panting, Kezza grinned. If they were going to arrest her, it was time to light the match.

Her smile stretched along with her arms. Her back arched as she locked her feet around her lyra's base and pushed forward. While her body provided momentum, a motor on the ceiling helped her along as the lyra circled around the audience. Kezza stretched forward, her arms curved like elegant wings as she absorbed the frenzied applause. Nothing felt better than this.

Barrett Juul sat alone in a balcony at stage right. He needed to be a part of this as well, so Kezza improvised. She leaned forward over the ring to audible gasps, propelling herself to the edge of the balcony without losing her tenuous grip on the metallic hold. Kezza placed her hands on the balcony's edge, her face a foot away from Juul's. Juul gaped, his lip almost quivering. She must have made for an imposing sight, with her shimmering black gloves and dress, the dramatic streaks of violet across her kohled eyes.

"It's happening," she whispered into his ear. "Time to invite your friends."

Then she pulled back, her fingers latching into the knot of his tie. It came away with her and she waved it triumphantly before the cheering crowd, before tying it around her own neck. Juul laughed appreciatively and clapped. The message to the crowd was clear enough – *we're in this together. We're on the same side.*

Before she could pull away from the balcony, Juul reached for a box at his feet. The hairs on Kezza's arms stood to attention. With an excited smile, Juul opened the box and pulled out a snake.

Kezza gasped along with the crowd. Animals of any kind were prohibited on Mars, but Juul must have smuggled the creature in. Juul met Kezza's eyes and she understood his intent. She swallowed and nodded.

Kezza shivered as he placed the snake over her shoulders. Its skin was smooth and surprisingly cool as she stroked its scales. The snake tightened its grip around her shoulders and she gave it a gentle squeeze back, a small handshake between worlds, as she remounted her lyra and pulled away from the balcony.

The crowd roared.

The snake coiled around her arms as she pushed the lyra into a rotating spin. She leaned back into a perfect back balance, letting her arms hang gracefully while her new performing partner maintained a firm grip around her shoulders and neck. The audience, upside down and spinning, rose to their feet, stamping energetically. She ended her routine with an ankle hang, an especially difficult and risky move while the lyra was in motion so fast. But Kezza felt fearless. With a forbidden lifeform entwined around her and a captive audience of fellow Martians holding its breath at her every move, Kezza, for the first time in her life, experienced power. Hopefully the audience, emboldened by Kezza and Juul's act of defiance in the face of the Corpsboard, would feel it too.

To a standing ovation and a hail of flowers, she disappeared toward upper stage left, where Calypso Security waited. One of them stepped forward.

"Ms. Sayer, if you'll come with us, please."

"If I must." She extended her gloved hands. Now that the moment had arrived, fear drained from her tired body. She had leapt in the air from deadly heights, boarded a space shuttle to the Obscura, incubated a mysterious illness – hired corporate thugs seemed benign in comparison. At least they were predictable in their threats.

"What's going on? We're about to do curtain calls," their coach Eddie protested, breaking away from the cluster of outraged performers.

"Stand back!" one of the guards yelled, louder than necessary. Kezza and LaValle exchanged a smile. *They're afraid.*

The guard who spoke cuffed Kezza's hands behind her back. The cold metal bit into her wrists. They pushed her toward the exit door, gripping her elbows. Exiting the arena required passing into the audience's line of view, and rapturous applause shifted into outraged cries at the sight of the circus's lead aerialist being dragged away in handcuffs. The guards quickened their pace at the swelling jeers and hisses. Kezza tasted a shift in the air's vibrations, the promise of impending violence. She raised her arms as far as she could behind her back, hands clenched into fists, and the crowd roared its response. On the balcony, Barrett Juul peered down at her. Their eyes met and he nodded.

She'd played every card in her limited hand. If nothing else, the Palmcorps activists would help Juul escape. But escaping without information out of Bokambe would accomplish little. Fortunately, that's exactly where they would lock up Kezza.

In the quiet of the hallway, the shouts of the arena fading, Kezza felt a twinge of self-doubt. Had she set herself up? Would Juul and his Palmcorps friends abandon her, leaving her to rot in a cell?

They advanced wordlessly down the hall. A burst of cursing, followed by the sounds of a scuffle, broke out behind her. Kezza craned her neck to find a complete stranger, a dark-skinned man with an elegantly trimmed beard, wrestling with one of the guards.

"Let her go! It's not right… What's her charge?"

He grimaced under the sharp blow of a baton.

"Where d'you think you are?" one of the guards holding Kezza sneered. Behind her, the man doubled over, but his eyes smiled at Kezza in the quickest of glances. Kezza turned away, training her eyes ahead. A friend from Palmcorps?

The guards marched Kezza down Calypso's narrow corridors and across an arched tunnel leading to the main domed section of the city. A thick double door loomed ahead, the words *Bokambe Research Sector* spread above the entrance. Kezza shivered. Her heart skipped a beat as she passed through the doors into a place where many never left.

A rough hand pulled Kezza's head back and the fluorescent hallway disappeared behind a band of darkness. A blindfold.

She stumbled ahead, gritting her teeth against the strong fingers digging into her elbows. Her arms ached and blood pounded in her ears. She inhaled, picking up a stale, medicinal smell.

Hands pushed her forward. Cold air blew against her clammy skin. A new room. A door clicked behind her.

With another rough tug, the veil over her eyes fell away. Kezza blinked, adjusting to the sickly green light.

She sat, hands bound behind her back, in a hybrid of a cell and a doctor's office. Syringes, hazard disposals and vials of clear liquid lined a counter. Kezza swallowed, trying not to imagine their purpose. A security guard stood over her, his expression thoughtful. Three other guards waited by the door, a heavy security detail for a lone, bound woman. Then again, Kezza had demonstrated what she could do with a well-placed kick.

"Kezza Sayer, you are charged with corporate theft, identity fraud and general social disruption," said the guard in a calm monotone. "Prior to formal processing, we are required to perform a basic health screening to ensure that you're fit to be charged and will not bring compromising viruses into a contained area."

Kezza laughed. She didn't find anything funny in the situation but needed to provoke the guards in those fleeting seconds of judgment. She needed to earn a high-security cell.

"What could I bring in that isn't here already?" she asked, relishing the unease that passed through the line of guards. "I know what you—"

A force knocked Kezza sideways. She pulled herself upright and the guard struck her again, sending her to the floor. Pain seared her left cheek, crawling all the way up to her ear. Gasping, she spat on the floor. A thick black substance splattered across the tile. Her eyes widened.

The guard stepped back.

"What the—?"

Kezza coughed again, deliberately this time. Cries of alarm, shouts for calm.

"She's got it!"

"Stand back!"

"Don't you dare run! We need to restrain her."

"I'm not dying over a damn badge theft!"

"Call the doctor in."

Retching, Kezza rolled over to one side, a thread of the black substance hanging from her lips. It tasted like chalk and ash, thick on her tongue. Steps thundered around her, feet seeking distance. She felt truly ill, her limbs shaking underneath her hot skin. The door swung shut, the click of a bolt echoing in her ears.

Kezza struggled to her feet, fighting back a wave of nausea. Her head became heavy and clouded, as though soup had been ladled into her ears.

She was alone.

"Kezza Sayer?" A voice boomed with godlike reverberation in the narrow room.

Or not alone. A mirror stretched across the far side of the room, which Kezza approached cautiously. She leaned forward, peering into her own reflection. Her skin resembled rotten synth-milk, sallow and graying around her weary eyes. She forced her face into a wry smile. An encore of her earlier performance.

"And to whom am I speaking?" she asked in a light voice.

A pause. Her reflection in the mirror faded, the glass clearing to reveal a man in a white lab coat. He stared back at her with saucer-like, light blue eyes.

"You appear to be unwell, Ms. Sayer." His thin, reedy voice belonged to a much older man.

"I've been better," Kezza rasped.

"For your safety, Ms. Sayer, we need to perform a full body health scan from a distance," he said. "Can you please approach the monitor on the medical counter and stand on the designated pad?"

Kezza mulled the request and found no reason to argue. She needed more time to think, to plan her next step. Her strength was abandoning her with alarming speed. Not just her physical strength – her mind stretched like gum, juggling her need for an escape plan, her fears over what awaited her in a Bokambe cell, and the fact that something was very wrong with her.

She stood on a pad several inches off the floor, marked by two neon pink footprints. The monitor whirred and a clicking sound followed, as the X-ray, 3D scanners and heat sensors all went to work. As she opened her eyes, a replica of her own body stood next to her, naked and straight-backed. Only flickers of static revealed it to be a holographic copy, one that the apparent doctor behind the screen could now unpeel like an onion. Kezza had long retired any sense of shame about her body, but the doctor's intent stare unnerved her. He was looking for something.

Her vitals danced across the monitor. A pulse of 125, high for an athletic woman, even one under unusual stress. A temperature of 104 – a high fever that should have knocked her off her feet, but only left her clammy and disoriented.

Next to her, her holographic copy switched to display her circulatory system, her heart clenching like a fist. A web of blood vessels spanned her body. Then her lungs came into view, expanding in time with her breath.

Kezza yawned and stretched her bound hands backward, watching her own lungs fill up with air.

"Please remain still, Ms. Sayer."

"If you're upset by my weight gain, there are less extreme ways to broach the subject," she sneered.

"Stop talking. Stop moving."

"Tell me what you see, asshole, or I'll start dancing," Kezza said. "Dabke or bhangra? I'll let you pick, because I'm feeling nice – ow!" A needle snuck sideways from the machine, piercing her arm. Cursing, she let it draw blood and retract. Another needle launched a surprise attack on her left arm, this time leaving a deeper, throbbing pain in her muscles. A chip of some kind. As though she didn't have enough of those already. She swooned under a sudden wave of dizziness and a measure spiked on the monitor.

The doctor's pale eyes widened into two liquid bowls. He gestured to someone invisible beyond the glass partition.

"Bring him," he said. A pause. "Have you encountered anything unusual in the last few months, Ms. Sayer? Someone who might be ill?"

Kezza forced down the fluttering sensation in her chest, ignoring the taste of bile on her tongue.

"You mean someone outside of the Bokambe sector?" Kezza asked. The cryptic, loaded question had the desired effect. The doctor scowled, his professional mask dropping.

"Don't test my patience, Ms. Sayer. I'm all that's between you and a Bokambe cell. But if you don't cooperate, I'll start their work for them and peel the truth out of you."

Torture? Kezza's stomach twisted, but she managed a smirk. For the first time in her life, she had to give that ridiculous circus doctor some respect. The worst he'd done to her was restrict her chocolate intake.

Another figure appeared behind the window. Kezza suppressed a gasp. Alan Schulz stood by the doctor's side, as nervous as he'd appeared during their first encounter in the loading bay, with some added bruises and circles under his eyes. So his desperate escape attempt off Mars hadn't succeeded. The last few weeks hadn't been kind to him. His face had already thinned, pasty skin sagging around his neck.

Kezza arranged her face into polite confusion. The doctor pointed at the medical results displayed on both sides of the door, talking to Schulz in a low voice. A second opinion. Though a prisoner and a traitor, Tier Ones remained a valuable intellectual resource.

"This one won't last long," Schulz said, not even bothering to mute himself from Kezza's room. "If we get a hazmat crew in, we can start examining her in more detail and run some tests."

"I don't think so," the doctor said with warning. "Do you not see? She's been a carrier for at least several weeks, but no one else in contact with her has been infected. And look! The proteins in her system are countering the effects, containing it further than the others. This one is different."

The words entered Kezza's ears like hot needles, but her body warmed with hope. She already knew she was sick with whatever the prisoners at Arabia Terra had. But could she avoid the horrific path the others had taken?

"What do you mean I'm different?" Kezza demanded, advancing on the two men. Unable to do anything else with her binds, she slammed her head against the window, the glass vibrating against her forehead.

A blaring, rhythmic siren drowned out the doctor's response. Red lights flashed in the corners of the room. A security alert.

Kezza backed away, heart pounding. Was this the start of a rescue attempt? Maybe Juul's rhetorical skills had paid off, and the people of Calypso were breaking into the sector.

Then, the beeping siren alternated with a mechanical voice, uttering the same word over and over.

Fire. Fire. Fire.

Kezza's blood froze.

Red lights flashed above the medical ward. The machines began to power down, preparing in case the water sprinklers were activated.

Back through the window, Kezza's jailers were gone. All had fled at the most feared warning on Calypso Corporate Campus.

Kezza balled her fists and screamed. It was a miracle that the flickering body scan didn't pick up the panic and fury radiating from her body. What planet did the Palmcorps people reside on? Certainly not Mars, if they deliberately set a fire.

It didn't matter. Loud footsteps and screams rose behind the locked door. Kezza stumbled to the medical counter, pulling herself onto its surface. She fumbled with bound, shaking hands for something sharp.

The mechanical voice continued its terrible chant. *Fire. Fire. Fire.*

Coursing with adrenaline, Kezza's fingers continued to rummage blindly behind her, until they curled around a sharp point. A syringe.

She gripped it and leapt to her feet, the room spinning momentarily. *Not now*, she thought. *Stay strong*. The door clicked open. A young guard, no older than eighteen, ran into the room. Kezza leaned back into a chair for balance as she shot her legs up. One foot found the guard's throat and he fell to his knees, retching. Still bound, she leapt over him and ran down the hallway with the syringe slipping in her sweating palms.

According to Calypso protocol, fires would be contained in their originating sector by automatic door locks. Individuals within the trapped sector would have exactly seven minutes to extinguish the fire before Calypso's systems automatically expelled all oxygen from the isolated area. Anyone unfortunate enough to be trapped at that stage would suffocate, if they didn't have an atmosphere suit handy.

Despite frequent drills, the only other real fire on Calypso killed all twenty-seven ore miners who'd been caught in the transport bay when a mechanical malfunction sent flames across the cluttered loading area. Threats of a miners' strike failed to motivate authorities to take measures to fireproof the bay. This was a corporate city and money overrode all concerns. All twenty-seven bodies, wrapped in white sheets, were incinerated in the Waste Room the next day.

Kezza sprinted down the Bokambe sector's labyrinth of hallways, dodging panicked workers spilling from all directions into a single tributary toward the main Calypso Campus. No one paid her any attention, despite her sequined costume and handcuffs. She continued to run and fumble with the syringe at the same time, attempting to pick her handcuffs open with the sharp needle. Despite her best efforts, the cuffs held.

Terror hovered in a low cloud above the fleeing crowd. Calypso authorities would likely show more care for their research base than their Tier Three laborers, but a fire was a fire, and no one could afford a campus-wide incident. If the fire originated or spread to Bokambe, the smoky air they coughed would be forfeit.

Kezza pushed against the current of Tier One and Two workers, deeper into the sector. If there was data about the illness or sick people, the evidence would be in Bokambe's most remote, hidden underbelly. Not knowing where this underbelly resided, she would go where others fled. Her shoulders throbbed from the effort of wrestling with the handcuffs until a large shape collided with her, sending her skidding across the floor. With a snap, her hands broke free of their binds.

The sirens continued their drumming mantra, drilling into her ears. *Fire. Fire. Fire.*

A sweet, acrid smell greeted her past another set of heavy doors. The same stench that settled in her mother's apartment during those final, agonizing weeks, and that lingered long after they sent her body for incineration. The smell of death, accompanied by a subtle antiseptic odor designed to conceal its traces.

Kezza hovered at the door, lost in memories. Cold hands and unseeing eyes, paperwork and sweet decay. She blinked tears away and reached inside herself for courage. At least it didn't smell like burning – there was no fire ahead.

She advanced down the hall in long strides, holding the bent syringe like a weapon. Flashing lights turned the corridor horror-film red.

A different light, fluorescent green, flickered from a room at the far, isolated end of the corridor. Her heart pounded violently, but she kept moving. Instinct drove her even as it warned her to run.

The small, clouded window on the door revealed nothing inside. With her pointy weapon still raised, Kezza kicked the door open.

Dark shapes took form under the flickering lights. The syringe slid from Kezza's hand. A row of bodies stretched across the floor, evenly spaced. Kezza's knees buckled and she sank to the ground, struggling not to vomit but unable to tear her eyes away from the patchwork skin, the scratch marks across pink throats and the dried blood forming dark puddles around each corpse. Death, everywhere. It filled the room, choking the air out of her lungs. The thought came before she could push it away – *I might die like this.*

Still on her knees, a shadow slithered in front of her. Hands gripped her shoulders, pushing her forward. Kezza screamed, struggling to her feet, but the hands shoved her back down.

She slid into the room of dead bodies, swiveled around to face Alan Schulz.

"Get back," he said. Though pale, he radiated a stern calm at odds with the surrounding chaos.

They were alone, not counting the scattered dead. Kezza lay on the ground, weak and coughing, in no position to inspire fear, but she snarled at Schulz anyway. The bastard looked way too comfortable surrounded by dead, zombie-like bodies.

"I let you escape once," she began, but his eyes hardened.

"How did that work out for you?" he snapped. A large canister swung from one hand and he removed a smaller container from his pocket with the other. The familiar symbol used for antifreeze. And the other one...

"Potassium permanganate," she whispered, before she put the two together. Wild terror seized her. "No, please!"

She scrambled to her feet, but he swung the liquid forward and she leapt back.

"You're sick, like them," he said. "For the good of this city, I don't have a choice."

He sloshed the remainder of the liquid across the front of the room, splashing several of the nearby bodies. Kezza trembled, unable to move or even scream. She was a trapped animal, paralyzed. He was going to set the entire room on fire. She would burn, powerless against the pain. She would die.

A loud crack filled the silent air, and Alan Schulz fell forward with a heavy thud.

A man in an atmosphere suit stepped over him, a metal pipe in hand. Breathing hard, Kezza stumbled and fell on her hands and knees. A strangled sob escaped her throat. She rubbed her eyes, to confirm she wasn't hallucinating. But there he remained. He lifted his vizor, eyes lighting up when he spotted Kezza.

"The woman from the circus." His voice was low, with a light, elegant accent.

Through her shock, she recognized him. The man who caused a scene as the police dragged her out of the arena, the one with the smiling eyes. One of Barrett Juul's friends from Palmcorps, the city across the Martian desert.

He held out his hand and she walked shakily toward him. His eyes darted in mild alarm at the gruesome state of the bodies.

"Bastard," he muttered. "What was he going to do?"

Kezza cleared her throat, finding her voice again. "Burn them, I think."

The man surveyed the scene and nodded. "Good idea," he said. "Excluding the part where he wanted to burn you, of course. Is that antifreeze?"

"What?" Kezza cried, outraged. The last thing Calypso needed was another fire. What kind of fucking pyromaniacs were they raising in Palmcorps?

"They're contagious," he said simply, gesturing her to stand back. "And we don't need Calypso playing with their bodies. I got my hands on their data cube, so we have the research we need. We can learn everything back on Palmcorps."

He hurled the remaining potassium permanganate into a puddle on the floor and unleashed the antifreeze. Flames rose obediently, catching the first body.

He shut the door. Through the portal window, the fire spread. The sealed door contained the crackling sounds and smells of burning flesh inside the room, but Kezza's stomach still lurched. At the first sensation of heat, they both took a reflexive step back.

"Seven minutes ought to be enough," the man mused. The oxygen would drain from the isolated room, but the damage to the bodies would be done.

The man grabbed her elbow, steering her away. The alarms wailed down the lonely corridors.

Inside the next open room, Kezza collapsed into a chair. Sweat from her clammy forehead stung her eyes. She shuddered.

"Can you move?" the man asked.

In response, Kezza leaned back into the chair, head limp.

"I'll stim you up," he said. "Give you enough energy to bail."

The man approached her with a needle in hand. Kezza groaned, having had her fill of syringes. He injected her with practiced confidence, the needle out of her shoulder before she could react.

A warm current flowed from her arm and the room sharpened into focus. Her body tingled with energy and her thoughts untangled themselves, shedding the conflicting fears and impulses of the last hour. Even her lungs felt fuller as she took several deep, renewing breaths.

"Suit up," he told her. "There's an extra one in that closet. Then we go."

"What's your name?" With her head clear, this detail became important.

"Amit Reddy, at your service," the man said with a mock salute. "I'm an old friend of Barrett Juul's from his Bangladesh project. Friendly enough to spend a couple years on this crazy planet waiting for him to arrive. What do you Martians call your home? Hell without the heat?" He laughed lightly, a sound that couldn't have been more out of place than here.

Kezza sighed. Another Earth guy. No wonder he was so frivolous with fire. But at least he saved her life, and seemed to know how to plan a daring escape.

"Only we get to call it that," Kezza said with a hint of a twisted smile. "You're a guest, buddy."

Amit grinned back. "Sorry. This place is lovely. Let's cross its scenic desert to another lovely city."

Suited against the elements, they ran down the corridor toward the Atrium. The stimulant propelled Kezza forward, overriding her urge to curl into a ball and hide. She had to escape. Fire awaited her on one side, unknown dangers on the other.

They reached the exit from the Bokambe complex only to find a mass of workers at the door, screaming and banging their fists. Despite their collective efforts, the door wouldn't budge.

"Shit! We're sealed in," Amit gasped, pulling Kezza around a corner before the workers could spot them.

Kezza exhaled, collecting her thoughts. Bokambe had other entrances and exits. The one they used to load prisoners, for example.

"Come with me," Kezza said. "There might be another way."

She charged toward the docking bay, Amit at her heels. The memories of the burning room drowned out the background noise of the sirens – heat against her arms, the mixture of antiseptic and decay burning her nostrils, the thick taste of smoke on her tongue.

The door to the loading bay neared, its oval window blinking at them at the end of the narrow hallway.

Kezza pressed the handle. Locked. *Shit.* She slammed her palms against the door.

"Hang on, I've got a Tier One badge," Amit said.

"Of course you do."

"How do you think I got to you? Save your snarky commentary for Palmcorps, my circus friend."

He pressed the badge to the security lock. After a pause, it blinked back in red. Access denied.

Kezza let out a wild, shrieking laugh. Even Tier Ones would burn to save Calypso.

Amit cursed, losing his cool for the first time since he knocked Alan across the head. Not an encouraging development.

Kezza balled her fists against the window, struggling to remain calm, to keep thinking.

A face filled the window. Kezza shrieked and stumbled backward. A dark-haired woman peered at them, tapping the surface with her knuckles.

Amit leaned forward with a triumphant smile.

"She's one of ours," he said to Kezza. "Evgenia! Get us out of here."

The woman raised both hands up to her ears and swung them forward in a universal, soundless gesture – stand back.

The door rippled and a white-hot light pushed through its center. It slid in an arch around the doorway like a hot knife through butter. Once the torch had carved a complete oval, the woman knocked it forward with a kick.

"Let's go," Evgenia said. Her sharp voice carried a thick Eastern European accent. "Nice to meet you at last, Kezza Sayer. We all enjoyed the show."

Kezza ran through the opening, careful to avoid its melting edges. The loading bay became a sinister cave without lighting or cargo to fill its concrete floors. Their footsteps echoed across the yawning space.

"We relocated the terrain vehicle here after we noticed the new cameras in the Waste Room," Evgenia shouted over her shoulder to Amit as they quickened their pace. "Some security, but we managed to slip by. We created the fire as a distraction after the show, so it's a good thing you came this way."

"You tried to burn the place down?" Kezza asked, outraged. As much as she despised Calypso, incinerating all life inside it seemed excessive.

"Not burn it down," Amit said, beginning to pant from effort. It amazed Kezza how out of shape people could become on Mars if they weren't mining ore or swinging on trapezes. "Just created a little diversion. Burnt a fake plant in the Atrium. But it spread to other fake plants like crazy and caused a damn stampede! So much panic, no one could get close enough to put it out quickly. But don't worry, they will."

A terrain vehicle waited in the darkest corner of the docking bay. Barrett Juul paced near a small group huddled around the door. His strained features brightened as Kezza approached. Kezza managed a smile back. Somehow, they'd both made it.

"We got the aerialist," Amit said. "Time to go!"

"I thought she'd be in the morgue by now," Evgenia said with impatience. "You Martians are crazy. Back in the Ukraine, we would never plan an operation like this without a clear escape plan."

"We had to act quickly," Juul said, a little testily. "The Calypso Corpsboard, it turns out, is even more reactive than we imagined."

"Is the fire under control?" Amit asked. "No air drains?"

One of the other Palmcorps activists, an old woman, beamed. "Barrett led everyone in putting it out. Security didn't know what to do. Shutting down the Atrium would have suffocated half of Calypso, so they did nothing. Barrett calmed the crowd and got a water chain going."

Kezza almost giggled at the image of Martian residents passing buckets to one another. But she exhaled with relief. In the course of a single evening, she'd been arrested, evaded justice during a fire evacuation, escaped from the most secretive wing of the city and witnessed a roomful of corpses incinerate. That was enough to process without innocent deaths on her conscience.

Juul shrugged, his posture stiff with embarrassment, but the corners of his mouth curled in triumph.

"How did you do that spin, by the way?" Evgenia asked Kezza in a more cheerful voice. "I'll give Calypso some credit, you know how to do live entertainment for your downtrodden masses. On Palmcorps, we've been making do with light shows and battle robots."

"I've got fifty credits on Katana 3.0," Amit said. "It's not so bad here. Hell without the heat – ha!" With everyone loaded inside, he fired up the engine and activated the bay's side airlock.

Within minutes, Evgenia was driving them at breakneck speed across the desert, the domed white shells of Calypso shrinking behind them. Twilight had reached their narrow sliver of Mars. The dimming landscape shuddered as the terrain vehicle bounced across the rocky stretches of Arabia Terra. Kezza drank in the sloping hills, her extremities tingling with adrenaline. Aside from a school field trip outside the airlock, she'd never left the borders of Calypso. Now the only home she'd known was disappearing behind clouds of red dust.

Good riddance. With luck, she'd never see it again.

Kezza's chest tightened at the sight of a lone statue in the desert, coated with red sand. A single, space-suited figure on one knee with a placard at its feet, commemorating the arrival of the First Forty on Mars. Kezza had seen it once before, as a child on that field trip. She'd memorized the names on the placard, knowing that they were important. Tamers of a new world. Makers of history. When this was all over, would Kezza have her own name carved into rock? She closed her eyes and smiled as the statue vanished beyond a high hill.

"You saw the bodies?" Juul suddenly asked Amit, businesslike.

Amit nodded grimly. "All dead. Whatever they've got, we don't want it following us to Palmcorps. We burned them."

"A DNA sample might have helped," Juul said. "But I'm no scientist."

"That's right, you're not," Amit said cheerfully. "Don't worry about that, semi-fearless leader. I got a data cube from a Tier One before I knocked him sideways. Once we unpack it, we'll know what they know. Including DNA insights."

At the mention of scientists, Kezza scanned the shuttle. The faces bumping together in the terrain vehicle did not include Juul's mother.

"Wait, where's Dr. Hamza?" Kezza asked.

A tense silence followed. Juul turned back toward Calypso, his expression dark.

"No," Kezza whispered.

"No is right," Amit said. "She's alive. Seems she managed to escape onto the Obscura station before we set up our distraction. She took the only shuttle up there, so she's fine for now."

"She's not fine," Juul said. "She's on a Calypso-subcontracted station with limited supplies and nowhere to go but back to Calypso."

"But she's safe," Evgenia said, as soothingly as her flinty voice allowed. Her eyes didn't leave the monotonous terrain before them. "Someone from the Corpsboard left with her. Meaning she turned someone to our cause. These are *positive* developments, Barrett."

"We're going back as soon as circumstances allow," Juul said. "Once we figure out what Calypso is infecting people with."

Kezza hugged herself, suddenly chilled. Every jerk of the terrain vehicle sent a pulse of nausea into her stomach. These people had gone out of their way to rescue her. The least she could do was tell them the truth.

"They tested me after they arrested me," she said quickly, before she could regret it. Alarmed expressions circled her. "I'm infected. I got it when I found the two Palmcorps people trying to escape. I touched the man who ran out the airlock, across the desert. I suspected it, but now I know it. I'm sorry," she added, addressing Juul.

The terrain vehicle swerved, kicking red dust over the windows as it screeched to a halt. Amit swore.

"Toss her out!" Evgenia yelled.

"No," Juul snapped back. "We need her."

"We need her out of this fucking enclosed space." Evgenia's voice rose several octaves.

"Wait!" Kezza cried. "I'm different, they said. Not infectious like the others. My body is…fighting back, somehow. Something in my DNA."

"Not good enough," Evgenia said. She rounded on Juul, the only person in the vehicle looking at Kezza without horror. "Did you know about this?"

Juul leaned back, as though considering his words. His gaze did not leave Kezza.

"I did," he said slowly. "But I've spent plenty of time with her with no adverse consequences. And seen her do remarkable things in the process.

Things that can help us on our new world. So it was a risk I considered worth taking."

Kezza nodded, blinking back tears. "From time to time, I've been coughing up this black stuff. But I'm also stronger and faster. I've been building muscle without trying. I even kicked a damn hole through the wall in the Atrium Tavern. It's only today that I've really felt...sick."

"Meaning that it's spreading through your system," Evgenia snapped. "It's just slower with you. We can't let her into Palmcorps, she's a walking time bomb!"

"She's an opportunity," Juul retorted. "If they're right and something in Kezza can fight off this...whatever this is, we have a responsibility to research it. It might even mean a cure. Kezza's been walking around Calypso for weeks without causing a plague. As far as we know, not even a single infection!"

Thick silence settled in the vehicle at his words. With a heavy sigh, Evgenia restarted the engine, accelerating with zeal over a steep hill. Sand hissed against the window, but the sound receded until nothing remained but the blood pounding in Kezza's ears and her own shallow breath in the vehicle's musty confines.

"So be it," Amit said. "I hope you like needles, Kezza Sayer."

"They seem to like me," she whispered.

Chapter Thirteen
Azad

MARTIAN DESERT
YEAR OF SETTLEMENT 1208

"I wish we could hear them," Azad said, holding on to the Glider's rails for balance.

"I'm not a genie, *hadir*," Feisal snapped. "You don't get wishes."

The Glider lived up to its name, floating above the rocky desert as though maglev tracks ran beneath its copper surface. It moved faster than the ancient vehicle that the legendary Barrett Juul, the circus performer, and the other early Martians took to escape from Calypso, forcing Nawalle to slow down repeatedly.

"Do we have to keep Barry running?" Nawalle shouted at Feisal over the Glider's steady hum. They all reeled from the effect of the quantum machine's whirring, the subtle shifts in dark energy that caused the ground to shiver and their own bodies to recoil under its gaze.

"Do you have any idea where these crazy people are going?" Feisal asked. He woke up in a foul mood, battling to keep Barry functional while the *Magreb* struggled to identify the people whose steps they meticulously followed over several days. They had to take breaks for the machine to recover, as well as decipher the remarkable past events they could see but not hear.

"Stop bickering," Zelle said, employing her best grandmotherly tone. "We'll break when we reach their destination."

Barry sat at the edge of the Glider, its most cooperative occupant. It dutifully projected the flickering image of a vehicle driving across

Arabia Terra, farther and farther from the unfolding chaos at Calypso. The vehicle had swerved and stopped for several minutes, confusing them all, before it continued its breakneck speed.

"So what we just witnessed," Azad said quietly to Zelle. "Those weren't the final moments of Calypso?"

She shook her head. "Still thirty Sols before the known flight from Mars. But events had been set in motion."

A thoughtful silence followed. All of them had been in awe at the sight of Barrett Juul in the ancient auditorium, leading people through riots and fire. The founder of Nabatea, the man they invoked in all things good and ill. Feisal had smiled at the sight of Juul wrapping the snake around Kezza's neck, touching the tattoo on his chest.

"It's our symbol, but we didn't know why," he said with an almost shy smile. Feisal lacked the tribal loyalties of many Vitruvians, but he had his moments. "Now I know a little something of where our history began. The creature mattered to Juul, and this woman must have mattered to him, if he trusted the snake to her. She's something, isn't she?"

She was something. Grace and power in equal measure. Azad stood transfixed by her dark hair and kohled eyes so expressive, they shone through Barry's grainy transmissions over a thousand years later. Bursts of intelligence, flickers of sadness. Even in the chaotic scenes after her performance, the woman stood out, as though a spotlight from her stage followed her everywhere. It was not attraction that warmed Azad's chest, but a strange kinship with the long-dead woman. He wanted to know everything about her, to understand her. To help her, even though she was long past helping.

Zelle had initially focused on Barrett Juul at the end of the performance. But when Juul stared at the female performer as she was dragged away, they followed her. They entered a private area of Calypso that the *Magreb's* AI confirmed was an infamous research complex called Bokambe sector, which Juul's autobiography characterized as a cruel place, a showcase for the worst of early humanity.

On that count, he hadn't exaggerated. In the complex, the dancer underwent a humiliating medical exam, only to be abandoned after lights began to flash. An alarm of some kind. Zelle's crew exited the Bokambe sector back to the main Atrium to find a fire spreading across the synthetic plants that wreathed the circular area. They didn't need sound to imagine the screams that echoed off the high dome, the cries of panic as crowds rushed to the far ends of the city.

"Why can't Barry capture sound again?" Nawalle had asked in frustration as she tried to read Juul's lips.

"Sound particles aren't captured in the quantum measurements that Barry detects," Feisal snapped back. "It's not impossible. I just need time to enhance it, time that our captain won't give me."

"We don't need sound," Zelle said. "We get the idea here. Fire in an enclosed space. They're screaming for their lives."

But Barrett Juul had leapt to action, climbing atop a food stand and waving his arms, pleading for calm. He stood rigid with shining eyes. The flames rose like a wave behind him, framing him in an orange glow.

"Well, we now know why the mythology describes Juul as a 'man made of fire'," Zelle said. Azad recalled Light Night at Khazneh Arena. The towering, flaming figure became almost comedic compared to the slight-framed man who stood over a sign in old Earth English, translated as 'taco', urging panicked Calypso residents to help him extinguish the fire.

But they did. While security blocked exits and swung their batons, a team of ordinary civilians passed buckets and wielded extinguishers. After a short but painful battle, they succeeded in putting out the fire.

"This appears to have been a turning point in Juul's attempt to recruit Martians for the Nabatean colony, although they may not have known it at the time," Zelle had said, the first to break the silence in the desolate, present-day Atrium. "He seized the moment to demonstrate that he was more than talk and would be on their side when their own leadership failed."

With the fire under control, Juul slipped away from the crowd with two men and a woman, leaving the chaos of the Atrium for the abandoned docking bay. After a wait, they were joined by none other than the aerialist, Kezza Sayer.

The scenes of the horrific fire and the dancer's equally horrific treatment clung to Azad, interrupting his usual worries about Ledo. These people, the same type of people as present-day Nabateans like himself, were treated as disposable cogs in a machine. Their lives weren't that different from those in modern Nabatea City, an endless cycle of work dictated by greater needs. But the woman on the trapeze fought back, as Ledo had. She escaped the Bokambe complex in pursuit of something else. But what?

Together, Zelle's crew reached the inevitable conclusion that the aerialist was an accomplice of Juul's, someone integral to his plans. While this was an interesting development, Zelle reminded the crew of another critical historical figure, one they rarely spoke of – Juul's mother, Dr. Hamza.

"This confirms Juul's account of his early days on Mars as tumultuous," Zelle said. "He's clearly escaping from something here on Calypso. But where is his mother? Odd that he would leave without her."

Zelle intended to locate and track Dr. Hamza. Azad, however, suggested that they first retrace their earlier steps and discover what fate befell Kezza during the fire and learn how she escaped. As important as Dr. Hamza may have been when she landed on Nabatea, Azad cared more about the performer at Juul's side. To his shock, Feisal agreed with him.

"We're already here," Feisal said to Zelle, patting Barry's side protectively. "And it's obvious this feathered circus lady is significant. She watched our crazy friend run out to the desert, she took the snake from Juul and their paths converged during this fire and escape. If we're not curious about her, then we have no business calling ourselves historians. It's not always the people who make the history books who have the most impact. For some reason, she was left out, despite being at the center of it all."

They'd watched her break out of a holding cell, only to discover a room full of the dead and dying. Nawalle clapped her hands over her mouth, muffling a scream, while the woman and her rescuer set the room on fire. Zelle and Feisal inched closer together, faces clenched in disgust. Azad turned away before the flames found the first body. Though not religious, he couldn't fathom the insanity behind such a sacrilege – the desecration of the dead. Rather than lessen his opinion of Kezza, however, it made him wonder at her desperation, to sink to such depths.

"This was a different time," Zelle reminded the crew. "Our ancestors didn't see the dead as we do. Back then, humans became objects upon death, like furniture."

And so here they were a day later, chasing Kezza Sayer and her companions across the dark, moonless desert. Azad had finally learned more than her name after careful examination of the earlier footage of the medical room, while machines scanned her naked body. Pausing the image and staring closely at the monitor, the *Magreb* translated the words on her profile.

Name: Sayer, Kezza
Sex: Female
Place of Birth: Cardiff, Wales – Earth
Date of Birth: August 12, 2167 (Earth calendar)
Date of Arrival on Calypso: Sol 562, 2171 A.D. (Martian calendar)
Professional Class: Tier Three (Code 0374: Entertainment – performer, non-sex worker)

Azad read her profile multiple times, as though the unimaginative words could yield new insights into this ancient woman. He had come here for Ledo, but instead found himself chasing a ghost in the desert and, to his shock, finding thrill in the chase. It was like nothing else. He gripped the Glider's rail, feeling the rush of wind against his suit. He, the reliable Nabatean doctor who never missed a shift, didn't know what would happen next – and that didn't frighten him. It exhilarated him.

"What are your theories, Zelle?" Nawalle asked.

"About this Sayer woman, or the roomful of bodies that she burned?"

"All of it, really. She watched that man run out of the airlock and kill himself, and then found a roomful of sick people in the Bak— sorry, Bokambe complex. And burned the dead. A horrible sacrilege. Are they trying to get rid of these people for showing Vitruvian features?"

On the other end of the Glider, Feisal huffed with perfunctory anger.

"I don't think Barrett Juul would order such a thing, given the world he ended up building," Zelle said. "Whatever this group wants, I don't believe it's just to kill the sick. The woman didn't force the man from the airlock – he went of his own accord. Similarly, burning dead bodies would suggest an attempt to destroy evidence of something."

"Or stop a contagion," Azad said.

Everyone turned to stare at him.

"I've been reading the *Magreb*'s archives on the history of early medicine," he said in explanation. "Our ancestors on Earth were quick to dispose of bodies during plagues, due to the frequency of airborne diseases. Mars relied on circulatory air systems, so the risk would be even greater. And don't forget fear – *if they don't understand it, they destroy it or suppress it*. That's what Juul said in his teachings."

He braced for Zelle's retort after daring to quote Barrett Juul, but she broke into a thoughtful smile through her vizor.

"I think you may be on to something," she said.

Nawalle shook her head in disgust. "But who are they? Why is Barrett Juul leaving Calypso?"

"My working theory is that we are heading in the direction of the fabled Palmcorps," Zelle said. "The secret, second city on Mars. Perhaps these people were from there or in their employ, and Juul is hoping for a more receptive audience than the one he received on Calypso. As for this Kezza Sayer, she may have been some kind of spy, or maybe just someone who keeps finding herself in the wrong place at the wrong time. Something about her interests Juul, which interests me."

"There's something there," Azad said, pointing in the distance. Darkness had settled over the desert, but a bright shape flickered in the distant hills. A light.

"Stop," Zelle said. Feisal disabled Barry and the image of the terrain vehicle vanished into the air.

"We're going up there, boss?" he asked.

"We are. We can re-follow our long-dead friends to Palmcorps, now that we have the exact date and location of their journey. But let's not lose sight of the present."

"Could be trouble," Nawalle said. Unease burrowed into Azad's stomach. Vitruvians. The short-range ship on the radar. This was not a historical relic in the desert but a modern outpost, lighted and possibly active.

"Maybe it's some natural phenomena," Azad said aloud, more for his own benefit. "Or maybe they came and left."

"It's all probability until we lift the box, *hadir*," Feisal said with a cheerful clap of his hands. "Let's open it."

Up close, the structure resembled a glowing worm rising from the sand, the door where its face would be. Its cream-colored surface sat windowless and partially underground. Man-made, without question, but designed for shelter rather than observation.

Zelle approached the outpost first. She raised her fist, as though considering whether to knock, but simply opened the door and walked through. His own fists clenched, Azad followed.

The airlock door sealed shut behind them. Feisal took off his helmet first, fixing his mustache before drawing a dramatic breath. He gave the crew two raised thumbs. Breathable air.

A little nervously, given that Feisal could function in most atmospheres, the rest of the crew followed suit. Cool air greeted them, tinged with a raw, biological smell. Sweat, blood and something almost sweet. Thin tubes ran along the tunneled interior like veins, circulating either oxygen or heat.

Feisal gingerly shed his atmosphere suit, revealing a deep crimson velvet jacket and striped pants in black and matching red. He adjusted his lapels, shrugging at the rest of the crew, who kept their atmosphere suits on, and certainly stuck to the recommended insulation suits underneath them.

They advanced together, descending the tunnel. The musty smell grew stronger, the air cooler. Azad fought the impulse to retreat. He focused on his breathing. Air in, air out, lungs rising and falling.

Nawalle turned to him with stern eyes and held a finger to her lips. Ahead of them, Zelle tied her locs into a knot at the top of her head and moved with unnatural calm, as though they were exploring a museum rather than a potentially deadly Vitruvian outpost.

The tunnel expanded into a round room. The only light came from an intricate web of phosphorous blue at the top of the domed ceiling, illuminating the center but leaving shadows around its perimeter. The light cast down on a trio of gurneys with loose straps. A holographic monitor hung in the center above the gurneys, switched off but still flickering around its edges.

Azad's insides clenched with horror. Additional shapes in the shadows came into focus as they entered. A metal cage, large enough to fit a den of Vitruvian asps. A cabinet on the other side, shelved with liquids and sharp instruments. Dark streaks smeared the rusted gurneys.

Zelle raised her arms to either side, blocking the others from moving further.

"What is this place?" Nawalle asked, her voice small and quavering.

A shape darted in the shadows. Feisal leapt over Zelle's outstretched arms, a streak of red and black. It happened in seconds. A shout of alarm, a rush of air, and Feisal's foot arching in a precise strike. Another cry, as a glinting shape clattered away.

Feisal dragged the tall shape into the light, revealing it to be a man in a white jumpsuit, clutching his stomach. His chest rose and fell in shallow breaths, the curve of a red and black snake peering through his collar.

A Vitruvian. An older one, if his haggard face and stringy white hair were any indication.

"Don't mind us, brother," Feisal said in a tone that could never be mistaken for familial. "We forgot to knock, but given this lovely reception, that was probably the right course."

"Who are you?" the man gasped. Under the light, it became clear that his problems extended beyond old age. His hand covered a partially healed wound in his abdomen – blood seeped between his fingers – the kind of injury that would have killed a normal human within hours without treatment, but one a Vitruvian could endure for days as their body chemistry adjusted, fighting back infection. His copper skin carried blotches of discoloration, angry flushes of purple and black. As he bared his small, sharp teeth, blood wetted his gumline.

"We could ask you the same question," Zelle said, stepping forward. Her face carried neither anger nor fear, only stern suspicion. "And since we outnumber you, I suggest you answer first."

Ignoring her, the man turned back to Feisal.

"Declare your vessel!" he shouted. "It's the law. Only the *Axel* has permission to operate in this section of the mother system."

Feisal smiled with bared teeth. "The *Magreb*. Ship of deviants, smugglers and historians. I'm Feisal MagrebTwo of Nabatea. Now answer my captain's question."

The man's mouth cracked open with a bloody smile.

"You take orders from her?" he sneered at Feisal. "Betraying your people to serve a non-Vitruvian? An orthodox lowlife? You must be the deviant on your list. Good that you leave the word Vitruvia out of your name – you're not one of us."

Calmly, Feisal strode toward the man, who cowered. Azad held his breath for the coming blow, but instead, Feisal's hand darted into the man's breast pocket, emerging with a blinking device.

"Is that the best you can do?" Feisal asked in a bored voice. He held the device up, squinting as he gave it a shake. "You're right, I'm not one of you. By choice."

The man's retort was lost in a fit of coughing. Feisal cocked his head in a mocking gesture and leaned to hear what the man tried to say.

"Stay back!" Azad said. "Keep your distance."

The man's coughing changed timbre, shifting into laughter.

"Smartest thing I've heard one of your type say," he said, but his smile faltered as he turned to Azad. Apprehension pooled behind his onyx eyes, flickering with something else – recognition.

Nawalle stiffened next to Azad. Zelle spoke first.

"It seems as though you've met our crewmember before," she said. "Or perhaps he looks familiar to you?"

The man's head jerked away as he avoided eye contact with the non-Vitruvian captain. But Azad wouldn't let this man dismiss him so easily.

"You've seen Ledo!" Azad said. "Where is she? Was she here?"

Taking his silence as confirmation, Azad rounded on the crew.

"We can see what happened here. Bring in Barry."

"Who's Barry?" The man coughed again.

"Barry can't fill in every gap," Zelle said. "We have a primary source to past events right in front of us. Someone who can help with the 'why' after we view the 'what'."

"And he's dying too," Feisal chimed in. "That much is clear. Look at this. Got his Archive Band all ready to download. Ready to send back to the *Axel* ship to keep his lifetime of cognitive vomit immortalized for all digital eternity." He waved the device in his hand teasingly in front of the man's eyes. "He can answer our questions and get his toy back, or die surrounded by enemies and have all his memories lost to eternal oblivion. Decisions, decisions."

"I have lived so long," the man gasped. "So many memories, so much knowledge to be shared. But I'd rather face oblivion than see it in the hands of traitors and criminals."

"Are you sure about that?" Zelle asked, and for a moment, the kindly, grandmotherly figure who descended the staircase in the Library of Souls returned. Someone who just wanted to help. "I suspect our motives here are not that different. We're all human. We all trace our roots back to this planet. We want to learn what happened here. Tell us what you know, and you'll get to witness something incredible before you die."

He spat on the ground. "I am more than human, you orthodox trash. I come from the stars and belong to the stars."

Feisal cackled. "I'll get Barry while Captain Starlight beams himself away."

Barry proved too large and cumbersome to wheel into the tunnel, but his smaller counterpart, the prototype used in the Library of Souls, was more than adequate. They were going back hours and days this time, not centuries. Nawalle set up the machine while Feisal stood guard over the Vitruvian captive.

"Let's just rewind the clock," Zelle said. "See how long our friend has been alone here."

The device whirred to life. Under Nawalle's careful hand, it began its reverse reel through time, starting with Feisal disarming the shape in the dark. She sped up. Little happened at first. The man crawled to different areas of the room, sometimes retrieving water or injecting himself with a medication from the cupboard. From time to time, he relieved himself or curled inside the cage to sleep.

"How is this possible?" the man whispered. He gaped at the sight of his own body going through its solitary motions. Tearing himself away from the surreal sight, he fixed his gaze on the dark lens as Nawalle held it steady.

"It's normally more interesting than this," Feisal said, helping himself to a freeze-dried pastry from the cupboard. "You've had some boring days on your lonesome. I'd at least be playing my oud."

"You've found a way to recreate past events," the man said. He addressed Feisal as the only possible inventor.

"Quantum-level wave function collapse visualization," Feisal said through a mouthful of k'nafeh. "A quantum historical projector. Opening up Schrödinger's box, where observation has occurred, and seeing which probability became observable reality."

"You discovered this…incredible technology and you shared it with… them?" The man's voice rose to a wild shriek of fury, before a renewed bout of coughing. Feisal shrugged, clearly enjoying the effect he had on his fellow Vitruvian.

"Wait, slow it down!" Azad cried.

The man was no longer alone. The cage now contained bodies. The man was dragging them back inside. When they switched to forward momentum, the scene became clear. The Vitruvian, grimacing under a fresh wound in his abdomen, dragged bodies out of the cage one by one, dissolving them in acid in a metal container. Tissue and bone and hair melted together, bubbling beneath a sickening green mist that Azad could almost taste on his dry tongue.

Nawalle screamed, dropping the device. Azad rushed to her, helping her to her knees, where she retched between whispered strings of Dusharan prayers. Feisal spat out the remaining pastry, his face pinched with fury. Even Zelle's face paled.

"Destroying bodies is a mother system barbarism," Zelle said with disgust. "Orthodox or Vitruvian, all Nabateans can agree on that. So why? We just witnessed a similar atrocity that our ancestors performed on Calypso campus."

"Probably for the same reason that I did," the man said. For the first time, panic found its way into his voice. "They were infected and dangerous. Even more dangerous dead than alive."

"That's impossible," Azad said. "Some viruses transmit through corpses, it's true, but they need living organisms to thrive."

"Not this one," the man said. "This one's most powerful with something that's freshly dead. Didn't matter to me at that point, but in case a rescue party arrived...you would have done the same."

"Perhaps," Feisal agreed, though he still surveyed the man with revulsion. "But how did they all get sick?"

The man closed his eyes. Thin droplets of blood leaked from his tear ducts, but he pressed his lips together in defiant silence.

Feisal picked up mini-Barry while Azad squeezed Nawalle's shoulders, letting her lean against him. His own heart pounded like an alpha-vessel's engine, so fast it was a wonder he didn't faint. But comforting Nawalle, worrying about her, helped distract him from whatever the prototype machine would display next.

The scene resumed. The bodies came out of the acid barrel in reverse, growing limbs and tissue like a blossoming plant before the man dragged them back to their cages.

Then he lay alone in the center of the room, dazed, as blood formed a dark pool from his abdomen onto the floor.

Then he was no longer alone.

Two figures, both female, ran backward from the tunnel into the center of the room, where they fought with the Vitruvian man. A flash of a blade jerked away from the man's stomach, blood leaping back inside. Swings of fists and sharp kicks. Dark hair whipping around, angry eyes alight like jewels.

"Ledo!" Nawalle cried.

It was her. Azad had wondered if the Ledo in his mind bore any resemblance to Ledo in reality. The details of her face, her mannerisms. But the young woman who came behind the man and swung a jar at his head could only be Ledo. The rounder, adolescent face he remembered had thinned, her features sharper even in the misted quality of the quantum historical projector's reading, but nothing else had changed. The ends of her straight black hair swung like blades and her pointed nose wrinkled in concentration, as it had done with any challenging task, while she went about the business of trying to kill a Vitruvian.

Nawalle gripped Azad's arms and their roles reversed as she steadied him. The device took them further backward, where Ledo lay strapped to a gurney before busting from her restraints. The other woman, it seemed, initiated the attack after an argument with the man. Ledo then joined the fray.

Another detail gnawed at Azad's cluttered mind. Tearing his eyes away from his sister, who lay on the gurney with a sullen expression, he followed the other female figure's movements.

"That's her!" he said. "The Vitruvian woman who died at the Central Nabatean Hospital. The one who knew Ledo."

"That traitor Nenah made it all the way back to Nabatea?" the man asked incredulously. "What happened to her?"

Nawalle looked ready to kick the man's head in, but Azad raised an arm to restrain her. Zelle was right – having him alive and talking was proving useful.

"She died on my table," Azad said to their captive. "Then Vitruvian authorities Archived her, wheeled her out and stored her in the Library of Souls." A sudden realization struck him like a blow to the head, and he reeled under its weight. "She was sick as well! You said corpses are contagious…could she have infected others inside the Nabatea hospital?"

"I'll caveat that statement," the man said after another round of coughing. His breaks between coughing fits were shortening. "Vitruvians, from our experiments in this hole, appear to be less contagious. They can transmit with direct contact to bodily fluids, but it spreads like wildfire through the orthodox. If only Vitruvians handled her, the damage might have been minimal."

His words failed to comfort Azad, and judging from the tense stillness in the room, the rest of the crew shared his fears. Feisal paused the reel. In the center of the room, the frozen figures of the Vitruvian man and woman faced each other with tight faces, the sparks of impending battle crackling in the air between them.

"You had better start explaining what happened," Zelle said. Her white hair shone under the blue light. Righteous anger radiated from her short but strong frame.

The man glanced from the woman to Feisal. Calculation stirred in his weathered face as he weighed the options for his final moments, deciding which one he cared for the least.

Feisal tipped the scales. "On my word as a fellow Vitruvian explorer, according to our laws and codes of travel, I will broadcast your neural imprint to the *Axel*," he said. "Unscrubbed. They'll see everything, except, of course, your last minutes here with us. We're fair but not fools. But only if you tell us everything you know."

Feisal turned to Zelle, asking for permission after the fact, but she nodded.

The man absorbed the offer. After a minute, an eon for a Vitruvian, he sighed.

"There's a reason we let everyone muck about to their heart's content on Earth but ban Martian passage to all except authority-approved Vitruvian vessels," the man said. "Several years ago, we made some interesting discoveries. Well, not exactly. On their own, they didn't amount to much, but together…they told the beginnings of a story worth exploring. Those of us who are Vitruvian explorers seek to understand our origins in relation to the less-evolved strain of humanity."

"You mean try to prove your inherent superiority to us," Nawalle said with a slight shake to her voice. The shock of witnessing bodies melted by acid lingered on her clammy face.

"That's right," the man said with venom. "Our inherent superiority. Why should we deny it? Our differences are evident. Our physicality, our intellect, our curiosity…take a side trip to Earth, or what's left of it, if you want to see what the orthodox did when they were the dominant lifeform. We eclipse you in so many ways, some even question whether we truly descend from such a primitive species."

"You deny Juul's own teachings?" Zelle asked, amused, but Feisal's eyes glinted with realization.

"You came here looking for proof that we're our own strain,"

Feisal said. "That we descend from somewhere else. A new origin story to persuade Vitruvians like me that we're something apart from our Nabatean brothers and sisters. There are more of us than ever who see our similarities more than our differences, and want to live more closely with the orthodox. You want to stop the new thinking, don't you?"

"Self-hating traitors," the man said with a snarl. "Living in the city, choosing monotonous domesticity over discovery. Some of us have come to the realization that Juul's teachings are inherently flawed, because Juul himself was flawed – he died an orthodox Nabatean."

Azad couldn't believe his ears. A Vitruvian, criticizing the founder of Nabatea. He drew several deep, steadying breaths to stay calm and focused.

"Do all on the *Axel* share this view?" Zelle asked with surprise.

"Of course not! And we don't reject Juul entirely. Had he evolved into one of us, we might have gotten a fuller set of teachings, one that didn't hide behind this 'separate but equal' nonsense that we all know is untrue. Teachings that would be clear on Vitruvian dominance, of the rest of humanity's role to serve."

"Too bad there's nothing for you to see but rock and ruin," Feisal said to the man. "And we've found no evidence of some fantastical Vitruvian origin story, so it looks as though you – *we* – aren't that special after all."

"Oh, we've found evidence! First, signs of collapse on a previously undiscovered colony on Mars, called Palmcorps—"

"Palmcorps collapsed, then. Interesting," Zelle said. The man raised his eyebrows but continued.

"And a body in the desert that clearly ran farther than possible without Vitruvian characteristics."

"Saw him," she continued with a cheerful smile. "Handsome face, until the blood started to boil."

"And then there's the crater," the man continued. When Zelle failed to conjure a retort, his ghoulish smile widened. "Our scanners sensed a stretch of Arabia Terra with biological properties. Mitochondria. Bacteria. We dug and unveiled something – yes, I'll say it – alien, deep within a crater in the desert. One that we believe our ancestors discovered."

Azad's breath stilled. Whatever he'd expected, it did not involve the word 'alien'. A surge of anxiety for Ledo ran like electricity through his body. What had she gotten herself into?

"Alien to Mars, or to our ancestors?" Feisal asked in a soft voice. He sat still like the Nabatean serpent on his chest, every muscle tense with anticipation.

"We believe it is alien to Mars itself," the man said. He coughed again, longer this time. "Perhaps imported from a crashed comet, or something foreign that predated human colonization, waiting for something carbon-based to interact with."

"And you believe we came from or were changed by exposure to this substance beneath the crater?" Feisal said.

The man grimaced, and in the shadow that passed over his face, the horror of his last few weeks manifested. The dead, the dying, the false hope and the failure.

"When anyone comes into direct contact with it, it kills them," he said simply. "The bacteria alter the mitochondria in our makeup in a manner that even Vitruvians cannot adapt to. We fight it, but the body becomes overwhelmed and we die. We wondered, therefore, if controlled or diluted doses would have a different effect. And if Vitruvians could still survive what others could not."

Dread settled in Azad's chest. The dead bodies in the cage clawed back into his consciousness. An experiment. As disposable as cells in a petri dish.

"We expected the non-Vitruvians to react differently," he said. "Recruited volunteers, gave them different levels of exposure. All died eventually, except one."

The cold floor swayed, the world tilting over the edge. Ledo. They had infected her, before she escaped. The only one to evade the barrel of acid.

"The girl survived," Feisal said with a barely concealed smile. "Where Vitruvians did not."

The man sighed. Nawalle's fists clenched and Azad knew her thoughts matched his – would this man hurry up and die already? They knew what they needed to know, save one detail.

"Where did Ledo go?" Azad asked. The man turned to Azad in surprise, as though just remembering him.

"The resemblance is striking," he said, voice rasping. "I wonder…if you would survive, too?"

Azad lunged forward. The man unleashed a surprised gurgle as Azad shook his shoulders.

"Where did she go?" Azad yelled. "Answer me!"

Strong hands pulled him back. Azad struggled, every particle in his body vibrating with fury, but proved no match for Feisal's grip.

"He doesn't know," Feisal said in a voice that was almost kind. "He's alone and powerless without the *Axel*. He's not worth your first kill."

Azad gulped for air, struggling even after he knew Feisal was right. The man stared up at him, his bloodied eyes oozing contempt and triumph as life's spark faded within them. Azad was nothing more than a toy to him. Something to be played with and discarded. Like Ledo. Like all orthodox Nabateans.

"You're wrong," Azad whispered at last. "Your experiments…all they proved was that this crater kills everyone it touches. We all die. You first."

They left the man to his final moments while they cleaned out the facility like scavengers. They stripped the medicine cabinets, the food supplies, but carefully avoided the cage and the spot where the dead turned to searing liquid. Nawalle focused on the supplies while Feisal and Azad turned on the quantum historical projector again, digging further into the past. They found pain, fear, slow disintegration. All the station's occupants trapped like sacrificial animals. The only useful piece of information came from evidence of the 'alien' substance itself – a shimmering, viscous blue liquid in an IV drip, shining like starlight trapped in deep water, snaking into unwilling veins. And Ledo. Talking with her inmates in their small cage, always defiant and fearless. Always fighting to survive.

The man watched them in his lucid moments as he slipped in and out of consciousness. His body relaxed between violent spasms, the demeanor of someone relieved not to be alone. Azad couldn't help but wish fear on him, for him to suffer as he made others suffer.

In his final moments, the man beckoned Feisal forward with a shaking finger and whispered. Feisal kept his distance to the last but nodded his head. True to his word, he held the Archive Band to the man's head as he drew his final breaths. A single, complete lifetime, trapped and humming inside a strip of machinery. Once the download was complete, Feisal stepped away from the dead man with speed. A dead body, according to the man, was even more infectious. They would need to leave quickly.

"What did he say?" Zelle asked.

"He gave us coordinates," Feisal replied. "For the crater."

"Do you think they're real?" Nawalle asked.

"Could be a trap," Feisal mused. "But I suspect not. He said everyone who came into contact with it died, and you know he wants us dead. What better way to kill us than a crater filled with lethal alien goo?"

"There's something else," Azad said. "Something I didn't want to say in front of him." He jerked his head at the fresh corpse.

"Go on," Zelle said.

"He said that the...whatever's in that crater affected everyone the same. Vitruvian or not. But when I tried to save Nenah at the hospital, I found something unexplainable in her medical readings. The medmechs couldn't find any evidence of a foreign infection inside her. It made no sense then, but I think I understand it now. If what's in the crater is some kind of virus, it was already part of her DNA. Her Vitruvian DNA. When she became sick, the machines found nothing foreign...because some element of this virus is already part of her genetic makeup."

"What does that mean?" Nawalle asked.

Feisal stepped forward, shaking his head. "Meaning our friend may not have been wrong in his theory that this crater and the Vitruvian bloodline are tied. But if this thing has already altered our ancestors' DNA, *hadir*, why does it still kill Vitruvians?"

Azad frowned, ignoring the insult in the face of an excellent question. "It could be that in its purest, raw form, this substance is still deadly. Maybe the originals who became Vitruvians weren't exposed directly to the crater, but a more diluted form of the substance. Something that made it compatible with their bodies."

"This is all nice and good," Nawalle said with a tone that suggested otherwise. "But we need to follow Ledo's trail out of here."

"First, we go to the crater," Zelle said. Nawalle's eyes welled with tears, but she said nothing. Azad was too numb, too shocked by the last hour's events, to muster his own protest.

Feisal snapped into action, packing up mini-Barry, but Azad and Nawalle stood where they were. Nawalle's face mirrored Azad's inner fury. Ledo was sick. Ledo escaped from a nightmarish experiment into the Martian desert. They had to follow her trail.

As though reading his mind, Zelle approached him with a thin mouth but kind eyes.

"Remember what I said when you first joined this crew?" she asked in a low voice. "We are here on a historical mission, not a rescue operation. We will return and trace her steps as far as we can, but we don't know where that will lead – it could take us to the *Axel* station or to a crash site back on Nabatea. For now, we must see this crater and uncover what our ancestors knew of it, how they may have used it. You heard the Vitruvian and what he wanted to do with his knowledge – this is bigger than you, or me, or Ledo, as much as we care about her. We will take this dead man's bait but with caution. This is my decision, and it is final."

Zelle enunciated every word of the last sentence. It looked to Azad that something inside Nawalle gave, her shoulders slumping back. She nodded and helped Feisal with the final loading.

Azad's skin prickled with frustration, but the captain's orders had made him the defiant minority. He snapped into line, though it pained him to load the Glider outside, where he scanned the Martian landscape in every direction, as though Ledo's head might emerge from a distant hill.

Guided by the new coordinates, they sped away in the direction of the crater. Away from Kezza Sayer, away from Ledo, into the unknown.

"We should have burned that man," Nawalle said. She gripped the Glider's rails, eyes glinting through her vizor.

"Not a chance," Feisal yelled over his shoulder, steering the Glider away from Kezza's original path. Clouds of red dust rose in the air. "Leave that fool as a diseased trap for any *Axel* explorers who try to grab him."

"I say the Dusharan funeral rites for everyone," Nawalle said several minutes later. "But not for him. Not for anyone like him."

"It makes no difference, Nawalle," Zelle said in a low voice. "Rites are for the living, not the dead."

Chapter Fourteen

Kezza

PALMCORPS CORPORATE CAMPUS, MARS
2195 A.D.

Where Calypso was a fortress, Palmcorps resembled an archipelago, a scattering of white islands in a red, windswept sea. The vehicle sped past low buildings with greenery peering behind their windows. Detached farms, where the city kept its crops separate. Other structures suggested laboratories or research facilities, with similar vehicles parked outside. Diversified risk – it was good planning, Kezza had to admit, although Palmcorps had the luxury of being the second corporate city on Mars, able to learn from Calypso's mistakes.

"Just received a warning from HQ," Evgenia said, businesslike. "They've shut down the underground emergency entrance to the med ward. Temporary security precaution, they say."

Amit swore. "What do we do then?"

"Same thing we always do," Evgenia said. "Go in through the main bay like the innocents we are. Quickly. Keep Barrett's presence quiet until we get into the Catacombs. And hope our Calypso refugee doesn't contaminate the station."

"I could keep my atmosphere suit on," Kezza said, ignoring the sliver of contempt in Evgenia's voice.

"Too conspicuous. You'll draw attention, which is the last thing we need. You've apparently been dancing and running around your own home without causing a new plague, so we can assume you're safe enough. Just don't cough or bleed on anything."

"I'll do my best."

The main campus loomed ahead, no part of it higher than Calypso's Coliseum. Kezza's heart panged at the low roofs – it meant most of the city was underground. But no one stopped them as they drove through the transport bay, which already earned Palmcorps several points over Calypso.

"We're close to the med ward," Amit said to Kezza. "It's staffed by allies, so we'll be able to run tests on you in peace there."

Kezza winced at the mention of tests, but Juul squeezed her hand reassuringly.

"This isn't Bokambe," he said. "You'll be safe."

"Any ID scanners?" Kezza asked as they passed the airlock.

Amit shook his head. "In secure areas, of course, but this is a large campus, where people serve multiple functions. Everyone has at least two professions here. Too hard to track everyone's movements."

The only secondary job a Tiered worker could find on Calypso involved crime.

"Interesting," Juul said. "I've experimented with multiple job roles in Unified Korea and it worked well. People like variety and they also like to be busy."

Amit and Evgenia exchanged a smirk. Barrett Juul, no doubt, knew how to keep them busy.

As they exited the Terrain vehicle, Palmcorps didn't differ too drastically from Kezza's home of over twenty years, at least on the surface. Still, Kezza drank it all in with wide eyes. New corridors, new uniforms, new faces, after decades confined to the same stretch of real estate.

True to its name, artificial palm trees lined the campus's Atrium, reaching up to the ceiling. Their fronds glowed with synthetic light, illuminating murals on the surroundings walls that reflected Palmcorps' corporate history. The Dubai skyline. Trains spinning through temples in Kuala Lumpur. Farmers from a simpler time harvesting grain. Not a hint of sugar in sight.

Kezza exhaled and turned to Juul with a smile. "So far, no regrets about being here," she said.

"A ringing endorsement if I ever heard one," Juul said with a wry smile of his own. "But we need to get you to the medical ward."

"Keep your hood on," Evgenia snapped at Juul. Obediently, Juul pulled his suit's hood over his face, his head low.

Two security officers patrolled the far end of the Atrium. Like their Calypso counterparts, they wielded large batons and bored, restless expressions. Kezza's shoulders tightened but she forced her face into practiced nonchalance.

"Don't look that way," Amit muttered. He moved so that he and Evgenia blocked Juul from the officers' view. They quickened their pace, but the officers shifted direction, toward an old man passing out pamphlets.

"No solicitation here, grandpa," one of them, a woman, said with a mocking edge to her voice. "What's this then?"

"Nothing," the man wheezed, but he reflexively took several steps back.

The other officer yanked the stack of paper out of the man's hand, causing loose pamphlets to scatter. Juul's face, with its familiar crooked smile, spread across the floor. Next to Kezza, the real Juul tensed.

"You better come with us."

"I'm not doing nothing wrong."

"We're not asking, old man."

"No!"

Kezza stared at her own feet, blood pounding in her ears. Seconds later, a loud crack filled the Atrium, followed by a pitiful cry. Juul closed his eyes, his dark cheeks reddening behind his hood. They passed the scene without breaking pace.

"He's one of ours," Amit muttered. "Figured we might need a distraction, and I was right."

"Did he have to take a beating to get us in?" Juul asked in a strained voice. No one responded, because the answer was clear.

They descended into Palmcorps' very own Catacombs. A familiar, musty smell greeted Kezza as they moved deeper underground, the smell of dirt, stale air and the sweat of too many people in a narrow space.

"No security in sight down here," Kezza murmured. "If people in Calypso knew about this, there'd be mass desertion. All this time, I thought you were just as trapped as we are."

"Don't be fooled," Amit said. "The same beast that runs Calypso is alive and kicking here in Palmcorps. The only difference is that we've been smart enough to make our Catacombs too…unpleasant for them to send their precious security into."

Unpleasant was a good, encompassing summary. The aroma of rotting trash hovered right at Kezza's nose level, making her eyes water. The walls carried decades of grime, paint stripped away. People of all stripes filled the hallways – workers, families, crowds of teenagers with nothing to do but occupy space. A scuffle broke out at the far end of the corridor and a mother dragged her two children into the nearest door.

"Home sweet home," Evgenia said with a sigh. "God, I miss Ukraine."

Down another level, graffiti fought with the grime for space on the walls. One word had been scrawled more than any other.

Juul.

His face covered several sections of wall, phrases from his speeches formed long, misspelled quotes in neon green and pink paint. Juul had not chosen Palmcorps for his initial visit, but the people of Palmcorps had clearly chosen him.

Kezza managed a smile, which waned at the sight of a man pointing in their direction. His eyes widened as he peered at the hooded Juul.

Amit stepped forward, giving the man a rough shove. "Back away," he spat.

The man turned tail but the lightning-quick exchange left a tight sensation in Kezza's stomach, unrelated to illness or hunger.

"To the ward," Evgenia barked over her shoulder. "I'll bring the boss in."

They ended up in a medical ward that was clean only compared to its surroundings. The wall grime looked fresher, the odor of trash countered by antiseptic fumes. Amit gestured Kezza onto a bed.

"We'll scan your vitals," he explained. "And also run some genetic tests."

The room blurred and swayed as Kezza's knees trembled. All of a sudden, it was impossible to move, to take another step into that room.

She had been scanned, poked, prodded, swabbed and measured without cause for most of her adult life. And now, as she coughed up black bile and struggled to stand, her body had reached its limits. She had reached her limit.

"What's wrong with her?" Evgenia asked.

"Give her a minute," Juul said. He moved closer to Kezza, whispering in her ear. "Trust me, Kezza. We'll do this on your terms. Want to draw your own sample?"

Fighting back tears, her throat burning, Kezza nodded. Through her exhaustion, fear gnawed at her. She feared what the tests would confirm, but having some control, however little, made the moment bearable.

Amit shooed away the others. Kezza removed her shoes and climbed onto the examination bed. Memories bubbled to the surface of similar rooms, aglow under fluorescent light. Gloved hands probing her, checking for imperfections rather than illness. And then her mother, progressing from screenings to tests to confirmation tests to treatments to experimental treatments to hospice. A wheel running downhill, nearing the final cliff. Kezza closed her eyes and opened them again, trying to blink the past away.

It doesn't matter now. Only the present matters.

Amit handed her a small thermometer-like device with a sharp point. A genetic processor.

"For the full tests, I'll need blood in addition to your hair and saliva," he said. "The sole of the foot tends to be the best place. We do it for newborns."

Kezza managed a smile.

"Well, if a baby can handle it," she said. Before she had time to hesitate, she pushed the needle into her heel. Its bite was sharp but fleeting. A red cloud filled the sheer portion of the tester and she returned it to Amit.

"Now lie back," he said.

The scanners worked their magic. Kezza lay still, falling into her usual dreamlike state when she wanted to be somewhere else. Pipes creaked and the walls groaned, reverberations from a Martian storm outside. Kezza closed her eyes, willing the winds to strip the landscape bare, revealing grass and streams underneath. Hopefully Juul's new planet would crackle with life.

"When will we know?" Juul asked beside her.

"It'll take a couple of hours to process the results," Amit replied, not looking up from his monitor. "But the head of the Palmcorps resistance knows we've arrived. He'll be here soon."

"What will he want?" Juul asked curtly.

Amit smiled. "Remember the economic minister back in Dhaka? A lot like him, this chap. When Kezza sent out that video of the sick people in Bokambe, he wanted to blast it out to both cities – hack the comms systems and show it across every screen in Calypso and Palmcorps. Evgenia talked him off the ledge, but not easily. Now that you're here, he'll want to trigger a coup and he'll want it now."

"Men of action can be useful," Juul said with a thoughtful nod. "When they're unleashed at the right time."

"I thought you were itching to get back to Calypso as soon as possible," Amit said. "Get your mother out of harm's way."

"This changes the dynamics," Juul murmured, glancing at Kezza. "My mother would agree."

The door to the medical ward flew open. A large man entered, Evgenia at his heels. The way Amit sprang to his feet revealed the man to be the leader of the Palmcorps resistance. He certainly projected authority, and not just because of his size. A tall, built figure with a network of tattoos webbing across his muscular arms, he reminded Kezza of the action hero toys she used to play with as a child. Unlike the toys, however, his eyes radiated intelligence and calculation, the look of a man always searching for the next opportunity.

"It is an honor to have the great civilizationist Barrett Juul under my protection," he boomed, his thick Martian miners' patois at odds with his formal choice of words. "It's a shame you didn't come here first."

"In hindsight, I can't argue," Juul said, standing up to clasp the man's hand. Next to the leader, Juul looked even more diminutive and delicate than usual, his Earth stature pronounced. "But here we are. Thank you for coming to our rescue – I know that carried a great risk."

The leader laughed. "You're a valuable friend to have, to be sure. But we also came in response to the horror you exposed on Calypso. A crime against humanity, even by the low bar the Corpsboards have set on this planet. Do you know we think that the first two to be infected were from Palmcorps? A married couple who strayed too far. We're assuming as much, anyway – Calypso took them."

"You're correct," Juul said, turning to Kezza for confirmation. She nodded.

"Their names are Evan and Nancy Kim," the man said. "What happened to them? We didn't see them in the footage you sent." His broad shoulders tensed, bracing for bad news, and Kezza's face flushed. The dead couple on the Waste Room floor had lives here, people who cared for them.

"Dead," Kezza said, ashamed at the bluntness in her voice, although a Martian miner wouldn't expect to hear the truth any other way. "They died before the rest. They might have been trying to escape, because I found them outside of Bokambe."

The leader swore, his large fists clenched.

"I'm sorry to hear that, even though I expected it," he said. "Two hard-working miners, in the wrong place at the wrong time. Shows that Calypso is no better than here – the same depravity festers in the higher ranks."

The man's eyes flicked in Kezza's direction, as though noticing her for the first time, and fear crossed them. Kezza allowed herself to cough for theatrical effect.

"I heard you brought a stowaway," he said, addressing Amit but keeping his eyes on Kezza, as though bracing for her to bite. "This is the famous Kezza Sayer."

"I wouldn't be here if it weren't for her," Juul said simply.

"Does she need to be under the bubble?"

"She doesn't appear to be contagious to the extent others are," Amit said. "The disease, whatever it is, is not airborne. But I'd keep some distance."

"Activate the bubble," the leader ordered.

A sheer curtain descended from the low ceiling, a transparent veil that reached the floor and circled Kezza's bed and surrounding equipment. She had seen them before, in the isolation wards she passed when she visited her mother. Though she could speak through the veil, the air system around her would be isolated – a costly endeavor on Mars, where air systems meant the difference between life and death.

"So you know my name," Kezza said with an arched brow. "Any chance I'm going to learn yours?"

The resistance leader faced her. His bulk would have intimidated her on any other day, but she lacked the energy for new fears.

"Of course," he said, with that same broad smile. "The name's Axel. Head of the resistance in Palmcorps."

Kezza suppressed a snort. Martians liked to give their children industrial-themed names. Axel, Hinge, Gear, Machina. Meant to symbolize their Martian heritage, a world where technology superseded nature. Ridiculous, but then again, her name was Kezza.

"We're going to take care of you, Kezza," Axel said, moving to the edge of the bubble. For a moment, he looked as though he might pass it and squeeze her shoulder, but he stayed back. "We're pleased to have a sister from Calypso here. You're under my protection as long as you're below ground, so if anyone gives you grief, if you need anything, you come to me. That means that you're also under my rules, but you'll find we have fewer of those than where you came from."

"Don't get in your way and don't cause a plague?" Kezza asked.

Axel laughed.

"A good start," he said. In spite of herself, she liked him. He was direct and firm about protecting his people, but he extended compassion to Kezza where it could be spared. No one on Calypso had ever called her 'sister'. Had Juul been right about Palmcorps? Could working Martians really band together under his leadership?

They'd have to try.

"On that note, there is something that we need regarding Kezza," Juul began. The atmosphere in the room shifted immediately, the friendly formalities over.

Axel gestured to the surrounding medical equipment. "We have everything here to keep her comfortable."

"We're thinking beyond that," Juul said with a careful smile. "I would appreciate any information you have regarding the location of the crater, the source of the infection. I need to collect a sample from it."

Whatever Axel had expected, it wasn't about the crater. Shock passed over the leader's face before he fixed it into stony calculation. He leaned against a nearby chair, veins bulging across his arms. Even Amit appeared slightly taken aback, either by the request or the bluntness with which Juul delivered it.

"You barely escaped Calypso with your life," Axel finally countered, raising his brows. "I'd have thought retaliating against the Calypso Corpsboard for your mother's arrest would be the next logical step."

"My mother's safe on the Obscura for now, with a turned Corpsboard member," Juul said. "We'll return to Calypso soon enough, but the immediate problem we need to solve is this mystery in the desert, before it becomes a plague or a weapon."

"It will only become a weapon if we allow the Corpsboards in both cities to remain in power," Axel said through gritted teeth. "I don't know what's going on in Calypso, if the population has been pacified by candy and circuses—" he nodded to Kezza, "—but the people of Palmcorps are at breaking point, and we're ready. We've been ready before your broadcast stunt from *Calypso One*. With or without you, we will overthrow the Corp and boil those who've subjugated us – but we'd prefer to stand with you. We will broadcast Calypso's crimes. The people will revolt."

Juul stepped forward, eyes alight. Kezza's shoulders had tensed to the point where a dull pain traveled up her neck, but Juul seemed to be having a great time. He was in his element – navigating an enormous change on a new world.

"Based on my experience on Earth many times over, you're right about one thing," Juul said. "The footage from Palmcorps will scare them, make them angry. But then what, Axel? The people already distrust the Corpsboards. They already know they're capable of anything – performing experiments, infecting prisoners, toying with lives. They might even revolt in both cities, but once again, then what? In my experience, it's not enough to cause fear. Fear makes people act rashly, but you need more than a common danger – to maintain power, you need a solution. A way to extinguish that fear and show that they can trust the people who replace the Corpsboards. To do that, we need to know more about this danger from the crater in the desert."

"So you want to find a cure?" Axel asked shrewdly. "And sweep in as the hero."

"And save the afflicted," Juul snapped, gesturing at Kezza through the bubble. "And secure our future survival."

"Evgenia tells me that your plans involve taking us off this planet, to an off-world colony," Axel said. "Isn't this the selling point? Rescue us all from this…virus, or whatever it is, by getting us far away?"

"This may be what we need to tip the scales," Juul said.

"So why go through the time and effort to cure it?" Amit interjected. "Not to mention the risk in getting a sample. I'm sorry, Kezza," he added, his brown eyes sincere.

"As I said, we need to instill confidence if people are going to abandon Mars," Juul said. "We can't just run from something – we need to run to something better. While I believe I'm offering that, I also think that this… disease, as we call it, may be an opportunity."

"Explain that one to me," Kezza said in a tight voice, and the group turned to her in surprise. "I might be dying. Where's the opportunity?" Juul's words about revolution and tipped scales charged through her like electricity but left a bitter aftertaste. She didn't just want revolution – she needed to be there when it happened. She needed to be a part of this new world they plotted together.

"But you haven't died yet," Juul said with renewed energy. He began to pace the room. "And you've not only lasted longer than others, you may have some…other benefits. Strength, for example. And greater endurance, adaptability. The man you found in the Waste Room, Evan Kim. You hinted once that something unusual happened before he died."

"Not unusual," Kezza said, her heart quickening. She was catching up with Juul's line of thinking. "Impossible. He ran out the airlock into open

Mars. He survived longer than anyone could have, without oxygen and protection. He kept running and running."

Their eyes met and even through the medical bubble, the air between them crackled with shared understanding. Juul had aspirations beyond a cure. He hoped to turn Kezza's affliction into a blessing. An asset.

"I'll go ahead and state what we're all thinking," Juul said with an air that left no room for challengers. "If something in the desert is infecting people, making them die or develop inexplicable characteristics, we might be dealing with an alien substance. An organism, a bacteria or virus. Perhaps even something intelligent, a gift we can use as we expand humanity's reach into the stars. Or maybe it's just a noxious gas released by drilling and we're best leaving it alone. We won't know until we investigate, and if nothing else, that is what I intend to do."

★   ★   ★

Kezza's body ached with exhaustion but she couldn't sleep as long as Amit sat nearby, mining every element of her biology for answers. The back of his head bobbed every few minutes but yielded no clues as he extracted indecipherable strings of data on the monitor. She nibbled at a cheese sandwich, bitter starch clinging to the roof of her mouth.

Barrett Juul had left the ward under tight security to confer further with Axel. His absence hung in the air like a mist. Without his words and promises to distract her, Kezza's own predicament fought to the forefront of her mind. *Infected*. The word conjured images of boils and sores, isolation and revulsion.

What had the Imam at Calypso's prayer room once told her? *Health is a crown upon the head that only the sick can see.* She saw it on Amit now, a halo of wellness that made him a distant object, part of a world that would continue on without her.

"Amit, am I going to die?" she asked.

Die. The word rolled so easily off her tongue, but its aftermath settled like a heavy pit in her stomach.

Amit turned around at last, face still as stone. He ran his hands through his hair, fumbling for the right words, and as he struggled, Kezza found a thread of hope and seized it.

"I'm different from the others," she said, her voice childlike in its pleading. "I haven't infected anybody. I have weak phases, but then I become stronger. I kicked a fucking wall open! I climbed up to the top of the Calypso observatory like it was nothing. Dying people aren't stronger than they were before. Maybe I can survive."

Amit's eyes softened.

"There might be some hope," he said gently. "I've been comparing your DNA against the other subjects who died in Bokambe, and I think I've found the cause for your different trajectory with the infection. It turns out that you have an uncommon genetic mutation, the MRC14. It becomes active with heavy pollution exposure. Where were you born on Earth, before you came to Mars?"

"Cardiff. Lived there until I was three, then my mother brought me here."

"It fits," he said. "One of the most polluted cities in northern Europe. I actually passed through there before I started working for Barrett – it hasn't improved with age. Anyway, this mutation seems to be interacting with the virus, allowing it to coexist in your body and integrate with your DNA. Producing proteins that keep the virus at bay."

"It's changing me?" Kezza's pulse leapt at her throat.

"Genetic mutations normally take generations to evolve and manifest in different characteristics," Amit said with a nod. "But whatever this is, it's not normal. In the others at the Bokambe complex, their bodies evolved at an alarming rate – unnatural bursts of strength, speed and coordination. Adaptation at the molecular level. The body adjusting to changes in temperature and atmosphere even, as you saw with Evan Kim. But then the virus overruns the body and their gains become short-lived. Thanks to your MRC14 mutation, you've taken a different course. The virus interacts with your system more gradually."

"But I can't beat it?" she asked.

"No. In the end, it will win."

The words washed over Kezza like water, churning in her ears and leaving her breathless. She heard them but struggled to sift through their meaning. Her tongue tingled on the roof of her mouth. Everything turned into fog. Her voice felt like someone else's voice. Even her body, the same body that carried her from trapeze to trapeze, became alien to her. It had betrayed her. Poison ran through it, eating at her until it would consume everything she had ever been.

Her face must have shown hints of her anguish, because Amit crossed into the bubble and took her hand. Kezza flinched but let him massage her palm.

"Don't panic yet," he said. "You're in trouble, I won't lie about that, but I've worked with Barrett Juul long enough to know what he's capable of. This infection, understanding it, is important to him and that's good news for you. He wants to find a cure and he'll do everything in his power to make it happen. As will I."

*   *   *

The ward's lights dimmed at night, but there was no way Kezza could sleep. The hospital bed creaked and she fidgeted in the dark. Did Juul really want to find a cure above all else? Or would he abandon all concern for Kezza once he succeeded in convincing the people of Mars to join his great experiment in the stars? It was an experiment Kezza would give everything to join. Doubts gnawed at her, but she didn't have the energy to chase them away.

Maybe not killing Juul was the best thing she'd ever done. Something primal, something *physical* within Kezza told her that he wouldn't let her die. She trusted him now, like he trusted all of these people around them. That might have been the best thing the civilizationist brought with him from Earth, including that snake – trust.

At his low-lit station, Amit ran his hand through his curly hair again. Despite herself, Kezza watched him at work, recalling his smell when he passed through the bubble, of cloves and something earthier, male. Kezza's skin itched with the urge to touch and be touched. An urge so foreign and infrequent to her, she barely recognized it when it began. Despite the aggressive marketing to the contrary back on Earth, Calypso was a sterile, sexless place. Life on Mars required order, and sex was messy. Complicated. On those rare occasions when she slipped into a VIP room with a visiting Earth dignitary or stumbled in a drunken haze into another Catacombs apartment, she always teetered on the edge of slipping away before it was too late, knowing the bittersweet aftermath that would follow. She would leave an hour or a morning later with her body altered – hair tussled, limbs sore, potentially satisfied for a fleeting moment – but the hollowness would linger within her like a scab.

But that satisfaction, however fleeting, was now out of reach. She was sick, infected, dying. A danger to everyone around her, however much they pretended otherwise.

★   ★   ★

Tangled in her own thoughts, Kezza didn't remember falling asleep, but she woke with a rude jolt.

Footsteps and shouts reverberated outside the medical bubble. Something was wrong. She opened her eyes. It was the middle of the night, but noise flooded in from the corridor.

Her eyes adjusted to the dark, revealing Amit and Juul donning atmosphere suits. The bubble around her had vanished. Juul gestured to her as Kezza pulled herself upright, blinking.

"We need to go," he said. "Suit up."

"What's happening?" she managed to mumble.

"There's been a coup in Calypso," Amit said. He helped Juul activate his suit scanners.

"A what?" Coups happened on Earth, where actual governments and functioning societies existed. Mars was less a separate world than a corporate outpost. How could it have happened?

As though reading her mind, Amit turned the nearest monitor toward Kezza.

"Look at this," he said, opening a headline titled, 'CHAOS IN CALYPSO: Corpsboard members executed in Atrium. REAL LIVE STREAM'.

He opened the link, which revealed grainy live footage from the Calypso Atrium. The same Atrium, except for the crowds massing in the center of the yawning room. Fists rose from the center of the gathering, moving in unison to an indecipherable chant. Other figures hovered around the crowd's perimeter, documenting the moment on their CALPals.

Kezza's heart dropped. Above the crowd, dark shapes swung from the rafters. Human shapes. Juul drew in a sharp breath at her side. The light from the monitor shone on Juul's face, giving his skin a greenish, sickly hue. No doubt he had seen similar events unfold on Earth, but he stood transfixed, eyes locked on the swinging bodies.

"Axel managed to get in touch with some members of your circus troupe," Amit said. "Following our escape, rumors spread around the city that Barrett had been arrested after putting out the fire, under torture in Bokambe. The protests grew until they breached the sector. It's not clear who's winning yet, but rumor is that Dr. Hamza is back in the city from the Obscura, suggesting that it's tipping in our favor."

Kezza sank back onto the bed. The camera zoomed in closer, revealing one of the hanging figures to be one of the Corpsboard women who had come to that private circus performance for Juul. Kezza disliked the woman. She disliked the entire Corpsboard, the Tier Ones and Twos, the system they upheld. Seeing it fall before her eyes left her transfixed, warm exhilaration flooding her veins. But nausea enveloped her at the sight of the swinging dead, the jeering crowd pulling shoes off their feet.

"Are there any other deaths we know about?" Kezza asked, her mind jumping to LaValle, Sergei and the rest of the troupe. The Imam at the prayer room, who always welcomed her. She closed her eyes against a wave of dizziness.

"It's chaos, that's all we know. Security fought back when people stormed the upper levels, so it's possible that a lot of people were killed and hurt. We don't know. But word's spread across Palmcorps. Everyone's on edge. Our own authorities are frightened of the same thing happening here, so you can bet they'll ramp up security quickly, maybe even try to round up our ringleaders. Axel's calling a meeting. They may try to seize the momentum and replicate the same thing here."

"He wants to release the footage across Palmcorps," Juul stated. Not a question, a statement of fact.

"Maybe he should," Kezza said. When Juul stared at her, brows raised, she continued. "If Palmcorps authorities are anything like the ones in Calypso, they won't take chances. People saw you. If they suspect you're here, they'll raid the Catacombs and we'll all be getting our fingernails ripped out in a matter of hours. We need to draw the first fire."

"You sound like Axel," Juul said. "That's almost verbatim what he told me when he shook me out of bed."

"She's Martian," a voice boomed behind her. Axel strode into the medical ward, pale but alight with purpose. "She knows how things work here. If you won't listen to me, listen to the dancer. This is our moment."

A tense silence followed. Evgenia trailed in the room behind Axel, a baton swinging from her hip. Amit met Kezza's eyes before he turned back to Juul, arms rigid. Juul looked at no one, his gaze turned inward and far away at the same time, lost in calculation. Finally, he spoke.

"Fine, release the footage," he said. "But to your and Kezza's point, I'm vulnerable once we escalate things on Palmcorps. A perfect time for our group to leave the city and procure the sample from the crater, now that we have the coordinates from your wonderful team. We'll return once the dust settles in whichever city is most secure, a solution in hand."

"Fair enough," Axel said. "Amit will accompany you to the crater."

Juul bristled, likely more accustomed to giving orders than receiving them.

"But your people had better get a handle on the violence that follows," Juul continued in a harsher voice. "You need to minimize civilian casualties. If the Corpsboard surrender, let them. If the guards put down their weapons, accept their surrender. If we become the villains, everything will backfire."

Axel nodded, although the steely glint in his eyes didn't promise mercy.

Chants rose from the hallways outside. A single name, barked through the airways like a siren.

Juul. Juul. Juul. Juul.

Barrett Juul slid his helmet on. He fumbled with the latches until Evgenia stepped forward, gently securing it. Kezza donned her own suit. She felt dizzy, her heart thundering against her ribs. Once the suit activated, it immediately went into alarm mode, displaying her racing pulse, her fever and state of near hyperventilation. She ignored the warnings and focused on her breath. Finally, her pulse lowered. She'd been waiting for this moment. Change was coming and she would ride on its first wave.

The Catacombs were already stirring. Crowds gathered in open rooms along the corridor, huddled around screens displaying the carnage on Calypso. Tension coiled the air around them like an electric charge, carrying the stillness that always precedes violence. Kezza felt it in the corridors of Calypso during the lockdown, and later when she was dragged from the Coliseum over the outraged cries of the crowd. In an hour, Palmcorps' walls would echo with stunner fire and screams.

And while the carnage raged within its confines, Kezza would see the crater. The source of their turmoil, the catalyst of the last few weeks that felt like years. Something trying to kill her nestled in the rocks of Arabia Terra, and she would meet it.

In the Catacombs' grimy, narrow docking bay, Juul turned to them with a strange smile.

"Let's go meet this crater."

Chapter Fifteen
Azad

ARABIA TERRA, MARS
YEAR OF SETTLEMENT 1208

The Glider slowed as it neared the base of a high ridge, at the bleeding edge of the crater. Warnings flashed, messages popped up, algorithms from the *Magreb* trying to save Zelle's crew from themselves.

Hazardous environment detected.

Indeed there was, although hazardous was a relative term. The very air around them was hazardous, although less so to Feisal. But the *Magreb*, sitting in its dark hiding spot while the Glider fed it data, detected a more immediate danger on the other side of the crater's edge. A chill ran through Azad. Even behind his atmosphere suit, a sense of the unnatural reached him.

The crater sat north of Calypso, in the no man's land in which the ancient Martian corporations mined for ore.

"A precious substance at the time," Zelle said, panting as they struggled up the crater's peak. At least, most of them struggled. Feisal strode several feet ahead of them with the miniature version of Barry over his shoulder, practically flying on air.

"So you think they discovered it back then?" Nawalle asked.

"We'll find out," Zelle said, nodding at Barry. "But I suspect it's no coincidence that the *Axel* station has taken such an interest in this crater, after searching for their origins on Mars. Whatever is in here might just be connected to why Barrett Juul and the Martians left."

"And dangerous," Feisal called out cheerfully ahead. "Killed an entire research station of people, aside from Ledo and that Vitruvian lady. May I suggest we proceed with caution?"

"Why do you think we're letting you go first?" Nawalle retorted.

At the top, Azad held his breath. The crater was massive, the size of the main hospital in Nabatea City, and unnervingly deep. Its dark floor stretched out before them, scarred with rocky hills and curving slopes of sand, the product of endless windstorms. In a dark corner, something shone back at them. Something blue.

"Water?" Azad asked, incredulous.

"Not likely, *hadir*," Feisal said.

They descended toward the crater's base, each step heavy with caution. Azad fumbled at his atmosphere suit, checking for any vulnerabilities, even though the suit's stat readings assured his safety.

"Look!" Nawalle rushed forward and picked something off the ground. Zelle drew in a sharp breath. Nawalle held it up to the group. A bronze pin shaped like a palm tree bent into a circle. Adrenaline rushed through Azad's veins.

"The Khazneh neighborhood pin," he said. "Ledo had one."

"She kept it," Nawalle said, her voice as choked as Azad's. "Had nothing good to say about life there, but she never threw it away."

"Until now," Zelle said. "Either she lost it or left it behind on purpose. A breadcrumb for someone else to find."

Azad gripped the pin in his suited hand, as though he could absorb something of Ledo from its smooth skin. He suspected she had been here, most likely involuntarily as part of the experiment in the research hole. But he had not expected to find a piece of her that was so familiar to him, a childhood relic.

A deeper pocket at the base of the crater opened into a cave. They advanced, following the blue light. As they drew closer, the phosphorous substance shimmered along a deep gash on the floor. It stretched down farther than they could see, lining the walls like honeycombs, filled with grooves and ridges. It looked alive, and Azad could have sworn he heard something beside the crew's sharp, shallow breaths, a steady rumbling.

"What is it?" Azad heard the words, then realized he had spoken them.

"According to our recently deceased friend, an alien substance," Feisal said. "A bacteria or virus, perhaps, given the effect it seems to have."

"Stay where you are," Zelle instructed the crew, her voice firm. "Don't get any closer."

Azad's doctoring instinct agreed, but his scientific mind itched with curiosity. "Is there any value in getting a sample?" he asked.

Zelle shook her head. "We're not here to conduct a scientific breakthrough. We're historians. What matters here is what others have done before."

They started with Ledo. Not knowing when exactly the Vitruvians had exposed her to this place, they had to uncover the timeframe the hard way — letting the quantum projector rewind through time while they waited. It required significant dark energy for the tracker to measure that many observational probabilities, forcing them to pause the device from time to time to allow it to regenerate.

Before them, the substance continued to pulse, waves of blue shivering along the crater's walls. Beautiful and terrible. Azad fought against two conflicting impulses — to run away and to reach out and touch its surface, to peel away its secrets. Instead, he let his feet sink into the ground.

"I'm worried about the *Magreb*, now that we know there's Vitruvian ships nearby," Nawalle ventured between one of the breaks.

"It's in stealth mode, isn't it?" Zelle asked.

"It is, but it's not far from Calypso. It wouldn't be impossible for Vitruvian reconnaissance to spot it if they were looking, and they might be looking now. Stealth mode has failed us in the past, if you'll recall, and the *Magreb* barely made it out." Nawalle spoke of the ship with the same weight she would assign a person, and after seeing the amount of back and forth the mechanic held with the ship, Azad could understand why.

A flashing of color interrupted the debate. Next to the substance, figures took form under the tracker lens's gaze, moving in reverse. Feisal slowed the device down and moved time forward.

Under the machine's lens, a group of about ten people in atmosphere suits approached the blue substance, pausing with the same hesitation as Zelle's crew. Several, however, immediately set to work. They sent mechs forward to bring samples. Once delivered, the figures raised vials of phosphorous blue toward the dimming sun, peering through their helmets. At another leader's beckoning, the rest formed a single line, like children in Township queuing up for class. Azad walked around the projected scene, scanning part of the line for a recognizable face through the vizors. None of them were familiar, although the Vitruvian man who died in the outpost might have been nearby, watching the proceedings from a safe distance while others put their lives on the line.

Several taller, leaner figures looked to be Vitruvian, a fact confirmed when one took off her helmet. The woman reeled for a moment before her chemistry went to work, acclimating to the lack of oxygen and the freezing temperature. With a grim face, likely amplified by the cold assaulting her bare skin, she wordlessly poured one of the blue vials into her mouth.

At the same time, another Vitruvian next to her performed a similar action, except he only consumed half of a vial. Both doubled over, the one who consumed the full dose collapsing to the ground with blood pooling around her eyes, dead, while the other merely stumbled back up the hill, where a vehicle or isolation tent presumably waited.

Azad stared in numb horror. Zelle drew in a sharp breath.

"And here you have proof of what I've always said, crew," Feisal said with a bitter laugh. "We Vitruvians are no more intelligent than the rest of you. Stronger and more adaptable, without a doubt. But we're just as prone to stupidity as the so-called mindless herd."

Recovering from shock, Azad, who had internalized the very opposite message all his life, couldn't help but agree. Stupidity laced with madness.

"So desperate to prove our superiority, they've demonstrated the very opposite," Feisal continued, anger rising in his voice.

Back under the tracker's eye, the remaining group awaited their doses. After witnessing the dead Vitruvian being dragged away, one of the suited figures struggled, only to be held down and administered an injection. Others received their own injections with different amounts, while another Vitruvian removed a glove, placing their hand directly into the substance with a shiver. Azad gasped. It was Nenah, the Vitruvian woman who escaped with Ledo. The woman who died under his care. After seeing what she had done, any lingering guilt about his failure dissolved faster than bodies in acid. She could never have survived, after this.

"What are they doing?" Nawalle murmured.

"Experimenting with doses," Azad said. "And degrees of exposure. Like the man in that awful place said…they were expecting Vitruvians and ordinary Nabateans to react differently. But they didn't."

A subset of the group stepped away, training weapons on the remainders, who shifted and struggled. The remainder of the Vitruvians, Azad guessed, had seen enough and didn't wish to commit suicide for their experiment. The orthodox 'volunteers', on the other hand, were disposable. A tremor of anger ran through Azad, knowing their later fate. Slow deaths, followed by the desecration of their bodies. All to prove Vitruvian superiority. But the scene before him told Azad all he needed to know about Vitruvian rule.

Azad walked closer, scanning through the line of helmeted figures for Ledo's face. She must have been among them, one of many to be dosed. The only one to survive.

"Azad, get back," Zelle warned. He hovered dangerously close to the blue substance, but Azad continued to pace along the line.

After the remaining Nabateans received their dose, the ringleaders ushered the group back up the hill. A solitary figure lingered in the back, facing the cave's depths. A small object slipped from her hand.

"Ledo," Azad murmured, rushing forward. The object fell at the spot where Nawalle had found it only moments ago. Within seconds, two figures seized her arms and dragged her forward.

"Let's follow her," Azad said.

"We know what happens because we've seen it already," Feisal said with an edge to his voice. "They go back to that outpost, everyone slowly dies and infects each other, and Ledo and your former patient escape. But we know something else now, Doctor. She got the smallest dose. Did you notice that? And another thing – she didn't come back here. The most recent human activity is what we just witnessed. So we'll go back and find out where she and her friend ran off to, after we see who else has been here during Juul's time."

"Wait," Nawalle said, surprised. "Did you just see what happened? Ledo's been directly infected. She could be dying as we speak. We have to look for her now."

"We're here for more than just a rescue operation," Feisal said, not unkindly. "Ledo made her choice."

"How can you say that?" Azad bellowed. "She was on your crew. She lived with you."

"*Was* on our crew. She left."

Azad and Nawalle faced their captain. Through the thick vizor, Zelle's face was unreadable but her voice, though soft, radiated authority.

"First we find out what happened here during Juul's time," she said. "Then we retrace Ledo's steps."

A standoff formed. Azad and Nawalle stood side by side, facing Zelle and Feisal. The Vitruvian's lean frame tensed, as though coiled for a strike at the first hint of insubordination. But Azad no longer cared. Seeing Ledo under the cave's blue light, the reality of her plight made the next decision clear. He refused to follow orders that would kill his sister. But this was about more than Ledo. He would not be part of a crew that, like the Vitruvians, put their lives second to a discovery.

Azad broke the silence.

"I'm going," he said. "I'm taking the Glider with me."

Nawalle gasped. Azad took several steps back toward the hill.

"I have made my decision," Zelle said, and the soft silkiness in her voice held more danger than any barked order. "You will remain here."

As though sensing his next decision before Azad knew it himself, Feisal took several steps forward, letting the tracker roll off his shoulder. His eyes shone through his vizor, a predatory gaze.

"I knew you didn't belong with us, *hadir*," he said with the same, ominous softness. "Can't think past yourself and your childish impulses. You don't even know the sister you're chasing."

"I know she matters, just like those people all mattered!" Azad yelled. Tears stung his eyes. "If you don't care enough to save her, then you're no better than them!"

Silence greeted his words, but the Vitruvian continued his slow, winding advance. If Feisal came after him, Azad wouldn't stand a chance. Everything in the Vitruvian's stance said that he would strike to kill. That he would even relish the opportunity.

And so Azad turned away from him and faced Zelle.

"I'm sorry," he said softly.

Azad would only have seconds, if that long. He pushed himself off the ground with all his strength, lunging forward. The captain's eyes widened. Shouts rang in his earpiece and movement flashed in the corner of his eye, but he charged at Zelle, his hand raised with Ledo's sharp pin. As they collided, his arm shot forward, puncturing Zelle's atmosphere suit just below her shoulder.

A furious cry followed. Azad rolled away, but not quick enough to evade a sharp kick to the side of his helmeted head. Red stars flooded his vision and the ground lurched, but he could breathe. Despite the dizzying force, the helmet stayed latched to his suit.

Azad scrambled to his feet. As he'd hoped, Feisal rushed to Zelle, who fought to close the tear in her suit. It wouldn't take them long to seal it. A comfort and source of fear, as he sprinted up the hill as fast as his legs and gravity would allow.

"You're dead for this, traitor!" Feisal yelled.

The Glider waited just over the hill. Azad crawled up the crater's edge, heart pounding in his throat. He sensed rather than saw another person at his heels. Afraid to turn around and leave his face vulnerable to an enraged Vitruvian, he hurled himself on the Glider's rails. A pair of hands gripped the rail next to his. Nawalle.

"Let's go," she said.

He didn't need to be told twice. The engine came to life. Barry weighed the Glider down, causing it to shudder before acceleration took effect, but the device sped across the rocky plain as Feisal charged over the crater. Red dust gave his tall frame an almost ethereal quality, a desert phantom as distant, but no less frightening, than the past figures they had chased across Arabia Terra.

Nawalle did not look back. Holding Barry steady with one hand, she trained her eyes forward with an unreadable expression. She adjusted the coordinates.

"Back to the outpost," she said. "And we'll follow Ledo."

"We'll find her," Azad said, for himself as much as for her.

Chapter Sixteen
Kezza

ARABIA TERRA, MARS
2195 A.D.

Kezza held out her hand as though in a trance, blinking back tears. How could something be so sinister and beautiful at once? The cave revealed a wall of crystalline blue. Veins of light radiated across the walls like a web, filling their surroundings with a vivid, otherworldly glow at odds with the monotonous Martian landscape.

The contrast made one thing clear – the substance was not Martian.

"How did it get here?" she said aloud. Nearby, Amit knelt in front of the blue wall, unpacking his equipment.

"Your guess is as good as mine," he said.

"A comet, then." A comet laden with organic matter crashing into a lonely, uncolonized Mars appealed to Kezza more than an alien spacecraft or bioweapon missile, both ideas that Amit volunteered as they first entered the cave. A comet felt more probable, an anchor of scientific plausibility Kezza could grasp.

Juul stumbled nearby, teetering dangerously close to the substance. He extended a gloved hand toward the rippling surface.

"Not by accident," he said. He spoke as though in a fever. "No coincidence…so perfect. Meant to be."

Amit made a clicking sound with his mouth but continued the practical work of obtaining a sample. A small mech slid toward the lower edge of the wall, vials stacked in its thin, metallic arm.

They found the crater abandoned, although tire tracks and outpost holes signaled earlier human activity. Kezza paced along the glowing wall, piecing together what she knew. Miners had been exposed first, along with Evan and Nancy Kim, and all were taken to Calypso for monitoring. How exactly they had been exposed remained unclear. No doubt they would have been wearing atmosphere suits. Perhaps one of the miners came into direct contact, falling through the cave into the substance, and exposed others in turn?

And now I'm here, of my own free will, Kezza thought. Contaminated, compromised and staring down her slow-moving killer in all its beauty and mystery.

"It looks alive," she said to Amit. "Is it…some kind of alien?" Her cheeks warmed. The question sounded absurd spoken aloud, but Amit didn't laugh.

"It's a virus, Kezza, so it's alive and not alive, depending on how you define it," Amit said. "It behaves like a virus, but not just any virus. It's been engineered."

"Engineered?" Kezza's pulse quickened. Nearby, Juul remained in his trance, muttering about beauty and fate.

"Viruses are great at mutating DNA," Amit continued. Using a pair of forceps, he scraped a vial against the wall, the glowing substance dripping into the container. Carefully, he handed the substance back to the mech for storage. "But most viruses don't have a fixed pattern in how they alter DNA. This one is different. It only affects a specific line of DNA, in every patient I've tested – including you. I'm not talking about symptoms, Sayer – I'm talking about the DNA itself. The fact that it behaves this way means that it's not a typical, natural virus – it's been intelligently designed."

Intelligently designed. But by what? And perhaps more importantly, why?

As though reading her mind, Evgenia chimed in her ear. "Could it have been put here by Calypso or some other Earth Corp?"

"Impossible," Juul said. He turned to Amit and Kezza as though he had just noticed them. "This is a gift from another civilization. It can't possibly be human. The technology to produce something like this doesn't exist."

"As far as we know," Evgenia said. The clipped tone in her voice, audible even through the long-distance static, suggested she didn't like Juul's answer. Kezza didn't either, for that matter. A human-engineered bioweapon, while horrifying, at least made sense. But another thought simmered, as Amit stored his samples with clinical precision.

"Maybe it isn't meant to kill," she said slowly. "It just kills us because we don't know how to use it. It makes people stronger, faster, able to even survive atmosphere without getting boiled on the spot. Maybe it's some kind of...evolutionary aid."

Juul turned to Kezza. Through his vizor, his eyes danced with a wild, joyful glow.

"Exactly, Kezza! We saw it as a threat only because we didn't understand it – we didn't know its potential. But if it comes from a civilization capable of traversing between worlds, and leaving traces behind, then we'd be foolish not to learn from it."

Unease gnawed at Kezza as she took in this new Barrett Juul, stripped of polish and decorum. An excited boy stood before her, one with big dreams and a limitless imagination who had just learned that magic, of a certain kind, existed. Part of her shared Amit's caution, aware that the substance inside her was slowly killing her. But what if Juul was right?

A loud screech flooded her suit's auditory system. Kezza collapsed to her knees, hands wrapped around her vizor. Nearby, Amit swore loudly.

"Evgenia, what's going on back there?"

After a pause, Evgenia spoke in a tighter voice than usual.

"Palmcorps Security are in the Catacombs," she said. "Fighting room to room. Axel's going to seal off the lowest two floors. I better move."

"Evgenia, are you safe?" Juul asked sharply, all business now. He moved away from the substance, as though tearing himself from an invisible spell.

"Trust me, I'm the hardest person in this city to kill," she said, a hint of a sneer in her voice, but the unmistakable screams and thuds in the background signaled that the Palmcorps resistance, and the people of Palmcorps by default, were in trouble. "Oh, shit! I better go."

Silence followed. Amit stood up.

"Back to the vehicle," Juul said.

An even louder crackling sound filled Kezza's ears.

"Did you hear that?" Kezza asked, but Amit raised his hand. He gestured toward the periphery of the cave, silent.

They were not alone.

Silently, they walked out to find five suited figures, bearing Palmcorps insignias on their atmosphere suits and stunners in their hands.

Amit slowly raised his hands, still holding the case with the substance, and Kezza followed suit. Juul spoke first.

"We surrender on the condition that—"

A force like wind struck Kezza, knocking her off her feet. The sky spun past her as she landed with a thud, sliding backward down the cave. Juul yelled through her earpiece, jumping in front of her to shield her. Arms reached forward, pulling him away while he struggled.

Kezza fought to stand but the ground wouldn't stop spinning. Her face numbed, her fingers tingling. Suddenly, she was back in the air again, carried by her arms and feet. Her mouth opened but no sound escaped. Behind her, the blue light from the cave grew distant.

Light flooded the crater. The ground rumbled, loose rocks chattering against the surface like teeth. Whoever carried Kezza dropped her unceremoniously. Yells in her earpiece, cries for help, followed by silence.

Her ears rang. Her senses returned, the numbness fading. A temporary stunner, designed to neutralize her without causing any real harm.

Shaking, Kezza pulled herself up. The five suited figures spread across the ground, unmoving. One lay on her back, vizor cracked to reveal a lifeless face behind it. All dead.

A large transport vehicle loomed above them, on top of the crater. The Calypso insignia shone on its side. Apparently, it had fired down on the smaller vehicle carrying the Palmcorps guards, eliminating the arrest party. An inter-corporate skirmish. Now, a new set of guards spilled from the larger vehicle. When they reached the trio, no one fought. Juul led the way in silence, flanked by the guards, while Kezza and Amit were dragged behind. Bile rose in Kezza's throat, but her body hung limp. Palmcorps authorities had followed them, only to be beaten by an even more lethal foe. They would return to Calypso, back to the Bokambe sector.

Kezza landed in a transport vehicle with a thud. Rough hands removed her helmet and she sucked in stale, circulated air. Amit lay on the vehicle's floor at her side, cursing.

"Are you all right, Kezza?"

"I think so," she gasped.

"What the hell is going on?" Juul spat.

"Barrett." A female voice.

In front of them, Dr. Saadia Hamza sat with her hands folded in her lap. Two armed guards stood behind her, faces stretched in triumphant smiles.

"I hoped to find you here," she said with a grin to match. "You can thank the Calypso Corpsboard for inserting a tracker in your friend here." She nodded at Kezza.

"Wha-what's going—" Juul sputtered.

"We've won. Calypso is ours."

Part Three

The Vitruvian Vector

Nature is inherently exploitative. Predator eats prey, plants feed off the soil and we feed off the plants. When it comes to human social systems, however, we abhor hierarchies and structures that exploit one group for the benefit of the other. It took our Earth-based ancestors centuries to reach that conclusion and even more time to war over it, as we veered back and forth between political systems and ideologies. Human hierarchies are bad, we all agreed, but what about hierarchies between different types of human? I do not refer to artificial constructs, like race and gender, but a true evolutionary split. If the Neanderthals survived us and lived among us, would we expect equality? Would we expect to be treated the same, to act the same? Hierarchies do not have to become evils, if they are logical, based in tangible truths, compassionately formed and serve to the benefit of all. Thus, in the early days of Nabatean settlement, I called upon those of us who are Vitruvian to continue my legacy and to build this city's workforce, its neighborhoods, its education and health systems, with a hierarchy in mind. A benign exploitation, where human nature's worst impulses are curtailed in the unevolved among us but its best impulses set free, unconstrained by labor, in the Vitruvian people.

From The Teachings and Sayings of Barrett Juul, Founder of Nabatea

But how could you live and have no story to tell?
'White Nights', Fyodor Dostoevsky

Chapter Seventeen

Azad

MARTIAN DESERT
YEAR OF SETTLEMENT 1208

Barry proved fitful when they first reached the outpost, as though sensing its parent had been replaced by less competent operators, but Nawalle brought him to life. They knew the exact time when Ledo and Nenah escaped from the outpost, so it proved easy to trace the moment when they emerged from the hellish hole in the ground. Ledo wore a clumsily assembled atmosphere suit but Nenah, being Vitruvian, had opted to rush into the nearest vehicle without one, and helped Ledo inside.

"And now we follow them," Azad said.

Nawalle nodded, keeping Barry's lens trained ahead while Azad started the engine. She barely spoke after their flight from the crater, except to wonder aloud whether Zelle and Feisal would find shelter before Zelle's oxygen supply ran out.

Their answer came an hour later, as they sped across the desert, struggling to keep up with Ledo and Nenah's powerful Vitruvian hover transport, which weaved in and out of Barry's line of vision. A scream rose from the sky, the ground rumbling. They craned their necks to find the *Magreb* flying overhead, tearing in the opposite direction.

"How…?" Azad began, once the screaming engine dimmed.

"I didn't think of that," Nawalle said. "There wasn't time to think. Feisal can call the ship."

"With his mind?"

"No, not with his mind," Nawalle snapped. "He has a device. A distress beacon. It can bring the *Magreb* to wherever he is." Relief and fear battled through her voice and Azad's skin crawled under a similar rush of conflicting emotion. Zelle and Feisal would survive. He was not a killer. But they had a powerful ship on their side, one that could catch up with them quickly if they felt inclined to chase them.

And if they didn't follow them, what then? How would they return to Nabatea if Zelle decided to abandon half of her traitorous crew? All their hopes for survival would hinge on Ledo – that she was alive, still on Mars and had been smarter than them in planning an escape.

"Look, up ahead!" Nawalle pointed.

White shapes emerged in the distant landscape like shells in the sand. Azad's mouth fell open. Palmcorps, or what was left of it. It could only have been Mars's second ancient city that Ledo and Nenah sped toward. Where Kezza Sayer must have gone, had they continued to follow her. All roads, it seemed, led to Palmcorps.

Palmcorps' surviving surfaces glinted like shards of glass ahead of them. Robots and larger, self-directed machines flooded the stretch of sand where Palmcorps once lay, conducting an elaborate excavation. Lumbering machines dug a large pit into the earth, through which mechs extracted pieces of concrete and pipes, while smaller robots went to work on digging up and scanning other sections of the scattered city.

"So the Vitruvians found it," Azad said through gritted teeth. "And Ledo went directly to them."

"Not necessarily," Nawalle said. "They've sent machines to excavate, but it doesn't mean that Vitruvians are there or even monitoring their activity directly. It's not unusual to send mechanized units to perform the dirty work on another planet before a human sets foot on the area. That's how Cerata was made livable."

The hover transport veered west and Azad followed its course. He ached for a way to peer inside the vehicle, to see Ledo's face. What had she and the Vitruvian woman planned, if they even planned at all? Only Nenah had stumbled into the Central Nabatean Hospital, on the piercing edge of death. Where had her path diverged from Ledo's?

Azad blinked back tears. Anxiety, Juul's teachings had emphasized, was the by-product of future-centered thinking. Better to focus on the moment and discover what he could. Even Barry couldn't unravel the future.

The hover transport ground to a stop in front of a small, unmistakably modern building on a hill overlooking Palmcorps. A Vitruvian outpost. Azad's hand twitched, itching for a weapon he wouldn't know how to use. About a hundred meters away stood a small launching pad, designed to propel ships directly upward into space. They shifted Barry in the pad's direction, revealing that a small recon shuttle had sat there when Ledo and Nenah arrived.

"No shuttle today, so hopefully no one's here to bother us," Nawalle said, echoing his sentiments. They had already had one unpleasant encounter in a Vitruvian outpost.

The two women emerged from their own vehicle, both now geared for the atmosphere. One of them hid a weapon across her back – a Vitruvian dagger. Azad assumed that was Nenah, but Ledo had proved herself dangerous. They stumbled toward the outpost, leaning on each other for support. Exchanging a silent glance, Azad and Nawalle disembarked from the Glider and followed them.

Thankfully, the present-day outpost proved empty, but the past version under Barry's lens showed an active Vitruvian station, shelves rich with supplies. And two Vitruvians inside. They shot to their feet when the door burst open. The suited figure with the dagger removed her helmet, revealing herself to be Nenah. She said something to the two Vitruvians, arms flailing in panic. As they moved closer to help, she swung her arm.

Azad had seen Vitruvian daggers in the Khazneh Arena, worn by Vitruvian dignitaries for ceremonial events, but had never seen one put to cruel purpose. Nenah spun with an incredible burst of strength, arm forming a graceful arc through the air. The two Vitruvians jerked back quickly, but not fast enough. The blade found both their necks, opening the skin like peeled fruit. Blood seeped out from the narrow wounds while at the same time, to Azad's horror, the veins around their necks darkened through their skin, spreading down their bodies and up to their heads, where their pupils swelled like black stones.

"I think Feisal said the blade is coated with something to mess with their circulation and respiratory system," Nawalle said. "Vitruvians can self-heal, but only to a point. The dagger shuts too many systems down at once."

Azad swallowed. Ledo removed her helmet, surveying the dead Vitruvians with indifference. Only a month into the past, she shone with sharp clarity under Barry's lens, so clear that they could have been standing in the room with them at that very moment. Up close, the subtleties materialized in Ledo's face – the way a dimple formed between her brows when she frowned, how her lips thinned when she prepared to speak.

The two women raided the supply shelves. They ate with primal urgency between gulps of water. Once satiated, they inhaled, ingested and injected various medications and stimulants. Both appeared ill, although Nenah far more so. The attack had taken its toll on her. She wiped sweat from her forehead and scratched at her arms between self-administered doses.

Though Nawalle and Azad could not hear their conversation, the two women appeared to argue over their next steps. Both gestured in the direction of Palmcorps, Nenah occasionally pointing upward before covering her mouth in a fit of coughing. They either came to an agreement or reached an impasse, because both women stood, embraced briefly and put their suits back on.

Outside the station, Ledo reentered the vehicle while the Vitruvian woman ran to the launch shuttle.

Nawalle paused Barry. "I wonder why they split up. Guess we're following Ledo, but I'm afraid I have an idea where she's going."

Nawalle's suspicions seemed to be confirmed when they resumed their cross-desert chase. Ledo's vehicle slowed.

"Palmcorps," she moaned. "Look, she's going right in."

They paused. Mechs flooded the ancient city, digging and scanning. If they were to follow Ledo, they would need a way to slip through the excavation site undetected.

Out of his depth, Azad let Nawalle pace across the Glider, letting the gears in her mechanic's mind spin with ideas. Or so he assumed – she muttered furiously under her breath, eyes flashing with bursts of thought.

"Feisal would probably go with that...no, too easy to run into surprises...but how do we lug Barry around and keep him hidden...oh!"

Nawalle's plan was close to perfect, provided they could succeed with the first, and most dangerous, part. They left the Glider hidden in the shadow of a steep hill and dragged Barry closer to Palmcorps' outskirts, on the edge of the excavation area.

They waited until a mech neared, rolling across the sand while it scanned its surroundings. Ledo's pin rested in the sand nearby and Nawalle shone a light on it. Catching the glint, the mech changed course.

When Azad had suggested throwing a rock to lure a mech, Nawalle explained that the machines were looking for relics and bones, not signs of life. Luring them with movement could be risky.

But move they would, once the robot drew closer. The mech rolled through a narrow dip in the hills, training its scanner on the pin. Nawalle crouched on one side behind a boulder, Azad on the other. Their eyes met. Nawalle held up her hand, shaking slightly, waiting, before she lowered it. Time to strike.

Azad leapt and jammed a metal rod into the mech's wheel. It tottered over before the scanner could turn. Immediately, Nawalle pounced on top of it, ripping its controls open. She yanked out its circuitry before carefully extracting a small chip from its bowels.

Azad dragged the deactivated mech behind the boulder while Nawalle went to work on Barry.

"Feisal's going to kill me for doing this," Nawalle muttered, opening Barry's complex interior. "But it shouldn't harm anything as long as I'm careful. Of course, Feisal might kill me anyway."

Azad stood over her in silence, searching for the right response.

"They'll forgive you, Nawalle," he said gently. "You've been part of the crew for a long time. And they know how you felt about Ledo. It's me that—"

"I knew what leaving them meant," she said. "We're very far away from home and we can't succeed if we're pursuing our own agendas. But Ledo is more than an agenda to me. I made my choice."

Azad nodded. She closed up the circuitry.

"Here comes the test," she said.

Barry whirred to life. Nawalle ran back to the Glider, turned on the system's scanner and raised her thumb in triumph.

"It reads as a Vitruvian device now," she said. "The locator chip took, so when we take Barry into Palmcorps, it will come across as one of their machines on an ID scan. As long as there isn't a sentient person looking around, we should be able to pass freely. We'll ride him in."

"But couldn't they still scan us and see carbon-based life?" Azad asked. If these mechs were like the medmechs back in the hospital, they knew the difference between metal and living beings.

"You're going to love this," Nawalle said. She shifted from foot to foot. "Actually, I'm lying. You're going to hate this. We'll have to make a run for it. Stand on the back of Barry, make ourselves as small as possible, and try to keep the mechs from spotting us."

"What?" Azad's stomach twisted. "But the second one of those mechs spots a living organism, they'll flag us."

"They're busy and we're smart," Nawalle said. "We've got Barry flagged as a Vitruvian vehicle. We just have to be quick and stealthy, and hopefully these little digger mechs won't piece together that they don't work for us."

Azad grimaced but nodded. Nawalle was right – any plan was going to carry risk, and this was the best plan they had. They couldn't avoid danger. And after all Azad had experienced on Mars, he no longer wanted the option free of danger, because that was usually the option where he surrendered what mattered most. He smiled grimly. Osbourne wouldn't recognize him now.

"Let's do it," he said. "But let's agree on a strategy if the mechs do spot us and try to take us hostage." The calmness in his voice surprised him.

"Worse comes to worst, we can flag the *Magreb*," Nawalle said. "And hope that Captain Zelle sees reason."

Azad sighed. In their current predicament, calling the *Magreb* would be its own form of danger. Azad feared Zelle and Feisal's wrath almost as much as the *Axel*'s Vitruvian crew. Nawalle must have been thinking along similar lines, because she patted Azad's shoulder, dark eyes alight with sympathy behind her vizor.

"I know contacting Zelle is the last thing you want to do now, but we have to keep the option open once we find Ledo," she said. "And we have to try to find her! We've come this far. Listen, keep in mind that these mechs aren't designed to hunt for wayward Nabateans – they're here to excavate and research. They won't be looking for us. If we're quick and stealthy, we have a fighting chance."

Gritting his teeth, Azad nodded and placed a gloved hand over Nawalle's. When it came to Ledo, they were united. She had ventured into this abandoned city alone – they owed it to her to trace her steps.

They switched Barry back on and picked up Ledo's trail into Palmcorps, standing together on the small footrest attached behind Barry. Azad's skin prickled at the sight of the first mech exiting a crumbling structure before them, but it continued its trajectory, oblivious.

Without any form of concealment, Ledo had followed their tactic of stealth and speed. She disembarked from her own vehicle once she neared the main building, zigzagging across the ruins and ducking for cover at regular intervals. On several occasions, a confrontation forced itself upon her. A mech would catch her darting from building to building and she would lunge forward, taking a move from Nawalle by ripping out their circuitry. Nawalle giggled softly each time, pride shining through her eyes, but Azad jolted at the sight of each mech. Bracing against the sand-swept winds, it was hard to tell past from present under Barry's gaze. The back of his neck tingled where Osbourne had once been to help him, to give him choices. But now his only option was to press forward and risk everything, as Ledo had done.

Ledo weaved around the site with surprising strength and unnatural speed. She leapt behind shelters with ease, her movements swift and focused.

Like Kezza Sayer, Azad thought. *Almost like a Vitruvian.*

They drove Barry deeper into the partially collapsed main building, revealing layers of structure underground. Another mech wheeled around the corner, facing them. Azad yelped. Nawalle raised a device in her hand – the call to the *Magreb* – but before she could act, the mech spun in a circle, oblivious, before gliding away.

"What just happened?" Azad said. He started to sweat under his helmet.

"It didn't register us," Nawalle said, pocketing her device. "That, or it didn't care. Interesting."

Azad gripped Barry's handles and crouched lower, not entirely convinced. The machine could have feigned ignorance and sent an alert to the *Axel*. But they pressed forward, passing the mech again on the other side of the building, with no response.

Inside the city, the mechs showed a stronger presence, their precise hands brushing away layers of rubble. In Ledo's world, however, she moved through the main building's interior with less traffic. Perhaps the excavators had not yet reached Palmcorps' innermost levels when she arrived.

Azad and Nawalle pressed together as Barry picked up speed across the open floor plan. But once again, the mechs in present time behaved oddly. Some did not perform their work at all, simply rolling back and forth or sitting immobile. The occasional mech spun in erratic circles, or attempted to push through walls, bumping into them repeatedly.

"What are they doing?" Nawalle said, frowning.

"It looks like they're operating without direction," Azad said, puzzled. "Or their directions are out of date. As if no one's managing them." *Like me without Osbourne steering my every move.* Was this how Azad looked to Zelle and her crew at first, like a mech who had lost direction? No more. No one, Vitruvian or otherwise, would make decisions for him again.

Ledo opened a heavy metal door in front of them. Azad opened the same door, surprised to find a fully intact hallway inside.

"It might be breathable," he said softly. He ran his suit's external scanner, detecting the right cocktail of oxygen, natural gases and temperature. He removed his helmet.

"Careful," Nawalle said, but followed suit when Azad failed to keel over. After hours in the open Martian desert, they needed relief and their suits needed a recharge of oxygen. Azad breathed deeply, cool air tickling his throat.

Ahead of them, Ledo glanced over her shoulder, where Azad and Nawalle now stood. Something startled her, and she sprinted down the corridor. They followed, Azad taking confident strides alongside Barry, emboldened by the fresh air supply and the unthreatening mechs. They descended a level down a winding staircase. Nawalle struggled to keep Barry stable.

At the base of the stairs, a mech twirled like the universe's least graceful ballerina, spinning and sputtering before it fell over. Nawalle kicked it aside.

Ledo ran down the corridor, vanishing through heavy double doors.

In the present, another mech moved with more specific purpose at the other end of the hallway. A guard mech, with stunners for arms, pressing against the heavy doors with a metallic foot. It struck at the door rhythmically, red lights flashing around its narrow head. A warning, or a call for backup. But no backup, it seemed, came.

The door flew open. The machine lost its balance in mid-kick, teetering to one side before a loud blast sent it flying into the nearest wall. Its limbs scattered like spiders across the floor. Smoke rose from its decimated center.

Azad and Nawalle stood back, stunned. The double doors pulled back slightly but before closing, a small head poked out, looking in both directions. A small head with dark hair. She saw them. They saw her.

Ledo.

⋆　⋆　⋆

She stepped into the hallway, peering at them. Azad sucked in his breath, reminding himself that it might be Barry, a flicker of the past, even though she seemed so real. Nawalle turned off the machine but the figure in front of them remained.

Ledo approached them with slow, hesitant steps. They stood in a triangle formation, staring as though they couldn't believe their eyes.

Ledo turned from Nawalle to Azad, and after a moment, shock crossed her face.

"Azad?" she asked.

Swallowing, too overwhelmed to speak, he nodded.

She frowned, the familiar dimple forming between her knitted brows, as though he were an unexpected factor in a complex equation. Neither joy nor anger marred her face, only surprise. He had seen her through Barry's lens more than once, but this was her first sight of him since she was fourteen years old, and she reacted accordingly. She scanned him up and down, taking in every detail, until their eyes met, seeing each other's face reflected in the other.

Nawalle broke the moment's spell by stepping forward and slapping Ledo across the face.

"Ow," Ledo cried, her voice high and hoarse. Nawalle shoved her to the ground.

"What in Barrett Juul's almighty toenails are you doing?" exclaimed Ledo.

"You…left…me," Nawalle panted, swinging her arms furiously while Ledo deflected the blows. "Thought…you were dead."

"I'm sorry, all right?"

"You're *sorry*?"

"Can we talk, or did you come all this way to slap me to death?"

Nawalle burst into tears. She wrapped her arms around Ledo's shoulders, cradling her like a small child. Ledo allowed herself to be held, hanging limp in Nawalle's arms. She pressed her lips together and kept her face away from Nawalle's. Her eyes met Azad's and her shoulders moved in the faintest of shrugs. *Let it happen*, her expression said.

Azad hovered at a respectful distance, swelling with his own conflicting emotions but unwilling to intrude on a more intimate reunion. After a moment, Nawalle wiped her eyes.

"I can't believe we found you," she said.

"You and me both." Ledo's voice remained hoarse but sounded stronger. She stood and shuffled with apparent discomfort before beckoning them through the doors. She had clearly been alone for some time, excluding the mechs.

Through the doors, they found the remnants of an old medical ward, repurposed as Ledo's base. Moldy blankets covered a rusted gurney, food rations lay stockpiled along a wall and a series of screens covered the counters, assembled through meticulous wiring. Up close, they revealed a schematic of the entire Palmcorps area, red dots indicating the movement of the functioning mechs.

"I've got everything tracked," Ledo said. "I've taken out most of the security mechs at this point, but there's a few stragglers. I didn't see you coming, though. You read as just another mech. You stole a locator chip?"

Nawalle nodded. "And snuck across the site, although we didn't attract a lot of attention. The machines are acting a little loopy outside."

Ledo smiled approvingly. "I could have used that locator chip three weeks ago, I'll tell you that. It's the guard mechs who are dangerous, but I think that hunk of metal was the last one."

"What are you doing down here anyway?" Azad asked. Ledo looked back at him with a sharp, inquiring gaze. *Who are you?* it asked. *Is that the first question you really have for me?* But she turned to her monitor and spoke.

"I needed to get evidence of what happened here long ago," she said. "These excavators, they're looking for what the Vitruvian higher-ups want them to find. But whatever they find, they won't tell the truth. A friend of mine was supposed to come back for me, after getting something that could treat us. I'm sick, by the way, so you might want to keep your distance, because there's no cure for what I have. But my Vitruvian friend never came back. Betrayed me," she added with venom.

"Was this Nenah VitruviaAxel3247?" Azad asked. Seeing Ledo's look of shock, he continued. "She died. In Nabatea hospital where I was working. I'm sorry. Had horrible, strange symptoms, but she recognized my face. That's how I knew you were alive, Ledo, after all these years."

Ledo grimaced. A shadow passed over her face at the mention of Nenah's death and a sadness lingered, albeit tinged with something else. Surprise and relief, perhaps, that Nenah hadn't betrayed her.

"I'm sorry to hear it," she said stiffly. "She was a good one, like Feisal and our vessel captain, Saje. Treated us all the same, as much as they know how. Knew the Vitruvians weren't gods or even smarter, just people with better reflexes and inner plumbing. Once she realized what was going on, she tried to help us. She would have made a great addition to Zelle's crew. Given Feisal someone to compete with and talk about whatever Vitruvians talk about amongst themselves. So that's how you knew where I was? But I don't understand how you found me here."

"We've been following your steps," Nawalle said carefully. "We got Feisal's machine to work, so we've been tracing your movements since the crater."

"The quantum historical whatever works?" Ledo's face brightened. "I hoped it would and that you'd make it here. That's why I sent you that recording."

"So that was you!" Nawalle said with a triumphant grin.

Ledo laughed. "Who else do you think would send you an encrypted transmission from the *Axel*? Got many friends or former lovers on the oldest alpha-vessel in the Greater Nabatean system? Unless Feisal has some old buddies who haven't pretended he got Blanked. Speaking of which, where are Feisal and Zelle? Did something happen to them?" The frown appeared again.

Azad took a deep breath. "I think we all need to take a seat and maybe have some coffee, if you've got it. This could take a while."

For the first time, Ledo smiled at him.

"Do I have coffee? I haven't changed that much, Azad. First thing I stockpiled, although I can't believe our ancestors drank this swill. No wonder they left."

"It might be expired."

"There are worse ways to die, dear twin."

Three rounds of coffee later, Nawalle and Azad had told Ledo everything they could recall. How they took Barry (Ledo cackled appreciatively at the machine's name) through Calypso Campus, tracking Kezza Sayer and Barrett Juul until the discovery of the sinister outpost changed their course. How they found a pre-Vitruvian man in the desert, dead by apparent suicide. They told her about their visit to the crater in Arabia Terra. With difficulty, Azad shared how they fought over whether to follow Ledo or the past, leading to the crew's painful fracture.

To Azad's surprise, Ledo listened with minimal interruption. At several points, including the moment Azad slashed Zelle's atmosphere suit, she let out a small exclamation or her face shifted. But once they finished their story, she spoke.

"This mystery woman, Kezza Sayer," she said. "Nenah told me they found her name on the first *Calypso One* roster, after they discovered her recording. She joined the Great Escape to Nabatea. But here's the interesting thing – she was never Archived in the Library of Souls."

Nawalle raised her brow. "But everyone who reached Nabatea got Archived, except for Barrett Juul and Saadia Hamza, of course."

"That we know of."

"What made her special?"

Azad frowned, swirling the vile coffee. "Everything we've seen suggests she is special. She played a big part in events on this planet."

"Then why haven't we heard of her?" Ledo asked, smiling slightly at Azad's indignation.

"Maybe she wasn't Archived because she never reached Nabatea?" Nawalle said darkly. "She said she didn't have long to live in the recording, remember?"

A pause followed, in which they all refilled their cups.

"How did the *Axel* ship discover Kezza's recording?" Azad asked. Ledo turned to him with a maniacal grin, as though she had been waiting for that very question.

"Now that's a story with a payoff at the end," she said with unabashed glee. "Hold on tight to your jaws, because this is a good one. The *Axel*, like all Vitruvian vessels, has a detailed log in its system of every command and action ever taken on the ship, dating back to its first launch. You can summon an abbreviated log history by typing in the usual queries – the date, the name of the person, and so on. Well, a bored Vitruvian was at the command station and decided to type in the date of the Exodus to Nabatea. Not only that, he used the original dating from the mother system, which made it year 2195 rather than the zero for our Year of Settlement calendar. And what do you know, but a video pops up with this lady's weird, pale face, talking about viruses and forgiveness."

"It was hidden in the logs?" Nawalle asked.

"Looks like it. Not an official recording, but something our girl wanted to slip into the system, for someone else to find years later. And it worked, although it took over a thousand years. No one likes using primitive search engines, so it wasn't the smartest approach. But do you see what this means?"

A pause. Then Nawalle's eyes widened like saucers; her mouth formed a silent 'O'. Azad frowned.

"Come on, brother."

"How could one of the original settlers place a recording on the *Axel*?" Azad asked, before a half-baked thought caught fire in his head. "Wait…"

"That's right," Ledo cried in triumph. "The *Axel* is *Calypso One*. They're the same ship!"

"How is that possible?" Azad asked. His head spun. The fabled *Calypso One*, the ancient vessel that transported the Martian colonists through the first wormhole journey to Nabatea, was the *Axel*?

"They kept the original ship and upgraded it," Ledo said. "Even the Vitruvians seemed surprised when they found the recording and put two and two together. Maybe some of the higher-ups knew, but I wonder. They've forgotten a lot of our early history. Or deliberately scratched out the pages, so they could rewrite them."

Nawalle, who had been sitting with her hands clasped over her mouth, leapt to her feet.

"We have to get on that ship," she said, running a feverish hand over Barry. "We can use Barry. We came here to find out what happened and why the Martians all left. Imagine what we could discover on the first voyage!"

"I actually think that's a wonderful idea, despite the obvious dangers of boarding a Vitruvian vessel," Ledo said drily. "It's what I've been trying to do for the last few weeks, without their knowledge, of course. Nenah said that my best chance of getting treated is on that ship. Although from what you've told me, twin, she didn't find a cure aboard."

The *Axel*, Ledo explained further, was still in Martian orbit but suspiciously silent. It had settled in geostationary orbit, on the other side of the planet. At this, Azad recounted the strange behavior of the mechs across Palmcorps. Ledo nodded grimly.

"That would make sense, if something happened on the *Axel*," she said. "If the ship's not directing the mechs, they go loopy after a time. Or maybe the *Axel* just abandoned the project on Palmcorps, but that doesn't make sense either. Like the guy told you in the outpost, they're here to gather a story to take back. In any case, we may not have a lot of time to get on that ship."

"Could there be a short-range shuttle nearby?" Nawalle asked. "One left for the machines?"

"Might be," Ledo said. "We could look, now that you're here with your fancy equipment. But didn't you also get here on a ship?"

Nawalle and Azad exchanged nervous glances. Nawalle had brought the long-range communicator Relay from the Glider, allowing them to contact the *Magreb*. But given how the crew had parted...

"Oh, for Juul's sake," Ledo exploded. "Do you want to join the skeleton collection on this miserable stretch of rock? Make contact! Worst case, we can get airlocked in space like civilized people. I'll vouch for you both. I'll tell Zelle I made you go against your better judgment with my irresistible charisma and natural wiles."

"Crazy in hindsight," Nawalle shot back, but she unfurled the Relay from her knapsack.

"I'm not going to apologize if they answer," Azad said to Ledo while Nawalle opened the Relay line. "Zelle wants to study the past, but she needs to remember why. I think she wants to expose the past for what it is, so we can look at the present in a different way. Imagine something better. We're not going to do that if we don't look out for each other. I was serving her mission better than she was."

Ledo raised her eyebrows. "Look at you, brother! Is this the same twin who used to cry when I got too close to the Sulpherlands?"

Before Azad could reply, the *Magreb* answered.

"We found Ledo," Nawalle said in a small, quick voice. "And she told us some incredible things. We know Kezza was never Archived. And the *Axel* station—"

"We found something as well," Zelle's voice crackled on the other end. Her voice was heavy but free of the anger Azad expected. "We found a massacre."

"What?" Nawalle frowned, glancing anxiously at the twins.

"Is the *hadir* still alive?" Feisal's voice interjected.

"Not now, Feisal," Zelle said with bite. "We have to get out of here, all of us. We're in Calypso but we'll come to you. Are you in Palmcorps?"

The door to the ward ripped apart in an explosion of heat and shrapnel, with an intensity to rival their violent landing on Mars. The sound thundered in Azad's ears, the force sent him reeling. He scrambled to his knees, checking for missing limbs or gaping wounds. Finding none, he crawled forward. Ahead, Ledo and Nawalle lay across the ground but stared at the source of the explosion.

A man stood at the shattered entrance, surveying them with cold appraisal through heavy, sunken eyes. His entire head was encased in a thin bubble, a headcover used by Vitruvians in open space to test their limits – or protect them from illness. A red and yellow snake tattoo reached out from his chest, coiling around his wiry neck.

"Ledo of Nabatea and friends," he said. "You're coming with me."

Chapter Eighteen
Kezza

CALYPSO CORPORATE CAMPUS
2195 A.D.

The white domes of Calypso shone ahead of them like bubbles on the night horizon, a surprisingly welcome sight. Next to her, Juul fidgeted as he grilled his mother for information. His joy at her safety and their control over Calypso proved short-lived, once the trade-off became clear – the surviving Corpsboard members and their enforcers had fled to Palmcorps, where they successfully suppressed the riot.

"How did they escape?" he demanded.

"I don't know, I wasn't there," Dr. Hamza said with a mother's forced patience. "But you saw the footage, Barrett. It's easy to slip out through chaos. They took a miners' transporter from the northern bay."

Tearing her gaze away from the vehicle's window, Kezza couldn't help but be impressed by Dr. Hamza's knowledge of Calypso's layout. The woman's silence, noticeable in comparison to her loquacious son, reflected a scientist's instinct to observe. The astrophysicist took in everything around her – the gadgets in the vehicle, the people and above all, the small briefcase nestled between Amit's knees. Juul was no idiot, but his mother was the real brains of the operation.

"Is it secure?" she asked.

Amit nodded. "Just get me back into Bokambe," he said. "And I'll run the samples."

"Don't get too comfortable," she said with a faint smile. "We won't be here much longer."

"We can't depart until we resolve the situation on Palmcorps," Juul said heatedly. "There are people there who risked everything for us, who want to join." He stopped short of saying the name – Evgenia – but Kezza had no illusion that she was the most valuable hostage on Palmcorps. She recalled the Ukrainian fighter's final sign-off over the radio – *I'm the hardest person in this city to kill.* Hopefully, that wasn't just arrogance talking.

"Of course," Dr. Hamza said. "My Corpsboard friend suspects they'll want a hostage swap. We have some of their Tier Ones and Twos, and likely others who wish to remain on Mars. We'll discuss it after your speech."

Juul sighed but nodded. The people of Calypso, who rioted on his behalf, would welcome him back as a conquering hero. They deserved a speech. Finally recovering from the effects of the stunner, Kezza's chest swelled, her breathing light again. *It was happening. Everything was going to change.*

The vehicle entered Calypso's main docking bay, from which they had escaped only a day earlier. Kezza coughed, inviting concerned glances from Dr. Hamza and her retinue. Juul pointedly held out his hand, helping Kezza descend the steps out of the transporter.

The sun had not yet risen, but the docking bay already stirred with the first waves of human activity. The *Calypso One* loading shuttle filled the far end of the room. A small team of workers directed mechs, who fed boxes and crates through the shuttle's open mouth like an offering to an ancient, demanding god. The retinue drew stares and pointed fingers as they crossed the docking bay. Juul raised his hand in a clumsy wave, triggering scattered cheers.

"So, *Calypso One* will be the ship that'll take us to…the new planet?" Kezza asked Juul in a low voice.

"It's the only long-distance transport ship available to us," Juul said. A shadow passed over his face, the glower of a man with a lingering problem to solve. "Now that Palmcorps leadership ordered their own transporter back to Earth, according to my mother. The journey began this morning."

Kezza considered this. A bold but risky move, one that allowed

Palmcorps to send valuable people and resources out of Juul's reach but left them shipless for another two years. Palmcorps' leadership had tied their fate to Mars.

A roar of approval greeted them in the Atrium. The same crowd they witnessed in the midnight livestream still congregated in Calypso's open space, reveling in their victory. Outstretched hands surrounded Juul, quickly repelled by the guards. Juul made a show of pushing past his own security, squeezing hands and offering one-armed embraces on the way to a high podium. Kezza and Amit followed behind.

A carnival atmosphere filled the room up to its high ceilings. Banners with crudely fashioned slogans hung from the wall. Afro-bhangra music blasted from a speaker. To Kezza's great relief, the hanging bodies had been cleared.

The circus troupe stood in a small cluster apart from the main crowd, near the food stalls. Even in the brave new world on Calypso, the performers, it seemed, remained at the bottom rung of the Tier Three ladder. LaValle ran to Kezza and lifted her off the ground in a tight embrace.

"Where have you been, Sayer?" he asked into her ear, his voice hovering between joy and a sob.

"Finding new ways to get into trouble," Kezza said, grinning as they broke apart. LaValle cast a wary glance at Juul before rejoining the rest of the circus.

The Imam from the prayer room stood near a group of mechanics. He nodded politely when Kezza caught his eye, but his face looked thin, tired. She beamed at him. He didn't know it yet, but he was about to make history with the rest of them.

Juul advanced to the speaker's podium, raising both hands in acknowledgment as the crowd roared.

"Good people of Calypso and those listening in Palmcorps...people of Mars! I have returned with a message for you all, and an offer of hope."

The crowd's cheers echoed off the domed roof. Cameras zoomed in on Juul's face, which projected across the Atrium's rotating screen. His eyes danced the way they had come alive in the cave, alight with possibility. Bodies jostled for space from the entrances to the Catacombs. The entirety of Calypso hung on Juul's every word, Kezza included.

"People of Mars," Juul continued. "After years of indentured servitude to the shareholders of Earth and their lackeys on Mars, you are finally free to chart your own course."

It took over a minute for the noise to abate enough for Juul to continue. He waited patiently, basking in the cheers like a snake in sunlight. Dr. Hamza smiled sedately on the other side of Juul, looking at everything and nothing at once. Her mind, Kezza guessed, was somewhere light years away.

"As you already know, I came here with a specific purpose. What you didn't know, and what it now thrills me to tell you, is that it was not to remain on Mars. You know this planet better than I do, and I'm sure you can understand why. We've all seen the horrors of the footage from the Bokambe sector. An already dangerous planet has been proven even more dangerous thanks to the virus discovered in Arabia Terra. Instead of protecting their corporate citizens, the Calypso Corpsboard decided to keep the discovery a secret. Not only that, they decided to endanger the most vulnerable people in the city for financial gain. They experimented on prisoners and hard-working miners, whose only crime was to be in the wrong place at the wrong time. And why? After procuring classified data cubes from the Bokambe, I can tell you – they wanted to sell the technology to Earth! They thought they could learn how to control the virus, develop antidotes and manipulate it to engineer human genetics. To use the bursts of strength and agility that are a side effect of this strange virus to turn people into better soldiers. To do what your Earth brethren have always done – kill each other in their endless wars!"

The crowd howled its outrage. Cries of *shame* echoed off the walls. Kezza's face flushed with indignation. This was new information, but none of it surprised her in the slightest. Of course, Calypso would find a way to turn a contagion into profit.

Juul raised his hands to appeal for calm.

"But while the leaders of Calypso decided to use this incredible discovery for experimentation and exploitation, my trusted friends have sought to overcome it, and are working on a cure as we speak."

Juul had not wasted time addressing the unspoken fear in the room. The crowd's faces, narrowed in concentration, relaxed at his words, and something shifted in the air. Kezza's mouth twitched. Juul had been right. Present a danger, then counter with a solution. He held the entire city in his palm.

"But a cure does not mean that Mars is a safe place! Danger lurks in its craters and more enduring, human dangers lurk in its power structures. I aim to travel to a better world, build a better society and fill it with better people. People who know hardship and struggle. The descendants of pioneers or pioneers themselves, those who have traveled to humanity's furthest outpost. And as Dr. Hamza and I extend that outpost to the other side of the galaxy, to the planet I've named Nabatea, I ask you to come a little further with me and be part of humanity's greatest experiment. Make the leap and join us into the stars."

The hesitation following Juul's first speech in the docking bay wasn't visible among the faces in this crowd. Even the circus troupe, cynics by necessity, joined in the applause and stamping feet.

"But please – I know I'm asking everything of you. Some of you may decide that your future remains on this planet, that the Martian experiment can continue and be saved. You may have families and entrenched lives here, and not want to risk the journey. To those of you for whom this applies, I have two things to say to you. The first is that I respect and support your decision to stay. The second is that you will indeed stay – there will be no return flight and no chance to join us in the future."

He paused for effect, letting the crowd process his warning.

"You must also remember that those of you born here cannot return to Earth, so your fate is locked on this planet, whatever becomes of it, whereas the planet discovered by Dr. Hamza, Nabatea, supports a similar gravity, one we can all live on. And remember this – as long as there is ore on Mars, the powers of Earth will always retain a vested interest in this planet's politics. I know this firsthand – I've spent years interacting with presidents, world leaders, CEOs and shadow investors. They care for power and profits above all else, and if they see that challenged on Mars, as we have done, their response will be swift and absolute. If another infection spreads through Mars, like the one we have narrowly avoided, you know how they will respond."

Like a conductor changing an orchestra's tempo, his words sent a dark, angry pulse through the sea of spectators.

"Our neighbors across Arabia Terra still live under the yoke of shareholders, but many there are looking to us for a new way. You will see our favorite mistress of the trapeze and silks, Kezza Sayer, at my side. She helped bring our like-minded allies in Palmcorps together in a battle against Calypso corruption and excesses."

The reception she received was louder than any of her performances in the Coliseum. Hundreds of faces turned to her, radiating kindness and respect. Some of those same faces had once greeted her with leers or contempt, if they even turned to her at all. With a barely perceptible nudge from Juul, she stepped forward. The crowd roared louder. Tears sprang at the corners of her eyes before she could stop them. They ran down her cheeks, stretched by her wide grin, as she stood at the podium's center. The crowd beamed back at her. This was not the Calypso she'd known and hated all her life. These people were her allies, and she was theirs. Juul had been the catalyst they needed, the ingredient that unified the once-voiceless Martian masses.

With effort, she stepped away from the limelight, exchanging a smile with Juul. No words in her arsenal could convey her gratitude for this slight, unassuming man who was about to lead them through the stars. When Kezza first met him, she wanted him dead. He represented everything she wanted gone. Now, they worked together for the same end – a better world, far away from this one.

Juul raised his hands and the cheering died down.

"But Kezza has done something even more important, something we must discuss seriously. The terrible footage from the Bokambe complex—"

A bright light flashed through the heart of the crowd in time with a deafening explosion. The force knocked Kezza back. Hot air whipped across her face and she curled into a fetal position, shielding every part of her she could manage with shaking hands. Orange flames rose, quickly drowned by a cloud of black smoke. Other objects flew in the air with a rush of heat, scattering metal and bloody tissue in every direction.

Screams rose through the din. Kezza scrambled to her feet, struggling for balance. Her ears rung with a rising pitch. Was she screaming as well? She couldn't hear, couldn't think.

Hands found her. Amit wrapped an arm around her shoulders, steering her off the podium. She let him drag her; her legs buckled underneath her. Juul ran several paces ahead, pulling Dr. Hamza down the steps. They retreated, all four of them and their guards, down the hall, past Bokambe into the Eden sector.

Kezza's ears rang. Amit's face hovered in front of her, his mouth moving. When she didn't respond, he took her hand and steered her toward Juul.

Sound returned as quickly as it had left. Distant screams, the pounding of her own heart.

In normal circumstances, Kezza would have drunk in Eden's opulence. But this time, Kezza could do nothing else but shake and run her hands across her torso, checking for missing pieces.

Juul yelled incoherently, his sharp face clenched in fury. Other wealthy residents spilled in through the doors, sobbing and screaming loved ones' names. With effort, Dr. Hamza steered Juul further down the hall, gesturing for the rest of them to follow.

Inside Juul's quarters, the civilizationist exploded.

"Cowards!" he yelled. "Trying to break us. If they want a war, they can have it!"

"We don't need a war," Dr. Hamza said, her soft voice clear and firm. Her skin, normally the color of milky coffee, had become whiter than chalk. "Barrett, take a deep breath. We're all in shock. We'll make decisions when we know what happened."

"We already know what happened," Juul continued, his widened eyes delirious with rage. "That was a bomb. Explosives, on Mars! Someone planted it, maybe even went down with it. Someone paid by the Palmcorps Corpsboard, or the Calypso snakes who ran into their laps."

"Calm yourself, Barrett, please," Dr. Hamza interjected. Juul ignored her; his voice rose to a shout.

"Those Calypso snakes have been waiting for this the second we stepped off the shuttle. They're fucking cowards, probably got some indentured bastard to do it by clearing his family debt. How did the affliction of martyrdom come all the way here? Do you know how hard it is to eradicate? Generations of families glorify it. But to do it not for a god, but a corporation…madness."

Juul paced and shook his head, projecting his own brand of madness. Kezza and Amit stood together in silence, not even daring a shared glance. At various times, Kezza had hated Juul, admired him, even pitied him. Now, for the first time, she feared him.

Dr. Hamza sank back into a plush red divan, hands folded into her lap. She closed her eyes.

"We've come too far to fail now," she whispered.

Dr. Hamza's elegant face had been stretched free of wrinkles but worry lingered in the shadows under her eyes. The image of a man dragged apart by cars flashed back into Kezza's mind. What else had this woman seen in her remarkable life? What other memories flooded her now, set loose from her subconscious by the explosion?

"Yes, we have," Juul said in a strangled voice. "The time for reconciliation and compromise is over."

The door burst open and they all jumped. A guard glanced around apologetically before striding up to Barrett Juul to whisper in his ear. Regaining his composure, Juul nodded and clapped the man on the back. After he left, the wild fury returned to his eyes.

"Twenty dead already," he said. "Twenty precious lives that will never see the new world. More wounded. Several say that a woman they didn't recognize had been pushing through the crowd moments before it happened. I'm sure the ID will come up as Palmcorps, or a Calypso Tier One. They won't even try to deny it. They want me to know."

Amit clenched his fists. Anger bubbled within Kezza at the thought of the Palmcorps and Calypso Corpsboards sitting together in a cushioned room, congratulating themselves.

"What do we do?" Kezza asked. "Evgenia and the others are still in Palmcorps. And so are other people who want to be here."

"A swap," Juul barked. "Our traitors and cowards who want to remain, for those in Palmcorps who wish to join."

"They'll never let that many people go," Dr. Hamza said. "Most of the Palmcorps workers will jump to leave, and the Corpsboard knows it."

"They'll consider it," Juul said slowly, pacing like a stalking animal. "Because they'll get all of Calypso campus when we leave. All the machinery. All the mechs. They'll consider it, or we'll do this the hard way."

Kezza opened her mouth to ask about the hard way but changed her mind. The conversation had come to its natural end. She backed away toward the front door.

"There's a suite next door," Dr. Hamza said. Her green eyes pierced Kezza like an arrow. "Get some rest there. The guards will keep watch outside."

"I suggest a stop at first into the Bokambe complex," Amit said carefully. "For everyone's safety, and so we can keep running tests."

"Yes!" Juul stopped his pacing, his attention back on Kezza. "Our trip to the crater, at least, was not wasteful."

"Why has Kezza reacted differently after exposure?" Dr. Hamza asked Amit. At her question, the tense atmosphere in the room eased, the group brought back to the next problem to solve.

"A genetic mutation called MRC14 that became active," Amit said. "Extreme pollution exposure triggers it, which Kezza experienced as a child in Cardiff. The radiation-filled trip to Mars back in the day probably didn't help. The mutation seems to…work with the virus by helping her proteins combat its worst effects. Lessens its toxicity while retaining some of its benefits. But it only slows progress. The virus will win in the end, unless we act quickly."

The group's eyes burned into Kezza. The room stiffened with the realization of death's presence among them, seated on the other end of the divan. A bitter wave of grief struck Kezza in the silence; amidst the chaos, she had not had a moment to think about the little time that remained to her. Escaping a sudden, violent death only served to remind her of the slower one waiting in the shadows.

Juul broke the silence. "But now that we have the substance, Amit, do we have everything we need?"

Amit nodded. "Now, it's just a matter of finding the right balance – almost like a genetic cocktail – between this substance and Kezza's mutation, the proteins it produces. Theoretically, if we test until we find the right balance, we will have a cure – one that allows the virus to coexist in a human body, allowing the benefits of the virus we have seen in Kezza but without the eventual deterioration."

Juul exhaled. "I knew you were special, Kezza Sayer, but I couldn't have imagined just how special," he said. "The happy accident of who you are will end up saving lives."

"I don't just want to save lives," Kezza said, the words spilling out before she could stop them, words chased by tears. "I want to live. I want to see Nabatea."

She was selfish that way. But was it a crime to want something better? She'd spared Juul's life because he offered her just that – a chance at life beyond Mars.

Juul knelt before her, grabbing her hand. His skin felt clammy, burning with his internal heat.

"If you haven't noticed yet, Kezza Sayer, I operate on my own schedule," Juul said with a reassuring smile. "We can do extraordinary things. Believe it. You will be there when we touch ground and sleep under a different sky. You have my word. You, of all people, were meant to join me across the stars."

★　★　★

Under the fluorescent lighting of a Bokambe medical room, Kezza submitted her veins to fresh needles, her insides to the medmech scanners. Juul stood to one side while Amit harvested samples from her body – slivers of tissue, saliva, the black substance she coughed up and blood. Lots of blood. He drew blood until the lights dimmed and the room spun, and Kezza marveled that she had any left.

On the way back to the Eden sector, Kezza stopped in the middle of the hallway. A familiar face caught her eye through a window, a lone man strapped to a chair inside a small, threadbare room. The same room where Calypso Security processed Kezza after her arrest.

An amateur guard stood outside. His uniform hung loose, his pockmarked face revealing a teenager filling in Calypso's sudden gap in law enforcement. Some security officials turned sides during the riots but many, fearing reprisals, left to join the suppression underway at Palmcorps.

With an approving nod from Juul, the young guard led Kezza into the room. Alan Schulz turned his head toward his new visitors, the way one would respond to a fly buzzing nearby. His eyes carried no recognition, and after a second, he switched back to the deck of cards in his hand, shuffling them with mechanical repetition.

"What happened to him?" Kezza asked. When she last encountered Schulz, he tried to burn her alive. But watching him now, he posed no threat. His jaw slackened, his eyes blank and broken. She scoured him for signs that he recognized her, but he only blinked back.

"We found him like this," the guard said with casual cheeriness. "They must have done something to him. Zapped his brain, according to this Tier Two gal who examined him. Stripped away the important parts of his brain, the pieces that separate us from the animals, and even more beyond. If you give him something to do – clean the floor, play with some cards, whatever – he'll keep doing it until you stop him. Doesn't seem to remember what came before, doesn't care what happens next."

Juul caught her arm before the dizziness crept on Kezza. She leaned against him for balance, eyes trained anywhere but at Alan Schulz. Had he known what would happen to him? Had he administered a similar punishment to someone else when he worked as a Tier One? It all seemed irrelevant now, especially to Schulz himself, who only cared about the cards flipping between his hands. Kezza knew, through the Catacombs grapevine, that all kinds of punishments were practiced within Bokambe. Physical tortures, ones that left marks and ones that did not. But this, somehow, seemed worse. An extracted fingernail left pain and a traumatic memory in its wake, without a doubt, but at least the fingernail would grow back, the person left whole.

"Horrible," she whispered as Juul led her out of the room. The door clicked behind them.

"Yes," Juul said, his voice soft and distant. "Yes, quite horrible. Quite."

Chapter Nineteen

Azad

MARTIAN DESERT
YEAR OF SETTLEMENT 1208

The Vitruvian man pointed his stunner weapon at them, holding a dagger at his side with the other hand. Azad, aware of what a Vitruvian dagger was capable of, shrank back.

Ledo stood her ground, surveying the man with cold appraisal.

"I remember you from the voyage here," she said carefully. "Tayyar, right? I'm touched you remembered my name."

"Address me by my full title, brat!" the man snarled.

"Who can remember all of those station names and numbers?" Ledo asked lightly. "Certainly not a dim-witted, helpless orthodox like me. How are things on the *Axel* by the way? Is Captain Saje still kicking?"

Azad's stomach clenched. The man, Tayyar, vibrated with nervous, angry energy. He had come with a purpose and it wasn't to banter. But while he glowered at Ledo, his weapon-carrying hand twitching, Nawalle shifted her arm behind her back. The Relay slid into her back pocket, the light still on.

Zelle and Feisal. They would hear everything. They could track them. Azad jerked his head away, back to the Vitruvian man. They needed to stall for time.

"Get up," Tayyar barked.

They obeyed. Keeping his weapon trained on them, he bound their hands. As the binds dug into his wrists, Azad clenched his teeth. He would not go the same way as the orthodox Nabateans they kept in cages. But he needed time. If he distracted the Vitruvian, perhaps Ledo and Nawalle could escape.

"What's that?" the man asked. He gestured at Barry.

"Our mobile transporter," Nawalle said quickly. "It carries our supplies while we travel."

"Not a lot of room to stand on and I don't see shelves," Tayyar said distractedly. He stared into the lens, inching forward. Nawalle and Azad exchanged nervous glances. Ledo scowled at Tayyar.

"This is what's been showing up on our readings," the Vitruvian continued. "Draining dark energy from the area. Leaving pockets of imbalance behind."

"Whatever's causing that, it's not this," Ledo said unconvincingly. "It's a transporter, like she said."

Ignoring her, the man traced his finger across the lens.

"We've seen it crop up around the area," he said, as though speaking to himself. "Captain didn't listen to me, didn't think it was worth investigating. But I knew we'd find something intelligent behind it." He snorted as an afterthought and cast a contemptuous glance at the bound trio.

"Ok, you've got us," Ledo said. Nawalle drew a sharp breath but Ledo continued. "It's a weapon. It harnesses dark energy to vaporize anything that lens points at."

The man took a light step out of the lens's view, surveying it with renewed interest.

"Very well then," he said. "You can give me a demonstration."

"It's complicated and dangerous to use," Nawalle said in a high voice. "Especially in a confined area—"

"Enough!" He struck her across the face and a sickening crack reverberated across the room. With a furious cry, Azad hurtled toward the Vitruvian but Tayyar jerked his knee and knocked him down easily. Azad and Nawalle lay on the ground, moaning, as the man dragged them closer together. Through her wheezing gasps, Nawalle shifted and arched her back, the Relay still on. No sound came from its speaker. Would Zelle and Feisal come for them? And would they get there in time?

Tayyar crept behind Barry and grabbed Ledo by her hair.

"I only need you, sick girl," he said softly. "Your friends were already dead when I came in. Now fire the damn thing and let's see what your toy does."

Shaking with fear or rage, Ledo activated Barry. She moved the toggles and dials with apparent confidence. Had Feisal shown her an early prototype? She paused, closing her eyes, and Tayyar raised his dagger to her throat.

"Now," he spat. "Shoot them. I don't have all day."

The lens swirled in wells of inky black, bright light swelling from its center. The ground around them shivered as present and past converged, the machine projecting the room as it stood once before. Cracked floor tiles under complete ones, shelves of equipment where Ledo's supplies now stood. And everywhere, all around them, the dead and the dying.

Tayyar's dagger fell to the floor with a clatter. On the ground, men, women and children clawed at their own throats, blood leaking from their eyes and mouths. Those strong enough to move stumbled in from the door, burrowing through the old medical ward's supplies for something, anything that could help them. Sprinklers on the ceiling rained liquid down on the room, passing through Azad and Nawalle like air. Mouths opened wide in silent screams and more collapsed onto the floor or fought their way outside.

Azad remained on the ground, in shock. More senseless death. Was this all humanity had to offer? Was history just the same cycle of cruelty and despair, with names and places changed?

"What is this?" Tayyar cried. At that, Ledo jumped on his back, wrapping her bound arms in a tight chokehold around his neck.

"Help me!" she shouted.

Tayyar swung wildly behind him and they both fell to the floor while Azad and Nawalle scrambled to their feet. With their hands bound in front of them, they joined the fray. The Vitruvian's foot reached out for the dagger lying nearby, kicking it toward his outstretched hand. Nawalle stomped on his fingers while Azad wrestled with the man's other arm, which still wielded the stunner.

"Don't touch his skin," Ledo yelled. "Don't rip off his mask." She referred to the bubble around his head, through which his sallow face harbored wild, murderous eyes.

Tayyar was incredibly strong but weakening under attack. Up close, he and Ledo bore an unnerving resemblance, their skin pale and papery like an onion layer, purple veins peering through. Around them, the mirage of chaos continued to unfold, bodies running and choking and collapsing to the ground.

The Vitruvian's legs kicked out, propelling him into a crouching position. His arm swung toward Ledo and Azad yanked it back. The stunner went off with a light crack and the figures around them vanished. Ledo, dagger now in hand, ran it across the man's jugular and leapt back. He gurgled, black bile pouring from the opening in his throat. The wildness faded from his eyes until they turned glassy and unseeing, blood crawling from their corners.

In unison, the group turned to the quantum historical projector. Barry's lens no longer swirled in its dark center. A small hole had torn through its body, gray smoke whistling into the air.

"No." The word escaped in a small moan through Azad's lips. Nawalle ran to the smoking machine, probing its torn metal with shaking fingers.

"Oh no, oh no, oh no."

Ledo, panting and cursing under her breath, dragged the man toward the exit.

"Can you fix it?" Azad asked. "Could Feisal?" If Feisal and Zelle had heard the scuffle, they hadn't made a sound. Nawalle pulled out the Relay. Tears spilled from her dark eyes. The communicator had been crushed in the struggle, no longer emitting a signal.

"I don't know," she said tearfully. "I don't even know if they can find us."

"Should we wait?"

"No!" Ledo barked from across the room. She had pulled the dead Vitruvian over her back like a knapsack, struggling with each step. "We have to take his ship and get onto the *Axel*. If we don't go now, we'll never get out of here. Hurry up!"

Before Azad could argue, his sister fell to her knees, doubling over in a coughing fit. He ran to her, but she held up a hand in warning, face still turned to the ground. A stream of black bile, thick like tar, streaked across the tiled floor. Azad's heart plummeted in his chest, his knees nearly following onto the ground. Not Ledo.

"What's happening to you?" Nawalle cried.

"I have what he had," Ledo rasped, gesturing to the dead man over her shoulder. "And what they had." She gestured with a swinging arm across the room, where the bodies had scattered centuries before.

"We need to get on the *Axel*," Nawalle said. "But how do we do it without getting Blanked or killed on sight?"

"We have to try," Azad said. He didn't have time to despair. Ledo needed him. Perhaps it was an instinctual twin bond, or he was becoming savvier at this dangerous life he had fallen into, but he guessed at why his sister was carrying Tayyar. "We might be able to use him to our advantage."

Raising her head and wiping her mouth, Ledo shot him the faintest of smiles.

"Now you're thinking, brother," she said.

★   ★   ★

"Identify yourself."

"Tayyar VitruviaAxel3247, back from reconnaissance across Arabia Terra."

"Copy, Tayyar, prepare to dock. Glad to have you back in one piece."

"One piece but struggling. Need medical attention immediately."

A long pause on the other end.

"Keep your anti-contaminants secured, Tayyar. We'll let you board."

"Received and appreciated."

Ledo exhaled loudly.

"This is madness," Azad muttered after Ledo switched off communications.

"Where'd you learn how to hack an Archive Band?" Nawalle asked her.

She had learned the trick in Cerata, as Ledo told the story, before joining Zelle's crew. She apprenticed with an alchemist on the Shadow Moon whose trade helped thieves impersonate Vitruvians. This mainly involved injecting a person with a steroid and stimulant cocktail to mimic Vitruvian strength and speed, should the situation arise, but also included extracting data from Archive Bands 'borrowed' from the Library of Souls. While it took Vitruvian quantum computing technology to decompress an entire Archive Band, the alchemist's algorithm could extract some essentials for criminal activity – the Vitruvian's voice and vocal patterns, memories tied to passwords, ship codes, people and locations. Tayyar's shuttle, once they reached it on the windy edge of Palmcorps, contained an emergency Archive Band they were able to attach to the recently deceased Vitruvian. A portable computer in the shuttle allowed Ledo to do the rest.

"It's a miracle you weren't caught," Azad said. "There's at least five Blankable offenses in there."

Ledo shrugged. "I only had to steal a couple of Archive Bands. I mostly spent hours in his study, running his code over and over. Good thing I left when I did though, because I heard they caught him in the end. He got Blanked. He's back on Nabatea, watering plants in the Slope Gardens."

Dread pooled in Azad's stomach. The dark behemoth known as the *Axel* ship loomed closer, filling most of the starry space out the shuttle's front window. An alpha-vessel, the oldest in existence, crewed by Vitruvian explorers who considered them to be inferiors at best, dangerous agitators at worst. They had already demonstrated their regard for non-Vitruvian lives.

And here they were, preparing to dock a shuttle with a dead Vitruvian in tow.

Once the course had been set and the airlock seal attached, they bound each other's wrists and settled in the back of the shuttle. Tayyar sat in the pilot's seat, slumped to one side despite his secure strapping. Without removing the bubble around his face, Ledo had attempted to wipe away some of the blood around his bruised cheeks, forcing the illusion of someone recently deceased.

"They're going to figure it out," Azad said abruptly.

"Keep calm," Ledo said. "Actually, act panicked and alarmed when they board, it'll sell it better. Remember, they think we're stupid and passive. They'll accept this version of events more readily than the truth of us overpowering a Vitruvian and commandeering his ship to the *Axel* ship."

The shuttle, thankfully, included a pre-logged return route to the *Axel*'s coordinates. The ship waited in geostationary orbit on the other side of the planet, giving them a scenic path around Mars after they left atmosphere. Azad grimaced as Arabia Terra vanished around the horizon. Had they made the right decision to leave Barry behind? Perhaps they could have removed key parts and taken them back to the shuttle. But Ledo's deteriorating health and the need to Archive Tayyar forced quick action, and wheeling a large, unpowered machine through Palmcorps' ruins and the desert would have lost them precious time. And better, he reasoned, to abandon Barry than to place the technology directly into Vitruvian hands.

But Barry's final projection would be lost forever. And if they didn't survive the next hour, they would have no story to share. All those people on Palmcorps, dying in unimaginable agony. The more recently infected test subjects from the *Axel* ship, dying for a senseless agenda. One thing was clear – the alien object in the crater had killed them all. But how? And why?

Kezza Sayer, the woman with the sad eyes on the flying trapeze. Her story would never be told. It wasn't possible that someone so integral to the history of Mars would have their story die in such an abrupt, undignified way. But perhaps that was just wishful thinking, given that he was likely to meet a quick end soon, his own story ending just as it had begun.

Shuttle and ship converged with the familiar whistle of the sealing airlock. They waited for what felt like hours before a knock rattled the door.

"Help us!" Ledo screamed. She bit her own tongue, drawing tears. "Please, something's wrong. He needs help now!"

The door flew open. A Vitruvian woman with bobbed black hair peered inside. Like Tayyar, she wore a bubble around her face and a full, fitted bodysuit. Azad gave her his best look of terror and bewilderment.

The terror, at least, was not difficult. He imagined himself Blanked, watering plants next to Ledo's alchemist.

The woman took in the scene with unreadable composure. The dead man in the pilot's seat, the three prisoners in the back. Seeing the Archive Band around his head, she wordlessly snatched it and handed it to a machine waiting behind her.

"He started choking," Ledo said in a quavering voice. "And put the band on."

The woman nodded. Her silence unnerved Azad more than any line of questioning or outburst. She studied them again, one by one, until her eyes settled on Ledo.

"You're still alive," she said. Her voice expressed neither surprise nor pleasure.

Ledo nodded, tears welling.

"And who are these two? One is your near-identical."

"My twin brother," Ledo said, taking a shaky breath. Azad couldn't help but be amazed by Ledo's acting, which wouldn't have been out of place in the Khazneh Arena. Her face shifted between fear and hope but gave no false sense of grief or affection for her captors.

"And how are your twin brother and this other individual in the mother system?"

"They're part of some rogue Nabatean crew based on the Shadow Moon," Ledo said, before bursting into tears. "They came looking for me. They broke the law, I know! Please don't hurt them."

"I know of the crew," the woman said. "Zelle of Nabatea's vessel. The so-called 'historian'. Where is she?"

"Dead," Azad said, surprised at how easily the lie flowed out of him. "We're all that's left."

The woman stared at him again, as though scanning every crease on his face for hints of a lie. But Azad arranged his face into blankness, forcing the terror to drain from his mind. He no longer cared what happened to him, he told himself, only that Ledo and Nawalle didn't pay for his mistakes.

If the Vitruvian didn't believe their story, the skepticism didn't reach her stern face. Perhaps she didn't care. After releasing their foot binds, she beckoned them to follow her out of the shuttle. As they passed Tayyar, Azad shuddered at the streak of black visible along his neck. Two armed mechs greeted them past the airlocked door.

"What about him?" Nawalle asked, gesturing back to the shuttle.

"He's infected and of no further use," the woman said in a hard voice. "He stays."

And with that, she pressed another button beside the airlock and a low rumbling followed. Through the portal window, the shuttle had disconnected from the ship, floating away.

Azad, naturally, had never set foot in a Vitruvian vessel before. This one didn't differ greatly from the *Magreb* in terms of aesthetic – bleak and utilitarian – but even within the narrow hallways, Azad sensed its immense scale. Silence filled the corridors, except for an occasional echoing sound, a banging against metal. They had walked for about fifteen minutes before Azad stopped, sharpening his ears. Something wasn't right.

"There's no one here," he muttered to Nawalle. "No one walking around. Only mechs."

"That's correct," the Vitruvian woman said ahead of them without turning around. "You are looking at the last functioning member of the *Axel* ship. Saje VitruviaAxel3247, although you may now call me Captain. This way, please." She motioned stiffly for them to enter a side room.

A medmech waited for them in a wide room unlike any Azad had seen. The walls had been painted a deep, dusky rose, the color of Nabatea City's cliff faces. The ceiling was the color of the Nabatean sky at night, dark with streaks of amethyst. Lanterns hung around the walls, the same ceremonial lights used for Dusharan Solstice Day. Azad gasped. He had been holding his breath. For a precious split second, he had forgotten how far he was from home.

Home. He had to get home with Ledo, but not to return to a Pod or live a Blanked life in a Nabatean park. If they didn't escape, all that they had learned would die with them. The Vitruvian authorities would continue to make the world in their own image, to write the history that suited them. Life on Nabatea would continue its dark, empty cycle.

"What is this place?" Nawalle said, running her fingers across one of the lamps. She mouthed a Dusharan prayer. *"For all who wander, home will follow like a shadow."*

"This is the *Axel* ship's biomedical research laboratory," Captain Saje said. "It was once the main passenger holding area. We try to make the areas we spend most time in resemble home as much as possible, to mitigate space madness. Yes, even Vitruvian explorers are not immune," she added at the sight of their faces. "And you may be spending some time here."

The medmech took swabs from their mouths while Captain Saje observed them with folded arms. She pursed her lips, the corners of her jaw tight. The soothing effect of the room dissipated under her calculating gaze. To Azad's right, Ledo and Nawalle sat close together. Ledo's face paled, her skin visibly clammy. She coughed and Saje took a step back.

"How are your symptoms?" she asked.

"They come and go," Ledo admitted. "I'll feel incredibly strong and then…" Saje nodded grimly.

The medmech returned, its head sliding back to reveal a monitor. After scanning its contents, the woman turned back to them.

"You." She pointed to Nawalle. "Your profession on the crew?"

"Mechanic."

"Good enough. You're coming with me to the command deck. You will do as I say without question. And you?" She turned to Azad.

"Doctor, gardener, traffic controller, personal—"

"All right," she said curtly. "I only care about the first one. You will stay here with your sister, treat her symptoms and run a full scan of her DNA. She is the longest functioning survivor of the Origin Element exposure, and we need to start understanding why. You will remain in isolation until we can return to Nabatea."

"I don't understand," Azad said. "How can she be the longest survivor? What happened to the rest of the crew?"

A shadow passed over Saje's face and Azad's heart leapt to his throat. The banging sounds in the corridor took on a new meaning.

"They're dying, aren't they?" he asked. "You locked them up somewhere on the ship."

"I had to," Saje said, raising her chin. Her voice was tinged with regret but firm. "We could not return to the Nabatean system with an infected crew and someone had to maintain command. Tayyar and I were the only two who tested negative. He went scouting for survivors on the planet's outposts and came back with you. He must have gotten compromised on the way. The others…most of them are gone by now."

Ledo gagged, a string of black tar hanging from her mouth. Saje jumped back while Azad helped Ledo lie down, lifting her legs in the air until color returned to her face.

"Get out," the woman barked to Nawalle. "You're still clean and I need you to remain that way! You will help me keep the ship functioning until this doctor can find a way to treat this disease."

"And if I can't?" Azad yelled, tears forming in his eyes. Ledo's hope of finding a cure on the ship had been a false dream. He was not a medical researcher. He could not find a cure for alien viruses. Not even to save Ledo.

"If you can't, we turn the ship's fusion rockets into a bomb and evaporate this vessel," the woman said without emotion. "I will destroy everything on this ship before I compromise our civilization's future. The dream of Barrett Juul will survive, even if we don't."

And with that, she exited the room with a sobbing Nawalle, leaving Azad and Ledo on the floor, stunned and shivering under the lanterns' ochre glow.

Chapter Twenty
Kezza

CALYPSO CORPORATE CAMPUS
2195 A.D.

On her final night on Mars, Kezza left the shelter of the Eden sector to swing on her trapeze and lyra one last time. It was two in the morning and the hallways were empty, but she tiptoed down the cold floors in her bare feet to avoid drawing any unwanted attention. Her last performance didn't need an audience.

The Coliseum had never looked so empty or vast. She would miss its openness during those months in transit to Nabatea. Nowhere to jump and fly, but a small price to pay to land on fresh soil across the galaxy, to breathe open air. To be part of something greater than any circus performance.

Kezza climbed to the top of the upper stage, dusting excess powder from her hands. She performed her most dangerous move – the Dead Drop, where she dove and grabbed the lower ring without support. She tasted cool air and adrenaline. Her body jerked forward when her fingers found the ring. She pulled herself up, crossing her legs in the ring so that it framed her, twisting and twirling in its center. Lady in the Moon, it was called – one of the easiest lyra moves, but one that made her feel elegant, beautiful.

Most of her performances had been choreographed and dictated from a team on Earth, who knew Mars's gravity in theory but had never experienced it in person. Kezza always tweaked them, added her own flourishes, but this time, her performance was hers alone.

She swung from the lyra to the first of three trapeze bars, starting with the highest. Seated, she leaned back, stretching her arm out to a phantom audience, waving a final goodbye. Her turns became wilder, freer, with each rotation around the Coliseum, until she tilted her head to the domed ceiling, the stars spinning above her.

By the time Kezza finished, her face was wet with tears. She had energy for a second routine but the first had been so perfect, so *right*, it felt pointless to continue. At that moment, a dark shape caught her eye. A lone figure seated in the audience. Dr. Hamza.

"Perfect," the scientist said as Kezza swung toward her on the ring before descending and landing lightly on the conductor's platform. "I apologize if I interrupted a private moment. I can't sleep and I can't lie in bed awake, either."

"It's fine," Kezza said, wiping her eyes. "I was just ready to stop."

Dr. Hamza gestured for Kezza to sit beside her. She pulled a small bottle of clear liquid from her jacket.

"You look like you could use a drink," Dr. Hamza said. She took a delicate swig before handing the bottle to Kezza. "Arak – a Middle Eastern classic. Not to everyone's taste but give it a try."

Surprised, Kezza raised the bottle to her lips. The alcohol burned her throat, leaving a strong but pleasant aftertaste of anise in its wake. She suppressed a cough and handed the bottle back.

"It's strong," Dr. Hamza said. "Normally, it's diluted with water, but I've been told that's something of a precious commodity here."

"To say the least."

"What do you think of my son?"

Kezza coughed, clearing her throat. The astrophysicist waited, unflinching. Kezza would have expected a different question, or the same question phrased less bluntly. How could she summarize her relationship with the great civilizationist? She scrambled for a response.

"I...I have faith in him. I believe he can do what he promises."

Dr. Hamza narrowed her eyes but nodded. She took another sip of the arak, her gaze shifting to the open stage.

"Before the war, I actually dreamed of playing in the Beirut Symphony," she said softly. "I played the clarinet. But by the time I arrived in Europe, I learned the hard way that I needed a…practical career. One that would give me influence and knowledge in equal measure, to best achieve what I needed to achieve."

She had certainly done well for herself. A pioneering astrophysicist fortified by an army of shadow investors and a son who redesigned nations.

Unsure where to direct the conversation next, Kezza turned the topic back to Juul. "When I first met…Barrett, he mentioned your time during the war. How he's naming the planet Nabatea for a place you loved."

Dr. Hamza's mouth formed into a grim line, at odds with the rest of her smooth, flawless face. "Barrett tends to romanticize what he has little experience of. There are worse impulses, of course, so I say nothing. I pick my battles, Ms. Sayer. What I fear more are his tendencies to… personalize every conflict and let his emotions run away from him."

The bomb in the Atrium. It had been four days, long enough for the initial shock to wear off but recent enough to make Kezza's fingers curl, her skin prickling at the memory of the smoke and blood in her nostrils.

"It wasn't just personal," Kezza said, inclined to defend Juul in this instance. "They killed twenty people. It was meant to punish and frighten everyone unhappy with the system in place here."

"I don't disagree," Dr. Hamza said, turning back to Kezza with a stern, confiding stare. "But that's how it always begins. You kill twenty of mine, I kill thirty of yours. It started with retaliatory killings in Beirut, one street pitted against the next. And it didn't stop for twelve years. Barrett knows my history and he carries my burdens. He feels them, acutely. His work is on a macro scale, millions of lives being designed and remade. It's too big for anyone to comprehend, so he sees my story in every story of suffering. Humanity's failings have become his riddle to solve, because it's the only way he knows how to make sense of my past, to balance out the senselessness of it all."

"Not everything happens for a reason," Kezza said, bitter. Her mother's last days carried no cosmic justice, no balance for an opposing act. Just the fate of a desperate woman, fattened up on promises and left rotting on the inside. Like Kezza.

Perhaps sensing Kezza's train of thought, Dr. Hamza leaned forward and squeezed her hand.

"I don't mean to be pessimistic. This journey we will begin tomorrow is the best chance we have to start a new world with a clean slate, and I have every faith in its success. Just as I believe that there is hope for you, Kezza Sayer. I'm just a mother, always worrying. Thank you for listening to an old woman's ramblings."

Kezza left the Coliseum in a fog, her brain a swirling cloud of arak and Dr. Hamza's confessions. The click of Dr. Hamza's heels faded down the corridor toward the Eden sector, but Kezza turned toward the prayer room. Morning prayers would not begin for several hours, but Kezza welcomed the chance for solitude.

She stopped at the sound of another set of footsteps, light and fast. The prospect of interstellar space travel, it seemed, had brought out everyone's inner insomniac. The entire city devoted their energies toward the journey to Nabatea. In the last two days, the Catacombs buzzed with activity – families packing belongings, workers loading cargo onto *Calypso One*, Dr. Hamza's employees from the Obscura collecting data.

Preparations included the hundreds expected to arrive from Palmcorps, after Juul announced that a swap had been negotiated – Palmcorps citizens who wished to join the exodus in exchange for those on Calypso wishing to stay. But the memory of the bomb lingered. Members of the Palmcorps Corpsboard would arrive to meet Juul as part of the swap and the prospect of their arrival, their bloodstained feet marring the Atrium, turned Kezza's stomach.

The footsteps grew louder. Kezza paused at a familiar smell of cloves.

Peering around the corner, she found Amit running down the pathway past the Atrium toward the docking bay. A shiny object glinted at his side. Kezza's heart skipped. Her feet bare, she followed him with long, light steps.

When she reached the docking bay, Kezza hugged the wall, running toward a stack of boxes waiting to be loaded onto *Calypso One*. A plant symbol had been stamped on their sides. Crops and seeds from the

Greenery, intended as sustenance for the journey and a food source to introduce to Nabatea.

At the other end of the docking bay, Amit greeted none other than Barrett Juul. They shook hands. The shining object in Amit's other hand turned out to be a large briefcase, the same type used to house the substance from the crater.

A new vehicle had arrived in the docking bay. A figure emerged from its side and Kezza gasped aloud at the sight of Axel, head of the Palmcorps resistance, walking toward the other two men. There was no mistaking his muscular frame, the confidence in his gait. After a brief conversation, Amit handed Axel the briefcase. Whatever lay inside was apparently heavy, because Axel's arm dipped under its weight. He laughed in surprise. The three men continued to speak for another minute before Axel returned to his vehicle.

After Axel left, presumably back to Palmcorps, Juul and Amit walked back to the docking bay's exit. Kezza struggled to remain still, to overhear their conversation over her thundering heartbeat.

"Timing has to be perfect...only in effect once the Corpsboard leaves the city," Juul said to Amit in a low voice. "Need to...water supply."

Their voices trailed down the hallway, and Kezza sat behind the boxes for at least half an hour before willing herself to her feet. Her knees shook as she stood.

The fact that Axel could move between cities suggested that the blockade had been lifted on the lower Catacombs. But what had Amit given to Axel, and why? A part of Kezza, the tired part, argued that it didn't matter. It could have been one of many things – part of the negotiations between Calypso and Palmcorps, perhaps an exchange of money ahead of the swap, or a more covert activity under the Corpsboards' noses. Whatever the three had planned, it did not concern Kezza, who had enough problems to contend with already.

But the conversation with Dr. Hamza followed her back to her room in the Eden sector, along with a sinking sensation in her chest, like an anchor tugging her heart to the floor. Though she lay in bed, all hopes of sleep gone, and tried to rationalize what had occurred in the docking bay, primal instinct, deep in her bones, told her that something was wrong.

★　　★　　★

Calypso Corporate Campus rose with the sun. Voices and smells of sugary, stale breakfasts filled the hallways. The ore miners' guild oversaw the final loading of cargo, many marking the occasion with a middle finger in the direction of the Arabia Terra mines. Others lugged personal effects, limited to one bag per person, children under five not included. Mothers cradled irritable babies, Tier Two employees attempted to sell excess clothing to lighten their loads and the stream of passengers into the *Calypso One* shuttles began. In a break from the usual procedures, Tier Three employees boarded first.

The Atrium transformed into a place of farewells. Those departing to Nabatea outnumbered those staying, but enough had chosen to cast in their lot with Palmcorps, the Imam among them. He stood apart in the crowd, as others recorded shared farewells on their CALPals, which would soon become obsolete in deep space. Kezza approached him stiffly. Several other congregants stood beside him, although most who attended prayers had opted to leave, encouraged by the fact that a Lebanese woman, Dr. Hamza, promised a chance to return to the best of the region's traditions.

"You decided to stay?" Kezza asked.

The Imam nodded. "Some decided to go, but I belong with those who remain, where we can face Mecca and help the new arrivals on each opposition. There is enough of God's creation and beauty to enjoy here."

With the dusty, barren landscape stretching across the window behind him, Kezza failed to see any beauty on Mars. She struggled for a polite response.

"This is a broken planet tied to a broken system," she said. Juul's words but hers as well. "You could see a new planet. Be part of something greater than yourself. People will know your name on both sides of the galaxy, as someone who took a leap of faith and started a new world. Don't you want to take that leap?"

Kezza hoped that the reference to faith would reach the Imam on a deep, personal level, but he only smiled.

"Fame has no temptation for me," he replied.

"It's not just about fame, it's—"

"I understand what you're trying to tell me," the Imam said with the same, reserved patience he bore at every prayer session. "But I don't need to be the first Imam to leave the solar system, or pass through a – is it a wormhole? I live a simple life here, but it's rich in many ways thanks to the people who need me. Who I need in return. This is where I belong, Ms. Sayer."

Kezza nodded, although she couldn't understand. She had tried. "I wish you the best. Thank you for accepting me in the prayer room every night."

"Don't stop, if it comforts you," the Imam said. There was a smile and just a hint of urgency in his voice. "You're never too far away to pray."

Kezza cleared her throat and nodded. Sadness followed her as she turned away into the crowd.

A scuffle broke out in the hallway near the Coliseum. Kezza followed the shouts to find a small group encircling a lone man, wreathed in bandages. She groaned. The Tier Two she kicked across the tavern. One of the men in the mob noticed Kezza and his face broke into an excited grin.

"Remember this one, dancer?" he asked excitedly. "He wants to go home to Earth. Sweet, eh? We're finishing the lesson you started."

"Let him go," Kezza cut in. Surprised faces turned to her, none more so than the Tier Two man's. Even through his fear and exhaustion, some haughtiness remained as he took in Kezza from head to toe. But Kezza felt nothing. Men like him had lost the power to puncture her ego, to earn her fury. They would have no place where she was going.

"We don't want his kind on Nabatea," Kezza said in explanation. "Let him rot on Mars for another two years."

The Tier Two man paled. Not entirely pacified, the group reluctantly followed Kezza's lead, backing away from the man. Kezza lingered behind for a moment. The man winced, but she turned away. She had nothing to say to the bandaged, broken man who avoided her eyes. She didn't want an apology. She let him stand alone, squirming under her gaze, before returning to the Atrium.

Juul and Dr. Hamza stood on the podium with broad smiles. The first passengers had taken the shuttle up to *Calypso One*. Dr. Hamza announced days prior that the quantum foam wormhole methodology had passed multiple simulations. No one understood it, but she explained it with such smooth confidence that everyone accepted her explanations without argument.

The hum of the crowd dimmed as a group of men and women entered the Atrium, flanked by a combined cohort of Calypso and Palmcorps Security. The Palmcorps Board, along with several familiar faces from the Calypso Corpsboard. Axel entered separately, taking a seat on the podium behind Juul. The Corpsboard remained in the center of the Atrium, lined up like a row of stony-faced prisoners awaiting execution. The Calypso members in particular looked pale and wary, undoubtedly remembering the violence in this very room that they had barely escaped.

Beyond the Atrium door, voices swelled. A long line of passengers crossed the hallway into the docking bay. Palmcorps residents who had chosen to join the journey to Nabatea. Many had answered the call. The line extended down the hallway and a row of transport vehicles waited outside, visible through the Atrium's windows, loaded with additional emigrants. The Corpsboard stared stonily ahead.

Juul approached the microphone and raised his hands, bringing the Atrium to silence.

"Whatever side of the debate you stand on, whatever your choice may be, be in no doubt that you are all witnesses to the greatest breakthrough in human history," he said without preamble. "The day we began our departure from our solar system. But we are not leaving our mother system as much as racing toward something new. A new planet, yes, but also a new way of living, of thinking, of interacting and treating one another. A society without isolation and loneliness, but one where we serve each other. I am a civilizationist. It defines me completely. It is my highest honor to be here with you, at the beginning of our evolution, of transcending our past and creating a new future. We will not look back."

Juul wiped his eyes. A deep silence followed his words, as travelers and loyal Martians alike absorbed their meaning. A member of the Corpsboard shifted his feet, glancing at his watch. The others made similar shows of impatience, eager to move past the theater. Kezza shot a venomous glare in their direction.

"I commend the Palmcorps Corpsboard for reaching a compromise," Juul continued, waving his arm toward the grim line. "And for showing vision beyond their counterparts here on Calypso. I hope you continue that spirit after we depart and remember that the wealth of Mars derives from the working people who toil to tame it."

Enthusiastic applause followed, forcing the Corpsboard to join in. But one woman among the Corpsboard, an elderly Southeast Asian woman in a sharp suit, stepped forward.

"I descend from the First Forty," she said. "I was born here and will die here, as my family have done. I know what it means to struggle. What is Juul going to offer that's different from what we already have? The early years were hard. It took generations to colonize Mars, to build from the ground up. Don't think this distant planet – if you even make it there – will be any different."

The crowd jeered and several members of the resistance advanced menacingly around the Corpsboard, but Juul waved them back. A faint smile curled on his lips. For a second, his eyes flashed with the same fury he had unleashed after the bomb. Dr. Hamza caught Kezza's eye, raising her brows.

"I appreciate the knowledge and experience you bring, Corpswoman," Juul said over the fading protests of the crowd. "Although who we all descend from won't matter where we're going. I have no illusions that the settlement of Nabatea will be easy. But we will be aided by the fact that we'll work and live for ourselves, not a cabal of shareholders on Earth."

At these words, the crowd renewed their jeers and the Corpswoman stepped back into her place in line. Kezza flushed with satisfaction, though there was plenty of truth in the Corpswoman's warning, whether the mob realized it or not. Guards gestured for the remaining travelers to head to the docking bay.

Kezza returned to her room in the Catacombs. The door opened with an obedient click and a musty smell greeted her. A pot of coffee sat unfinished. Clothes had been yanked out of her drawers, scattered across the room, no doubt the aftermath of a ransacking by Calypso Security following her escape.

She only needed one thing. She fished through a box underneath her bed and pulled out a silver bracelet – her mother's. Her mother brought it from Earth, her only valuable possession to leave Kezza when she died. Supposedly, it was a gift from Kezza's father, who left her a year into life on Mars, after selling her on the lie. *It'll be an adventure, love,* she reassured a screaming, three-year-old Kezza when they boarded the precursor to *Calypso One* so long ago. She found a sad stream of men during her time on Calypso, but only cancer and Kezza remained with her at the end.

It hadn't exactly been an adventure, but without her mother's romantic impulses, Kezza wouldn't be here, about to board a ship on the farthest journey ever taken. Gripping the bracelet in her hand, Kezza touched the door before leaving, a silent goodbye to her mother, to the only home she had known. She smiled. The bracelet would have the unique honor of visiting three planets, as would she.

Kezza returned to a nearly abandoned Atrium. All who planned to travel to Nabatea had left for the docking bay, while those who wished to remain were boarding Palmcorps' transporters. The Imam's white hat disappeared down the hallway and Kezza felt a twinge of sadness that he hadn't changed his mind.

On the other end of the Atrium, close to the Coliseum's entrance, Juul and Axel faced the Corpsboard.

Kezza froze. Two bags, long canvas sacks, lay in between both parties.

"As agreed, your deceased workers," Barrett Juul said solemnly. "Evan Kim and Nancy Kim. It was the Calypso Corpsboard's decision to hoard and desecrate their bodies for research, but in the absence of their worst members, I apologize for their crimes."

"How do we know it's them?" the elderly Corpswoman asked. "Show their faces."

"You don't want to do that in front of all these people," Axel said in a rough, loud voice. He gestured toward the remaining Calypso employees waiting for their shuttle. "And you won't be able to ID their faces. Run a DNA test when you get back. That's the goal, anyway – research what happened to them."

"After you're passing through a wormhole?" another Corpsman sneered.

"Do you think we want to carry two corpses through space? Scour the entire Bokambe complex for all we care. You've got your dead, now take your people and go."

"Time to go." A member of the resistance appeared at Kezza's shoulder, scowling.

"I was just getting—"

"I said *move*."

As Kezza exited the Atrium, the door shut behind her, the lock bolt clicking in place.

Kezza's knuckles whitened as she gripped her backpack over her shoulder, quickening her pace. Why lock the door? Another realization hit her – how did they retrieve Evan Kim's body from the desert? It was certainly possible that someone on Axel's team had unearthed the corpse, but hadn't Nancy Kim's body been burned with the other infected when they left Calypso? Kezza's stomach lurched. If the bodies in the bag weren't Evan and Nancy Kim, then who were they?

Calypso One did not leave until Juul and Axel boarded hours later. As a transporter vessel, the ship boasted an impressive section for living quarters, though it must have seemed compact for the Earth-based colonists it transported. After the ride with Juul up to the Obscura, Kezza handled the ascent to *Calypso One* with ease. She entered a ship pulsing with excitement and something even more unusual – joy. Families helped one another settle in sleeping quarters, strangers smiled at her, everyone set about the task of preparing for launch together.

Is this what life on Nabatea would resemble? Her tension after leaving the Atrium lessened. Juul had a plan, and it would succeed.

Recognizing Kezza, a guard informed her that she would stay in the ship's medical ward under a 'loose quarantine'. Kezza vowed that upon landing on Nabatea, she would never set foot in another medical ward again.

She found Amit there, poring over tables of data on a large monitor.

"I'm going to need a few more samples of your DNA at some point," he said.

The ship rumbled as the fusion rockets activated. Kezza lay in her cot, her teeth rattling, while cheers rose down the corridor from the living quarters. A voice boomed over the ship's speakers.

"My fellow travelers," Juul said. "We're on our way."

Kezza closed her eyes, battling for control over a wave of nausea as the ship propelled forward. Once in motion, her body settled, but her mind continued to play its own reel. The explosion. Light footsteps in the night. The click of the bolt on the Atrium's door.

Chapter Twenty-One
Azad

AXEL SHIP, MARTIAN ORBIT
YEAR OF SETTLEMENT 1208

Hours passed without a sign of life outside of the laboratory. Azad stretched Ledo onto a bed, propping several pillows under her head as her body heaved with coughs.

"I'm fine," she said, but even she couldn't act well enough to hide the fact that she struggled for every breath.

"You need oxygen," Azad said and the medmech obliged, wheeling in a nearby tank.

"What happened to Nenah?" Ledo asked. "When she…was near the end?"

Azad squeezed his eyes shut, looking away. Composing himself, he reached for his sister's hand.

"Don't let your mind go there. You're going to be fine. We have the best medical equipment and data at our fingertips. You'll be ok."

Ledo snorted, which triggered another bout of coughing.

"I know how she died anyway," Ledo rasped. "I watched all of the others go before me. It's like a tug of war. They get strong, their bodies fight, then this…thing fights back harder. With aliens out there like those, I may have to rethink this exploring life."

She laughed but stopped at the sight of Azad's face. He worked silently, preparing a blood sample kit. When the medmech advanced, he waved it away. He would do this himself.

"It wasn't about you, by the way," Ledo said softly. "Why I ran away. I know it must have hurt after I left. But nothing could have made me stay."

"I didn't speak to anyone for weeks," Azad said. He didn't mean to sound angry, but a dam inside him had burst and the words flowed out. "The rest of the community told me to forget you, stopped saying your name aloud. You became a Problem to ignore. But I kept looking up to the night sky, wondering where you were. When you would come back. I felt so alone without you, Ledo."

Ledo seemed at a loss for words. Her lips parted to speak but she remained silent, staring at her hands. The skin on her knuckles had begun to crack.

"And you did it again," Azad continued, filling in the silence because he couldn't bear its weight. "To Nawalle and Zelle and Feisal. They care about you. Nawalle loves you, anyone can see that. When are you going to stop wandering, Ledo? When are you going to be happy with what you have?"

Ledo's eyes shone at something Azad could not see.

"I don't know," she said softly. "I keep waiting for that day to come, when I'm not looking for something else. But the universe, Azad…there's so much of it. More than anyone can ever hope to see. I want all of it. The present, the past. All of its borders, in space and time. It's crazy, but that's what I want."

"You can do all of that with Zelle's crew," Azad said, calmer now. "You can live a great life and not be alone. I understand now, Ledo, I really do. Why you left and why you could never go back. Because I can't go back now, either. You were right to leave – it just took me longer to realize that I should have done the same. But being free doesn't mean you have to be alone."

Ledo coughed again. She gasped, holding her hand in front of her mouth. When she pulled it away, streaks of red painted her fingers. A trail of blood ran down her nose.

"Guess I won't be having any more adventures, with or without the crew," she said with a weak smile.

"No." Azad pulled out the kit, holding a swab before Ledo's lips.

"We're going to beat this. Here – let me—"

"Stop, I'm a coughing and bleeding mess. I'll infect you."

"We'll sink or swim together, then."

He extracted a DNA swab, handing it to the medmech for processing. Ledo wiped a tear from her eye.

"Just let me go. It's over, brother. But I'm glad you're here."

A deep, rumbling sound interrupted them. They paused, glancing toward the door. Nothing.

Ledo rested, eyes fluttering occasionally at the whir of the busy medmech, while Azad faced the monitor, poring over Ledo's genome.

A sharp rapping sound came from the door. Ledo opened her eyes.

"What's happening?" she slurred.

Tentatively, Azad stepped closer to the door.

It flew open, its hinges screaming as metal collided with the wall. On the other side, Zelle and Feisal stood with stony expressions.

"How-how did—?" Azad managed to stammer before Feisal charged in, knocking Azad aside.

"Who on this Juul-cursed vessel destroyed Barry?" he said, his feverish eyes passing over Ledo and the medmech. "He's mine."

"A Vit-Vitruvian n-named Tayyar," Azad stammered.

"Who?"

"He's dead, floating on a detached shuttle in space."

Feisal spat. "I hope it was unpleasant."

"Very."

A crooked smile broke through Feisal's curled mustache and he turned to Azad again.

"You've survived longer than expected, *hadir*."

"Feisal, if you call me that one more time—"

"Oh, fine then," the Vitruvian said with a dramatic wave of his hand. "I guess you've earned an upgrade, even if you had to commit mutiny to prove you're not an unthinking robot anymore."

Azad turned to Zelle, meeting her cool dark eyes.

"I'm sorry," he began.

"Not now," she snapped. "Where's Nawalle?"

"The captain took her. Needed her to help commandeer, since she's one of the few functioning people left on this ship."

Zelle nodded. "To the command room, then."

"Let me come," Ledo gasped, pulling herself off the bed.

"You're not well," Azad said, but Ledo turned to the medmech, pulling back her arm's sleeve.

"Stim me," she said.

The machine acted before Azad could counter it. A syringe jabbed into Ledo's arm and she shuddered. After shaking her head several times, blinking with frightening intensity, she looked up with a bright smile.

"Ready. Great to see you, Captain. You too, Feisal. We'll avenge Barry together." She cackled at those last words, but Feisal pulsated with grim focus.

"Stay behind me," Feisal said in a low voice. "I'll deal with this captain."

Ledo staggered sideways every few steps but found her rhythm as they advanced through the ship's passageways. They entered the mezzanine of a two-story space, an area with a combination of lounge chairs and computer stations. The arched ceiling was a window into the outside, an imposing telescope aimed at the stars.

"Scouting room," Feisal said in a low voice. "This is an exploratory ship, so the crew would spend most of their time here, surveying new planets and so on."

"Where's the *Magreb*?" Azad whispered to Zelle.

"Docked to this ship," she said with a smile. "When we traced your departure out of Palmcorps with that dead man, we knew there was only one place you would be crazy enough to travel to. I expected us to get shot down on sight, but clearly, this ship has other distractions."

A banging sound erupted from below. After a pause, it resumed with less fervor.

Feisal dropped down to the lower level, standing near the door where the sound came from. He tapped at the door, resulting in a louder, more frantic knock from the other side. He flipped a switch near a control panel.

The walls along the side turned transparent, revealing the lit room behind them. Azad drew in a sharp breath, standing in front of Ledo as if to shield her. Through the glass, bodies spread across the floor. At least twenty lay dead, while a quarter of that number lay dying, twitching and crawling, leaving bloody streaks across the floor. One remained standing. Seeing Feisal through the wall, she pressed her hands to the glass, mouthing a silent plea. When Feisal only stared back, she punched furiously at the partition, striking with potent force.

Ledo observed the scene with a strange, dreamlike expression. Azad couldn't look away. This is what awaited Ledo. Every punch the dying woman threw thundered in his chest, his teeth rattling. Though the dead Vitruvians beyond the partition probably cared nothing for him, it gave Azad no joy to watch their suffering.

"Is there no way to help them?" Zelle asked Feisal. She clenched her fists, shooting a nervous glance at Ledo.

"Not at present," Feisal said. "Not without introducing unnecessary risk. She'd do the same or worse to us." He forced his gaze away from the gruesome scene, returning to the mezzanine. Zelle pointed across the walkway to a flight of stairs leading up another level. The command room.

They climbed the steps. Voices floated through the door. The group paused for a moment, considering their next step, when the door swung open and they came face to face with Nawalle.

Her mouth formed a perfect 'O' while Captain Saje's head rose behind her. Feisal leapt over Nawalle and charged at the Vitruvian captain. The woman pulled a stunner from her waist belt. Azad grabbed Nawalle and yanked them both to one side, just in time. Captain Saje fired and Feisal jumped straight in the air at incredible height, the stunner's pulse passing below his feet. Saje sprinted forward, ready to strike before he landed. Feisal kicked the stunner from her right hand while she pulled a Vitruvian dagger with her left.

"No!" Nawalle cried.

Captain Saje swung and Feisal barely dodged the strike. With a roar of frustration, Feisal swerved to the side, evading her swings with light, frantic steps.

"Feisal!" Zelle threw something at them. Both pairs of eyes darted away for a split second, but Feisal managed to catch the device one-handed, duck low and swing it at Saje.

He struck her with a light, swift crack. The Vitruvian captain screamed, curled into a ball and shuddered. Feisal kicked her across the head, rendering her unconscious.

"Don't kill her," Azad said quickly. "She treated us decently. Directed me to study Ledo while Nawalle helped with the ship."

"She was a little rude," Nawalle muttered under her breath.

"What kind of monsters do you think we are?" Feisal asked, panting slightly. He pulled the unconscious woman up to the command chair, strapping her in with zero-gravity binds. "This is her ship, after all. But we have questions."

Nawalle hugged Zelle and Feisal in the quiet lull. An uncomfortable moment followed as the crew stood together, united for the first time since the crater. Zelle turned to the trio of Azad, Nawalle and Ledo, arching her brow.

"I should never have disobeyed orders," Azad said.

"You were wrong to do what you did," she said, addressing Azad. "But I was also wrong to choose a historical trail over Ledo. After what we've seen in the last few days, I hope we can be forgiving of each other."

Nawalle exhaled loudly, blinking back tears.

"I'm just too charming, boss," Ledo chimed in, concealing a cough.

Zelle rounded on her.

"You've created a veritable tempest around yourself," she said with such conviction that Ledo took a step back. "Sent my crew into a tailspin, nearly got yourself killed, pulled your brother out of Nabatean life – all because a Vitruvian in a bar dangled something shiny at you, offered you a new adventure. A *month* away from our journey, but you couldn't wait."

"But I sent you that recording," Ledo said with forced cheer. "Gave you something to look for on Mars."

"And can we remember who the real criminals are here?" Azad asked, cheeks flushing. "The Vitruvians of the *Axel*, who tricked Ledo and others like her. They killed people for an idea."

"Thank you, brother. He's right, Captain. And by the way – we're on *Calypso One*."

Zelle sighed but her shoulders relaxed.

"That's what we hoped," Zelle said. "We watched Juul and the Martians leave Calypso – which was not easy with the smaller version of the quantum projector, by the way – but couldn't see the ship itself. They boarded in their primitive way of the time. Shuttles breaking atmosphere, to connect with a ship parked in geostationary orbit. We could only see Juul and the Martians leave. We saw it after Barrett Juul and his henchmen killed the remainder of the Martians on Calypso campus."

Nawalle gasped. Azad's head tingled, his tongue thick like cotton. Juul, founder of Nabatea, whose every quote he knew by heart – a killer.

"They spoke to a group of people," Feisal added, mustache twitching in disgust. "And two fighters burst out of body bags on the ground, started shooting down everything that moved with their old weapons. Everyone started screaming and running but they had locked the doors. Picked them off one by one while Juul watched with his hands behind his back."

"Lies."

Captain Saje had regained consciousness. She wrestled against her binds, throwing a snarl in Feisal's direction.

"The Founder gave the Martians every opportunity to choose their fate," she said. "Despite the corruption inherent in their primitive society. But he killed no one. That is a hideous slander."

Feisal readied a retort but Zelle held up her hand.

"This is painful for all of us," she said. "Believe it or not, I did not come here to slander our Founder or create a different narrative. I came to learn the truth and we have proof of that truth."

"Zelle of Nabatea, I presume?"

"If you have to throw unnecessary titles at me, I would prefer Captain Zelle of the *Magreb*."

Saje snorted. Feisal fiddled with Zelle's weapon, and the *Axel*'s captain eyed it warily. When she noticed Ledo in the corner, however, she recoiled.

"It's not airborne, genius," Feisal said with irritation. "It takes direct physical contact or exposure to the dead. One of your shipmates told us as much before he moved into the eternal ether. The way you locked all those poor souls up in that holding bay was a bit excessive, if you ask me. Just don't kill her or kiss any of us and you'll be fine." He paused for a flickering moment, as though rolling this new idea around his head, when Saje spat on the ground.

"My entire crew has been dying before my eyes," she said. "One at a time, until I commandeered a ghost ship. Have you any idea what that feels like?"

"Sadly, no," Feisal said with a searing stare at Azad. "But unless you were having orgies in the canteen area, my guess is the contagiousness came down to how you interacted with the corpses. We don't desecrate bodies, but there's a reason our ancestors did. They remain contagious."

Saje nodded. "Something we didn't know until we received the Archive download from our comrade in the Martian desert. But by then it was too late. Was that your doing, getting the download up to the *Axel*?"

Feisal inclined his head in a mocking bow.

"Indeed, it was. I honor our laws to a point. It's also how we tracked this ship. Picked up the coordinates during the transmission process."

"While this is fascinating," Zelle said with a hint of dryness, "let's get back on topic. Feisal, would you bring Barry in from the *Magreb*?"

Azad's heartstrings twinged with a pang of guilt. "How'd you manage to find Barry in those ruins?"

"Who or what is Barry?" Saje groaned, looking ready to be knocked unconscious again.

"We got enough of a signal from Nawalle's Relay to track your location on Palmcorps," Zelle explained while Feisal practically skipped out of the room. "You were gone by then, but we found the machine in a room, amid a lot of defunct mechs."

"Did you fix Barry?" Azad asked.

"We did," Zelle said. "The stunner shot didn't strike anything crucial, so the repairs turned out to be straightforward. You wouldn't know it, though, from the way Feisal reacted."

On cue, Feisal returned, wheeling Barry through the door. Saje flinched as she took in the imposing machine, with its dark, unblinking lens.

"And before you ask," Zelle added in a more serious tone, "we retrieved your footage from Palmcorps. All of it."

They started with the Calypso footage captured by the smaller device, downloaded to Barry's server. Azad understood what Zelle meant when she said that the past had been harder to capture without Barry; the smaller machine displayed a grainier image with a narrower radius in front of them, but the events unfolded clearly enough. Martians congregated in the city's old communal area, carrying luggage and saying goodbyes.

Still bound to her seat, Captain Saje's jaw hung open.

"This is incredible," she said with feeling.

Azad's heart hammered as a dark-haired woman moved through the crowd, addressing an elderly, bearded man.

"It's her! Kezza Sayer. She returned from Palmcorps."

"After you and Nawalle took your side trip and I got Zelle patched up," Feisal said with ice in his voice, "we fulfilled the plan to find out what happened at the crater in their time. Took a while, but we traced Barry back to the point where Juul discovered the crater. Kezza Sayer and some others we don't care about joined him as well. Gaped at it, took a sample. And then a vehicle came, attacked them, another vehicle showed up, attacked the previous vehicle and then took our Founder and his friends back to Calypso."

"Interesting," Azad said. Their ancestors lived undeniably violent lives.

"It only gets more interesting from that point," Zelle said. "Observe."

In Calypso, the crowd applauded as Barrett Juul spoke from a podium. At some point, he had transitioned from a guest of the corporate city to its leader. Feisal forwarded the footage. After the ship's passengers dispersed, Juul and another man remained behind and began speaking to a row of imposing men and women.

"From their different outfits and lapels, I believe we may be looking at the 'Corpsboard' of the other city, Palmcorps," Zelle said. "In the mother system, before we had orthodox Nabateans and Vitruvians, private companies governed their people on Mars."

"I recognize that man," Saje said. Her arms bound to the chair rests, she gestured with her head. "The one next to Juul. That's Axel, believed to be one of the first Vitruvians who evolved during the journey. This ship is named after him. His head is in the restricted section of the Library of Souls."

Silence followed as they absorbed this information. Zelle moved toward the holographic display, peering hungrily into the man's face.

"If that's true, you won't like what follows," Feisal said. "Watch."

The image spun to the other side of the room. Feisal must have pointed the device's lens in the opposite direction to focus on something. Kezza Sayer entered the room, only to be pushed out by a guard.

"It seems your girl isn't part of what follows," Feisal said to Azad with a smile in his eyes. "They rushed her out pretty quick."

The display spun again, back to Juul, Axel and the Corpsboard. The discussion continued with unmistakable tension. Two body bags sat between the two parties.

Azad held his breath. Though he already knew what would come, he still jolted as the bags ripped open and two masked figures burst through the tattered fabric with weapons in hand. The lined row of the Corpsboard barely had time to react. The closest two received shots to the head, dropping to the ground. The guard who had ushered Kezza out of the room joined in, picking off the scurrying crowd.

In the middle of the chaos, Juul stood still with arms folded. Through the grainy image, his face looked troubled, but he made no effort to move. Axel stayed at his side but, with his own weapon, occasionally fired at a civilian attempting to break through one of the sealed doors. The massacre lasted several minutes, during which Azad was sure he would faint. But it ended, and Juul and Axel stepped calmly over pools of blood on the way to the door.

Zelle spoke first.

"Barrett Juul led the willing people of Mars to Nabatea," she said. "But ensured that no survivors would remain behind on a world he hated, populated by people who betrayed and rejected him. This is evidenced not only by the fact that he killed off those in Calypso who chose to remain, but by the fact that a similar massacre occurred at Palmcorps.

"After we traced your steps and found Barry, we did more investigating around Palmcorps. We didn't have the time I would have liked, since we knew you were in danger, but we found the evidence we needed. Men in full atmosphere suits dumped a dismembered corpse into the city's main water tank."

The bodies on the ground in Palmcorps. The way they clutched their throats, collapsing to the ground when they realized there was nowhere to run. Water, falling from above.

Azad nodded. "The ceiling sprinklers switched on around the city. They were everywhere, in case of fire. They reached everyone."

"I will bet my right arm and my head of hair that that corpse had been infected with the virus from the crater," Zelle said. "The entire city exposed in an instant. And those that avoided the first wave would find themselves compromised in a city full of corpses and no place to escape. Is that what you were looking for on Palmcorps?" Zelle turned to Saje.

The Vitruvian woman shook her head. Color had drained from her face. Her eye twitched as if to blink away everything she had seen.

"We had not been aware of a second city on Mars before, so we set about excavating it," she said. "When it became clear that something catastrophic occurred there, we sought out evidence of natural disasters, system failures. But it did occur to us that the Origin Element in the cave might have caused the failure, and the authorities back on Nabatea City encouraged this theory. It would bolster the notion that the virus only killed non-Vitruvians, and those who had left Mars had been 'blessed' somehow. Special enough to adapt to the virus and take along those who could not evolve."

"Except there's a roomful of dead Vitruvians downstairs that prove otherwise," Feisal said. "And there's your little outpost in the desert. Only two made it out alive from there, and one is standing right here." He gestured to Ledo, who coughed on cue.

At the mention of two survivors, Saje's skin turned even paler.

"Nenah," she whispered. "She made it back here in terrible shape. By then, half of the ship was compromised. I immediately tried to isolate her, ordered the mechs to lock her with the others. When she saw that no one would help her, she ran back to her shuttle and detached from the *Axel* and passed through the wormhole. It astounds me that she made it back."

Ledo flushed, a feverish glow in her eyes. Azad guessed at her thoughts. Nenah had tried to seek help for them both. When that failed, she turned back home, in a last-ditch attempt to survive.

"Apparently, Nenah thought that the answer for a cure might lie here," Azad said, careful not to say anything that would upset Ledo further. "Was she right?"

Saje shook her head, grim. "We learned enough from the experiment in the desert to understand the virus better, but not to cure the infected. There was one key breakthrough that might help us. From our samples, we broke down the properties of the alien virus and found that Vitruvians, and only the Vitruvians, had DNA that appeared to share remarkable properties with the viral vector. Meaning that at some point, the people we know now as Vitruvians had been exposed to the vector. The rest of Nabatea had not."

The room held its breath. Even Feisal appeared stunned. Azad flushed. He had posed the same theory back on Mars, albeit without evidence, that the Vitruvians had a connection to the virus. He had been right.

"If that's true, then why does everyone die equally when exposed?" Feisal managed.

Saje nodded, apparently expecting the question. "First of all, they don't quite die the same. Notice how some downstairs are still alive? To be Vitruvian is to be adaptable. When we are deprived of oxygen, our bodies try to exist without it for as long as possible, slowing our circulation. When exposed to the virus, our bodies fight it harder than you could, but the vector always wins in the end. But to answer your question, it seems that *direct* exposure to the substance in its pure form is deadly, regardless of whether our DNA had been previously altered at some point in our evolution. But this is where the mystery lies. How did Vitruvians come to be, then? It appears that we were exposed to the virus, but *something else* allowed it to exist in our bodies and thrive. Our ancestors must have found a way to alter it."

"There's still an anomaly in all of this," Zelle said. "Ledo is still alive and doesn't appear to be contagious. An orthodox Nabatean who received a direct dose. She's not well but has outlasted most."

"And that," Saje said with a sad smile, "is why I wanted her here. Why Tayyar went scouting for her. Something about her is different, but we sadly may not have the time to find out what it is."

"Kezza Sayer," Azad said.

Everyone stared at him.

"Don't look at me like I'm crazy," he said, heat spreading across his cheeks. "We've been following her, and she was different as well. Strong for her size, like a Vitruvian, but she coughed up black liquid. They arrested her in Calypso, scanned her body. They knew something was unique about her. That's why she went to the crater with Juul. They knew she was the key to this virus."

To Azad's surprise, Zelle beamed at him. For a moment, her steely gaze dissolved, and she became the warm, grandmotherly figure that first greeted him in the library.

"I believe our doctor may be on the right path," she said. "I haven't forgotten that you proposed this same idea in the outpost. Time to put those ideas to the test. We know this ship is *Calypso One*. And we know Kezza Sayer made it on the ship. Feisal, how will Barry respond to the laws of space in this instance?"

The question made no sense to Azad, but Feisal scratched the back of his neck, lost in thought.

"We aren't on the same path in space that *Calypso One* took to Nabatea," he said slowly. "But we are in the same confines where the probabilities of the past journey became observable realities. So I believe that if we run Barry through these hallways, we'll see what occurred on this ship hundreds of years ago. But only for the parts of the ship that existed back then. It would help to see the schematics, to see what's original and what was built on to," he added, arching a brow at Saje.

Captain Saje observed the crew as though they were an alien species. Conflict raged behind that bob-framed face, but something had softened in her eyes, a sense that, if they were not yet allies, they shared an interest in survival that required them to cooperate.

"Certainly," she said after a pause. "If we can discover how our ancestors neutralized this virus, we can treat the afflicted. We must. We cannot pass through the Emigrant's Wormhole back to Nabatea until we ensure we're not a danger to our system."

"She threatened to blow up the entire ship earlier," Azad added, earning a derisive snort from Feisal.

"Give us time, Captain," Zelle said in a more respectful tone.

"Do I have a choice? But we may not have unlimited time. Since Nenah made it to Nabatea after I became captain—" Her voice cracked, and Azad guessed that she had only become captain after most of the ship's chain of command fell to the virus. "I flagged her as dead, assuming her ship wouldn't go far, given her state. But since she survived the trip, the authorities in Nabatea City may be aware of our plight and take matters into their own hands."

"Meaning send a vessel our way and shoot us into dust?" Nawalle asked.

The captain nodded.

"She survived to make it to the hospital where I worked," Azad said, a terrible chill flooding his senses. "They Archived her. Put the band on, placed her in the Library of Souls."

"Which we stole," Nawalle reminded him, but Captain Saje's face confirmed Azad's fears.

"They review Vitruvians with unexplained deaths immediately. I would assume that they managed to copy or comb through the Archive Band's data before you made off with it. Once they piece together her memories of the virus and the infected ship, they'll come for us."

An agonizing pause followed. Ledo's life, all of their lives, hinged on piecing together clues from the Great Escape, the original journey to Nabatea, and extracting a cure. If the virus failed to kill them, the Vitruvian authorities would finish the job.

"I can run an analysis on Ledo's DNA," Azad said. "But we need to find out what happened on this voyage that caused Vitruvians to come to be. Kezza Sayer is the key. She *has* to be. If we find out what happened to her, then maybe we can find a way to contain this virus. It's that or die, and I have things to do before I die."

The group stared at him. Ledo winked at him before coughing with alarming intensity. Feisal and Saje shared a glance that veered between surprise and amusement, to hear an orthodox Nabatean speak so assuredly. Nawalle stole an anxious glance at the radar, as though expecting a Vitruvian vessel to burst into view at any second. But Zelle smiled at Azad.

"I think our task is clear, then," Zelle said. "Feisal, time to put Barry back to work."

Chapter Twenty-Two

Kezza

CALYPSO ONE, MILKY WAY GALAXY
2195 A.D.

"Let me go!"

Kezza pushed Amit aside, struggling to comb her hair with one shaking hand while the other held a compact mirror. She never cared much about her hair on Mars, any more than her profession required, but self-care had become critical on the journey. She never felt clean. The rotational gravity, supposedly identical to Martian gravity, didn't feel right. Her stomach flipped at the sight of the soy-compressed meals. And her whole body cried for the sleep her nightmares denied her.

"Why would they bolt the doors?" she kept asking aloud. *Space madness,* she overheard Amit tell Juul once. Others had it as well. *The wormhole was traumatic to many of us. She'll be herself again before long. Give her space.*

Traumatic barely began to describe the wormhole passage. Dr. Hamza had performed the calculations, throwing out jargon about quantum foam and dark energy, but even she couldn't guess what the experience of crossing through would be like. The warning came before they approached it, a wormhole conjured by Dr. Hamza's quantum wizardry, and everyone lay down in a fetal position, as recommended. The ship roared and creaked, lurching as though dropped from a great height, and Kezza's body turned inside out. Her brain leapt out of her skull, her bones burst through her skin, her lungs clapped together like two hands. It felt as much, anyway, but when the universe righted itself on the other end, her body looked no worse for wear.

Screams had filled the ship, cries of terror, once they made it to the other side. Some vomited while others lay down, catatonic. But they survived. And once the trauma faded, crowds congregated around the ship's windows, gaping at the sights outside. Some fell to their knees in a moment of reverence at creation's beauty.

Kezza lingered long after others had resumed daily life, spending hours with her face pressed to the yawning window on the ship's front deck. Their new home sat on the opposite end of the galaxy but closer to the Milky Way's glowing heart. The dense band of light stretched like a river through clusters of purple gas, arms of light bleeding from its center. Stars scattered away from the heart like clouds of dust. Its beauty made her feel both small and powerful. Though a comparatively small piece of carbon-based matter, she was alive, one of the first of her kind to witness the universe's vastness from a new vantage point.

They passed a dark planet covered by swirling clouds, an imposing behemoth against two satellite moons. A gaseous planet, Juul explained. They would reach Nabatea in eleven months.

"Kezza, we need another blood sample."

"Do I look like a bottomless well?" Kezza scowled at Amit but raised her foot. Back on Mars, her doctor with the cockatoo hair mined her body on a monthly basis but at least gave her tangibles in return. Medications, massages, muscle therapy. Even food credits, if she stayed thin. Everything Amit took disappeared into computers and petri dishes, offerings to a god of discovery that performed no miracles and gave no answers.

"It's extraordinarily complex, Kezza," Amit said. "The proteins your mutation produces need to fight off but not overwhelm the viral vector. To cure it, we must test until we find the right cocktail."

"If you're going to bring up cocktails endlessly, you could at least make me one," Kezza snapped.

If only they needed less blood. Her body felt weak, and in those bouts of weakness her mind followed, until doubts battled each other through the fog. *Why did they lock the door?* The question consumed her waking hours, her dreams, the nightmares that woke her each night. Or at least, the hours that the ship considered night. En route to their new home, days had lost their planetary cycle, but they adhered to a routine of night and day out of biological necessity, the ship turning dark during the requisite ten hours. It was in those hours that Kezza struggled most, turning in her bed, closing her eyes but unable to extinguish the fears burrowing into her subconscious.

Several pints of blood lighter, Kezza's head sank into the pillow while Amit worked. Blood pounded in her tender, aching skull. Her whole body ached with exhaustion. She must have faded at some point because when her eyes next opened, a large figure bent over Amit's desk, pointing at the monitor. Axel. She could smell the engine grease and steroids radiating off of him.

Kezza's eyes snapped shut. She slowed her breathing to mimic sleep. They spoke in low voices, but with concentration their words were clear.

"We'll start with the snake, of course, but at some point, we need human testers," Amit muttered.

"Don't worry about that," Axel said, in his best impression of a subdued voice. "We have a list. A select group with unquestioned loyalty to the vision on Nabatea."

"It might be better to broaden the test group to the physically fit and those who want to volunteer."

"No, it wouldn't. I want to make something very clear. When you figure out how to make this work, it's not going to be available to everyone."

Kezza suppressed a gasp, covering it with a deep sigh. Her eyes twitched and her feet itched with the urge to kick the cartilage off of Axel's nose.

"What do you mean 'not available'?" Amit asked, his voice rising slightly. A pause followed, perhaps to check that Kezza remained asleep. Her heart fluttered but she kept her eyes closed, drawing a deep breath.

"Meaning that the entire ship doesn't need to evolve into superhumans," Axel continued in a low growl. "It doesn't fit the model Juul put together. Something about not making the majority too adaptable. Only those in leadership need the cocktail."

"It's supposed to be a cure," Amit said.

"And it is. If our circus friend here fucks her way through the crew and infects someone, we'll treat them."

"Is that really necessary?" Amit asked, angry. Kezza's jaw tensed but she kept her eyes shut.

"All I mean is we'll do what we have to do if others get sick. But this is not going wide. If you have a problem with that, take it up with Juul."

Their conversation shifted to the technical details of Amit's progress. Kezza's ears burned as she tried to contain herself, to avoid leaping out of her bed and screaming at the pair of them. Instead, she forced each muscle to relax, the way she loosened her body before a big jump on the trapeze. She knew what to do.

Axel may have misinterpreted Juul or simply been pushing his own agenda. *Not for everyone.* Wasn't that the opposite of what Juul, what the resistance, stood for? Once the coup ended, they hadn't retaliated against the Tier Ones and Twos who cooperated. Some of them were even on this ship.

Kezza needed an explanation directly from the source. After all she had done, this was her future world as well.

She found Juul the next day in his private room.

"Ah, Kezza! Needed a break from the medical room?"

"I need a permanent break from all things medical," she said, grabbing a protein cube from a bowl on his desk and peering over his shoulder. He let out a forced chuckle but tolerated her over-the-shoulder reconnaissance. Being a civilizationist, Kezza had discovered, involved more mathematics than she would have expected. Simulations had to be run using quantum computers to predict everything from population growth, human settlement and interaction with the biological world. Juul's work in the Koreas had been ground-breaking for predicting famine cycles to the day, accounting for climate changes and food consumption habits.

Now, Juul practiced his simulations on an alien planet, using images taken from *Calypso One*'s telescope, already relaying detailed images of the planet's topography.

"Where does my dream house go?" Kezza said, chewing the cube with an open mouth. Juul laughed again.

"Actually, see these mountains here? It might be more effective to carve living spaces into them, rather than build houses in open fields. The sun will be more intense here than what we're used to, you Martians especially. There's signs of underground water, and—"

"And what about the 'leaders'?" Kezza interrupted, unable to stop the venom from leaking into her voice. "Where will they live, with their virus-enhanced bodies?"

Juul pushed his monitor away, resting his hands on his lap. He stared down at them, his long hair falling over his eyes.

"Who spoke to you?"

"No one."

"Then why do you—"

"It was Axel. I overheard him and Amit talking. He said that the cure for the virus wouldn't be open to everyone. It would be a secret."

Juul stood up. Barely taller than Kezza, he looked her squarely in the eye.

"You don't approve."

"To say the least."

"Don't be flippant!" Juul slammed his palm against the table. "I've never met such a naturally intelligent person so ruined by bad thinking and poisoned ideas. You live in a fantasy world, Kezza, if you think we can establish a new society without some limits in place. In case you've forgotten, I'm the civilizationist here. Not you! You're a circus performer aware of her own unimportance in the dark, scary universe, fighting for relevance by latching on to others' dreams. You don't matter, and that scares you more than anything else."

"If the civilizationist gig doesn't pan out, you could make an excellent living as a rent-an-hour therapist," Kezza said lightly, masking the deep cut his words had carved. "But we both know you're going to try to convince me that creating a group of superhumans is somehow a good idea and in our best interests. That's what you do. So, get it over with."

"Has living on Mars taught you nothing?" Juul asked. "It is not enough to simply live in a hostile environment. We need to adapt to our environment if we're going to have a viable future in deep space. Humanity must evolve. This...virus is a gift, an opportunity to traverse the stars without our crude biological constraints. You carry the key to opening it, Kezza. You want a place in history, a way to leave a meaningful legacy? This is it. This is all that's left. Let us use your illness for a higher purpose."

"What higher purpose?" Kezza exploded. "You're going to create the same system we had on Mars. Two groups of people. The powerful and everyone else." It did not escape Kezza that Juul no longer mentioned her chances of surviving. He didn't expect her to live, but now appealed to her deep, consuming desire to live on in other ways. To make history. But what kind of history would she help create?

"Hierarchies are not inherently evil. They are evil on Earth, where they create artificial constructs and consolidate wealth and power with a select few. But if you calm down and listen to me, that is not what I'm planning for Nabatea. We need equal but different roles—"

Kezza laughed. "I can't tell you how many times I've heard 'equal but different' being thrown out at me. Funny how some groups get to be different in ways that are more valued." -

"No, no, no!" Juul's face turned pink. In that moment, the great civilizationist resembled an angry child being challenged for the first time.

"We were supposed to be equal, all of us," Kezza said. Tears burned in her tired eyes. Had all of Juul's speeches, his soaring words, been lies? "Those little communities you talked about. Everyone taken care of, everyone sharing the workload. *Everyone* equal."

"There is no equality between species!" Juul said, voice rising. "That is what will occur here – two different species of people. When the vector is contained, we will have a new type of human in all respects. One that could adapt to different atmospheres on different planets without thousands of years of evolution, heal at faster paces, possess the strength and speed of a predator. These will be society's makers and innovators, the ones who advance art, medicine, philosophy and exploration. But in every human civilization, very few have the luxury to cultivate their talents and advance humankind, so trapped in their basic survival. And then there are others, the majority who will never have the ability or capacity to make significant contributions – in fact, attempts to try such feats make them miserable. They hate change, they hate excess choices, they simply want to live quiet, fulfilling lives with people around them that they care for. On Nabatea, there will be no anxiety or ambiguity over which class a person belongs to. We will have the workers who make up Nabatea's backbone, never bored or alone. And those with enhanced genetics will be freed up, bolstered by the labor of the majority, to do as they please and push humanity's boundaries. That is why everyone cannot have access to the vector! That is why everyone cannot *know* about the vector. Even those who are blessed with its advantages will lose their knowledge of their origins, how they came to be different. I have planned it that way – they will simply consider themselves a different type of human with a different purpose under one single, unified, orderly civilization."

Kezza backed toward the door. Though he wielded his usual eloquence, Barrett Juul couldn't convince her. Not this time. She'd lived too much and learned enough history to know when a plan would fail. Her hopes, her faith, deflated within her like a collapsed lung. She had been deceived. Taken advantage of, as she had been countless times on Calypso. She could've prevented this, a long time ago, by killing Juul when he first arrived on Mars. But she'd let herself be fooled by his dreams and schemes. She was a gullible idiot.

Kezza couldn't help it. She burst into tears.

"Kezza," Juul said slowly. He advanced toward her while she continued her slow retreat. "You and I are the same at heart. I saw it when we first met. We think beyond ourselves. Your sacrifice, should you fail to survive before a cure is found, will be the greatest gift for human evolution. You will never be forgotten."

"I'm going to—" she whispered before stopping herself. What was she going to do? Make Juul's plans public? On the narrow confines of a spaceship, filled with passionate followers who believed Juul would lead them to a distant, promised land? Stop Juul in some other way? Kill him? She certainly had the strength to do some damage – for now.

An inkling of Kezza's thoughts must have made their way onto her face, because Juul lunged forward, grabbing her by the throat. Kezza gasped.

"You will cooperate," he whispered in her ear. "And remain silent.

You will accept your legacy and for once, understand when the battle is over."

Kezza kicked him, landing a sharp blow on his right knee. He grimaced in pain, sinking down and relaxing his hand. Kezza burst through the door, running along the ship's main walkway. She needed to find LaValle, or someone else from the circus. Someone, anyone, who would listen to her.

"Help!" she cried. "He's insane, he—"

A rush of air whipped at her hair but before she could turn to its source, a force struck her head with a violent crack. The walkway tilted, until her face touched its cold grating and the world around her receded.

★   ★   ★

Kezza woke up strapped to her bed. The somber group standing around her scrutinized her as though she were a mental patient. Dr. Hamza, hands folded, with a perfunctory, sympathetic smile. Any acknowledgment of their previous confidence had been erased from her smooth features. Evgenia, bored and impatient. Axel, his thick eyebrows lowered like a canopy as he frowned. Juul, radiating fury and wounded betrayal in equal measure while Amit sat in the corner, a different type of concern on his face.

"We're all friends here," Juul said. "We all know what's at stake. Kezza, you were given freedom on an isolated ship despite your contagious nature because you were a friend. Your friendship was integral to this entire enterprise. Your privileges have now been revoked. You will remain here where you can no longer harm others."

The group began to file out of the room. Kezza opened her mouth to retort, but her tongue slid to one side out of her mouth, heavy and swollen. She tried to raise her head and failed, the room spinning. A gurgling scream escaped from her throat.

"It's ok." Amit's voice. A hand appeared, brushing hair away from her eyes. "They gave you a sedative, but it'll wear off in an hour. I'll be here with you."

The tears didn't come again. Kezza wouldn't have been able to wipe them away, bound and silenced. She may as well have been back on Calypso, reduced to a collection of body parts to be mined and used by others. Her friends had become vampires, stroking her hair while they drained her dry.

Time passed in starts and stops. She drifted in and out of consciousness and when she woke up, she had to remind herself of where she was and why. True to his word, Amit remained close by. Her binds had been removed. A metal tray lay close to her head on a nearby table, filled with several vials of blood and a scalpel. She kept a careful eye on Amit while her hand darted up and grabbed the scalpel. She brought it to her side, running a finger across its sharpest edge.

Seeing her lucid again, he sat beside her with a sad smile. She whispered his name and he leaned closer.

"Kezza, what did you say to Juul?"

Kezza lunged forward. In a single, swift motion, she grabbed Amit's throat, her other hand pressing the scalpel to his neck.

"What did you give Axel in the docking bay the night before we left Mars?"

"What?" he gasped, eyes widening as she pressed the sharp point against his skin.

"I saw you. You gave Axel something."

Amit's left hand wandered toward the medical tray, but Kezza rose from her bed, her face inches away from his.

"Don't try it," she said. "I'm more than willing to infect you. Think a cough in the face will do it? Some spit in your eye?"

Amit groaned, squeezing his eyes shut.

"I didn't want to," he said in a soft voice. "But I have to follow orders. He didn't want any loose ends on Palmcorps. He didn't want the Corpsboard to survive."

A knot formed in Kezza's throat. "Tell me."

"We infected that man, Alan Schulz, with the virus," Amit said. "Using your blood. Put his remains in the water supply. The plan was to activate the sprinkler system as the others came back to Palmcorps.

Everyone who stayed would be compromised. All of the Tier Ones, the security who suppressed the revolt."

The room spun. The Imam, his remaining congregants. Families, children, anyone reluctant to leave the only life they had known. All dead or dying as she lay there, Amit's face inches from hers.

"Murder," she whispered.

"Revenge," Amit said. Sweat formed on his forehead. "But yes, it wasn't right to kill them all. We could have stopped with the Corpsboard."

The locked doors in the Atrium. Whatever had happened, Juul clearly ensured that the Corpsboard met the same fate as the remaining citizens on Palmcorps. Everyone on Mars, dead, to ensure that the failed Martian experiment could not happen again.

Kezza pressed the scalpel deeper into Amit's neck, puncturing skin. A low whimper escaped him as a bead of blood ran down his neck. But Kezza paused. She couldn't bring herself to infect another person. Thousands on Mars now struggled for air, clawed at their throats, likely fought each other for survival. Infecting Amit could cause a similar chain reaction on the ship.

Instead, Kezza jerked forward, striking Amit's head with her own. He reeled and she shot out of bed, finishing him off with a kick. He crumpled to the ground, unconscious.

Wincing, Kezza yanked the IV drip from her vein, eyeing the door. She knew what she needed to do.

She needed to die.

To stop Juul, she would not only have to die, but obliterate herself to the point where no part of her remained to harvest. Samples of her DNA had already made their way to the incinerator in the fusion rocket, disposed of by Amit once he was done with them. Now the rest of her would follow.

They would curse her name, and then her name would become a curse word itself. But she wouldn't let Juul win, after what he'd done. She would not be part of a future even worse than Mars. She'd stop him from creating his twisted new world, even if it meant turning into ash in a single, terrible second.

She left the ward, advancing down *Calypso One*'s narrow corridors. Laughter drifted down the hall from the main living quarters. Through a crack in the door, several men and women stood in a circle around a solitary light, talking through the sleeping hours. LaValle and Jen stood in a dark corner, whispering. Kezza's heart clenched. She couldn't say goodbye, so she continued down the hallway.

She found the communications room. Normally used to relay updates to Earth and Mars during the periodic opposition journeys, it now sat empty, used only for storage. No need to communicate back to Earth, and no one remained on Mars to communicate with.

With shaking hands, Kezza switched on the recorder. She tried to select the option to send her recording back to Earth, but the system denied her request – either Earth was too far away, or Juul had restricted communication by design. Instead, she chose to enter a log in the ship's archives. No one on the ship would listen to her now, but some day, they might. Maybe her sacrifice would be known by someone not yet born, in a place far away.

She began her message, but the words dissolved into the air as soon as she spoke. She could not recall what she said, her thoughts scrambled and urgent. Soon, she would be dead. Nothing less would stop Juul. Death hovered over her shoulder, its breath cold on her neck.

A rap on the door interrupted her recording. She switched it off, entered her message into the ship's log with a password, and hid behind the door.

Another loud rap. A pause, and footsteps trailed away.

She waited another minute before forcing herself to venture outside.

Kezza opened the door, coming face to face with Amit. His bruised face widened with shock and he grabbed her wrist, pushing her back into the room. She struggled but a wave of weakness overcame her, forcing her to her knees.

"What are you doing in here?" Amit asked. He glanced over her shoulder at the communication room's array of equipment.

A half-truth might suffice. "Recorded a goodbye in the logs. It's hidden with a password. I wanted to leave something of myself behind in this ship, before I die."

He yanked her by the wrist, pulling her to her feet. "Kezza, you don't have to die. I'm close to a cure. Trust me. You're losing your mind. All you need to do is calm down and think clearly."

"I am thinking clearly," Kezza said, tears springing to her eyes. "That's why I have to die."

"Kezza—"

"I can't be a part of this any longer. I can't live on another version of Mars, which is what Juul is going to create. Please, Amit. Just let me go."

Amit's brown eyes wavered, his grip loosening. He understood. He may have even empathized. Hadn't he been ordered to poison innocents on Juul's orders? A haunted look passed across his face. Kezza seized that moment and twisted out of his grip, running out of the room and down the hallway.

She ran to the other end of the ship, only looking back when she neared the engine room, where no passenger was meant to go. Amit had not followed. The incinerator remained within her reach, but she had to be quick.

Kezza descended the stairwell. Her mind felt both stretched to its furthest frontiers and oddly blank, filled with a singular focus. Only one option had been left to her. All that remained was to carry it out.

The bowels of the ship groaned and creaked as she traversed the walkway. Her knees rattled. Was it fear? Or just unsteadiness after a lifetime on solid ground? The walls closed in around her. Minutes became decades, each forward step a mile, as time closed in around her.

Would it hurt? Would it be quick? Even if it was quick, would there be a moment of excruciating pain before she entered eternal oblivion, her last moment of consciousness one of such agony, she would not want to survive it? No – she couldn't think that way. The questions meant nothing – the answers to them would change nothing. She would do what she had to, regardless.

Heat greeted her as she opened the door into the engine room. Empty, as she expected. Long gone were the days when crew manned ships. Computers did the heavy lifting, humans intervened only when necessary. Her final walk would be lonely.

She crossed the room into the upper walkway. Signs warned her of danger, not to enter except in extreme emergencies when the ship was in operation.

Through the door window, the main fusion reactor groaned and rumbled below. A narrow gangplank ran along both sides of the massive engine sector, overlooking the main propulsion system, which powered the fusion rocket. The main heat resided outside of the ship, but the plasma rocket, where energy was converted, resided within the interior engine room. A walk through the door and a jump from the gangplank would plunge her into the plasma heat source, obliterating all past and present traces of Kezza Sayer.

A portal window to Kezza's right unveiled the canvas of space. Stars blinked back at her through clouds of cosmic dust, a golden band of light. Somewhere, on the other side of that band, Mars glowed.

Her throat tightened. Even saying goodbye silently could trigger her instinct to live, to survive at all costs. Already, her muscles turned on her, tightening around her neck and twitching at her hands as she reached for the interior engine room door. Inhaling deeply, forcing calm into her limbs, she turned the handle.

The handle didn't turn. Locked. She tried again, pressing her weight against the door. Nothing. She scanned the room, searching for a heavy object to swing at the lock, as she had seen in countless movies imported from Earth.

She froze. A face looked back at her from the outer engine room's entrance, the one she had passed only moments ago.

Kezza ran to the door, panic bubbling in her like a poison, spreading across her battered body. She grappled the handle, a strangled noise erupting from her throat, but Barrett Juul had locked her in on both sides. She slammed her hands against the window, against his stony, unsmiling face.

"Let me go!" she yelled.

He didn't respond. At last, he had run out of things to say to her. Like Kezza, only action remained.

He gestured to someone at his side, someone who Kezza could not see but who had betrayed her. Betrayed everyone on the ship. Amit? Or someone who just happened to spot her wandering down the hallway, deciding to alert Juul? She would never know.

A warning sign flashed above the door. For several moments, nothing happened. She faced Juul, defiant as she could manage. Then the room spun. She drew in breath but found none.

Oxygen drained from the room, from her lungs.

With her last remaining air, she screamed. She pounded with all her strength on the door. Fury, terror replaced air in her veins, until she couldn't see in front of her, only red light that seared her vision. Tears spilled out from her eyes, snot fell from her nose, her courage shed away from her body. She needed air. Every particle in her screamed for air, for life.

The pressure lessened, focus returning to the room as it had once done on a stairwell in Calypso, when a criminal stealing her hard-earned money kicked her to the ground. Another criminal watched her through the window now, pale but patient, while her body fought to survive.

Agony returned, worse than before, worse than she thought possible. She gagged, thick, black liquid filling her throat, her mouth. Her eyes burned. She touched them, finding blood on her fingers. She slammed a hand to the window, leaving red streaks across the glass over Juul's face. She tried to scream again, but her legs buckled, her lungs burned, pain licked at her hands, her mouth and feet.

Then the fear evaporated. The face through the window dimmed and flickered like a candle flame, and for a second, it changed into someone else. Her mother? *Mummy*. She became a child again, lying in bed while her mother sobbed nearby. Old memories danced before her like a movie reel. A sample of an old song. A classroom. A moment of joy, of spinning through the air.

Suddenly, she lay on the ground. Her head found the window and the stars gazed back at her. The ship moved so fast, but the stars stayed still through the glass, ancient and uncaring. Each one a throne of light, around which worlds gathered.

Peace flooded her. She was almost home.

Chapter Twenty-Three
Azad

AXEL SHIP, MARTIAN ORBIT
YEAR OF SETTLEMENT 1208

Azad couldn't breathe. His vision narrowed into a tunnel, the world around him receding until only Kezza's face remained. Terror scarred her face as she struggled for air, black tar seeping through her lips, and Azad, separated by a door and over a thousand years, could feel the horror of her final moments in his very bones.

"Why is it taking so long?" Azad asked.

"Her body's fighting it, looking for ways to stay alive," Feisal said. He spoke with his head bowed, his face fixed in somber rage. "She was our first Vitruvian."

Kezza stopped pounding at the door, panic draining from her face. Her eyes glazed over, filled with the peace only known by the drowning, before she collapsed to the floor.

Azad pushed the door open, walking through Barrett Juul's ghostly image, so Barry could view Kezza beyond. She lay on the ground, head tilted to one side.

The crew stood around her in silence. Azad knelt, following the path of her gaze. The image flickered out.

"What's happening?" Captain Saje asked.

"Barrett Juul and the others must have looked away," Feisal said, and sure enough, the civilizationist no longer stood at the doorframe. "We can only view what has been observed."

Barry's projection returned, Kezza still on the hard floor. Several figures stepped inside, lifting Kezza up and carrying her away. The crew followed their path.

They placed her on a table, in the same room where Saje had locked Azad and Ledo. The room's original incarnation couldn't have differed more from the current one – cold and threadbare. She lay there, as people came and went, discussions held over her graying body. Juul sat alone with her for a time, head buried in his hands.

"He killed her," Nawalle said heatedly.

"She made that recording and headed to the back of the ship, toward the rocket," Zelle said. "If we're going to get technical, she may have tried to kill herself, in a bid to halt whatever Juul had planned for her. Perhaps she learned what we learned about Juul."

Azad shook his head. He preferred Nawalle's interpretation.

"But why did he follow her then, and watch her die?" Nawalle asked, tears starting to form.

Azad frowned. "They were taking her blood and other DNA samples in the earlier images we saw. Maybe Kezza had enough." His voice cracked but he straightened his back, composing himself. Like him, Kezza wanted to regain control over those who had power over her, even if it meant dying. But she had been denied that control in her final, horrible moments. They chose how she died.

"Now comes the moment of truth," Zelle said. "What did they do with the first Vitruvian?"

They dismembered her. When the archaic medmech first drew a scalpel, Nawalle covered her face and gave a low sob. Feisal wrapped his long arms around her, staring stonily at the scene. Azad fought the urge to look away, to run out of the room, but the need to save Ledo anchored him to the horrific sight. The need to witness how Nabatea had been made.

Juul stopped the medmech. He took the scalpel and stood over Kezza. He raised his arm but faltered, his shoulders racking with sobs. Once he composed himself, he made the first incision. He then handed off the scalpel to another man, curly-haired and dark-skinned, who accepted it with a shaking hand.

They cut off pieces of flesh and placed them in petri dishes. They removed organs, limbs, sections of bone. And the blood. She had been dead long enough that it no longer flowed from her desecrated body, but they salvaged every drop left.

"I can't watch this anymore," Nawalle said, rushing out of the room. Captain Saje's face suggested she was ready to follow suit.

"Why would they do this?" Saje managed to say.

"They're harvesting her DNA," Azad said. The initial shock of Kezza's death had lessened and Azad understood exactly why Kezza had snuck her way to the back of the ship, toward heat and fire, instead of airlocking herself into space. She intended to deny them this very opportunity.

Sorrow welled in Azad's heavy heart. Kezza may have hoped to make a final stand and change the course that Juul had set for them all. Instead, she had been forgotten. *Until now.*

A soft thud jolted Azad back to the present. Ledo curled on the floor, retching.

"Get her on a gurney and contain her," Saje shouted. A medmech sped over, armed with a bubble like the one Saje wore.

"No, Ledo," Azad said in a low voice, his pulse pounding at his throat. "Not yet, just a little longer."

Her face was small and a sickly gray behind the bubble. Red pools formed in the corners of her eyes. She lay on the ground as though in a daze when, without warning, fear flooded her eyes and she let out a single, long wail. The sound cut through Azad like a blade. He helped the medmech load her onto a wheeled chair.

"Azad, he'll take care of her," Zelle said. "Back to Barry."

"I'm staying with Ledo."

"We have to keep going," Feisal said. "We don't have time to panic. Get over here, we need to focus. *Azad!*"

Startled at hearing his real name on Feisal's lips, Azad turned back.

"If you want to save her, the best chance we have is finding out what they did," Feisal continued, pointing back to the macabre scene unfolding in front of Barry's lens. "They discovered a way to change the virus's course. Let the medmechs treat her and help her another way."

Feisal was right. Azad cast a final glance at his sister as the medmech wheeled her away, deeper into the medical ward. He turned back to the crew.

"Let's see what they do next," he said.

An overhead speaker played a trio of musical notes, a simple but ominous melody. Nawalle's voice followed, crackling in the air around them.

"I need help at Command," she said in the high voice that preceded panic. "A message received from the Vitruvian *Cana'an* vessel."

Saje swore. "So it begins."

"Stall them," Zelle said. "We need all the time you can give us."

"What do you suggest I do?" Saje asked with ice in her voice. "Lie? Fire at them?"

"Make for the Emigrant's Wormhole," Feisal said. "Full speed. They'll give chase but the *Cana'an* is a behemoth, it'll be hard for them to keep up. And they won't risk following us through the wormhole if it comes to that."

"You want us to commit suicide by leaping through an unstable, unsupported wormhole?" Saje said with a wild, angry laugh.

"We came here that way in the *Magreb*," Feisal said with a shrug and a crooked smile. "What's a second roll of the dice?"

Another warning chime, more urgent, erupted from the speakers. Saje sighed.

"I'll talk to them for as long as I can," she said. "Stall them. And then set off for the wormhole."

She spun her feet around, her bobbed hair bouncing, and left them. Feisal stared at the spot where she stood a moment ago, apparently lost in thought, before turning back to the group.

"Time to give Barry a challenge."

They jumped forward in time after Kezza's dissection several days at a time. The curly-haired man occupied the room, formulating injections and running calculations on his monitor. Azad's stomach clenched. This part would be the challenge. Hours, days, even months of an ancient man conducting lab work, and they had to find the critical outcome of his research, the moment when he made a discovery they could replicate. But how would they manage in time?

"Can you speed up the projections?" Azad asked as they watched several figures stare at a computer.

"Not without overstraining Barry," Feisal said in a tense voice. "I can move a sequence of moments forward and back, as you've seen, but this machine is unveiling macro-level aggregates of wave function collapses over a thousand years ago. I can't just hit a speed button. We tried that in the crater and it nearly shut Barry's smaller cousin down."

"We have to do something," Azad said, expecting such a response but still struggling to accept it. "Let's cut a week ahead."

They found a group in the laboratory. Juul, Axel, Dr. Saadia Hamza and several others. The medical researcher injected an electric-blue substance into a snake. The same snake, it appeared, that Kezza wore around her neck on Calypso, the night of their escape.

The snake, sensing a disruption, struggled in the man's hands but slumped as the injection took effect. They observed it for several minutes, but the snake simply curled inside its container, raising its head lazily.

"Why the snake?" Feisal asked, brushing his long fingers against the tattoo on his chest.

"An animal control," Zelle said. "Based on archive records, this was a common practice back on the mother system. They tested a new product on animals before braving it on a human subject. They had more forms of life to play with than we have on Nabatea."

"Barbarians," Feisal spat. "The Vitruvian asp is practically sacred."

"And what we're witnessing now is probably the reason why," Zelle said. "This may be the first successful injection of your DNA line."

An hour passed while they jumped Barry through several fruitless days, before they found a breakthrough. Two large men, one of them Axel, dragged a smaller man into the laboratory. At the sight of the equipment inside the room, the man struggled, shouting. They wrestled him to the ground before strapping him on the same table that once hosted Kezza's remains. The medical researcher stood there for several minutes, so long that Azad waited for him to resist, before something inside him drained away and he injected his patient's arm. Immediately, the man's muscles tensed and his eyes bulged, tearing with blood.

"They're doing the same thing the *Axel* crew did down on Mars," Feisal said.

"Not quite," Azad said. When they set Barry on a new day, Azad scoured the scene for medical evidence – readings on computer monitors, measurements in test tubes. So far, without evidence of a cure. "They're mixing the viral vector with Kezza Sayer's genetic mutation, this MRC14 string that keeps popping up on every screen, seeking the right balance. They probably got close with the snake, as it's still alive. But they don't have the combination right in humans yet."

An idea struck Azad. Tearing away from Barry, he issued a command to a diagnostic medmech.

"Run this mutation of Kezza Sayer's, the MRC14, against Ledo's diagnostics," he said. "Is there a match?"

The medmech did not recognize the term MRC14, so Azad pulled up a DNA mutation chart and highlighted the impacted sequence.

"Mutation confirmed on patient Ledo Axel3248," the medmech replied. "Pollutant-based mutation is highly rare, affecting only point zero three percent of the Nabatean population."

Ledo had the same genetic mutation as Kezza Sayer. Ledo, the longest modern survivor after exposure to the crater's virus.

"This is why Ledo's survived this long," Azad said, spinning wildly to face the bewildered crew. "She has the same genetic mutation that Kezza Sayer did! Pollution triggers the mutation, and it allows the body to fight off the virus better than most. It's rare because we don't have the pollution our mother system did, but it triggered in Ledo somehow. Looks like her runs into the Sulpherlands paid off."

His elation was short-lived, however. The shared mutation explained how Ledo had lived so long but like Kezza Sayer, she was only the first step to a cure. Now they needed to find the moment when their ancestors discovered the right balance, transforming the virus into Vitruvian genetics.

Warning lights flashed above them and Captain Saje's voice filled the air.

"Preparing to leave Martian orbit and accelerate," she said with clinical composure. "Secure yourselves."

The chase had begun. Grumbling, Feisal secured Barry against the wall. They rushed to the back of the medical ward and fastened themselves to a long bench with chest straps. Nearby, Ledo lay on her hospital bed. Her head, enveloped in a thick bubble, turned and her eyes found Azad's. Her bloody mouth cracked in a weak smile. The engine roared and Azad's spine pressed against the back of his seat.

After several, teeth-rattling minutes, they stood up, shaking. Feisal reassembled Barry.

"There has to be a more efficient way," Azad said. "There are eleven months left on the journey and we don't know how long it'll take them to find the right balance. If they even figured it out before they landed on Nabatea."

"Let me know when you think of one, Doctor," Feisal said.

Axel ran a hand through his hair, straining not to yell, to scream in frustration. They didn't have time to run Barry through each day on the journey, hoping to stumble upon the exact moment that Juul's followers made the breakthrough.

An idea struck Azad with sudden force. A possibility, however reaching.

"Feisal," Azad began. "Are there any dates on the calendar that are significant to Vitruvians? Any special events or commemorations?"

The Vitruvian frowned. "The start of every Nabatean year is Resolution Day, where we make plans and then burn them, to show ourselves that we don't live by routine, like you orthodox folk."

"Anything else?" Azad asked, refraining from further comment.

"And then…there's Sol 150. On the one hundred and fiftieth day of the Nabatean year, we commemorate past Vitruvians, firstly Barrett Juul's mother. We launch a small, empty spacecraft in the direction of the journey she took alone after Nabatean settlement."

"Where did the date Sol 150 come from?" Azad asked.

"Your guess is as good as mine. Maybe she left on Sol 150. But what's the point? Are we going to keep running Barry or not?"

But Zelle's eyes met Azad's, alight with shared understanding.

"Perhaps it has deeper origins," she said. "Let's move Barry back based on that date."

"Remember that the Nabatean calendar differs from the calendar they used during space travel," Feisal pointed out, but he was already activating Barry and toggling with the next date.

"It's worth a try," Azad said. "Let's try the one hundred fiftieth day of the journey, based on their own calendar."

Feisal ran Barry. Nothing. The medical researcher sat alone, feeding chemicals into test tubes, but without signs of progress.

The ship creaked and they all steadied themselves for balance. Azad pressed his palms against his temples.

"Try the fifth of January on the mother system calendar," Zelle said. "One for the month, five for the day. Based on their logs, that would be about two-thirds of the way into their journey."

Feisal adjusted the dates and activated Barry.

A group formed a circle, including Barrett Juul, Dr. Hamza, Axel, the medical researcher and another dark-haired woman. The gathering appeared oddly ceremonial, their faces stern and expectant. Juul spoke, his mouth moving but his words in this critical moment lost to time. Then, one by one, the medical researcher injected them with the same electric-blue substance, all except Juul. After a moment, the man injected himself. Zelle inhaled loudly, as though she had been holding her breath. No one reacted with surprise when the researcher skipped Barrett Juul, known by everyone in Nabatea to have been unevolved to the end.

Why did you not take it? After all he had seen of the founder, Azad assumed the motive had been a calculated, political one. Perhaps Juul wished to avoid alienating the remaining population who would never become Vitruvian. It also bolstered the 'different but equal' notion that had been drilled into Azad's head in Township. How could the Vitruvians be a ruling class if Vitruvians revered an orthodox human founder?

Feisal froze the image, leaving the group suspended under Barry's eye.

"Everyone search," he said. "Look at the computer monitors, scan what's on the tables that could show what went into those syringes."

Feisal and Zelle walked through the frozen scene, peering into every test tube and piece of equipment they could see. Above them, an unnerving rumble came from deep inside the vessel.

Azad stared at the circle of Nabatea's founders, the first Vitruvians. He did not need to view what occurred next to know that the injection had succeeded. Axel, Dr. Hamza, the other Vitruvians who stepped off the ship onto Nabatean soil had all lived to old age, commemorated as the first humans to be kissed by starlight. He scoured his memory for the names of the other first Vitruvians, matching them to the other man and woman in the room. Amit Reddy. Evgenia Zelenko, who would give birth on Nabatean soil, the first Vitruvian born on the planet.

The monitors revealed nothing. Something had been hand-scrawled on a desk, but no one could read it. They rewound the events of the day. The cure had been formulated, assembled by a mech, but nothing helped them understand how to replicate it.

"Any other ideas?" Feisal snapped.

Another shudder from the ship sounded overhead, the chatter of an exhausted engine. They were so close. Juul's followers had found the cure. It was there, in front of them, in a still image. How could the medical researcher, Amit Reddy, not leave a trace of it behind?

The realization struck Azad like an electromagnetic current.

"Have you been Blanked?" Feisal shouted. "Going to stand there until we get blown to dust?"

"The logs," Azad said aloud, his voice croaking.

"What are you babbling about?" Feisal asked, but when his eyes met Zelle's, he could see the idea churning in her head.

"Kezza made that recording to confess what happened on Mars," Azad said. "What if that recording wasn't the only thing hidden in the ship's logs? The man, Amit, found her in the log room. Maybe he realized what she did and decided to do the same."

They burst into the command center, finding a very frazzled Nawalle and Captain Saje manning the ship's controls.

"I hope you have good news," Saje said through gritted teeth.

"We need to access the ship's logs," Azad said.

"The logs? Can't you see we're a little busy?"

On cue, a loud bang echoed down the ship's spine and they all toppled forward.

"Status!" Saje barked.

"Indirect strike on the lower-right hub," Nawalle said in a controlled voice. She spoke with the mechanical automation of someone trained to do their job until the end. "Vacuum detected, sector is losing air."

"Seal the hub," Saje said, before turning back to Azad with a blood-draining glower.

"I want to enter a date into the logs, the way one of your people did when you discovered Kezza Sayer's hidden message."

To her credit, the Vitruvian woman understood immediately, even if she didn't like it.

"So you've found nothing useful with your…machine," she grumbled, but she stepped aside, gesturing Azad toward the monitor in front of her seat. She pressed several keys, which unveiled a painfully archaic, two-dimensional log search screen.

Before Feisal could mount a righteous defense of Barry, Saje turned to Zelle.

"I'm leaving this room under your command until I return," she said to a collection of shocked faces. "You and Nawalle keep us on course to the Emigrant's Wormhole while I man the ship's guns. Some counter-fire might slow them down. If we remain under pursuit, you have my authorization to pass through."

It had come to the lesser of two evils. Face certain destruction at the hands of a superior Vitruvian vessel or face potential implosion through an unstable wormhole. Zelle nodded, placing her hands on the back of Nawalle's chair.

Saje rushed out the door and Azad went to work on the ship's log.

"Let's try the ship's landing date on Nabatea," he said. "In mother system years."

Zelle recited the date with almost mechanical reflex. "It's 03142196."

The log yielded a long list of actions – landing maneuvers, atmosphere scans, disembarkation procedures. But nothing from Amit.

"The date they injected the first Vitruvians," Feisal said. "Try 0105195."

Nothing.

The ship shuddered again, followed by several loud cracking sounds. Azad grabbed the nearest seat for balance, avoiding a detached wire above his head.

"Another hit," Nawalle said. "We're seven minutes from the wormhole, but I don't know if we can pass without knowing the damage."

"Scan for damage and maintain speed," Zelle said simply, but her bones jutted through her knuckles as she gripped the seat.

"There's another option," Nawalle said in the same mechanical voice. "The *Magreb*'s connected to this ship as an ancillary shuttle after you and Feisal boarded. No signs of damage yet. Saje will go down with this ship, but we could return to the *Magreb*, try to pass through the wormhole alone." She expressed neither encouragement nor hope at this proposal, only a pilot's relay of remaining options.

Azad tensed. They might survive the passage if they abandoned ship, but Ledo would die.

"We stay," said Zelle after a pause. "The cure is on this ship. Our hope of survival is here. We succeed or fail here."

"Come on," Azad muttered, running his fingers feverishly over the log screen. Then it came to him.

"What's the date that Kezza died?" he asked Feisal. Scanning Barry, Feisal gave him the day.

Azad added the date and pressed enter. Time held its breath and Azad's heart skipped a beat. And then, to a surge of joy, a string of text and numbers flew across the screen. Distance logs. Personnel shift changes. And buried amid the banality of ship life, an unmistakable genome sequence. The measurements for an injectable vector.

Azad cried in triumph, leaping from his seat with a fist pumped in the air. His joy was short-lived, however, as the ground slipped out from under his feet. The side of his face struck the side of the command board, pain bursting through his jaw.

"Hold steady!" Zelle yelled. She shoved Azad aside, taking a seat.

"Get down to the medical bay," Nawalle yelled.

"No time!"

Pain licked at Azad's teeth, his mouth filling with blood. He had come so close. The riddle to Ledo's life, to an entire human evolution line, in front of him but out of reach. It didn't matter. They would all be dead in minutes. The secret of the Vitruvians' origins gone with them.

At least she didn't die alone on Mars, Azad told himself. *I found her. We'll all go together.*

Screams surrounded him, rising in pitch alongside whistling pipes as they burst above them. Even the floor seemed to be screaming, its metal rattling like chattering teeth. He started to crawl, pulling himself across the floor with heavy arms. He needed to reach Ledo. She needed to see a human face before...

Then the floor dropped and the world turned inside out. Azad tried to scream but his lips had been welded shut under the weight of an invisible gravity. His insides pressed together in agony, organs and bones and tissue churning like a stream of water through a narrow tunnel. He waited to die – surely, no lifeform could survive this sensation, this pain. His skull constricted, choking his rattling brain, and when darkness finally reached for him, he welcomed its embrace.

Chapter Twenty-Four
A Middle Way

"Look at that, he's back with the living."

Opening his eyes proved challenging, but Azad forced his lids open after several exhausting attempts. A bright light greeted him, threatening to add blindness to his list of physical complaints.

He turned away, toward the soft curve of palm trees, black against a gentler, orange light. It took several seconds to realize that the trees had been painted on the wall. He was still on the *Axel* ship, in the room where Nabatea's secrets had been laid bare.

And where Ledo lay dying.

"Welcome back, brother," a soft voice said. Azad whipped his head around, pain shooting down his neck, to find Ledo sitting at his side. Her long hair hung around a warm, almost shy, face.

"You're ok," he croaked, noting the color in her cheeks and the fact that she sat upright, free of tubes and IV needles, while he lay in pain. "How—"

"You found the treatment, remember?" she said with a smile. "After we passed through the wormhole, Captain Saje put the machines to work on replicating the injectable. It worked! Took a while, but Saje said my proteins started attacking the excess virus in my system, balancing everything out. You became the problem patient – you didn't react well to passing through the wormhole conscious. Spent a good thirty minutes screaming and babbling."

Had he? Azad recalled nothing after the first pull, the way his insides fought their way out. He gathered his thoughts. They had passed through the wormhole. The ship was intact, meaning that the Vitruvian vessel had not given chase and shot them to oblivion. The others had managed to cure Ledo using the injectable, a combination of Kezza Sayer's fighting genetic mutation and the alien viral vector. Meaning...

"You're now a Vitruvian," Azad said to Ledo.

"An earlier version, at least," Zelle said. She squeezed Ledo's shoulder with grandmotherly affection before sitting beside her. Feisal, Nawalle and Captain Saje also filed into the room, gathering around Azad's bed. Nawalle beamed at him. Even Feisal and Saje exuded less hostility than expected. Feisal carried his oud under his arm, sitting cross-legged at the foot of the bed. He had changed from atmosphere gear into his trademark leather jacket and red pants. Saje, still in her crisp uniform, looked upon her fellow Vitruvian with the strained tolerance usually reserved for excitable children.

"I'm not that different," Ledo countered. "I check all of the basic boxes. You won't get me to ruin this perfect skin with one of those tattoos, though. I always thought they were ridiculous."

Saje's mouth twitched in a near smile before she explained, "By receiving the injectable, she shares the traits of the first Vitruvians who landed on Nabatea. But we have evolved over many generations, become more adaptable. So while Ledo could probably function on Mars, should you ever return, I doubt she should attempt open space any time soon."

Ledo shrugged.

Azad turned to Zelle. Her eyes twinkled.

"You found something else, didn't you?" Azad asked.

"While you were out, we took Barry around the ship and found more clues," Feisal said, plucking a few strings with long fingers. "Followed our new Vitruvians throughout the journey, although we've got more to see. But we connected a few more pieces together."

"The remaining open question," Zelle said. "Mainly, how Vitruvians came to be what they are now."

After a foggy moment, Azad understood what Zelle meant. "No one injects themselves now to become Vitruvian, right? Vitruvians are born to other Vitruvians. The mutation must have made it into the germ line."

"We confirmed that fact." Captain Saje spoke again. "Using...Barry.

They modified the embryo that Evgenia Zelenko was pregnant with, introducing the vector into the germ line. Once the DNA gets into the germ line, it can evolve and be passed down generations. They changed being a Vitruvian from an injectable treatment into something that was inherited. And at some point in history, that knowledge was lost to us. We all learn that one is either born Vitruvian, to Vitruvians, or one is not."

"I suspect that history was lost on purpose," Zelle said. "That Evgenia and the first wave of Vitruvians let the secret die with them, at Juul's instructions. Juul wanted the line between Vitruvian and non-Vitruvian to be clear, so everyone in his perfect world knew their place. Easier to do if one is simply born with a fixed fate."

Ledo and Azad shared a nervous, excited glance. For the first time in a thousand years, that line had been blurred. Nabateans of different castes never formed sexual relationships or crossed bloodlines, the idea comparable to a human reproducing with a cactus. Regular Nabateans lived in districts like Khazneh, had children that were an amalgamation of the community's DNA, while Vitruvians formed couples when it suited them. But now, the unthinkable had occurred – an orthodox Nabatean had become a Vitruvian. The magnitude of this new reality hung thick in the air around them.

"It's good," Azad said to a circle of surprised faces. "The more the lines between us are blurred, the more we can be ourselves and live the lives we want. So many Nabateans think they have no other options. I used to think it would be impossible for me to live without the routine of Nabatea City. The authorities want to keep us thinking that we're inherently different, so they can keep things the way they are."

"That desire to keep separate roles is what drove us back to Mars," Captain Saje said after a pause. "The lines are already blurring in different ways. You, Azad, may have noticed this back on Nabatea City. More Vitruvians choosing stability and routine over exploration, some even forming Vitruvian communities in imitation of your Nabatean social structure. It disgusted the authorities, this violation of the natural order. I'll admit, it disgusted and frightened me at first. I joined this expedition because I wanted to find proof of our different origins and remind our people of who they are. And look at what we've learned instead – we're the result of an injection."

Azad recalled that last night at Khazneh Arena, with the group of Vitruvians standing in a circle with drinks in hand, drawing curious stares.

"I'll admit, the idea of living like a *hadir* chills the soul-conscious," Feisal said. "I joined a Nabatean crew who all left. Why would anyone choose that path?"

"We all want what we can't have, on some level," Saje said. "Perhaps becoming more like the orthodox isn't the worst thing for all. And if anything, you have revealed your capacity to be more like us." She inclined her head at Zelle, Nawalle and Ledo. And then Azad.

"How do you think the authorities will react when they learn about all of this?" Zelle asked, gesturing toward Ledo. She stood up with an air that drew everyone to attention. Feisal even placed his instrument down. "We carry some important and terrible truths about our origins. Nabatea came into being through blood and lies. It was born through a genocide on Mars, the death of an innocent woman and a people deceived into a system that could never be fair and free."

The bluntness of her speech sank into Azad like a weight. He had grown up believing that life on Nabatea had been a correction of the mother system's mistakes, but by erasing history, Juul had managed to repeat it, the same theme in a different setting. A theme of some people beneath others, of a person's story written for them before it had begun.

"The people, all of them, have a right to know," Azad interjected. He flushed as heads swiveled in his direction, Zelle's included, but he had to speak. "You said that we have to know our history to avoid its mistakes," he said to Zelle. "I didn't realize what that meant at first, but I do now. We owe it to Kezza Sayer and the others who died to tell the truth. Her name needs to be known. She mattered. She tried to keep us from repeating history, even though that may have been impossible. But for better or for worse, she helped make Nabatea what it is today. Let's blast the footage from Barry out to the Nabatea system. If we can access the radio wave channels on Nabatea City, there's no stopping it. Tell the whole story!" He sank back into his bed, winded from his speech. Ledo shot him a wink and an encouraging smile.

Zelle stared at Azad, her face a mask. She turned to Captain Saje, who raised her brows.

"What do you think our next course should be?" Zelle asked Saje. "As captain of this vessel, I think you have a critical say."

If the Vitruvian woman was taken aback by Zelle's overture, she brushed past it quickly. Saje frowned and began to pace in front of them.

"There are two key truths you possess, and I feel they should be looked at individually," she said. "One, there is the fact of Juul's ordered massacre of the remaining Martians on Calypso and Palmcorps. While the actual evidence is shocking to witness, I don't know if that will change things on its own. Let me explain my reasoning. First, the authorities will try to frame it as lies and slander, and if you are able to debunk those claims before they come after you – and make no mistake, we are all being hunted now – they will shift gears and find excuses. Juul had no choice, they will say. We already have been taught to see the mother system as barbaric beyond redemption. They will frame Juul's assault as justified, claiming he had been provoked by a corrupt system trying to thwart his vision of a future on Nabatea."

No one responded. She let the idea settle before continuing.

"The second truth is the origin of Vitruvian lineage, which has deeper implications," Saje said. "We have learned that Vitruvians were not blessed by some cosmic force en route to Nabatea or the product of some inherently superior trait, but the result of trial and error, by splicing a genetic mutation with a virus. One that, thanks to our discovery, anyone can access. That fact will not sit well with the authorities at all, or with Vitruvians in general. It will cause anger and suppression, but I don't even believe it will cause upheaval. Do you think the population will really rise up and demand the right to live as Vitruvians do? After all they have been conditioned to believe for so long?"

"Maybe you underestimate us," Nawalle said. "I left. So did Zelle, Ledo and now Azad. Maybe we're not all docile and happy with our lot."

"Maybe," Saje conceded. "But I don't see a good outcome either way. Either they struggle to accept this truth and carry on with the system en masse. Or they do accept it and revolt in some fashion. Who has the arms? Who controls technology, entries and exits from Nabatea and has the will to maintain the status quo? The Vitruvian authorities. I would be interested to take your machine to Earth, Zelle of Nabatea, and see how past revolutions ended. See what the cost was."

Though the truth of her words soured him, Azad felt a grudging wave of respect for this Vitruvian captain. She had adjusted to new facts with remarkable speed, even become an ally in the span of a frantic chase across the galaxy. Her adaptability to difficult truths was more impressive, in Azad's eyes, than adapting to an oxygen-starved atmosphere.

"So you advise us against pushing what we know out to the system and seeing what happens," Zelle said. "What do you suggest we do instead?"

For the first time, Captain Saje smiled. It emerged slowly, curving into her sharp cheekbones until it shone in her dark eyes. A smile laced with danger, but a conspiratorial understanding that she would cast in her lot with them, whatever the consequences.

★   ★   ★

When the *Axel* vessel emerged on the other end of the Emigrant's Wormhole, Nawalle and Zelle set their course away from Nabatea planet and deeper into the system, where Vitruvian authorities no longer went. Saje only modified their course slightly, casting them toward a pair of nomad planets far from the Nabatean sun's gravitational pull.

Azad and Ledo paced the corridor, passing a wide window that unveiled the rich, painted canvas of the stars beyond the system. Nabatea had become a distant, glowing disc, no more than a flickering cosmic bulb behind them, Cerata hidden behind its mass.

"I'll never get tired of that sight," Ledo said. "Just think, on that little red circle, our former neighbors are getting up for whatever job's on their schedule today, walking down the streets and planning their nights with Osbourne's help."

"Do you miss it at all?" Azad asked, oddly moved that Ledo had remembered Osbourne. He touched the back of his neck. The scar itched but felt smooth under his calloused fingers.

"I miss parts of it," Ledo admitted. "The palm trees, the fresh air after rain. The tall buildings down the main road, but also the low huts around Khazneh. I miss those smells of baked spice bread and the sweets."

"I thought you might mention the sweets," Azad said with a smile, earning a punch on his shoulder.

"Nothing is all bad," Ledo continued. "I think Captain Saje was right, the more I think about it. Let's do it smartly, so we fix what's wrong with Nabatea but don't lose everything. Look at Mars. It became a graveyard. Even Earth died out. We're all that's left."

Azad had nothing to say in response, so he put an arm around her shoulder, letting her overtake him down the walkway. She leapt onto the side rail, balancing perfectly on her toes. Azad gasped as she leapt down off the mezzanine to the lower level, landing with a soft thud.

She raised her arms in triumph, blessed now with Vitruvian reflexes. Azad rolled his eyes.

"Show off," he said.

"If nonessential crew are not busy," Nawalle's voice cut sharply through the ship's speakers, "*essential* crew could use assistance in the mechanic's room!"

With a shared look of shame, Azad and Ledo obeyed. Nawalle's main task, now that the addition of Feisal and Zelle had made the ship steerable again, had been to find and disable all communications equipment that Vitruvian authorities could use to track the *Axel*. This proved challenging, given the size of the ship and the Vitruvian dedication to sharing information with other Vitruvians. Nawalle's mood had also been fouled by the damage done to the *Magreb* during the wormhole passage. The ship came out the other end, still attached to the *Axel*, but would not fly on her own. Nawalle tended to the *Axel* with an aura of guilt, as though she were cheating on a loved one.

"We can't be followed," Saje had insisted once the crew agreed to her plan. "If the authorities discover that this place exists, they'll destroy it faster than a Nabatean running out of the Sulpherlands. When I first heard of it, that was what I intended to do – to stop abominations occurring under Nabatea's nose."

Azad and Ledo found Nawalle covered in grease and her own sweat, wielding a gear like a Vitruvian dagger. Her eyes flashed as they entered the room.

"We only have days," she said with a voice verging on hysterical. "I've taken out all of the built-in comm transistors but what about the mechs? Do you know most of them can relay to central databases on large Vitruvian vessels? I need some help – they don't like being tampered with. They'll obey any command except one that overrides central command."

Ledo's newfound speed still had the power to surprise Azad. She had always beaten him whenever they raced across the Arena and along the Khazneh waterways, but she moved now with a predator's reflexes, cornering mechs that Nawalle lured into the hallway, tackling them with kinetic fury. Azad and Nawalle would then disable their communicators and cloud functions, letting them wheel away, disgruntled but intact.

"Happy, boss?" Ledo asked Nawalle with a sly grin.

A range of emotions passed over the mechanic's eyes before she settled on a returning smile.

"Happy enough for today," she said, brushing paint off Ledo's shirt. The two women, Azad sensed, wanted to pick up where they had left off, but neither was quite ready. No one on the crew could return to the status quo. With Vitruvians on the hunt and a terrible secret in their possession, they had more pressing concerns.

Several grueling days of chasing mechs and playing with wires left Nawalle satisfied that the *Axel* now served its crew and that crew alone, an island in a dark, infinite sea. The vessel slowed as it neared its destination, the crew all gathered in the command room at the sight of the asteroid's gray, desolate surface. Smaller than Cerata and just as dark, it was dwarfed by a nearby rogue planet that emitted a faint, purplish glow.

The ship docked on the asteroid's surface, the airlock connecting to a spoke-shaped building outside. The rest of the city, Saje explained, lay underground.

An elevator took them below. The door opened to a cavern teeming with people. They moved in and out of tunnels, a web of entries and exits around the open space. A crowd gathered to greet the new arrivals, smiling but curious.

Ledo nudged Azad's arm, pointing at the crowd. A couple stood together, a child on the man's shoulder. The woman at his side bore a black and green snake tattoo.

"He looks orthodox," Nawalle whispered.

They were not the only odd couple. Groups of orthodox Nabateans and Vitruvians mingled, dressed alike. The orthodox did not step aside for Vitruvians in their midst, while children ran around the cavern, their humanoid class unclear. Judging from the couple, they could be something different entirely.

The crowd parted as the crew stepped out. Saje smiled, enjoying the look of bewilderment on Feisal's face. The glowing lights along the rocky walls shone on Zelle's white hair as she also stared, shaking her head.

"Incredible," she whispered.

"A colony of Vitruvians and non-Vitruvians living together," Feisal muttered. "I never would have believed it."

"I suspect we have even more to learn from them than they from us," Zelle said. "But if anyone will be receptive to our discoveries, they will be here." She inclined her head at Saje.

Azad walked slowly through the crowd, trying not to stare at any particular person. It was incredible. Something that he had expected generations to achieve was already happening on this small, hidden asteroid. Orthodox Nabateans and Vitruvians, living as equals. As partners and friends.

A child extended her hand and Azad shook it with a broad smile. He, Ledo, Nawalle and Zelle were not exceptions to a rule. Nabateans could all live differently, if they were shown another way. When asked for a plan, Saje offered one in two-fold. First, share the discoveries on Mars and the *Axel* with allies on Cerata. The Shadow Moon, with its comparative free-thinkers and rebels, would be more inclined to accept the truth about Nabatea's origins and to spread the word organically, creating an undercurrent of skepticism toward Vitruvian rule. This information-sharing was insurance, in case the authorities managed to find them, ensuring their secrets would not die on the *Axel*. Second, they would find a safe haven in a place few knew of, an experimental colony on the dark edges of the system, founded by Nabateans seeking a different way.

They would hide here and plan their next step while the story of Zelle of Nabatea's crew spread across Cerata. They would learn how this asteroid society existed, lessons that could be taken back to the inner system. And perhaps, if it became safe to return, or even if it didn't, they would return to Nabatea with Barry, and learn more about Juul's early days on Nabatea, uncovering more of his carefully woven plans.

An old man with white hair approached the crew, extending his hand to Saje. The Vitruvian captain bowed before introducing Zelle.

Azad smiled, taking Ledo's hand. The future waited for them within this strange city. Its rocky tunnels beckoned them inside.

Acknowledgements

This novel underwent a long journey, predating the pandemic, from a half-baked idea in my head about space-traversing historians to a published book, and there are many people to thank for that. First of all, my amazing agent Naomi Davis, for their early support of this story and helpful feedback on what was and wasn't working with those initial drafts. And to my editor at Flame Tree Press, Don D'Auria, for his sharp eye for the small details and for helping me grow as an author through multiple books – I'm finally learning to stop making characters hiss, and realizing that a person can't be in handcuffs one minute and swinging a weapon several paragraphs later. You are both a joy to work with.

To the rest of the Flame Tree Press team – Nick Wells, Gillian Whitaker, Olivia Jackson, Mike Spender and all of the other talented folks who designed the incredible cover, supported production and made this book a reality – thank you.

A special thanks to Jacob Hernandez, an early reader and talented writer who gave me great feedback on the early manuscript. Thanks to the book club crew for hearing my trials and tribulations as I navigated dual timelines, pacing and other writing struggles over many months. Thanks to Justin Casey for explaining the science of viral vectors and DNA, helping me make the premise of an alien virus at least somewhat scientifically grounded. And to my family, especially my mom, who is always an early reader and champion of my stories, I appreciate your support always.

And to my husband, Colin – the extrovert who always gives me my quiet, introverted time to write for hours on end, the optimist who lifts me up when I face setbacks and rejection, the fearless soul who makes me believe in the possible – thank you for being you.

About the Author

Nadia Afifi is the author of the *Cosmic* trilogy and numerous science fiction short stories. Her debut novel, *The Sentient*, was lauded as 'staggering and unputdownable' in a starred *Publishers Weekly* review and recommended by *Booklist* for 'readers who love a thrilling narrative and welcome moral and philosophical questions in their science fiction.' *Analog Magazine* describes her as 'a brand-new voice in our field, and one you should become familiar with.' *The Sentient* is the first novel in a near-future series about a controversial cloning project, human consciousness and a high-stakes conflict between religious fundamentalism and science, and was followed by *The Emergent* and *The Transcendent*. Nadia's short fiction has appeared in *The Magazine of Fantasy and Science Fiction*, *Abyss & Apex* and *Clarkesworld Magazine*.

Nadia grew up in Saudi Arabia and Bahrain, where she read every book she could get her hands on, but currently calls Denver, Colorado, home. She is a member of the Rocky Mountain Fiction Writers organization. Her background as an Arab American who lived overseas has inspired her fiction writing, particularly her passion for exploring complex social, political and cultural issues through a futuristic lens.

When she isn't writing, she spends her time practicing (and falling off) the lyra (aerial hoops), hiking through Colorado's many trails, jogging through Denver's streets and working on the most challenging jigsaw puzzles she can find. She also loves dogs, travel and cooking. Follow her latest musings and adventures on her website (nadiaafifi.com), Twitter/X (@nadoodles) or Facebook (nadiawritesscifi).